1989

It's 1989, and Allie Burns is back. Older and maybe wiser, she's running the northern news operation of the *Sunday Globe*, chafing at losing her role in investigative journalism and at the descent into the gutter of the UK tabloid media.

And there's plenty to keep her occupied. The year begins with the memorial service to the victims of the bombing of Pan Am Flight 103, but Allie has barely filed her copy when she stumbles over a story about HIV/AIDS that will shock her into a major change of direction.

The world of newspapers is undergoing a revolution, there's skulduggery in the medical research labs, and there are seismic rumblings behind the Iron Curtain. When kidnap and murder are added to this potent mix, Allie is forced to question all her old certainties.

VAL McDERMID

1989

Complete and Unabridged

CHARNWOOD
Leicester

First published in Great Britain in 2022 by
Little, Brown
An imprint of Little, Brown Book Group
London

First Charnwood Edition
published 2022
by arrangement with
Little, Brown Book Group
An Hachette UK Company
London

*A catalogue record for this book is available
from the British Library.*

ISBN 978-1-4448-4944-8

Published by
Ulverscroft Limited
Anstey, Leicestershire

Printed and bound in Great Britain by
TJ Books Ltd., Padstow, Cornwall

This book is printed on acid-free paper

For Jo on the occasion of her 20th birthday.
Don't worry, it'll all work out.

On reflection, I think the 1980s were an
absolutely terrrible, abysmal time
PETE BURNS

When I look back at the 1980s, I pinch myself.
Did I really do all that?
CYNTHIA PAYNE

Prologue

Finally the weather turned. He only realised how tense his shoulders had been when he felt them relax. He'd had just a week's holiday, and as the days flew past bringing more Atlantic gales, he'd thought he was going to have to abort his plan. But at last, on the fourth day, the wind dropped enough to make sailing a proposition. He slipped anchor from Tobermory Bay on a cold blue morning and motored out into the main channel heading north-west.

The wind was from the south-west, around a force four, he reckoned. It wasn't perfect, but he set his sails to catch the wind to his best advantage and settled down for what he calculated would be around a four-hour sail out past Coll to Ranaig. And 'sail' was the operative word. He wanted to use the motor as little as possible so nobody would be able to estimate how far he'd travelled.

The boat he'd hired for the week in Tobermory was a bit of a tub but she didn't take much getting used to and she was well suited to single-handed sailing. There was a muscular swell on the sea that would have made most people feel queasy. But he'd learned his sailing off the coast of North Wales, braving the Irish Sea in all weathers. Sailing solo on a small boat in fair weather held no terrors for him.

The wind whistled in the sails and the water hissed along the hull yet they were no distractions from his thoughts. He'd been working out how to kill Wallace Lockhart for months, evolving and discarding plans one after the other till his researches had eventually led him to this. It matched his existing skills, it embraced elements of poetic justice, and it had the added beauty of not requiring an alibi. A man would die, but the timing was impossible to predict. Whenever it happened, his avenging angel would be far away. The only downside was that, as he lay dying, he would not know which of his inhumanities he was dying for.

It was early afternoon when he lowered the sails and motored into the bay on the Atlantic coast of Ranaig. There was a small wooden jetty, exposed to the elements beyond the tidal barrage that provided power to the island, and he tied up his craft securely to the iron stanchions. He grabbed his tall rucksack and climbed ashore. He stood on dry land and took a long deep breath. The air smelled of salt and seaweed, and that was all. He was alone on the island; he knew the housekeeper and the bodyguard were only in residence when its owner was due. And he was giving evidence to a Parliamentary committee this week. When he wasn't being questioned himself, he'd be watching his rivals closely.

There would be nobody standing between the intruder and his intended goal.

There was a faint track up from the bay which joined a tarmacked path that ran between the helipad and the house. It was easily wide enough for the golf buggy that sat under a carport at the back of the house, protected on three sides from the weather by log cabin timbers. He crossed the path and approached at an angle, the machair springy beneath his feet, treacherous pockets of wet peat ready to suck the boots off him.

From the shelter of the carport, he checked out the positions of the security cameras. The island's lord and master clearly thought there was little risk on Ranaig. The cameras at the back of the house were fixed and they covered a wide arc including the path. But the corners weren't within their scope.

Nevertheless, he took a balaclava from his pack and pulled it on. Gloves next. Then a folding aluminium ladder just long enough to put him in reach of the guttering. It was cast iron and firmly secured to the stonework and the fascia board with heavy bolts, designed to withstand the wild weather that would blow in from the ocean. Finally, a lumpy plastic bag whose handle he slipped over his wrist.

With little fuss, he unfolded the ladder and propped it against the wall. He took off his boots, scaled the ladder and pulled himself on to the roof, grunting at the effort. He crawled up the roof till he reached the first of the long dormer windows. He clenched his fist and drove it hard into the window. The glass crazed and he hit it again. This time it broke, the hole large enough for him to reach inside and unfasten the catch. The window swung abruptly open, carried by the wind, and he rolled over the sill and into a bedroom.

Stepping carefully over the broken glass, the man opened the carrier bag and emptied the dead seagull on to the carpet. He'd picked it up off the beach the day before. By the time Lockhart's people arrived, the obvious conclusion would be that the gull had crashed into the window in a storm. It happened. Occasionally, it was true. But it happened.

This was obviously a guest bedroom. Well appointed, but impersonal. He emerged on the landing and tried the next door. Another guest bedroom. He crossed the landing and as soon as he opened the door, he knew this was the master suite. Vast picture windows looked out across the sea to a distant vista of small islands and big mountains. It would be a treat to wake up to this, he thought.

It wasn't the bedroom he was interested in but the bathroom. The plan he'd finally settled on had been formed after reading an interview with the island's owner in Condé Nast's *Traveller* magazine. There was a sidebar on Travel Essentials —What I Never Leave Home Without. Among his target's necessities were his vitamin capsules. 'Individually tailored to his needs by a top Swiss naturopath.' And a photograph of a scatter of dark green capsules, their overlap obvious even at that small scale. Two cylinders with open ends, one nesting tightly inside the end of the other.

The bathroom was roughly the size of the intruder's living room. A bath that would comfortably contain a very large man and plenty of water; a separate double shower cubicle. A toilet, a bidet and a pair of sinks. Why one man needed two sinks was beyond him, but what did he know of a life of luxury like this? He opened the bathroom cabinet and there, among the toiletries and assorted medications — it pleased him inordinately to see three preparations for easing haemorrhoids — he found what he was looking for.

He unscrewed the jar and took out a capsule. They were dark green, he'd read, so they wouldn't deteriorate in sunlight. From his pocket, he took out a small vial of white powder. With infinite care, he separated the two halves of the capsule and tipped the contents down the nearest sink. Then he replaced the vitamins with the white powder and reassembled the capsule.

4

He compared it with a couple of others from the jar, and was satisfied. He closed the jar and put it back in exactly the same place. He ran the tap briefly to wash away any trace of the vitamins then retraced his steps.

Across the bedroom, across the hall, through the window. Closing the catch was more tricky but he managed it. Inching down the roof to the ladder, then feet in boots and back to the boat. Back aboard, he stripped off his gloves and balaclava. He'd drop them overboard somewhere on the way back, along with his folding ladder.

At last, he allowed himself to relax. He had a half-litre bottle of good Polish vodka in his rucksack and he poured himself a small measure. He raised a silent toast, threw it down in one and plotted his course back to Tobermory.

He didn't know when the cyanide would catch up with its intended victim. But it was only a matter of time.

1

A steady drizzle fell from low clouds that echoed the slate roof of Dryfesdale parish church and leached colour from the red sandstone walls. The world was monochrome with grief.

Good intro, Allie Burns thought, hating herself even as the idea crossed her mind. She'd come to the church before dawn, knowing she'd have to beat the rest of the world's press to the Lockerbie bombing memorial service if she was going to stand any chance of a decent exclusive that would hold till the Sunday paper. The main door of the church was still locked but she'd lurked among the worn sandstone grave markers until a florist's van turned into the access road. She sidled through the headstones to the front of the church. A middle-aged woman in a nylon overall under a rain jacket was struggling with an impressive load of floral tributes.

'Let me give you a hand,' Allie said, not waiting for a reply to get stuck in to unloading the flowers. 'Thank goodness. Are you with the church?' the woman asked.

The correct answer would have been, 'No, I'm the northern news editor of the *Sunday Globe*.' Allie opted for the less problematic, 'I couldn't see you struggling by yourself.'

Between them, they unloaded the van and carried the flowers in through an unobtrusive side door. Allie quickly took in the typical Church of Scotland spartan interior, the simple wood pews, the plain communion table and the pulpit built from blocks of local stone. The gallery above boasted a barrel roof, its panels painted a surprising pink in contrast to the white ribs. Towards the rear of the church, a young boy sat with bowed head.

'Oh, my,' Allie's new friend said. 'That must be the wee laddie that lost his mum and dad and his brother.'

Allie knew exactly who she meant. He'd gone to a friend's, to play table tennis. When Pan Am flight 103 had disintegrated above the small Scottish town thanks to a terrorist bomb, part of the scatter of wreckage had obliterated eight houses. One of those houses had been home to the boy's family. Four days before Christmas.

Now she had an even better intro.

Before she could say more, two burly men in dark suits hustled in the side door with a harassed air. They gave the florist a cursory glance then glared at Allie, betrayed by her belted black raincoat and fashionable footwear. 'Who are you?'

Allie's smile was conciliatory. She held up her hands, palms facing them. 'I'm out of here,' she said.

The younger of the two was faster than he looked. A hand shot out and grabbed her arm. 'Not so fast. What are you doing here?'

'Nothing sinister. I'm press,' she sighed. 'I'd just arrived, and this lady looked like she needed some help.' With her free hand, she reached in her pocket and produced her NUJ press card. 'I'll get out of your way, if you'll just . . .' She nodded at the fingers gripping tightly.

'You're not supposed to be in here,' he snapped. 'Have you got no shame? This is a memorial, not a press conference.' He let her go. 'Away and join the

8

rest of the vermin.'

Allie squeezed out a smile. Never let them see you're intimidated, no matter which side of the good guys/bad guys fence they are on. On her way out she nodded to the florist, whose expression gave no clue to her reaction.

While she'd been inside, the security cordon Allie had anticipated had been set round the church. The dozens of police officers were no surprise, given that the service for the 270 victims of the presumed terrorist attack would be attended by the prime minister and the American ambassador. Not to mention another seven hundred mourners from the town and far beyond.

Allie spotted the press corral, dozens of reporters and photographers hemmed around by a subsidiary cordon. Nothing for her there. Today was Wednesday, and the nuts and bolts of the memorial service would be detailed many times over by the daily paper reporters that were covering it. With luck, her early exclusive would hold till Sunday. But it wouldn't hurt to try and find something else. She kept her distance, joining the growing crowd standing in the rain along the pavements of the main street. She managed to get a good line of sight to the main gate then pulled a folding umbrella from her satchel and snapped it open.

The mourners began to arrive, some wearing white carnations, some carrying posies and bouquets, many unable to hold back the tears. Allie had struggled to imagine the shock and grief that gripped them. Two weeks on from the catastrophe that had claimed 270 lives, it could scarcely have penetrated the shell of natural denial. If Rona had been one of those sudden dead, Allie doubted she'd even manage to stand, never mind walk into a church under the eyes of the watching world.

But thankfully she wasn't one of the bereaved, even though she'd walked those streets the night the plane had disintegrated, scattering debris and human remains around the town and its surrounding fields, turning roads into rivers of fire. Allie had stumbled on stray rivets and cut her leg on a jagged piece of metal, she'd inhaled the terrible varied smells of burning, she'd spoken to locals who could hardly manage sentences. She'd come close, but she had no right to grief today. Sympathy, pity, anger, yes. But not grief.

It dawned on Allie that for the first time in two weeks there was no rattle of rotors overhead. The military helicopters that had been quartering the skies in the search for wreckage were absent, presumably out of respect. The streets were empty of traffic too. Instead there was a heavy stillness in the street. Allie had never been in such a silent crowd. There was no conversation around her, no speculation about who was attending the service. Not even condemnation of the supposed bombers, or conjecture about who might be behind the attack. Just the gentle patter of rain on umbrellas.

But when the public figures arrived at the church gate, she heard a low murmur run through the crowd. The PM and her husband, the leader of the Opposition, the US ambassador, assorted half-recognised faces of politicians. And walking close on their heels, the unmistakable bulk of Wallace 'Ace' Lockhart. A couple of inches over six feet, solid legs bearing the wide body of a heavyweight boxer gone to seed, the newspaper proprietor was upholstered in a double-breasted black coat with an astrakhan collar. He topped it off with the inevitable homburg that Allie believed he wore solely because he thought it lent him a resemblance to Churchill, especially when he was smoking one of his Cohiba Esplendidos.

Typical of Ace Lockhart. Muscling in on an occasion where he had no business other than the bizarre form of showmanship that he inhabited. Ace Lockhart, the sole architect of all her present ills. As if today wasn't rough enough, here came the chopper to chop off her head.

She considered slipping away before the mourners left the church. Anything to avoid seeing her boss twice in one day. But before she could manage to find a gap in the crowd behind her, he turned his head, as if her malevolent gaze were magnetic. Their eyes met and she knew it would be more trouble than it was worth to leave before he did. If she'd learned one thing from her years inside the testosterone tent of national newspapers, it was never to give a bully fuel for his fire.

And she'd seen enough of Ace Lockhart at close quarters to know quite how much of a bully he could be. She'd been happily running the investigations unit of the *Sunday Globe* when Lockhart had bought the Globe & Clarion group in the wake of Rupert Murdoch's breaking of the print unions. Lockhart had decreed that investigations were a waste of money — too much time spent for too little return, he said. Because he only counted return in cash terms, not respect or moral authority. Then he'd decided the paper's northern operation was a waste of money too. Lockhart had fired all the journalists apart from Allie, two football reporters and a single photographer. The rest could be handed over to freelances.

He'd added insult to injury by giving her the meaningless title of northern news editor. Boss of sweet fuck all. A herder of freelances, a harrier of contacts, a chaser of headlines and no time at all to do the kind of stories Allie lived for. He'd stripped her of the job she'd clawed her way up to, then handed her a poisoned chalice and dared her to react with anything but magnanimity. Because what he'd done to all her colleagues had been worse. Allie knew it, and still despised herself for going along with Lockhart's darkhearted game. Sorry, restructuring plan.

So she turned up her coat collar and cooried in against the cold, glad of the fleece lining of her slouched mid-calf boots. They'd been a freebie from a fashion shoot her partner Rona had been running for *She* magazine; Allie had benefited from the disdain Rona showed any footwear (apart from walking boots) with less than a two-inch heel.

It wasn't idle waiting. It never was with Allie. Her eyes were busy, ranging over the crowds, the police, her fellow hacks. Her ears were alert too, ready to pick up anything that might add colour or texture to whatever she'd end up writing for Sunday's paper. Or that might provide a lead she could pass on to one of the freelances she used now instead of colleagues. She might not be an investigative journalist any longer, but the instincts she'd cultivated over a decade refused to lie down and die.

The service was impossible to avoid, hymns wavering on the air, the indistinct sound of prayers and readings and eulogies carried from the church and from the live transmissions that leaked around them. The minister spoke of the importance of valuing

12

forgiveness over revenge. As if there were anyone obvious to wreak revenge on, Allie thought.

At last, the doors opened and the mourners emerged. Heads down in grief or against the weather, their shades of black rendered them almost indistinguishable. All but Lockhart, who made his way down the path, head held high, elegant eyebrows raised, scanning the crowds. As he reached the street, he peeled off and made for Allie. He leaned over her and spoke, his treacle tones at odds with the steel in his words. As usual. 'Burns.' A pause. 'Make sure you include me in whatever your story is on Sunday. There's a couple of photographers here from the *Clarion*, they'll let you have some shots to choose from.' Then the smile, bestowed on the crowd around her as much as on Allie herself. One hand twitched upwards, as if he'd been about to give them a gracious wave then thought better of it. *How very unlike him.*

Only four days into the new year, and already Allie was despising herself for being at the beck and call of Ace Lockhart's monstrous ego. Not for the first time, she wondered how her dreams and ambitions had slumped so low.

2

The sound of Enya's *Watermark* greeted Allie when she opened the front door, rapidly followed by the insanely happy arrival of their Border terrier Germaine, her tail wagging like a stubby metronome. Allie bent to scratch her ears, then headed for the source of the music. It was only a Wednesday, but when Allie walked into their kitchen after the gloom of Lockerbie, it was as social as a Saturday-night dinner party. The remnants of a cheese course were scattered round the table and Rona was holding court, close to the punchline of an anecdote Allie had heard before but still relished. Her purple silk shirt shimmered in the lights, adding even more drama to her tale. Around her sat three of their friends, rapt and already chuckling. For a moment, no one noticed Allie and she drank in the room. These were some of the people who had embraced them since their arrival from Glasgow half a dozen years before. The people who had made them feel less like exiles.

Alix Thomas, rock drummer and record producer, passionate, innovative and provocative, her halo of glossy black curls an inheritance from her Barbadian father, her sharp features and startling green eyes from her Manc mother, relaxed in a black knock-off Sergio Tacchini shell suit; Jess Jones, research chemist with a pharmaceutical giant, whose blonde blue-eyed innocent English-rose prettiness masked an intelligence that took no prisoners and a cynical wit that cut the feet from under anyone who tried to write her off, in her usual uniform of pressed white shirt and jeans; and Bill Mortensen, a private eye whose fair Viking appearance couldn't have been less noir and whose brilliance with computers was matched only by his restless quest to find the right woman, probably hampered by his fondness for primary-coloured polo shirts and wrinkled chinos. They'd arrived severally in Allie and Rona's lives and now it was hard to remember the enforced narrowness of their life in Glasgow. There, it had been hard enough to be taken on anything like equal terms as a woman; to be out would have been professional suicide for both journalists.

They'd managed to stay under the gaydar for a few years, each maintaining their own homes but spending the nights together in one or the other. But it had all become too much for Allie when she'd been handed a story by the newsdesk about a social worker who'd abandoned her four children to the care of her lorry-driver husband so she could move in with another woman. A former client to boot, just to add to the tabloid salaciousness. Allie had done some digging and uncovered evidence that the husband had a history of violence towards his wife. But when she'd explained this to the deputy news editor, he'd literally rubbed his hands in glee. 'That's even better, Allie. The heartless bitch leaves her kids with a violent husband. Ya beauty!'

She couldn't get out of writing the story, so she'd made it as dull as she could manage — woman forced to abandon her children to escape brutal husband — but what had appeared in the paper had been transformed by the subs' desk into a half-page sen-

15

sation whose homophobia was matched only by its misogyny.

And so she'd put the word out that she was looking for a job in Manchester, a city variously known in tabloid terms as Gaychester, Gunchester and Madchester. It took only a couple of months before she heard that the Sunday Globe was seeking to expand its investigative team in the North. It felt like a miracle — Allie's dream job opening up in the very city where she wanted to live. Her only concern was what it would mean for her relationship with Rona.

She should have known better. Rona had responded with a gleeful whoop, a chest-crushing hug and the bottle of Lanson Black Label that had been sitting in the fridge waiting for a celebration. 'Manchester! Bloody amazing,' she'd said, toasting Allie. 'A feature round every corner. With my contacts, I'll be in clover.'

'I don't understand.'

'Freelance, Allie. I can jack in the tramlines of the *Clarion* women's page and finally cover all the stuff I love. Fashion, design, music, theatre. *Coronation Street.*' Her eyes were shining. 'We're moving up in the world, Allie.'

And so it had seemed. Allie had sold her flat, Rona had rented out her mews cottage with its Alasdair Gray mural, and they'd bought the house in Chorltonville with a mortgage that still felt immense to Allie. But the money came flowing in, thanks to her new improved salary and Rona's apparently endless stream of articles. They'd made forays into the city's gay subculture, tentative at first, but more openly as their anxieties subsided and they made new friends.

Now Allie watched her partner, animated and

16

self-assured, blond hair glinting in the bright light of the kitchen, and felt the familiar surge of pride and love, still as strong after nearly a decade since their first kiss. 'But Chaz had misremembered the room number,' Rona said, filling her voice with suspense. 'Instead of 354, he'd told the night porter 345. And that, my friends, is how I was wakened at four in the morning by a naked photographer in my hotel room.' And as everyone laughed, Rona jumped up and crossed the room to pull Allie into her arms. 'You're back,' she murmured into her ear, then gently kissed the corner of her mouth. She drew Allie to the table, where Alix had already poured her a glass of red.

'How was it?' Jess asked as Allie shrugged out of her coat and took a deep draught of wine.

'Draining. I feel like I've been swimming in other people's sadness.' Allie sighed. She caught a con-cerned look from Rona. 'But they did it all with so much dignity.'

'I've been amazed by the lack of strident calls for revenge,' Bill said.

'I do think people are still in shock. As soon as the intelligence services identify for sure who's behind it, you can bet there'll be reprisals.' Jess reached for the grapes and broke off a small bunch, putting them on a plate with a few oatcakes and placing it in front of Allie. 'Eat,' she said, pushing the remains of the cheese towards her.

'Sorry, we finished the beef stroganoff,' Alix said.

'I'm not that hungry.' Allie carved a chunk of crum-bly white Lancashire and a wedge of Camembert. 'As if the funeral wasn't hard enough, bloody Ace Lock-hart had to make a point of monstering me.'

'What do you mean, Burns?' Alix leaned forward,

frowning. Everyone knew the stories about Lockhart and his war of the tabloids with Rupert Murdoch. Being friends with Allie had let her friends feel they had the inside track on the larger-than-life figure that the rest of the media maintained a love-hate relationship with. They despised him but they couldn't resist him; he was perpetually good copy.

Allie sighed. 'The usual ego trip. He spotted me on his way into the church then hit me up afterwards with a demand that I include his presence in whatever I write for Sunday's paper. It's so galling. He destroys my career then expects me to join his fan club.'

'He probably thinks he's made your career, not wrecked it,' Jessica observed. 'After all, he made the whole of the northern team redundant except for you. I bet he's convinced you owe him big time.'

Rona opened another bottle and topped up the glasses. 'If he spares you a thought at all. The likes of us, we're just dust beneath his chariot wheels.'

Allie grimaced. 'Enough about Lockhart. I'm sorry I brought him up. Cheer me up, guys. Somebody must have had a better day than me. Jess, what have you been up to?'

'It's actually been an exciting week, believe it or not. My group is prepping for a clinical trial of a combined therapy to prevent HIV-positive people from developing pneumocystis. We're excited about it, because it's such a major life-threatening infection for patients with AIDS. And I also heard today that one of the research groups reckons they've got some promising leads towards a vaccine against HIV.'

'That'd be a game changer,' Bill said.

'No kidding,' Jess said. 'I'm thinking of applying to join the team. But it's probably going to be based at our research facility in Groningen and I'm not sure I want to move to Holland.'

'Very flat, Holland,' Rona said. 'You'd miss the hills.'

'More importantly, I'd miss evenings like this.' She grimaced as the music changed to the *Chariots of Fire* soundtrack. 'Though maybe not the background music.'

Allie shrugged. 'It's only dinner-party wallpaper. But Jess, we relocated and it's the best thing we ever did.'

'Second best, surely?' Rona said with a cheeky little smile. 'Jess, you really should go for it. You'd miss us and we'd miss you, but there's flights every day to Amsterdam and we'd visit. And there are plenty lovely dykes out there to change your life with.'

'Not to mention that it'd be so exciting to be out there at the leading edge of research that could change the world,' Allie said drily.

'And God knows this is one bit of it that needs changing,' Alix sighed. 'Bill, do you remember Matt Singleton?'

Bill tugged at his beard. 'Bass player? Used to be with Trudge? Were you not in the Anarcho-Syndicalists with him back in the olden days?'

Jess sniggered. 'Catchy name.'

Alix shrugged. 'Catchier than our tunes, trust me. Hence the past tense. Somehow Mattie always ended up being the best musician in an average band, so when I started the studio, I got back in touch with him. Always need good session players, you know?' She pulled a leather tobacco pouch out of her pocket and began skinning up with a casualness born of long practice. 'I knew he was doing heroin, but for a long time it looked like *he* was running the game, not the drug.' She crumbled some dope into the tobacco. 'But sometimes the need beats your good sense, and he shared his needles.' She sighed. Allie knew what was coming. 'And boom, HIV ambushed the boy.'

'High price to pay for a moment of stupidity,' Rona said. HIV, they all knew, was the death sentence. The only question was how long it would take AIDS to reach you. But it didn't matter if it was a crawl or a gallop, the end result was the same.

'Yeah. So what I was doing today, Allie, was a little bit of personal grief. I went to see poor old Mattie who isn't dead yet but is literally at death's door, finger poised above the bellpush.' She forced a smile that went nowhere near her eyes then licked the adhesive on the Rizla, closing the joint with neat expertise.

Allie reached out and covered Alix's free hand with hers, just as Bill put an arm round her thin shoulders. 'That's shit,' he said.

Alix faked a laugh. 'Yeah, no idea where I'm going to get a decent bass man now.' She withdrew her hand from Allie's and sparked up her lighter. She took a deep drag on the joint, then passed it to Bill.

'Is he being looked after?' Jess asked.

'He's in the rehab unit out at Prestwich. Well, they call it rehab, but these days it's more like a warehouse for the dying.' Alix gave herself a little shake. 'That's not fair, I'm sorry. The staff are great. And they're running clinics for the patients who are HIV positive but haven't developed full-blown AIDS yet. Helping them to get clean and stay off the smack.' She looked straight at Allie. 'You know what the funny thing is? This fifteen-bed unit in north Manchester? More than half the guys there are your lot.'

Genuinely puzzled, Allie asked, 'What do you mean,

20

my lot?'

'Scotchies. It's not just whisky you're exporting these days. It's junkies too.'

3

There was nothing outside the tinted windows of the Jaguar to distract Genevieve Lockhart. The grey sweep of the motorway that whisked her from the airport to her father's house was dull enough in daylight; after dark, she could have been anywhere. What, she wondered, lay behind Ace Lockhart's latest summons? He'd groomed his only child from her earliest years to inherit the empire he'd built with single-minded determination; there had been no choice but to give in. And besides, he'd always painted it as an exciting prospect. But he liked to keep her guessing and she had no idea why she'd been called away from supper with friends to board the Ace Media private helicopter. That ignorance provoked a niggle of anxiety.

They left the motorway and drove down a wide street lined with tenements. Suddenly those gave way on one side to tall spiked railings, behind them a line of mature trees, bare now but in the summer a colour chart of green — limes, sycamores, oaks, beeches, birches, alders and rowans side by side, their trunks obscuring the parkland beyond. A quarter of a mile passed, then the car swung into a wide driveway. The driver pressed a button on a remote control and the elaborate wrought-iron gates stuttered open.

Every time she arrived here, Genevieve couldn't resist a wry smile. If anything was a tribute to her father's deal-making, it was Voil House. The Palladian mansion had been built on the proceeds of the slave trade, and stuffed with valuable furniture, paintings, ceramics and silver. The extensive parkland had been designed to showcase an unrivalled collection of rare plants. The rhododendron collection alone was world class. The last of the Voils, Sir Alexander, had died childless in 1956 and he'd left a will of infuriating idiosyncrasy. The house and grounds were left to Glasgow City Council with the proviso that the plant collection should be maintained and open to the public for the same price as a ticket on the city underground. The house and its contents were to remain intact and were not to be open to the public. If the council failed in its obligations, the whole estate was to be sold to the highest bidder and the proceeds donated to the Royal Horticultural Society. In vain, the city council had gone to court to vary the terms of the bequest. They were stuck with the off-white elephant.

Their unlikely saviour had been Wallace Lockhart. In exchange for a peppercorn rent, he agreed to maintain the mansion. There was nothing in the will to say the contents had to remain in the exact spot where they'd been when Sir Alexander Voil had died, so Ace had moved everything he disliked upstairs to the attic floor. The dining room and one of the drawing rooms remained in their full magnificence to impress visitors, but in the rooms he and Genevieve routinely used, he'd installed comfortable modern furniture. The one thing he hadn't been able to budge them on was installing a helipad in the grounds.

That evening, she found him in the room he called the den. Half the size of a football pitch, it was furnished with vast sofas, marble-topped tables, a lavish drinks cabinet and the biggest TV screen Genevieve had ever seen. Instead of gilt-framed portraits, the walls were lined with photographs of Ace in the company of heads of state and film stars. He was sprawled in the only armchair, designed to his own specification, his feet up on a wide leather pouffe. His shoes lay askew where he'd kicked them off and his tie was a crumple on the rug by his chair. On his kettledrum stomach, he balanced a tumbler with a thin meniscus of what she knew would be an absurdly expensive rare malt whisky. Its rarity was his excuse for his sparing measures; Genevieve suspected it had more to do with his need always to be in control. She had never seen him drunk.

'Ah, Genny,' he groaned, raising a hand in greeting.

'Hello, Ace.' She crossed the room and planted a kiss on his forehead.

He muted the TV and nodded towards the drinks cabinet. 'Help yourself to a drink.' He delved into the bowl of Twiglets on the side table and crammed a handful into his mouth.

'Don't turn it off on my account. I know you can't bear to miss the news.' She poured herself a generous schooner of Tio Pepe. She turned back, catching sight of the Lockerbie memorial service on the screen. 'You were there, weren't you?'

He swallowed and grunted. 'Maggie made a meal of it. These people, they don't know what tragedy is. How many died in this bombing? Two hundred and seventy, for fuck's sake. The Nazis murdered more people than that in my shtetl. No memorial service for them, though. No prime minister dabbing her eyes with a hankie for my family.'

'They had families too, the people who died on Pan Am 103, Ace,' she protested. 'They're suffering the way you suffered when our family was wiped out.'

24

He let out a puff of breath. 'I know, sweetheart, I know. And I'm not callous about their individual pain. But I can't help feeling this kind of public memorial is a mere indulgence. How many people there today actually had any personal stake in this? It's little more than a performance of grief, not the real thing.'

'Nevertheless. You'll plaster it all over the first five pages of every one of your titles tomorrow. The *Clarion*, the *Globe*, the *Mercury* — they'll all be vying for the most tear-jerking copy.'

He sipped his drink. 'That's showbiz, Genny. It sells papers. But I bet you that none of that crowd will take their grief and make something out of it, not even the ones directly affected. Not like I did.'

It was a story Genevieve knew so well she could almost lip-synch it. The village in the debatable lands of Eastern Poland. The arrival of the Nazis and the rounding up of the Jews. The sound of gunfire, the crackle of flame. The screams. And Chaim Barak who hid in the dung heap in the byre till the shtetl grew eerily quiet. Then the escape, sleeping in ditches, eating roots and berries, making contact with General Anders's fledgling Polish Army. Then the Middle East, the hell of Monte Cassino, the oak leaf medal for gallantry, the liberation of Berlin, the discovery of a stash of German scientific research papers and the brilliant idea of helping himself to them. 'Liberating knowledge,' he self-righteously dubbed it. Even Genevieve could see it had an unscrupulous side to it. But in 1945, scruples had often been hard to come by.

She let him wind up the story, then said, 'Let's hope the Americans don't jump on this as an excuse for vengeance.' She curled up in a corner of one of the sofas.

'They're still not sure where to jump. The smart money's on Libya, but there's a distinct dearth of evidence.' More Twiglets, washed down with a tiny sip of whisky.

'So why am I here, Ace? Are we planning what to do for next year's big celebration?'

There was a momentary flash of surprise, quickly hidden behind a smile. 'What exactly are we celebrating?'

'Don't tell me you've forgotten? Glasgow, European City of Culture in 1990? I presumed we'd be planning some cultural extravaganza to blazon our name across the heavens?' Her voice was light with mischief.

He flapped a hand at her. 'I'm confident someone below your pay grade can handle that.'

'So, if it's not that, why am I here?'

He graced her with his loveliest smile. 'It's not enough that your old dad wants your company?'

She snorted. 'If that were all, you wouldn't have sent the chopper. You're too cheap. You'd have told me to get on the sleeper.'

His smile turned down at the corners, an exaggerated clown's grimace, his eyebrows high, perfect arcs. 'It's as well my enemies don't know me like you do.' He shifted his heavy body more upright in the chair, his belly appearing to move independently of the rest of his torso. 'I need you to do something important. Not for me, but for the business.'

'You know I'll always do my best for us.' Faced with her father's seriousness, Genevieve straightened up, planting her feet on the floor. The tragic death of her mother before her fifth birthday had meant there was no one close enough to temper her father's enthusiasms. And when things turned against him, as they sometimes had the temerity to do, she was the one who capered and cajoled him out of his disappointment and rage.

'You know my motto. When opportunity knocks, throw the door open wide.' Lockhart heaved himself to his feet and shambled across to the humidor that sat on the drinks cabinet. 'Well, tonight, opportunity has taken a battering ram to our back door.' He took out a cigar and fiddled with it, chopping off the end. On his way back to the chair, he lit it with the battered brass Zippo he'd used since 1942 and puffed at the cigar. 'America, Genny, America.'

This was news to Genevieve. But she held her tongue, familiar with her father's habit of setting the scene before he got to the point. Instead, she nodded redundant encouragement.

'Simon Levertov was one of the mourners today.'

It was a name she knew well. Levertov was the head of a family empire that controlled a sprawling web of local papers throughout the Midwest. Its flagship titles were city papers in Chicago, Minneapolis/St Paul, Cincinnati and Indianapolis. The outlier was the New York *Daily Globe*. Rupert Murdoch had come close to buying it, but the family had rebuffed him. The word was that Murdoch's tabloids left a bad taste in the mouths of the conservative Levertovs. Her father had been assiduously courting the family ever since. 'What was he doing there?'

'Thirty-five students from Syracuse were on the flight. The Levertovs own one of the local papers.'

She nodded, understanding. 'Did you get the chance to speak to him?'

He exhaled a blue cloud of aromatic smoke. 'He

27

sought me out. They're ready to sell the *Globe*. It's the perfect fit for us. It gives us a prestige foothold in the US, a springboard to drive us forward into new markets.'

Genevieve knew how much her father craved the New York *Globe*. He loved the idea of new worlds to conquer, but even more than that, he loved anything that reeked of victory in his pissing contest with Rupert Murdoch. To win a trophy the Australian press baron had been chasing would be more than the icing on the cake. But that didn't mean it was the right choice. Wary, she said, 'There's a reason they want rid of the *Globe*, Ace. It's losing money and circulation like a runaway train.'

'Of course it is,' Lockhart said, waving away the objection as if he was batting away an annoying fly. 'Because the Levertovs have no idea how to produce a vibrant paper that speaks to the working man.' Seeing her frown, he added hastily, 'And woman, naturally, Genny. But in our hands, we'll reverse that downward trajectory. I'll send my best team from London to get the show on the road, and then we'll show New York what it's been missing.'

His obvious passion for publishing and the power it brought was irresistible. His boisterous delight in success had infected Genevieve at an early age. There was, she knew, little point in arguing. Ace Lockhart was the only god in his universe. 'Have you set up talks?'

Lockhart guffawed. 'Genny, we've done the deal,' he said. 'We sat round a table in a dismal little hotel after the memorial, we agreed a price and we shook hands on it.'

She knew she was supposed to rejoice, and she

managed a decent facsimile. But she couldn't help a sense of dread creeping into her gut. If it was that straightforward, why had he summoned her to Voil House with such urgency? Even though this was the biggest acquisition he'd made since he'd bought the *Clarion* and the UK *Globe*, he could easily have told her over the phone, leaving the celebration for their next meeting in a few days. She knew her father well enough to understand that there was more to come. She reminded herself he'd taken some dramatic and unusual routes to success, but that was a measure of his originality and nerve. Neither the intellectual rigour of St Andrews University nor MIT had managed to shake her belief in her father. So she summoned up a smile and raised her glass to him. 'What a coup.'

He shifted his bulk in the chair, pushing himself more upright with a creak of leather. 'There's only one problem.'

Here it comes, she thought. 'What's that, Ace?'

'Liquidity. We've extended ourselves to the limit to build the new printing plants in London.'

Which are nowhere near up and running yet, never mind washing their faces. Genevieve tried to hide her dismay. 'Can we borrow?'

Another cloud of smoke. 'It might be complicated. And it would definitely be expensive. Not to mention, a sign of weakness. I want us to go into America looking powerful, not cap in hand to the bankers. Murdoch would love that.'

A snatch of panic in her chest. So far, she'd had nothing to do with the flagship newspapers and magazines that defined Ace Media in the world's eyes. The cash cow that kept everything else afloat was the academic and scientific publishing, and that was

29

where he'd installed her. A year of intense intern-ships in every department, and now she was running a publishing house that had grown to rival the most prestigious university presses. 'You're not going to sell Pythagoras?'

He laughed in genuine astonishment. 'My goose that lays the golden eggs? Don't be silly, Genny. Besides, you're doing such a fine job there. No, I have another solution.' Lockhart gave her his most benev-olent smile, but Genevieve knew him well enough to understand this was often a Judas kiss.

'Tell me.'

'The pension funds. Pythagoras and Ace Media are carrying huge surpluses. Half a billion, Genny. Half. A. Billion.'

'But that's not company money,' she protested. 'It belongs to the pensioners, present and future.'

'I know that. What do you take me for? Some kind of robber baron?' His indignation sounded like the real thing. 'I'm proposing a loan.' He waved his cigar air-ily. 'A temporary arrangement. I know I can turn the New York *Globe* around in short order. This would be exactly the same as borrowing from the bank. Except that it would be a private transaction.'

Genevieve hid her unease. She knew if she showed it, he'd pounce. 'Is it legal?' was as far as she felt she could go.

His smile was sweet. 'Of course it's legal. All I need is for you as the MD of Pythagoras to countersign the papers.'

It wasn't a question.

She'd seen her father's rage rip against anyone who dared to impugn his integrity. She wanted never to be on the end of that fury. Even more, she didn't want to provoke the look of mournful disappointment that transformed his strong features when one of his trusted employees let him down. His eyes became moist, his lips parted, a bewildered frown creased his forehead. It was a moment that was usually followed by a sacking. OK, she knew he couldn't sack her. Being his daughter was a fixed point. But she'd seen him throw some of his oldest friends out of the charmed circle and knew how much that had hurt him. Genevieve loved her father; she couldn't have borne being banished from his affection and respect.

She took a deep breath. 'Pass me the pen.'

4

Allie loved watching Rona taking off her make-up last thing at night. The mask that faced the world disappeared, revealing the naked beauty that was just for her; it always felt like the most private intimacy. The buzz of the dope she'd smoked earlier had combined with the alcohol to ease the darkness of the day, leaving her feeling relaxed. And maybe just a little bit sexy? She stretched languorously.

'That was a weird little snippet Alix dropped on our toes tonight,' Rona said, sweeping a cotton pad across her eyelids.

'What?' Allie yawned. 'The Scots in the rehab clinic?'

'Yeah. I mean, I know Edinburgh's supposed to be the AIDS capital of Europe, but I didn't know they were actually fleeing the country.' Now for the mascara.

'Is it really that bad up there?'

'So I've heard. Last statistic I remember reading was that one per cent of the male population of the city is HIV positive. Which doesn't sound much, till you translate it into actual bodies. Four thousand or so in a wee city. Plus they'll not be stravaiging through the Georgian elegance of the New Town, will they? They'll be concentrated in the most deprived parts of town. And of course, nothing gets reported down here.' She opened her mouth to wipe off the lipstick, distorting her speech. 'Faraway place of which we know nothing, and all that. Not to mention it's the untouchables — the druggies and the gay boys.'

'You think there might be a story in it? Why the Edinburgh junkies are heading south?' Now Allie was alert. The prospect of a lead to dig into never failed.

'No idea. But it might be worth checking it out? If they're leaving because the NHS can't cope with the numbers, you could go either way. NHS swamped, locals complain other ailments are being ignored? Or HIV patients forced to leave because their city wants them gone?' The last of her foundation removed, Rona patted toner on her skin, then finally applied a layer of expensive night cream that smelled deliciously of lavender and geranium.

'Did they fall or were they pushed?'

'You never know what you'll find till you go looking.' Rona raised her eyebrows in the mirror.

'You're right. Whatever it is, I should take a look at it. Maybe tomorrow, if I get a couple of hours spare.' As Rona slipped under the duvet next to her, Allie reached out. 'But right now, I've got more pressing matters on my mind.'

'So have I,' Rona said in a different tone. 'Are you sure you're OK? When you walked in tonight, you looked like someone had put you through a mangle and squeezed all the life out of you.'

'I thought I'd dealt with the night the plane came down. Put it away in a box at the back of my head and moved on. But seeing the grief on those faces today — it all came rolling back.' Allie inhaled deeply. 'But I'll be fine. It's done now.'

'I'm not so sure about that.' Rona stroked Allie's hair. 'The things you see, the things you hear on the news beat — I see it eating into you, Allie.'

Allie scoffed. 'It just takes wee nibbles, Rona. Then it heals over. Deep down, I'm OK. This is what I do. This is who I am.'

Rona looked dubious, but said no more. She lay awake long after Allie had drifted into an apparently untroubled sleep, unconvinced by her partner's words. Germaine, alerted by the instinct that draws dogs to humans, nestled tight to her side. Rona turned on her side and pulled Germaine close. Between them, they'd have to find a way to rescue Allie from herself.

* * *

Between dealing with a royal visit, yet another political scandal in Liverpool and a clutch of tedious TV spin-off stories, it took Allie more than a month to find that couple of spare hours to chase the AIDS story. Being a one-woman roadshow meant the demands of her job were constant. Every Tuesday she had to have dug up enough stories to pitch at the weekly conference. Then she had to assign the ones that made the grade to a freelance, which meant chivvying and chasing them, a task as frustrating as trying to corral toddlers in a playground. In the interstices, she needed to maintain her own contacts and mine them for possible stories she could pursue herself. Keeping on top of the greedy demands of the London news-desk left virtually no time for pursuing the stories that truly interested her. Not a day went by that she didn't mourn her investigative berth.

In the end, Allie went into the office one Monday afternoon in early February. Technically, Monday was her day off, but that didn't stop the London features desk calling to instruct her to set up jobs for later in the week; or the picture desk demanding contact numbers for whoever they wanted to photograph for the colour supplement.

She hooked up with Rona in the kitchen over a plate of soup at lunchtime. 'I might as well go in,' she said. 'It's the only way I'll get peace from the bloody phone. I need to get up to speed on AIDS and HIV before I take a proper look at this Edinburgh idea. I'll hide away in the library — nobody will think of looking for me there.'

'Ironic but true. While you're there, can you do me a favour?'

'Always. What do you need?' Although, as a freelance, Rona had no right of access to the *Globe* library, Allie reckoned it was the least that Ace Lockhart's empire owed them.

'Can you do a cuttings check on murders in soap series? I've heard a whisper about a murder coming up in *Coronation Street* and I want to be ready to roll with the background features as soon as I can bottom it.' Rona gave Allie a mock-beseeching look.

'Who's for the chop?'

Rona shook her head. 'That's for me to know and you to find out from a third-party source.'

Allie grinned. 'I'll see what I can find for you.'

'And don't steal it.' They both knew Rona's words were a tease. They'd established the principle of Chinese walls when they'd moved to Manchester. Back in Glasgow, they'd both been working for the same title. From time to time, one would turn up a story that they both agreed was better suited to the other's department, so the finder would hand it over. But now Allie couldn't afford to have her boss in London think she was passing stories to a freelance who might sell them to the opposition. So they'd agreed not to share. Except when Allie's boss spiked one of her stories. Few things gave Allie more pleasure than seeing one of her rejected stories make a page lead or a magazine feature somewhere else.

'You could always sell it to me,' Allie said, rising to put her bowl in the dishwasher.

Rona chuckled. 'You don't pay enough. I can think of at least three newsdesks who'd outbid you.'

'Fair enough. All the more for you to lavish on me.'

★   ★   ★

Although Ace Lockhart's swingeing staff reductions had cut the newsroom to the bare bones, he'd listened to whoever had persuaded him that the library represented an irreplaceable asset. Admittedly, these days it was only staffed between noon and eight in the evening, the duties shared by one and a half librarians. They struggled to keep up with the cuttings, but at least the archive remained. For now.

An afternoon of poring over the files gave Allie a working knowledge of what had been written in the UK media about HIV and AIDS since the first cases had been identified. It left her fingers black with newsprint and her heart filled with a slow burn of rage at the virulent homophobia and lack of empathy she'd encountered. Whether it was the tabloids with their lurid 'gay plague' headlines, or the broadsheets with their equally censorious faux-scientific condemnations, this was a disease whose coverage blamed the victims for their own fate. Even in Manchester, with its gay village at the heart of the city's nightlife, its citizens had been told by their chief of police that people with AIDS were 'swirling in a human cesspit of their own making'.

There were even lowlifes who seized AIDS as a pulpit to preach their hatred. It was God's revenge on gay men, a modern-day Sodom and Gomorrah, sent to punish them for their deviant ways. The only flaw in their argument, as Allie always enjoyed pointing out, was that, taken to its logical conclusion, it established that God was not only a woman, but a lesbian, since lesbians were the lowest group on the totem pole of risk.

It was a riposte she always delivered with a note of savagery. For Allie herself had lost one of her closest and dearest friends to AIDS only eighteen months before. She'd bonded with Marcus on their journalism training scheme and they'd stayed close, their connection only strengthening when her feelings for Rona forced her to examine her own sexuality. Marcus was darkly funny, endlessly smart and constantly embarrassed by his own kindnesses. He'd been a talented subeditor, rising to the position of deputy night editor on a regional daily in the Midlands when he'd fallen ill with a strain of pneumonia most commonly found in sheep. Less than six months later, Allie had read a poem at his funeral. So the pile of AIDS clippings felt like a very personal slap in the face.

The slap to the other cheek was that the efforts of pharmaceutical researchers like Jess earned barely a paragraph. The attempts to find drugs that would either cure HIV or temper the effects of full-blown AIDS clearly provoked little interest from newsdesks. There was a certain level of ghoulish fascination with the obscure and humiliating conditions that afflicted AIDS patients, and, inevitably, the occasional heroic

37

celebrity who actually hugged one of the twenti-
eth-century lepers. But other than that? It was simply,
as one of her cynical colleagues back in Glasgow had
called it, 'God's pruning fork'.

By the end of the afternoon, Allie had worked up
a head of righteous anger. If there was a story here,
she was going to find it. She set the duty librarian to
researching Rona's request and called Alix. 'Hey, girl,
how are you doing?' Allie opened.

'Been better, been worse,' Alix said. In the background was the faint clash of electric guitars. 'You still
on for dinner at mine on Sunday?'

'Wouldn't miss it. I'm not ringing to call it off. I've
got other motives.'

Alix laughed, a deep throaty chuckle. 'Nothing new
there, then. What can I do for you, Burns?'

'I want to follow up on the conversation we had a
few weeks back about the AIDS rehab facility. But
first, how's your friend Matt doing?'

The guitars stopped on a discord and Allie heard
two indistinct male voices argue under Alix's deep
sigh. 'He's not great, to be honest. They're talking
about weeks at the most.'

'I'm sorry.'

'I know. Why are you asking?'

'What you said about the Scottish patients moving
down from Edinburgh? I want to take a look at it.'

'What's your angle?' Alix was her friend, but that
didn't mean she was a pushover for whatever story
Allie wanted to chase.

Now a drum break rattled faintly in Allie's ear. 'I
want to find out what's going on. What's driving the
exodus? Is Manc being dangled as a kind of Great
White Hope, or is it that Edinburgh is so shit for

them? I want the story behind the bare facts, Alix.'

'I don't think talking to Mattie is a good idea, Allie. He's got lesions on his brain now. A lot of the time, he's not lucid. He doesn't know who I am, or where he is.'

Allie had suspected as much. 'I get that, Alix. What I was wondering was whether you'd made connections with any of the Edinburgh lads? Or staff. Doctors, nurses, who might talk to me. Off the record, if that's the only way of getting them to talk.'

A crash of cymbals. Distracted, Alix muttered. 'Oh, for fuck's sake. I need to sort these bloody children out. Let me think about it, Burns. I don't want to throw anyone to the wolves.'

Allie stared at the dead phone in her hand. Just when exactly had she become one of the wolves?

5

Allie pulled up outside Alix's studio. The only clue to what went on inside the squat brick building in the low-rent street behind the city's high-security prison was a small metal plaque that read SOUND AND FISSION above a graph with a jagged line like a life support machine on a hospital soap.

They'd spoken late the previous evening, Alix intense and protective, Allie reassuring and driven. In the end, Allie had been just persuasive enough. Now, Alix came striding out bang on time, hair tripling the size of her head, a long leather coat swirling around her. She got into the car and leaned in to brush a kiss across Allie's cheek. 'Sorry I made it so hard for you,' she said.

'Don't be. It's OK to be careful.'

'I totally trust you on my own account, Burns. But other people are more fragile than me. These guys? A lot of them have already been rejected by their families and colleagues. They don't want to be judged all over again.' Alix gave her an apologetic smile.

Allie nodded her understanding. 'So, I need directions. Prestwich, yeah?'

It took them just over twenty minutes to reach the HIV facility. The two-storey Victorian building was set in the grounds of a small general hospital. If it had been built from stone, it would have had the Gothic air of Castle Dracula, but the Accrington red brick made it look more like something created by a pre-teen in

Lego. Turrets and balconies gave it an unexpected glamour that belied what lay within. It might have been a minor resort hotel or a convalescent home. What it did not look like was a place where people came to die.

Alix led the way inside to a cramped reception area, clearly carved out from a much bigger space. The walls were painted a bilious mustard, the only decoration the familiar tombstone poster that urged, *AIDS. Don't Die of Ignorance.* Allie thought the people coming here were well past the point where that would have been a useful message. The middle-aged woman behind the desk clearly knew Alix. 'Hello, love. I'll just give the ward a bell and check Matt's up for a visit.'

'Thanks, Denise. Is Dr Rob around?'

Denise picked up the phone and dialled. 'He is. Did you want to see him?' Then she held up a finger and spoke into the handset. 'Julie, it's Denise at the front desk. How's young Matt today? Alix is here to see him.' She listened and nodded. 'Thanks, love.' She replaced the receiver and smiled. 'Up you go. Is your friend going with you?'

'Yes, if that's OK,' Allie said.

'You'll have to sign in, love.' Denise pushed a clip-board towards her. 'Alix knows the drill.' She turned back to Alix. 'I'll tell Dr Rob you're looking for a word.'

Once they were past the reception area, all the visual signals indicated that this was definitely a hospital setting. That, and the smell of disinfectant that left only the faintest traces of what it was hiding. They emerged from the lift to face a nurses' station. Alix waggled her fingers in a wave to the nurse on duty and carried on down the hall. At the end of the corridor, they turned into a high-ceilinged room with a pentagonal bay window. On either side of the room was a bed; in both beds, a man propped up on pillows. At first glance, they seemed quite old. But when Allie looked more closely, she saw they were young men gaunt with illness and pain. One had the familiar purple blemishes of Kaposi's sarcoma, a cancer whose rarity had been trounced by AIDS. The other man had some sort of rash on his throat and cheeks.

Alix made for the one with the skin irritation. A smile spread thin on his face. 'Alix,' he said, his voice faint and scratchy. 'What's new, babe?'

'This is my friend Allie. I told you about her?'

He studied Allie. 'Yeah, you did.' His voice trailed off and he frowned. His face cleared and he nodded. 'You're the hack, right?'

'I am,' Allie said, offering a hand to shake. Matt raised his arm and dropped his fingers into hers.

'Remember I told you Allie wants to write about the Scotch lads that have ended up here?'

Matt tipped his chin in a nod. 'You need to talk to Jamesie.' One finger raised, pointing to the other bed. 'He's from Edinburgh.'

'That's right,' a throaty rasp came from the other bed. 'What's your interest, pal?'

Allie drifted across the room. 'My name's Allie Burns. I'm a reporter. I used to work in Glasgow but now I'm based here in Manchester.'

'Who do you work for? I mean, none of the papers has a good word for guys like us. I don't want to get tricked into saying shit that'll get twisted.' His accent was Edinburgh. Not the posh bray of privately educated lawyers and politicians, but the sprawling vowels and slurred consonants of the housing schemes.

'I'm an investigative reporter.' It wasn't exactly a lie. 'I want to write about why people with HIV and AIDS are leaving Scotland. I suspect there's a story there about a lack of provision in the Scottish system. I work for the *Sunday Globe*. But I don't twist stuff. That's the whole point of doing the investigations. It's to get behind the lies and the corruption, not to make it worse.'

A short bark of laughter, then an explosion of coughing. 'Fuck,' he groaned at the end of it. 'What's in it for me?'

'I'll be honest,' Allie said, pulling up a visitor's chair to Jamesie's bedside. 'I suspect I'm too late to the party to be any use to you. But if we can shame the authorities into doing more to prevent the spread, and to treat people that haven't dodged the bullet better than they have been doing? Well, that's kind of a legacy.'

'Legacy. Fuck. My legacy's probably passing this disease on to all the guys that have sucked me off. Or everybody I've ever shared a needle with.'

He wasn't wrong, she thought. 'You didn't know you were passing on anything more than a bit of fun. It's not your fault this disease came out the woodwork.'

Jamesie gave an approximation of a shrug. 'Mibbes. But I can't blame anybody else for getting hooked on the smack. That was down to me.'

It wasn't the time or the place for Allie to protest about the confluence of social circumstances and government policies that had contributed to the epidemic of shooting up drugs. Instead, she said, 'I wish I could make it easier for folk to avoid getting drawn into that black hole. But what I can do is try to change how people like you get treated. You could help me with that. What have you got to lose, talking to me?'

A bitter laugh that turned into a clatter of coughing. Jamesie shook like a rat in a terrier's teeth. 'Fuck's sake,' he moaned at the end of the spasm. 'Aye, all right. Ask away.'

Allie reached out and patted his arm. 'Thanks. So how did you end up here?'

There were few surprises. Leaving school with no qualifications, unemployment, drugs, petty theft, hepatitis B, then a bunch of weird symptoms that didn't fit any obvious pattern. Finally, the diagnosis. HIV+. 'It didn't make me special in Muirhouse,' Jamesie said. 'Sometimes it felt like half of north Edinburgh was staggering about, either stoned or sick. Or both.'

'What about treatment?'

He shook his head. 'There isn't any treatment, is there? Not once you've got full-blown AIDS. They can't make us better. All they can do is warehouse us in places like this. But there's not nearly enough places like this. In Edinburgh, I couldn't get into rehab or any other treatment after I was diagnosed. There were no beds. No spaces. What clinics there are, they're bursting at the seams. We're just dumped on a scrapheap. If you've not got family or pals to look after you, it's just curtains. And guys like me, we don't have anybody that wants to take care of us. No cuddles from Princess Diana for the likes of us. So I came down here, where nobody knew I was HIV positive. I thought I could escape that feeling that I had a target on my back.'

He sighed. 'I cut right back on the heroin. I even got a wee job, working in a café. But I couldn't hack it. The drugs, man. They're even cheaper down here, and my life was shit. So I stopped trying. Started using again. Then I got sick. And here I am. One of the lucky ones.' Another bitter laugh, this time without the paroxysm of coughing. 'That's what they tell me. I've got a place here. I don't have to lie in my own piss and shit in a scummy bedsit, waiting to die.' He shook his head. 'I don't feel very fucking lucky. You know how old I am?'

Allie knew whatever guess she hazarded would be way off. All she could do was make a joke of it. 'Sixty-five?' she said.

He gave a harsh bark of approval. 'Aye, right. I'm twenty-four. And I'm going to be dead before I'm twenty-five.'

'I'm sorry,' Allie said, meaning it. 'Nobody deserves this.'

'You wouldn't think so, to read what you bastards write in the papers. We're the lowest of the low, junkies sharing needles. Even in here. Wait till you hear this. Some of the staff wanted to run a poster campaign — 'Don't jack up with a Jock.' Is that not racist, or what?'

Shocked, Allie was quick to respond. 'At the very least, it's insensitive. I told you, that's not the kind of story I'm writing.' She looked around the room. 'I hear there are a quite a few of you down here from Edinburgh.'

'I came down with three other guys. We were wanting away. Wanting to be some place nobody could point the finger at us all the time. I kind of hoped that there might be clinics where I could get medication that would stop me getting the full-on AIDS. You're always hearing rumours like that.' He shook his head, sadness in his eyes. 'But it's just bullshit. Once you've got the HIV, it's a death sentence. The only question is how long it takes you to get to the finishing line. Do you run or do you crawl? And that, my friend, is a lucky bag.'

It was hard to argue against that analysis. 'So how are your mates doing?'

Jamesie looked away, staring out at the trees stark against the winter sky. 'One dead, one down the hall, and one doing whatever it takes to get by out there on the streets.' He glanced quickly at her then away again. 'Not exactly a great strike rate. And we're just the tip of the iceberg. Last count, there were five other guys from Edinburgh in here.' He shook his head. 'We're here because there's nothing for us there. How are you going to change that?'

Allie had no answer. But she was spared by a voice from behind her.

'And since you can't change it, what the hell are you doing here?'

46

6

The man standing behind her was clearly a doctor. The white coat and the stethoscope were the giveaway. Allie gave him her best smile. 'Hi. I'm guessing you're Dr Rob?' 'It's Doctor Butler. You're a journalist, is that right?' There was no welcome in his voice or his expression.

Allie began to explain her reason for being there, but she'd barely managed the first sentence before Alix had joined them. 'She's one of the good guys, Doc,' she butted in.

He didn't look convinced. 'No such thing, when it comes to hacks.' Butler looked weary, dark smudges under his eyes and a downward turn to his mouth that had the air of permanence. He didn't look old enough to seem so defeated. 'Your tribe are not welcome here,' he added.

'I appreciate why you feel so hostile —'

'Hostile? You think this is hostile?' he scoffed. 'You people are the experts in hostile. You're the ones who dubbed my unit 'the Plague House'. You're the ones who knocked on doors along this street asking people how they felt about having drug addicts and male prostitutes spreading the AIDS virus in their community.'

'I don't condone that,' Allie insisted. 'But we're not all the same. I don't condemn the whole medical profession because some doctors and nurses refuse to treat people who are HIV positive. Look, I'm a lesbian, I know all about homophobia. And I've already lost one of my dearest friends to AIDS.'

'She's telling the truth,' Alix weighed in. 'Give her a chance, Doc.'

'I'm not even here to write about your clinic specifically,' Allie added.

'Then what are you doing in my clinic if you're not here to find a cheap headline?' His belligerence was fading now. Allie thought that had more to do with weariness than taking her at face value.

'I won't deny that I'm pursuing a story. That'd be pointless. But it's not about this place, except in relation to the number of people with HIV and AIDS turning up here from Edinburgh. As you can probably tell from my accent, I'm Scottish. And I was genuinely shaken to hear that the treatment facilities in Edinburgh are so oversubscribed that desperate people are uprooting their whole lives in a bid to get treatment. That's the story I want to write. The failure of my people' — here, Allie clamped a palm to her chest — 'that my people are letting guys like Jamesie down.' There was genuine dismay in her voice and she saw it hit home.

'So I told her she should speak to you,' Alix said. 'It's not right that people have to run away to get treatment. Plus, frankly, they're taking up beds that local people need just as badly. It's not like we've got any shortage of sick people round here.'

Butler shook his head. 'I don't discriminate on the basis of where people are from. Our patients are referred by local GPs and clinics. We assess them and we admit them when we have a bed on the basis of how ill they are. It's not my job to make judgements about other facilities.'

'Aye, but you know all about it,' Jamesie interrupted. 'You know because we've all told you how shit it is in Edinburgh. It took bloody ages for them to set up needle exchanges. The longer they held out, the more of us got infected from shared needles. And when it comes to getting off the drugs? Jeez. Don't get me wrong. There's some doctors and nurses working their arses off to help us. But there's a hell of a lot more who wish we'd just crawl into a corner and die. They fucking hate us.'

Butler ostentatiously looked at his watch. He sighed. 'I can give you fifteen minutes. But I'm warning you, any sign that you've got a hidden agenda and you're out that door a lot faster than you came in.' He turned abruptly on his heel and marched out of the ward. Allie raised her eyebrows at Alix and followed him.

He led her briskly down a corridor and unlocked the door at the very end. It led into a small turret room filled with light from a pentagonal bay with high windows. The other walls were lined with shelves crammed with books, folders and sheaves of loose papers. A desk was set side on to the bay. At one end was a pile of files, but the rest of the surface was clear. Butler waved Allie to a visitor's chair sitting at an angle to the desk, back to the watery winter sunlight. 'I have to keep it locked,' he said. 'These files are confidential. Nobody wants their HIV status to be public property.'

'I get that. Can you give me an idea of the scale of the exodus from Edinburgh?'

He shook his head. 'A lot of the information we get is anecdotal, but it's a significant number. We're seeing a few dozen, and that's only the ones that are making it as far as us. Multiply that by other cities with a fair-sized gay community . . .' He spread his hands. 'And every one of them is a vector for the disease. What I hate is you lot blaming people for getting sick. We're all careless of our lives in one way or another. It's just that some of us have worse outcomes than others.'

Allie bit back a defensive retort. 'Is that where the 'Don't jack up with a Jock' came from?'

It was as if she'd flipped a switch. His eyebrows lowered, his expression darkened. 'Is that what this is about? Making us look as prejudiced as the rest?'

Realising she'd mis-stepped, Allie responded quickly. 'Quite the opposite. The fact that you never ran with it told me all I needed to know about your attitudes here. But the fact it was even mooted indicated that there were a lot of Scots arriving on your doorstep.' In an attempt at diversion, she added, 'What happens to them when they get down here?'

'They're generally in free fall. They struggle to find somewhere to live. With no address, they can't sign on for social security. So they end up stealing or dealing or resorting to prostitution. And then they get sick.' Butler sighed heavily. 'They hear about us on the grapevine sooner or later.'

'How many beds have you got here?'

There was no humour in his smile. 'Fifteen.'

'And how many do you need?'

'It doesn't matter, does it? Nobody's going to wave a magic wand and give us another fifty. We're not even the Cinderella service. We're the ugly sisters.'

'How did you get into this?'

He shook his head. 'You said this isn't about this clinic. So don't try to make it about me.'

Allie held up her hands in surrender. She could

always look him up in the office copy of the Medical Directory if she needed more background. 'What about medical research? Are they making progress? Are you working with any of the pharmaceutical companies?'

Butler ran a hand through his thick dark hair, leaving it in an untidy crest. 'We're not big enough. We wouldn't give them the statistically significant results they need. I know there were some trials going on in Edinburgh, but I don't know what happened.'

'What do you mean, what happened?'

He shrugged. 'Your guess is as good as mine. They just stopped.'

7

Rona looked puzzled. 'They just stopped? What does that mean? Is your Doctor Butler out of the loop? Or is there more to it than that?'

'I don't know. I was hoping Jess might be able to help me out, but she's gone off to Holland to see whether she wants to join this new team over there.' Allie took a brick of chilli con carne from the freezer and dropped it into a small casserole dish. While it spun slowly in the microwave, she grated cheese into a bowl.

'So what are you going to do about it?' Rona asked, rummaging in the bread bin for a couple of pittas.

'I can either wait for Jess to come back or I can go up to Edinburgh and do some digging there. The thing is, with what I've got already from Butler and the three Edinburgh patients I eventually got to speak to, I've got enough for a great page lead. I might as well run with that now.'

'Really? It sounds to me like there might be a much better story lurking beneath the surface of the cancelled drugs trials.'

Allie put the block of cheddar back into the fridge, ignoring Germaine's eager nose prodding her leg. 'No, dog, you've had your dinner.' She absently leaned down, scratched the dog's head and turned back to Rona. 'A bird in the hand, though. The drugs trials thing might be a damp squib. Plus, if I've got my byline on a story with a positive spin about AIDS

52

patients, there's more chance of people thinking I'm on their side and talking to me.'

'Good point. By the way, I was talking to a senior executive on one of Lockhart's magazines today. There's muttering in the undergrowth that he's planning big production changes in the newspaper empire.' Rona took a couple of broad bowls from the cupboard and laid them on the kitchen table with forks and spoons.

'What sort of changes?'

'The rumour is that he's bought a building south of the Thames and he's installing a new line of presses, kitted out for direct input by journalists.'

Allie gave a low whistle as she took the chilli out of the microwave and dished it up. 'How very Ace. He let Rupert Murdoch fight the war and beat the print unions into submission. And now he comes along in Murdoch's wake and dips his bread in the gravy. It was only a matter of time, once he'd turned Manchester into a satellite printing operation instead of a proper newspaper office. The printers know they're beaten before they start. There'll be no strikes this time.'

'At least you're safe. You're the last one standing. He can't cut you.' They sat down to eat.

'More's the pity, I think some days. I hardly have the time to chase my own stories. And I'm always on the front line when the big stories break. Take Lockerbie. I drove there the night the plane blew up and I was there pretty much constantly till the memorial service. And then four days later, another plane dropped out of the sky on to the M1. And because they're short-staffed too, London decides my patch extends all the way down to the bottom of the East Midlands.

And I'm back in the thick of another mass bereavement, leading the team, doing the key interviews. In the firing line when the opposition gets something we missed. Back when we had a team of reporters, at least the shit got shared out,' Allie grumbled.

'You used to complain that the Lone Ranger dumped on you more than anybody else,' Rona reminded her.

Allie gave a wry smile. 'Moaning about your news editor is compulsory. But the Lone Ranger did enjoy fucking with our private lives more than most. God help you if you mentioned it was your anniversary or your kid's carol concert. You'd be guaranteed a trip to the sticks. 'Go straight to Scunthorpe, do not pass go, do not collect £200. Just book yourself into some scabby hotel and await instructions.' He was a shit. But at least he was an even-handed shit.'

'I never thought I'd hear you being wistful about him. What was it you said to him that time he sent you to mid-Wales on my birthday?'

Allie grinned. "I hope your next shite's a hedgehog.' I slammed the door, too. He just laughed.'

'You do have more freedom now, though. The London newsdesk can't keep tabs on you the same way. When you answer your pager, you could be anywhere. You could just go off to Edinburgh and chase your drug trials story and they'd be none the wiser till you'd nailed it down.'

Allie ate in silence for a couple of minutes. 'That's all well and good till they tell me to be in Barnsley in forty minutes . . .'

'Just do it, Allie. There could be a really good story there. You've got your 'Scots escaping AIDS' story in your back pocket to cover you if the desk does find out you're in Edinburgh when they expect you to be here. You know it'll just eat away at you if you don't chase it down.'

She was right, Allie thought. The idea that there might be something worth investigating about the drug trials had already triggered her investigative instincts. If she was going to start ignoring those feelings, she might as well throw away her notebook and take up cross-stitch. 'I'll write a draft tonight to cover my back. And I'll head up there in the morning.'

8

Although the new printing plant Ace Lockhart was building was emphatically without frills, he had not stinted on his own quarters. They had been completed first, ahead of the installation of the press lines or the newsroom. His office was large and airy, and beyond it, he'd installed a lavish dining room with rich wooden panelling and a gleaming walnut table with a dozen matching chairs. It was served by a kitchen that would have satisfied a Michelin-starred chef, with its plancha, its salamander and its hanging array of copper pans. There were only four hours in the day — 2 a.m. to 6 a.m. — when there was no chef on duty to cater to the whims of Ace Lockhart's appetite. He was as likely to demand cheesy beans on toast as lobster thermidor. Staff turnover was already high.

Whenever Genevieve came to dinner, however, the table was dressed to impress. Ever since he'd been widowed, Ace believed it was his job to make sure his daughter was never deprived of what a mother would have provided. That evening, they'd started with chicken liver pâté and Melba toast, and Ace's butler had just sliced through the golden pastry shell of a Beef Wellington to reveal steak cooked perfectly medium rare, as Ace decreed it should be. They waited in silence while the butler served the steak and placed chafing dishes of dauphinoise potatoes and crisp battered courgettes in front of them.

As her father loaded his plate, Genevieve took a

mouthful of the Château Lynch-Bages he'd chosen to accompany their meal. Not so much Dutch courage as something to moisten her dry mouth. He wasn't going to like what she was about to say. 'I was wondering,' she began, then tailed off.

An interrogative raise of the eyebrows opposite. 'Unless you spit it out, you'll remain in a state of wonderment,' Lockhart said through a mouthful of food.

'It's been more than a month since you borrowed the pension fund cash to pay for the New York Globe. Do you have any sense of when you might be able to start repayments?'

He chuckled indulgently. 'What? You think I'm going to welsh on the arrangement, Genny?'

'Of course not. I'm just a little uncomfortable about the position. We do have a Pythagoras Press audit coming up in a few months and I don't want awkward questions being raised.'

He shrugged. 'Inter-company loans happen all the time, there's nothing to concern the auditors.'

They concentrated on their food for a couple of minutes. Then Genevieve said, 'This isn't an inter-company loan, though. The pension fund is a separate entity.'

Lockhart shook his head. 'The pension fund belongs to me, as much as the companies do. Where do you think the money came from?'

'A lot of it came from the employees.' It was a stark truth that it took some nerve to point out.

'And they trust the pension fund will invest it wisely. Lending it to me is about as wise as you can get.'

She felt at a disadvantage now. Genevieve knew her own business inside out, but Pythagoras Press was only one part of the empire. Although he'd promised that one day it would all be hers, she wasn't privy yet to the financial details of Ace Media. She knew there had been moments when the ice had been thin beneath her father's feet, but he had an uncanny skill for turning things around. And he'd always turned his critics' words against them when she'd questioned him. Really, she had no reason to doubt him. 'I suppose so,' she said.

'Stop fretting about this, Genny.' He cut the remains of his steak into small pieces. 'There are more important matters to be concerned about.'

'Is that why I'm here tonight, Ace?'

He bestowed a gracious smile on her. 'You know I always delight in your company. But as it happens, I do have something to share that concerns you.'

'That sounds intriguing.' She took a last mouthful of courgettes and placed her knife and fork together among the remains of her meal. 'What's up?'

'Gorbachev.' Lockhart helped himself to another slice of the Beef Wellington. 'What a bloody mistake he turned out to be. None of us expected his bloody reforming zeal.' He carved off a chunk and stuffed it into his mouth. She waited patiently while he chewed and swallowed. Food was always his recourse when he felt stressed. '*Glasnost*, telling the world enough of the dirty little secrets of Chernobyl to put the fear of God into them. And then *perestroika*. And now, with Bush in the White House, he's cosying up to the Americans.'

None of this was news to Genevieve. But she didn't interrupt, accustomed to her father's habitual need to set the scene before getting to the point.

'There's a low rumble of discontent running right through the Soviet bloc. You can hear it from here if

58

you have ears to listen. The natives are getting restless, Genny. So much of our profit comes from there. Both from what we publish and from the . . . indirect arrangements we have with Moscow. I'm concerned about what Gorbachev's policies might mean for us. We need to talk behind closed doors with the allies we've cultivated over the years.'

Genevieve's mouth twisted in a sardonic smile. 'All those hagiographies of heads of state that they made their citizens buy.' She caught his frown and laughed. 'Don't worry, Ace, I'll never say that outside these four walls. We were of course satisfying a need for the citizens to be informed about their leaders.'

He topped up their wine. 'I can't do a tour of our client states. My very presence will set alarm bells ringing. But we need to know what's really going on beneath the surface. *You* can get them to take meetings because you're my daughter and they owe me.' Seeing her bridle, he hastily added, 'And you're the most senior executive in Pythagoras. But what we need right now is to reach out where you and I can't go.' A dramatic pause. He smoothed one of his eyebrows in a characteristic gesture.

'What do you mean?'

'We need to get a toehold with the dissidents. Listen to what's being said in the universities and the bars and the underground meetings. Information is power, you know that. And if the Soviet Union's going to go tits-up, I want to know who we should be talking to when the dust settles. What do you say?'

'It makes perfect sense, but —'

'And the perfect man for the job is Stephen Lavery,' he announced with an air of triumph.

Stephen Lavery. A man who turned into a human

oil slick when her father entered the room. Worse, a senior executive in Ace Media. He'd be reporting directly to her father about things that concerned the future of *her* business, leaving her out of the loop if he could. 'An interesting choice,' she said.

'He's very able.'

'Yes, he is. But he doesn't have a network in the East.'

'You can connect him with your people,' he said, nonchalant. 'They'll warm to him.'

'Surely it would make more sense for me to take this on? I already have the connections, and I know how things work. The nuances. Different territories need very different approaches. If you want to get ahead with this right away, it would waste a lot of time for me to bring Stephen fully up to speed. And you know what they're like in the East. It can take a long time to build trust. They'll go through the motions, but they won't do anything they're afraid might get them in trouble with the authorities.'

He looked affronted and her heart sank. Then suddenly he smiled. 'You really want to take this on? As well as your other responsibilities?'

She drank some more wine. 'Pythagoras is my baby now, Ace. I want to prove to you how seriously I take that responsibility. If we're planning for the future, I want to be at the heart of those plans. And that means driving the car, not sitting in the back seat.'

He leaned back in his chair and shook his head affectionately. 'I didn't want to overload you, but I see now you are more than capable. I should have known better. You are your father's daughter, after all.'

The track she'd been listening to at least once a day for months echoed in her head. *The only way is up, baby.* Genevieve grinned. 'When do I leave?'

9

Darkness had fallen by the time Allie reached Edinburgh. She'd delayed her departure long enough to brief three of her regular freelances on stories she wanted them to pursue. 'I'm going to be on the road,' she told them. 'I'll be on my mobile if you need me.' She loved saying that. Even though her Motorola cell phone was like a small brick weighing down her bag, it still drew attention and envy whenever she pulled it out to answer it.

The first mobile phone the office had issued her with had been the size and weight of a car battery, with a handset on top. When she'd brought it home, Rona had roared with laughter. 'It's about as mobile as a fridge freezer,' she'd exclaimed. Even though the network coverage was better these days, the reception was still dodgy enough to drive news editors crazy. Now that Allie was running her own ragbag of freelances, she'd lost count of the number of times she'd heard, 'You're breaking up, love,' when she was handing out an unpopular task. Partly they did it to avoid whatever it was she wanted of them; partly it was the cost. Allie could never work out how the phone companies had the nerve to charge their customers for receiving calls from a mobile as well as making them.

She drove through the outskirts of Edinburgh, past the wealthy enclave of Barnton to Cramond Village, and parked up with a view of the black waters of the Firth of Forth. Across the wide estuary was East

Wemyss, the village where she'd grown up. She'd only been back a couple of times since the move to Manchester; there was nothing to draw her back, nothing to feel nostalgic for. She felt like a stranger; it certainly wasn't the return of the native.

The lights of Fife twinkled in clumps that marked the towns and villages along the coast. Invisible beyond a corner of coastline was Kirkcaldy, where her parents now lived. They'd moved three years ago to a neat little bungalow overlooking Ravenscraig Park. She imagined them sitting down to their evening meal somewhere round that corner, the TV on in the background. She had to use her imagination because she'd never crossed the threshold. All she'd seen of their home was what she'd glimpsed doing a slow drive-by one summer evening when work had brought her back to the patch where she'd grown up.

Her loving Rona had been incomprehensible to them. She'd delayed telling them for more than a year after they'd shared their first tentative kiss, but she didn't want Rona to think she was ashamed of their relationship. That Rona's parents and siblings had embraced Allie as one of their own only made her feel worse. 'They might surprise you,' Rona had said when Allie tried to explain her reluctance.

They hadn't. The three of them had sat round the kitchen table eating Sunday dinner, making desultory conversation over roast chicken, peas and mashed potato, Allie struggling to swallow at the thought of what she'd decided to do. When her mother began to gather up the plates, Allie cleared her throat and said, 'I've got something to tell you.'

'What's wrong?' Josie Burns demanded, knowing her daughter well enough to understand this wasn't good news. 'Has something happened at work?'

Allie drew in a deep breath. 'I've met somebody. We're in a relationship and I'm very happy.'

Her mother gave a hesitant smile. 'But that's good news?'

David Burns was less sure. 'You don't look happy. What's the problem? Is he married?'

'David,' Josie scolded him. 'Why would you think such a thing? We brought Allie up better than that.'

Allie stared at her plate. 'Nobody's married.' Screwing up her courage, she lifted her chin and said, 'It's not a he. It's a she.' The silence seemed to swell, pushing the air from the room.

Her mother flushed, as if someone had slapped both cheeks. Her father's lips pressed tightly together, momentarily bloodless. Then he said, 'That's ridiculous. You'll say anything to get attention. I thought you'd grown out of that childish behaviour.'

She bit back her anger. 'I'm a grown woman, Dad. Believe me, if I thought I could avoid this conversation, I would. But I'm not ashamed of who I am or who I love. Call me crazy, but I thought you might be pleased that I've found someone who loves me, somebody that makes me happy.'

He made an explosive sound. 'Happy? How can you be happy with a woman?'

Allie couldn't help herself. 'Well, you claim to have managed it.'

A red tide rose from his neck and engulfed his face. 'How dare you compare your mother and me to this . . . this filth.' He pushed his chair back and stood up.

'You've always had boyfriends,' Josie said, plaintive and placatory.

'I did. And they never made me feel the way I thought they would. Not like the love songs or the movies.'

'You just haven't met the right one.' Her mother looked desperate.

'I have met the right one. Her name's Rona. Rona Dunsyre. She's kind, and funny and clever and beautiful, and I still can't believe we found each other.'

David Burns scoffed. 'And is she sponging off you?'

Allie shook her head. 'Money's got nothing to do with it. But if you're worried — she earns more than I do. Dad, for the first time in my life, I feel I'm in the right place.'

He stepped back, almost recoiling. 'You disgust me. You've been brought up in a good Christian home, and this is how you repay us? I think you need to go away and have a long look at yourself, Alison.'

'It's maybe just a phase, isn't that what they say, David? You read about it in the papers, young people experimenting, then coming to their senses?' Josie was pressing her fingertips along her jawline, panic in her eyes.

'Of course it's —'

'It's not a bloody phase,' Allie said tightly. 'Rona is the person I want to spend the rest of my life with. If we could get married, we'd do it tomorrow.'

Her father scoffed. 'Well, that's never going to happen. We're a civilised Christian country here in Scotland. How stupid can you get? How can queer perverts be married? You can't have children. That's what marriage is supposed to be about.' He stepped behind his chair and tucked it under the table, his controlled fury obvious.

Now Allie was on her feet. 'You're behind the times, Dad. Lesbian families are all the rage. Look, if you

64

can't accept my choice, there's nothing more to be said. You're not going to change my mind.'

'I think it's time you left.' David gripped the chair-back so tightly his knuckles were white.

'I think you're right.' There was a long moment where they all refused to meet each other's eyes.

'Allie . . .' her mother pleaded.

Allie turned abruptly and walked out of the room. Her father's words rang in her ears as she grabbed her coat and made for the door. 'And don't come back till you've come to your senses.'

That had been the last time she'd been in the same room as her father in more than eight years, unless you counted her Uncle Andrew's funeral service in the crematorium. Her mother had stayed in touch, with occasional phone calls and, while she was still working in Glasgow, awkward lunches near Queen Street station. Every time, Allie suggested Rona join them; every time her mother had said she wasn't ready for that.

The impact of that Sunday lunch had hung in the air between Allie and Josie, like the aftershock of an earthquake. She'd sensed something similar in the living rooms of the bereft from time to time. It was as if someone had ripped their lives in half — before the disaster and afterwards. It wasn't as if she'd been close to her parents. There had been little in common to stitch them together. But she'd never gone through the hostility that friends had experienced in their teens and beyond. There had always been a vague lurking hope that they might find more common ground now she was an adult. But that was never going to happen. Rona was her home now, her family. And she was fine with that.

10

A dog barking woke Allie from a deep sleep. For a moment she was confused, thinking it was Germaine, and wondering why the window was in the wrong place. Then she put the pieces together. She wasn't at home; she was in Sarah Torrance's spare room in the north Edinburgh suburb of Trinity, where the quiet streets were lined with solid Victorian villas. Sarah was a fellow journalist, covering fashion and theatre for a Scottish broadsheet. She'd originally been Rona's friend but she'd happily drawn Allie into their circle. When they'd moved to Manchester, Sarah had insisted they should stay with her whenever they were in Edinburgh. It was an offer Allie was always glad to accept.

She'd arrived in time for dinner with Sarah and her teenage daughter Meriel. Sarah's husband was a BBC foreign correspondent, perpetually shuttling from one overseas crisis to another, currently somewhere in the Caucasus. They sat down to steaming bowls of venison chilli, glasses of red wine to hand for the grown-ups. 'Why can't we have beef like everyone else?' Meriel complained.

'Because it's absolutely laden with fat,' Sarah said. 'You'll thank me one day when your arteries are still functioning.'

Meriel harrumphed and ostentatiously mixed the meat sauce with rice. 'Are you here for a story, Allie?' she asked.

'What? Did you think she's just here because she loves us so much?' Sarah teased.

Meriel scowled. 'No, Mum. Rona would be here too if it was a fun trip. I was trying to take an interest, like you're always telling me to.'

'I am here chasing one story for sure and another one for maybe,' Allie said.

'That sounds weird. How come?'

'I've got one story more or less nailed down. I just need to firm up the Edinburgh end of it. And I got the lead on the other one when I was doing the first one.'

'Intriguing,' Sarah said. 'Can you tell us what it's all about?'

Allie would have deflected that request from most journalists, but she knew Sarah could be trusted not to run off to her newsdesk with the tip. So between mouthfuls, she told them what she knew so far.

'There's drugs everywhere in Edinburgh,' Meriel said, with all the lofty assurance of a fourteen-year-old whose life is as safe as her parents and her expensive school could make it.

Sarah put her cutlery down. 'Not around here.'

'Mum, just because the only used needles you ever see are the ones granny does her knitting with doesn't mean they don't exist. Muirhouse and Pilton are just down the road. And you've said yourself that burglaries and car break-ins are massive in our lovely Trinity.' Meriel smiled sweetly to sugar the sarcasm.

Allie smiled, rueful. 'She's got a point, Sarah. There's a major drugs problem in the city, and it's mapping right on to an AIDS epidemic.' She'd driven around Muirhouse and Pilton herself on the way in, and it had been a depressing experience. The high flats, low-rise blocks and mean little houses looked unloved and run-down. It reminded her of photographs she'd seen of post-war Soviet housing, right down to the scrubby grass and churned-up mud. Weak lights glowed through thin curtains; other uncovered windows showed the flickering colour palette of invisible TV screens. Hardly anyone was out on the streets. A handful of youths lurked in a bus shelter. A couple skinny as fashion models hurried into a block of flats, the woman teetering on blocky heels. Two men walked towards her car, their jackets too thin for the weather, their frail faces tucked into the collars, their shoulders hunched. Everyone she'd seen looked ill and pinched, apart from a pair of middle-aged men emerging from an off-licence with carrier bags that explained the barrel guts they carried before them. Tomorrow, she was going to have to find people from these grim streets to interview. For most people, that would be an unappetising prospect. For Allie, it set her journalistic juices flowing. Finding the right voices to tell a story was what she lived for in her professional life. And giving a voice to people whose lives had left them silenced was always worth doing. 'Well, at least some of them are taking their problems to other people's cities,' she said wearily.

'That's hardly a solution, though, is it?' Sarah picked up her fork and resumed eating.

'What about the other story? The drugs trial? How will you find out whether there's a story there?' Meriel asked.

Allie smiled. 'Are you rehearsing for a career in journalism?'

'No. I'm thinking about joining the police after I've been to university.'

Sarah groaned. 'Not this again.'

'I don't know,' Allie said. 'There's plenty of scope for smart and thoughtful people in the polis. Especially women.'

'I want to be on the murder squad,' Meriel said. 'I bet I could do better than most of the detectives there.'

'It's not like *Taggart*, you know. Most murders, there's not much to solve. They're either domestics or drunken brawls.'

Meriel rolled her eyes. 'I know that. But sometimes it's not. Sometimes it's like Bible John or the Yorkshire Ripper, and they need really good detectives. That's what I want to be.'

Allie didn't know whether to laugh or cry. She didn't think many of the cops investigating the Lockerbie bombing would ever have dreamed of facing an atrocity like that, never mind seeking it out. She exchanged a look with Sarah. 'Aye, well. Plenty of time before you have to make a decision about the rest of your life.'

'I'm not going to change my mind, you know. So how are you going to find out about the drugs trial?'

She was persistent enough, Allie thought. 'I've got the name of a local GP. I'll take it from there. I'll tell you tomorrow evening if I get lucky.'

★ ★ ★

Fuelled by coffee and a bacon sandwich, Allie checked in with her freelances. One of them had copper-bottomed the story he'd been chasing, which gave her something to placate the London newsdesk with. Then she headed back to Muirhouse. As she drove, she remembered something Jamesie had said to her.

'People don't care about drug addicts. We're the people who rob your car and steal your granny's wedding ring and give your daughters AIDS.' It was a shorthand version of what the press had been screaming for a while. She had two mountains to climb — first, to persuade Edinburgh's HIV victims to talk to her, and then to persuade her newsdesk to run the story. Two separate pitches, and each as crucial as the other.

Before she reached the housing estate, she stopped at a newsagent and scoured their limited card selection till she found one that didn't wish a happy birthday or sincere condolences. The watercolour of a heather-covered mountain bore no relationship to anything within fifty miles of Muirhouse but it was blank inside, which was the main thing. Back in the car, Allie sucked her pen for a minute, then wrote.

Dear Dr Diack,
    Please excuse this intrusion on your over-worked and intensely busy practice. Although I am a journalist, please don't dismiss this approach out of hand. My name is Alison Burns and I'm the northern news editor of the Sunday Globe. I have great sympathy for those caught up in the HIV/AIDS epidemic — I'm gay myself and I have lost dear friends to this terrible disease. I'm not here to demonise them as so many of my colleagues have done.
    I've recently become aware that there is something of an exodus among HIV+ patients from Edinburgh to other UK cities. I've spoken to several of those who have left and it seems that one reason for this is insufficient facilities in Edinburgh and the failure of Lothian Health

Board to address this. I know you're one of the key medical professionals bucking this trend and I want to talk to you about your work and also what you think is needed here to improve the situation. Half an hour of your time is all I'm asking. I'm happy to fit in with your schedule. I plan to be in Edinburgh for the next couple of days.
Sincerely, Alison Burns

Years on the front line had taught Allie how to write a begging letter, though she held out few hopes for this one. Sometimes the judicious application of flattery worked wonders, especially if it was seasoned with a bit of personal interest. But any doctor working in a practice with so many habitual drug users had probably been exposed to a myriad hard-luck stories and lies. She feared he'd be immunised by now. But she had to try. She always had to try.

The group practice where Dr Derek Diack worked alongside three other medics was housed in a single-storey brick building with metal grids over the windows and roller shutters protecting the entrance. A single slash of graffiti across a neighbouring wall read, *THE WHITE HORSE OF HEROIN WILL RIDE YOU TO HELL.* Allie pushed open the door and walked into a reception area that felt as if the promised destination had already been reached. Among the posters and leaflets on the wall was the unmissable tombstone poster. A couple of smaller HIV+ support group circulars flanked it. There were the usual walking wounded of a GP's waiting room — whining infants and small children, an elderly woman hunched over a walking stick, a teenager with his arm in a sling. What was less usual,

71

in Allie's experience, were half a dozen grey-faced hollow-eyed men and women who either couldn't stop twitching or else appeared to be on the verge of catatonia. Nobody bothered with anything more than the most cursory of glances at the new arrival.

She crossed to the reception desk, where three receptionists sat behind screens with cut-outs at the bottom barely big enough for a hand to pass through. Allie pasted on her best smile and slid the envelope across. 'I'd appreciate it if you could give this to Dr Diack. It's kind of urgent. I'm happy to wait for a reply.' She nodded at the waiting-area chairs. 'I'll just sit myself down.'

'Are you a drug rep?' The woman glared at Allie.

'No, nothing like that.' Allie walked away and sat in the nearest chair.

'His surgery's full this morning.' The receptionist wasn't giving up.

'I'm not in a hurry.' Allie took her copy of Gillian Slovo's *Death Comes Staccato* from her bag and opened it at her bookmark. Allie loved the new wave of feisty feminist private eye novels that had made its way across the Atlantic. She knew enough about the business from her friend Bill Mortensen to know the fiction was just that, but it was a form of escapism that reinforced her own love of investigative reporting, so she devoured it avidly. Even so, she managed to keep her peripheral vision on alert. Patients came and went, the receptionists called out names, children grizzled and people coughed. No doctors appeared. Occasionally, a receptionist would disappear through a second door at the rear of their area. Allie noticed her envelope accompany one of those trips.

Gradually, the reception area emptied and by

half past noon, nobody new came to replace the treated patients. At last, there was only Allie and a middle-aged woman hunched into a stained beige raincoat, a crumpled bloodstained tissue held to her nose. The receptionist looked up. 'Dr Diack will be out in minute,' she said. It sounded as if she grudged every word.

Allie smiled her thanks and put her book away, relieved not least because she barely had ten pages left. The door opened and a stocky man with a blaze of thick red hair and a pink, freckled face strode through, thrusting his arms into a tweed jacket. He took one look at Allie and stopped in his tracks. 'I know you,' he said.

It sounded like an accusation. And Allie knew there was no denying it.

11

It was a salutary reminder of what Allie had almost forgotten — that in Scotland, Stanley Milgram's theory of Six Degrees of Separation seldom made it past three. The man standing before her was the ex-boyfriend of Rona's cousin.

Their paths had crossed at a family wedding a few years previously. Allie stood up and greeted Dr Derek Diack with a smile. 'I never knew your surname.'

'And I never thought of you as 'Alison',' he replied, closing the gap between them and extending a hand. 'I came through that door fully intending to give you the bum's rush.' He shrugged. 'But since it's you . . .'

'I appreciate it. Are you breaking for lunch?'

He scoffed. 'Lunch? You've got to be kidding. I hardly manage a toilet break these days. No, I'm off to a meeting. The health board wants me to set up a clinic for drug users. Fat chance. I've no time for that. I've already been ambushed five times today — they get me when I park my car, they sneak in behind legit patients. Not that I blame them. They're desperate.'

'We could talk on the way?'

He looked at his watch. 'OK, I'll drive.' He made for the door, Allie following him. She had no idea how she'd get back to Muirhouse or if her car would still be there when she did, but she had to make the most of a lucky break. She followed him out, hurrying to keep pace with his long strides, switching her micro-cassette machine to record as she went.

74

His car was a Ford Cortina, too ancient to hold any attractions for thieves or joyriders but the engine started smoothly enough at the first attempt. 'So you're chasing a story about Edinburgh exporting its AIDS epidemic down south?' He was as sharp as she remembered. No point in trying to bullshit him.

'I'm more interested in why it's happening. I've spoken to a few of the guys who have gone to Manchester and I've heard three different explanations.' She outlined what she'd been told and he nodded his agreement.

'All of that's true. Edinburgh only has one dedicated clinic for treating drug users. They've got four beds for addict rehab. Just one of those beds is for Pilton and Muirhouse.' His voice was bitter. 'We've got something like four hundred heroin users in Muirhouse. No wonder anybody who can manage it is getting out.'

'Why is the service so inadequate?'

He scoffed, again. 'Edinburgh's always tried to deny it's got an underbelly. It's all about the church, the lawyers, the academics. They've got a crick in their necks from looking the other way, ever since Burke and Hare were raiding the churchyards to provide bodies for the anatomists to dissect. They don't want to acknowledge there's a problem.'

'So it gets worse?'

'Exactly. It took them forever to set up a needle exchange. There was nowhere in the city to get a clean needle. We caught people stealing used needles from our sharps bin, for God's sake. Raking about, exposing themselves to other folks' infections.' His voice was a low growl, but his driving was still thankfully attentive. 'There's a new campaign group got going, they're trying to raise money for an AIDS hospice. It's an uphill struggle — most people don't want to be associated with AIDS. But those guys are determined. Good luck to them.'

They were in the city proper now. Allie worried they were running out of time. She needed to make a move on her second story. 'I heard one of the drug companies was running a research project in Edinburgh. Were you not part of that?'

He flashed her a quick glance. 'Where did you hear that?'

'I've got a friend who's a researcher for a drug company, a different one. Did I get that wrong?'

He frowned at the traffic lights that were holding them up. 'No. You heard right. There was a drug trial. But it got stopped in its tracks. No warning, they just closed it down. I don't know, I wasn't directly involved.' Diack turned into a car park behind a decaying 1960s office building tucked between an office block and a tenement. He turned off the engine and looked at his watch again. 'This is me.'

'Who can I talk to about this?'

'Dr Death.' He smiled at her shock. 'Paul Robertson. He runs the rehab unit I was talking about. They call him Dr Death because, they say, if you have a consultation with him, it means you're going to die.' He pulled a face. 'They're mostly right.'

'Where do I find him?'

'Notebook?' He gestured at her. Allie handed it over. Diack scribbled on the pad. 'I'm trusting you here, Allie. Don't let me down.'

★ ★ ★

Allie had very little idea of where she was, other than somewhere south of the city centre. She walked back to the nearest main road and waited in the biting wind for a taxi. The driver was surprised at her destination, muttering something about danger money. 'You sure you know what you're doing?' he asked. 'I wouldnae want my wife going down there by herself.'

'Just as well I'm not your wife, then.' For all sorts of reasons, Allie thought.

Her car was where she'd left it, minus its hubcaps. It could have been worse. Though she couldn't quite believe there was enough of a market in second-hand hubcaps for it to be worth the effort. She drove back down to the sea and parked with a view across the water to Fife. Time to wear her news editor hat. She spoke to two of her freelances, seeking updates on what they were working on. Allie was aware that none of the men she used as hired guns liked working for her. What galled them even more was that they couldn't accuse her of having slept her way into the job. So it was no surprise that neither of them had much to report. Allie suggested some lines of inquiry to both, stressing that she wanted something positive by the morning or she'd pass the job to someone else. It was no empty threat; the clear-out of journalists across the tabloid empires of Ace Lockhart and Rupert Murdoch meant there was no shortage of hungry operators.

The third freelance wasn't on the end of a phone. Presumably out on the road doing what Allie was paying him for. Either that or in the pub. She paged him, asking for an update, then checked in with the London news-desk. 'What's cooking?' the deputy news editor demanded. 'Have you got a juicy page lead for me, Burns? A shocking revelation from *Coronation Street*? Or some rock twat throwing a wobbler at the Hacienda?'

'Steady on, Ronnie. It's only Wednesday. I'll have something for you, never fear.' She ran through the freelance assignments — a Yorkshire MP allegedly having an affair with a cricketer's wife; a soap star reportedly diagnosed with breast cancer; new developments in the search for the Lockerbie bomber.

Ronnie gave her a grudging seal of approval. 'It's a start. You've got the talking brick with you, haven't you? Do they have mobile phone signals up there in the heather?'

'I'll be here if you need me, Ronnie. Now, I've got work to do. And so have you.' She endured another exchange of banter then escaped. According to her A-Z map of Edinburgh, Dr Death's clinic was across the city in a former infectious diseases hospital in Liberton. Plenty of time to get there before close of play. Thanks to Rona's cousin's taste in men, things were breaking her way for once.

12

It had clearly been a long time since the hospital that housed Dr Death's AIDS ward had been state of the art, Allie thought, dodging the potholes in the car park in search of a space. It was a crumbling red-brick building with the kind of metal window frames that produced condensation on the inside nine months of the year. The ground-floor windows were all frosted glass; good for privacy and interior gloom.

Allie responded to a couple of pager messages, dealing with a freelance, then picking up a tip from a local paper reporter and passing it on to yet another of her superannuated stringers to flesh out. Then she made for the entrance.

Nobody challenged her as she walked in with an air of confidence. It smelled like a hospital; disinfectant with bass notes of school dinners and bedpans. Diack had told her to look for Ward 17 and she spotted the sign in time to avoid breaking stride. Up a flight of stairs and down a hall, a faded track worn in the vinyl flooring. She passed the entrance to the ward, looking for the door on the left behind which she'd find Dr Paul Robertson's office.

It was an unassuming door, looking more like a janitor's cupboard than a consultant's office. There was no nameplate, as Diack had warned her. 'Otherwise people would just barge in constantly.' Allie knocked. No response. Without much hope, she tried the handle. From behind her, a light tenor voice with a strong

Glasgow accent said, 'Are you trying to break into my office?'

She turned swiftly to face a tall thin man with a narrow head and dark brown hair cut close to his scalp. His features were sharp and two frown tracks separated his eyebrows, but his eyes were warm and the lines that sprang into definition when he smiled had clearly been etched by good humour. 'Dr Robertson?' Allie cursed herself for sounding so jumpy.

'That's me. Are you the lassie Derek Diack warned me about?'

Thirty-five, and still men were calling her a lassie. As usual, she bit back a retort and smiled. 'I'm flattered. Didn't realise I merited a warning. I'm Allie Burns, *Sunday Globe*.'

He gestured towards the door and she stepped aside to allow him to unlock it. 'I'm normally wary of you lot,' he said as he waved her inside. 'I've been burned too many times by hysterical headlines. Big black lies that blight my patients' lives.' He looked her up and down and pointed to a chair set at one corner of his desk. 'But Derek says I've to give you a chance. Which in my book means giving you enough rope to trip yourself up. Soon as you do? There's the door.'

Allie sat. 'Fair enough. Did he tell you what I want to write about?'

'The exodus. I can't blame them for going. When they told me I could have a treatment unit, I asked for fifty beds. They gave me four. We take patients in extremis. They endure medieval deaths. Diseases of sheep. Tumours in the brain.

Convulsions, vomiting blood. The worst of it is that they've bought into the media message. Mostly, they think this is what they deserve. Running down south

80

is their last act of defiance.' His style was dramatic. She could imagine him in a health-board meeting, making the bureaucrats squirm. But not quite enough to change their minds.

'You run outpatient clinics as well?'

He shrugged one bony shoulder. 'For what it's worth. Eat better. Try these steroids. Here's some extra-strong antibiotics for your pneumonia. Oh, and some soothing cream for that rash that makes you scratch till you bleed.'

'What about the pharmaceutical companies? Are they working on more effective drugs?' She made it sound casual, but he'd been warned.

A sharp cackle of laughter. 'Derek said you'd try to corner me on that one.'

'I'm not trying to corner you, I'm trying to find out what's going on.'

'Derek said he explained the general lack of enthusiasm?'

She nodded. 'Not enough profit to be made.'

He nodded, approvingly, and leaned his elbows on the desk, steepling his long bony fingers. 'But now we've got evidence of heterosexual transmission, and the so-called innocent victims of contaminated blood products from the US. Which means a couple of research institutes have the foresight to see this is only going in one direction. And we are the perfect petri dish. We've got the facilities for all sorts of testing, and we've got a significant population of infected patients. Do you know how we know we've got such a big sample?'

Obediently, Allie said, 'How?'

'It's not because they're all so concerned for their health that they rush off to get tested. For all sorts of reasons, the longer you can kid yourself you're not positive, the better. No. What we had in Edinburgh was an epidemic of hepatitis B that was reaching its peak round about the time HIV was infiltrating our intravenous drug users. And for some reason that escapes me now, we froze the blood samples we took from the HepB testing. Then once we had a test for HIV, some bright spark thought it would be a good idea to defrost all the HepB samples and test them for HIV. And we discovered we had an epidemic on our hands. One surgery had a hundred and sixty-four positives.' He pursed his lips and shook his head. 'Unimaginable.'

'I'm amazed you got that many patients to consent. Knowing what it would mean.'

He closed his eyes and sighed. 'It was done without consent.'

Allie was too shocked to curb her response. 'But surely that's unethical? Don't people have a right to decide if they want to be tested?'

He waggled his hand indeterminately. 'Scientists sometimes get overexcited. Yes, they should have been consulted. But they weren't. Bad for them, good for science.' He jumped up and crossed to a small fridge on the floor by the desk. For a moment, Allie wondered whether he was about to produce some fiendish experiment. He looked over his shoulder and grinned. 'Diet Coke or Irn Bru?'

It was no contest when she was back in Scotland. 'Irn Bru, please.'

He passed her a can, took one for himself then sat down again. They tore off their ring pulls almost simultaneously and let them fall to the metal desk with a tinkle. It was a tiny moment that broke the ten-

82

sion. 'So that's why the researchers came to you with the drug trials?' Allie asked after they'd both taken a swig.

'We were the obvious choice once the word got round. To begin with, it was just observational studies, trying to get a sense of the progression of the disease. There's such a wide variation. Some people are dead within months of a diagnosis; others are still doing OK three, four years on. The researchers were keen to try to identify what factors impacted the speed of the development of full-blown AIDS. That's going nowhere yet. But now we're starting to get somewhere with DNA analysis, who knows? We might crack the code.'

'But until then, we need medicines.'

He frowned at her. 'What's your interest in this? What's the story?'

'You had a drug trial going on here that came to a sudden halt. Why?'

'That's hardly a tabloid story, is it?'

'I'm curious.' Allie let her answer hang.

Robertson took a long pull on his fizzy drink and stifled a burp. 'It started quite well. Patients reported feeling less weak, their appetites started to return. Their T-cell count rose slightly. Then they turned a corner and collapsed. Three of them suffered heart attacks, two fatal. Three others went into respiratory shock.' He stared at the desktop, unmoving.

'How many were in the test study?'

'Twenty-four. All volunteers. Twelve on the drugs, twelve placebos. All the problems were with patients on the drugs.'

'What happened?'

'The researchers wanted to carry on. They made a

strong case for the problems being with the patients, not the drug. I refused to continue. I stopped the trial.'

'And that's the end of the story?'

'It should be, shouldn't it?' His gaze was speculative.

'But you don't believe it? You think they're still trialling the treatment?'

He said nothing.

'Dr Robertson? If people are being put at risk, should they not be told?'

He met her eyes. 'They should. But not everybody lives in a place where they have control over their own decisions.' He got up and crossed to a filing cabinet. He took out a slim folder and extracted a single sheet of glossy paper. He passed it to her. 'This is the company we dealt with. Zabre Pharma. It's not hard to find out where else they operate.'

'Can I keep this?'

He nodded. 'Getting an HIV diagnosis is a death sentence. Chances are, it won't always be. But right now, it is. Patients don't deserve to be robbed of what little time they have. If we're going to start treating victims of this illness like they don't matter, where do we stop? Treat smokers with lung cancer like guinea pigs? Inject weird drug cocktails into morbidly obese people with heart problems?' He stood up. 'Fuck that. Away you go and do your worst, Miss Burns.'

13

By ten that evening, Allie was willing to concede that she'd covered all the angles her Edinburgh stories had to offer. She'd spoken to a pair of charity support workers, to the woman who ran the needle exchange, and to four regular users of the service. She had it all, from the tragic tales of dead friends to the police who staked out the needle exchange in the hope of arresting dealers, from the angry parents of a young haemophiliac infected by US blood products to the father whose two children had been born with HIV they'd contracted from their sex-worker mother.

And to the girlfriend of one of the men who had died during the aborted drug trial. Janine denied she had a drug habit herself. 'I smoke a wee bit o' dope. No' every day. I never got into the heroin. Gordie once took me to a squat in that block in Muirhouse they call the Terror Tower. It was full of folk off their faces. I hated the whole thing — sharpening old needles on matchboxes, washing syringes out with their own blood. Honest to God, it gave me the dry boak. I said I was never going back.

'Gordie tried to quit, but he never managed it. The drug had its claws in his heart. Then he got on Dr Robertson's drug trial. We were over the moon.' She'd looked piteously across the table at Allie, trembling fingers clutching her vodka and Coke. 'I still loved him. In spite of everything. He was my world. I thought the doctors could fix the AIDS, and he'd manage to get off the heroin.' Her eyes filled with tears, but she blinked them back. 'He was doing well, Dr Robertson said. And then, boom. Out of nowhere. He took a massive heart attack and that was that.' She took the last cigarette from her pack and crushed it fiercely. 'No more Gordie.'

It had been a difficult interview. Allie couldn't avoid the intensity of Janine's grief and it ate a hole in her own defences. She'd felt a complicity she couldn't justify. Journalists were only supposed to empathise for as long as it took them to nail down their story, not to struggle with the emotional response. It seemed to be happening to her more often these days. The interviews she'd done after Lockerbie, the bereaved families she'd spoken to after the M1 air crash weeks later, the frustrations that doctors and community workers had shared with her about the AIDS nightmare — these conversations were leaving her hollowed out and drained. Maybe it was just that her new role was demanding too much of her. Or maybe, as her male colleagues had never tired of insinuating — or saying to her face — women like her just couldn't take the pressure at the top.

Allie walked back to her car. She knew she'd be welcome back at Sarah Torrance's, even at this late hour. But after the day she'd had, the thought of light chit-chat over a nightcap or dealing with Meriel's inquisition over breakfast made her want to lay her head on the steering wheel and weep. If she set off now, she could be home around three in the morning. Six hours' sleep and she'd be on top of her game again, running her freelances, putting together a news schedule, writing her copy. And arranging to meet Jess to pick her brains about pharmaceutical companies.

It was a plan. Allie was always happiest when she could convince herself she had a plan. She turned the key in the ignition and headed for the apparently random combination of A-roads and motorways that would take her across Scotland to the M6 and home. As she drove, she rummaged one-handed through the box of cassettes she kept in the car, eventually settling for a Scottish mixtape she'd made herself. Aztec Camera, Deacon Blue, The Rezillos, Annie Lennox fronting the Eurythmics, Bronski Beat with wee Jimmy Somerville, the Cocteau Twins. If singing along to that didn't turn her spirit bright, nothing would.

She reached Carlisle just after midnight and pulled off to fill up with petrol. There was no signal on the mobile, so she called Rona from a phone booth to tell her she'd be home. It took her so long to answer, Allie knew she'd woken her up. Nevertheless, as soon as Rona heard her voice, she perked up. 'We've missed you. Waking up to Germaine just isn't the same.'

Allie chuckled. 'I thought I'd better let you know I'm coming home in case you thought we were being burgled. I'll just crash out in the spare room. I don't want to disturb you again.'

'You think you can get into the house undetected? You know the dog'll wake the neighbourhood. Come to bed, my love. You know you want to.'

She was right. Even after a decade, she was right. 'OK,' Allie said. 'Go back to sleep, I'll see you later. Love you.'

'Mmm. Drive like the polis are watching.'

★ ★ ★

Once she was asleep, Allie knew nothing until Rona woke her with a coffee just before nine. 'I wish I could sleep like you,' Rona said. 'I swear you will sleep through the end of the world.' She perched on the bed next to Allie, fragrant from her shower. The dog followed, rather less fragrant. 'We've already had a wee jog round the water park.'

Allie groaned. 'I wish you'd never done that feature about retraining your body.'

'You do enough running around on the job. And let's not forget, you are the queen of the dance floor. So how was Edinburgh? Did you get what you needed?'

'I've got the exodus story nailed down, all four corners. And enough of a thread to tug on with the other one. I'll try to get hold of Jess today, see whether she can pull a rabbit out of a hat for me. I got some great quotes. One woman said to me, 'Don't say this is an Edinburgh problem. We don't live in Edinburgh, we live in Muirhouse. There's people lived all their lives here and never walked down Princes Street. Edinburgh's another planet to us." She sipped her coffee. 'What about you? What have you got on today?'

'I'm off across the Pennines to Sheffield to interview Neil Morrissey.' Seeing Allie's faint frown, Rona added, 'He played the biker guy in Boon, remember? He's in rehearsal at the Crucible for *William Tell.* I've already sold it twice over.' She kissed Allie then jumped up. 'I need to get a move on.'

'Me too,' Allie sighed. The day had started too early for her. She wrapped herself in her cosy dressing gown and made a list at the breakfast bar while a fresh pot of coffee brewed. Rona passed through like a blonde tornado, and Allie started on her phone calls. Freelances first, then a call to Jess, who was intrigued by the story so far. 'I don't know anything about this drug trial,' she warned. 'I've only heard of Zabre Pharma because one of my colleagues moved there a couple of years ago. I'll see what I can find out. But it's always good to have an excuse for lunch.'

Allie couldn't put off writing her copy any longer. It was always the same with stories she knew didn't fit the strict parameters of what the newsdesk considered their readers were interested in. The knowledge of the fight ahead always made it hard to get started; she had to make the story powerful enough to strike a knock-out blow against objections. This was one of the few occasions that she missed the few colleagues she'd had camaraderie with over the years. She could have bounced her ideas off Marcus, back in the trainee days, or Danny Sullivan at the *Clarion* back in Glasgow, their thoughts sharpening her own focus. But these days, she was on her own. She went through to her office and turned on her Amstrad PCW, watching the familiar green letters crawl across the black screen. Deep sigh, then she created a new file.

Scores of seriously ill patients are being forced from their homes because there aren't enough places to treat them. The resulting exodus threatens people all over the UK with the spread of an incurable disease.

That should grab the attention of the newsdesk, she thought. Hopefully without whipping up their knee-jerk anti-AIDS hysteria.

Dozens of Edinburgh patients who are HIV+ and even those who have developed AIDS are abandoning the city because the NHS has turned its back on them.

With every passing week, the numbers grow.
They are travelling to cities in England because they believe they have a better chance of medical care there.

James Forrester, 24, left his flat in Muirhouse, Edinburgh for Manchester, where he is now being cared for in a city hospital. He said, 'In Edinburgh, I couldn't get into rehab or any other treatment after I was diagnosed. There were no beds. No spaces.

'What clinics they do have are bursting at the seams. We're just dumped on a scrapheap. If you've not got family or pals to look after you, it's just curtains.

'So I came down here, where nobody knew I was HIV positive. I thought I could escape that feeling that I had a target on my back.' Sadly, James has since developed full-blown AIDS and has only weeks to live.

Gus, 26, fled Edinburgh to escape the stigma of being known as HIV+. He refused to give his surname to preserve the life he's trying to build in Manchester. 'There are no secrets in Muirhouse,' he said. 'But down here, nobody knows I'm HIV positive. I've got a part-time job in a bar, and I go to an outpatient clinic. HIV is a death sentence, but I think I've got a right to a life for as long as I'm able.'

Jackie Green, who runs a support group in the Scottish capital, said, 'How can we call ourselves civilised when we treat sick people like this? Imagine if that was your child, your sibling. How could you bear it?'

Edinburgh doctor Derek Diack has hundreds of HIV+ patients on his books. He explained the problem. 'Edinburgh's always tried to deny it's got an underbelly. They don't want to acknowledge what's going on.

'There's a new campaign group trying to raise money for an AIDS hospice. It's an uphill struggle - most people don't want to be associated with AIDS. But they're determined. Good luck to them.'

Dr Paul Robertson runs the AIDS wards in an Edinburgh hospital. He revealed, 'When they told me I could have a treatment unit, I asked for fifty beds. They gave me four. So we can only take patients in extremis. Before they get to that point, running down south is their last act of defiance.

'Patients don't deserve to be blamed for being ill. They don't deserve to be robbed of what little time they have. If we're going to start treating victims of this illness like they don't matter, where do we stop?'

A spokesman for Lothian Health Board said, 'We don't discriminate against any patients. However, our resources are limited and we have to make difficult decisions about how to allocate them most effectively.'

Allie read through her copy and made a few tweaks. She hoped she'd managed to keep enough of a lid on her sense of outrage to slip past the newsdesk. She saved the story then dialled up the office connection. There was the usual procession of whines, trills and ringtones as the modem connected and started to transmit her story. While it was uploading, she took a quick shower then returned to check it had actually gone. Often, there was interference on the line, which corrupted the process and meant she had to start again. This time, she'd been lucky. Now it was in the lap of the gods.

14

As usual, the pub was busy. Its unique selling point was bread and cheese in copious quantities, which was the main reason Jess always chose it. She'd arrived first and snagged a table in the window, already furnished with two kinds of bread, three different cheeses and two pints of beer. Allie squeezed through the bodies and greeted her with a quick hug. 'I thought I'd better grab the grub while I could,' Jess said, nodding towards the crowd around the food service area. 'Good thinking. The brie I recognise, but the other two?' 'The green-veined one is Sage Derby. And that's a smoked cheddar.'

The important business out of the way, they loaded their plates, striking their usual balance between talking and eating. Allie filled Jess in on her trip to Edinburgh; Jess talked about the tempting offer to relocate to Holland. 'The cheese is a bit naff,' Allie pointed out.

'They don't think so. The guy who was showing me round said, in all sincerity, 'Edam does not go off but rather, it hardens, making it a great Dutch cheese to take along as you travel.''

They both roared with laughter. 'I'll remember that next time I'm packing my case. And speaking of abroad, what's the score with Zabre Pharma?'

Jess carved a slice of brie and applied it to some granary bread as she organised her thoughts. 'I was barely aware of them before they made Colin

Corcoran an offer he couldn't refuse. Did you ever meet Colin?'

'Doesn't ring any bells.'

'You probably wouldn't remember even if you had. He's pretty forgettable. Geek chic in the wardrobe department. He'd last about ten seconds on a dance floor. Early thirties, medium height, receding hairline, the kind of face you'd struggle to recall the day after you'd met him. The most noticeable thing about his appearance is he's got these big wire-framed glasses, like giant aviator specs. He says it's so he doesn't miss anything in the lab, but honestly, they're that close' — she held her index finger and thumb a fraction apart — 'to being goggles.'

Allie chuckled. 'Definitely no bells ringing. Is he a researcher like you?'

'We worked on the same projects but he was much more involved in designing the clinical trials process. I think he's very impressive, actually. He's good at taking a 360-degree approach to a project. I liked working with him, he was passionate about getting good drugs to market. He lived with his mum, and then she died about eighteen months ago, and he didn't really know what to do with himself. So when Zabre came calling, he was ripe for the picking.' Jess speared a chunk of the smoked cheese and nibbled it with tiny bites, like a cartoon mouse. 'Mm, that's good.'

'OK, so they plucked him like a peach. What do they do, this Zabre? What's their thing?'

'They bumped along on the generics train for quite a while, then they made a bit of a killing a few years ago with an eczema treatment that worked better than anything else around, especially on kids. It wasn't a game changer, but it's been a nice little earner for

94

them. Then when AIDS came along, they realised it was here to stay and they've been trying to develop a combination therapy that will slow down the progression from HIV to AIDS.' Jess drained her glass.

'Another one?'

'Just a half, I need to be able to look down a microscope and not see double.'

Allie pushed through the bodies at the bar and returned with a couple of halves of bitter. She picked up the thread of the conversation. 'That's pretty much the Holy Grail right now, isn't it? Stopping the HIV developing into full-blown AIDS?'

The corners of Jess's mouth turned down. 'And it's about as likely to be found as the Holy Grail. The best we can hope for is seriously slowing it down. We just don't understand enough about how retroviruses work yet. And AIDS is not a sexy disease in terms of attracting either massive amounts of funding or — whisper it — the most brilliant minds.'

'Really? I'd have thought being the team that cracked this one would be high prestige.'

Jess shrugged. 'Yes and no. There's so much stigma attached to it. A lot of people think AIDS victims don't deserve a cure. The real prestige would come with a breakthrough that would lead to applications for other illnesses.'

'So Colin bucked the trend and went off to Zabre? Would he have been involved in this aborted trial in Edinburgh?'

Jess shrugged. 'I've no way of knowing.'

'Where are they based, this Zabre?'

'Their main production site is in Dusseldorf. But they've got an outpost in West Berlin as well.'

'Dusseldorf I get, but why West Berlin? Does that

not create all kinds of supply problems? It's not like you can just nip down the road with a truckload of drugs.'

Jess seemed uncomfortable with the question. 'I imagine it's not entirely straightforward.'

'So why?' Allie persisted. Just because Jess was her friend didn't mean she had to give her an easy ride.

'OK, so a lot of drug trials get done across the wall.'

'In East Berlin?' Allie was taken aback. 'Why?'

'Not just in the city, in East Germany generally.'

It felt as if Jess was avoiding the question. 'But why?'

Jess pushed her plate away. Allie read that as a sign things were getting serious. 'To do clinical trials properly isn't cheap. The protocols have to be set up and followed. The patients have to be closely monitored, often residentially. The paperwork has to be done thoroughly. East Germany's desperate for foreign currency so . . .'

'Come on down, the price is right?'

'It's not just because they're cheap,' Jess said. 'To be blunt, the patients are more used to doing what they're told, so the drop-out rates are a lot lower.'

Allie scoffed. 'And the patients are a lot less likely to sue if the wheels come off, right?'

'I suppose. I don't have any direct knowledge, we've never worked with them.'

'Is it possible that if a trial was aborted here because of adverse side effects, it might be moved to East Germany? Where it would be easier to body-swerve scrutiny? Sweep the bad things under the carpet?'

Jess sighed. 'It would be pretty unethical. Like I said, I don't have any first-hand experience.' She filled the uneasy silence by returning to the last of her cheese.

'Are you still in touch with Colin?'

Jess shook her head. 'He sent me a Christmas card, which kind of surprised me. It's not like we were friends.'

'So it wouldn't be weird if you got in touch with him?'

Jess rolled her eyes. 'Of course it would be bloody weird. Why would I do that?'

'You don't think he was maybe reaching out to you? If he was worried, he might do that?'

'Allie, he didn't say, 'Help, Jess, I've got into something over my head.' He said, 'Merry Christmas, let me know if you're ever in Berlin.' It's not exactly a bloody cry for help.'

Allie sighed. 'OK, OK. I don't suppose he gave you his phone number?'

'What are you planning, Allie?' Jess knew her well enough to let her misgivings show.

Allie opened her eyes wide. 'I'm just interested.'

'My arse,' Jess said. 'You're going to ring him up and put the fear of God into him.'

Allie grinned. 'The innocent have nothing to fear from me.'

Jess snorted in derision. 'Luckily for Colin, all I have is his address.'

Allie held out her hand. 'Gimme. You know you want to. If there's anything dodgy going on, you've got to want to know. It's in your interests that your industry cleans up its act. And what about those poor sods in East Germany? You think anybody there gives a flying fuck about them?'

'You've got no basis for thinking there's anything unethical going on with Zabre.'

'Except that Dr Robertson said they fought with him to continue the trials even after they were getting adverse results. He said they blamed the patients, not the drug.'

Jess pulled a face. 'Sometimes you do get a badly chosen cohort. Doctors put forward patients for emotional rather than scientific reasons. Look, I know you're missing being an investigative reporter, Allie, but you're seeing stories where there are none.'

Allie gave a dry little laugh. 'If you knew how often I'd heard that line ... Please, Jess, humour me. I promise I won't monster Colin the geek. I'll just pop over to Berlin and buy the boy a few beers, see what's happening. Maybe take Rona with me, let her loose on the Berlin scene.'

'Now that really would put the fear of God into Colin.' She sighed and pushed her chair back. 'I need to get back to work.'

'The address?'

'I'm not even sure I kept the card.' Jess got to her feet, making a fuss of getting her coat on.

'I've been in your house, Jess. You never throw anything away. Please? I'm trying to get some stories in the paper that have a bit of heft to them. Ace Lockhart is dragging us so far down into the gutter, I swear some days I feel like I'm up to my chin in raw sewage.' Allie tried for a laugh to hide the desperation that had slipped through her protective mask.

Jess sat down again and put her hand over Allie's. 'You need to find another job,' she said softly. 'This is killing you.'

'Easier said than done. Used to be we did proper reporting as well as the trivia. Investigations. Revelations that didn't involve soap stars. But there's nothing left. And the broadsheets would just laugh at somebody with my track record rocking up for a job. I had a drink with the northern news editor of the *Guardian* a while back. I said I'd always fancied working for them. He literally snorted beer out of his nose, then said, 'Once a tabloid hack, always a tabloid hack, my dear girl.' ' Allie forced a smile. 'So all I can do is try to keep the aspidistra flying.'

'I'll dig out Colin's address this afternoon,' Jess said. 'Don't break him.'

Allie promised, knowing she'd probably fail to keep her word. She watched Jess make her way through the thinned-out crowd, the cold slither of guilt reminding her how manipulative she'd just been. Sometimes, she despised the depths she'd sink to when she had the whiff of a story in her nostrils.

15

Saturday night and Manchester was buzzing. There was a broad arc of the city centre that was busier between 10 p.m. and 3 a.m. than it ever was during daylight hours. For Allie and Rona, Saturday night was either sitting round a table eating and talking and drinking with friends, or clubbing like they'd never left their twenties. They loved to dance. In their early years together, they'd sweated the nights away to hi-energy but when the late eighties hit, improbably they both felt like they'd been waiting all their lives for acid house. Rona had found it first, when she went along to a Hot night at the Hacienda to write an 'I' piece. 'Honestly, I was probably the oldest person on the dance floor by a generation, but Allie, it's insane. You have to come with me.'

So they'd gone together one night in 1987 and it felt like they'd found their lost tribe. Every time they returned, there was some new bolt-on, some invader from outside that had tweaked the sound, and they loved it. They didn't care that they didn't fit; the cool thing was that nobody else seemed to care either. The door team treated them like their favourite aunties. They avoided the drugs. 'The inside of my head is mad enough without E's.' Rona always said. And they danced.

The bonus was that sometimes they even fell over a story. Mostly Rona; features were easier to bump into. But occasionally, one of the regulars would drop a word in Allie's ear that would pull her towards an unexpected page lead.

The Saturday after she'd come back from Edinburgh, they'd dressed for dancing. Rona in denim shorts and a black camisole top with lace across the yoke and wide shoulder straps, a white leather jacket like Chrissie Hynde had worn on the last Pretenders tour slung over it; Allie in black leggings and a V-necked short-sleeved tee with scarlet piping on the seams that picked up her red Converse shoes. They were a bold contrast to Rona's black heels. God alone knew how she could dance the night away in shoes that would have Allie weeping inside an hour. Finally, Rona touched up her lipstick, a dark plum to change her vibe. Now they were ready to hit the town and shake off the week.

Exhausted and exhilarated, they left the club just before two, heading for Kai's, their favourite of the Chinatown restaurants that stayed open till breakfast time. Allie demanded a detour via the all-night news stand on Piccadilly Gardens so she could pick up a first edition of the *Globe*.

'Leave it till morning,' Rona pleaded. 'You know it'll only wind you up.'

'I want to see what they did with my story,' Allie said.

'You have a streak of masochism that troubles me.' Rona, teetering on high heels, hooked her arm through Allie's. They swung along the pavement, the music still coursing in their bodies. They bought an armful of papers, Rona snatching the *Globe* from Allie. 'No,' she scolded. 'Wait till we're at least sitting down with a bottle of Tsingtao.'

The moment the sweating bottles of beer arrived

in front of them in the busy restaurant, Rona passed Allie the *Globe*.

Allie flicked swiftly through the pages, scanning the columns with a practised eye. Her spirits sank as she delved further into the paper. If they'd run the story at all, they'd buried it way back. Then she stopped, snagged by her byline. 'What the fuck?' she exclaimed, loud enough to turn heads at the next table.

'What did they do?'

Allie held up a hand, demanding a pause so she could digest what was in front of her. It was the lead on page 23. In bold black capitals, she read, 'SICK SCOTS EXPORT AIDS TO ENGLAND.' She felt her heart contract. This was exactly what she'd tried to avoid. She could hardly bring herself to read on. 'English cities are being flooded with killer infection as Scots flee Europe's AIDS capital.

'Junkies and gays carrying the lethal HIV bug are trying to escape the stigma of their disease by moving south from Edinburgh, where many hundreds are already carriers.

'And a health official in Manchester warned, 'Don't do drugs or have sex with someone who's come down from Scotland."

Allie couldn't bring herself to carry on. 'Those bastards.' She threw the paper across to Rona.

Rona skimmed the ten paragraphs. 'You didn't write this.' It was a statement, not a question. 'You've been stitched up.'

'Like a bloody kipper.' Allie groaned. 'The fucking news-desk. They've gone behind my back and set a freelance on the story. That supposed health official quote — that's not mine. If I'd been going to write that kind of shite, I'd have quoted the 'Don't jack up

102

with a Jock' line.'

'I know that.' Rona reached across the table and squeezed Allie's hand.

'They've burned me. I can't go back to any of these people.' She picked up her beer and downed half the bottle. 'Alix is going to nail me to the wall.'

'Alix knows you wouldn't write this shit.'

Allie stabbed a finger at the page. 'It's got my name on it. Everybody will think it's me. One piece and my credibility in the gay community is shot to ribbons.' She shook her head. 'This is what Ace Lockhart's done to the Globe. We'd never have gone this far down bigotry road before. Murdoch led the way, but Lockhart's running as fast as he can to catch up.'

A waiter appeared. 'You ready to order, ladies?'

Rona looked at Allie. 'The usual?'

Allie nodded. 'Not that I feel much like eating now.'

'You'll change your mind as soon as you smell the hot and sour soup,' Rona promised. She gave the waiter their order, adding another couple of beers.

'I thought things were getting better,' Allie sighed. 'We came down from Glasgow to get away from the worst of the homophobia. But look at this.' She slapped the paper. 'It's just as bad as what we left behind. The only difference is that we've got places to go and have a good time. To fiddle while Rome burns. No, not Rome. The whole bloody world.'

'It's because of AIDS. We know now it's not a gay plague, but there were a few years when it was a brilliant focus for everyone who hated gays. Gay men in particular. Us lesbians, we pretty much got off the hook, Allie.'

Allie scoffed. 'We got off the gay plague hook, maybe. But now we've got Section 28 and that gives all the bigots licence to put us in our place. 'You're not real women, I don't want you teaching my daughters or in the same gym changing room as my wife.' And anybody that thinks we're not still staring down the barrel of misogyny only has to do a shift in our newsroom to have their eyes opened.'

'It only feels so bad because you persist in staying in news. The world I move in isn't half as bad. I get respect from most of the people I work for.'

'Lucky you,' Allie muttered as the waiter arrived with the soup. 'I used to think I got a bit of respect when I was working investigations. Now I think that was barely skin deep.'

'They kept you on, running everything north of Stoke-on-Trent. And fired all the guys, babe.'

'Only because I was the best. And because I didn't disappear to the pub for two hours every lunchtime.' She dug into the comforting bowl of complex flavours, her sinuses clearing with the first mouthful.

Rona watched her, and gave a sympathetic smile. 'There's nothing that a bowl of soup can't ease,' she said.

Allie rolled her eyes. 'I'll remind you of that the next time you break a nail and it's like the end of the world.' More soup. 'But honestly, Ro, what am I going to do? It's not just shit like this. It's the other stuff too. Lockerbie, the M1 plane crash — it's draining and there's no downtime. You go one of two ways — you empathise, you listen to the loss and that destroys you one way. Or you build a wall and hide behind it, and that destroys you a different way. At least doing the investigations, I took away something positive. I might have been exposing total shitehawks, but I felt like I was doing good in the world, not just wallowing in other people's misery.'

Rona put down her spoon. 'Then maybe you need to think about getting out.'

The response shocked Allie. It wasn't that the notion hadn't crossed her mind. But to hear it from Rona was a different matter. Rona understood the passion Allie felt for nailing stories — and writing them — because she shared it. That she could say the unthinkable brought Allie up short. 'What would I do?' she said. 'I've got no other skills, Ro. I'm rubbish at taking orders, I hate working nine to five and I've got the lowest boredom threshold in Manchester.'

'Don't oversell yourself,' Rona teased. 'Allie, you're the smartest woman I know. You could turn your hand to anything.'

'I think you might be a wee bit biased, Rona. Name one thing I could walk into with any prospect of being successful.'

The soup occupied Rona for a minute. Then she said. 'You'd be a brilliant private eye. You've got all the skills. You can get a Trappist monk to talk. I bet Bill Mortensen would take you on in a heartbeat. He's always complaining he's got more work than he can handle. Mortensen and Burns. It's got a ring to it.'

Allie burst out laughing. 'Me? A private detective? Are you kidding?'

'Why not? You're always reading those American women private-eye novels with their kick-ass heroines. You could be V. I. Warshawski or Kinsey Millhone or . . . what's that English one called?'

'Anna Lee?'

'Yeah, that's right. You could be a Scottish Anna Lee.'

'Rona Dunsyre, that's the maddest thing you've

ever suggested. Besides, I don't want to work for Bill, much as I love the guy.'

Rona wagged a finger at her. 'I know that. I'm not suggesting you'd be working *for* Bill. Working with him, that I can see. Don't dismiss it out of hand, my love.'

'And what about my writing skills? I love knocking a story into shape and I'm good at that, Ro.'

Rona sighed. 'Good point, well made. But there's no reason why you couldn't still do bits and pieces of journalism. Hell, maybe you could even write your own private-eye novels.'

Allie choked on her beer. 'Now I know you've had too much to drink. There's no way I could make stuff up. I don't have that kind of brain.'

'Some would say that being a tabloid hack is all about making stuff up,' Rona said, a wicked glint in her eyes.

Suddenly sobered, Allie shook her head. 'You know that's not me,' she said. 'I feel guilty rewriting a quote when somebody stumbles over their words.'

'I'm worried about you, my love. You give so much of yourself to the job, you let it take so much from you. What happens when you run out of Allie?'

'There's no chance of that, Ro. When I come home to you, it's like being plugged into the mains. Nights like this, all the stress leaks out of me and I get refilled with the good stuff.' She reached across the table and tenderly ran a finger down Rona's hand. 'I love that you're trying to fix things for me. But I'm going to have to dig my own escape tunnel out of this one. And I don't think it's Bill Mortensen.'

16

When it came to travel arrangements, Genevieve Lockhart moved in a different world from Allie and her fellow employees. She only drove when she wanted to; there was always a driver available to take her to the office, to the shops, to parties and to dinners. Either her father's helicopter or his private jet were generally available for longer journeys. Staff organised her travel and hotels, and they knew only too well the standards that were demanded. Someone would have packed her case if she'd wanted it; that she always chose her own travelling wardrobe was something Genevieve believed was a mark of her attitude to the staff. She wasn't a spoiled princess, for heaven's sake. She could fold her own blouses.

That winter evening, Genevieve was alone in the penthouse flat that sat above the Pythagoras Press operation, making final preparations for a trip to Vilnius. She'd been researching this project ever since she'd elbowed Stephen Lavery out of the picture, setting three of her most trusted staffers the task of identifying the new radicals in a clutch of Eastern bloc countries that were important to Pythagoras Press, either as scientific contributors or eager consumers. She'd analysed the intel her team had accumulated and decided Lithuania would be her first target. When she'd told her father, Lockhart had raised his eyebrows in a quizzical look. 'Why Lithuania? It's not one of the big players in our market.' He puffed strenuously on his cigar, releasing a cloud of blue smoke that obscured his expression. It was a trick he loved to play in negotiations. He banned people from smoking cigarettes in his presence because he considered the smell disgusting, but he used his own smoking habit to powerful effect.

Genevieve counted out the reasons on her fingers. 'Ever since we published that ridiculous biography of their beloved leader, we've had a good relationship with the existing government, so it won't seem strange for me to turn up on a visit. They're a good market for PP — they've got a young population with frustrated ambition. We've got a great fixer there in Tavas Nagaitis. He's a devious little shit, but he's our little shit, and I suspect he'll know exactly who to talk to on the other side of the fence. From what I can gather, there's already a head of steam building up in favour of change in all the Baltic republics. And Lithuania is small enough that I can get a real sense of what's going on.'

Lockhart stared hard at his daughter, as if he was trying to penetrate her skull to see what lay within. 'It's not a bad place to put your toe in the water. And your Russian and German are both good. Do you have a list beyond that?'

'Bulgaria next. Zhivkov loves you. He actually believes what we said in the whitewash biography we did for him. He wants you to move there. He'll be thrilled to see me. He'll be giving me a guided tour of all the lovely palaces he'd rent to us. But my people tell me there's real unhappiness bubbling under the surface. They're only about seven hundred miles from Chernobyl, and that's no distance at all as the wind blows. When Gorbachev did his Chernobyl

108

revelation, it freaked people out. They were all, 'So what else have they *not* told us about?''

Lockhart grimaced. 'Bloody Gorbachev. But I think you're wrong to prioritise Bulgaria. For a start, you don't have the language —'

'But we've got good people there,' Genevieve protested. 'The people in power all have Russian. And the forces of change — they'll have an internationalist perspective. English, German —'

'Turkish, Romani, Genny,' he cautioned her. 'Look, I know Bulgaria. And they're held tight in the party grip. Even if Zhivkov is forced out, and his politburo with him, there won't be a revolution. A few hotheads, maybe, but conservatism has a tight hold there. Bulgaria drops down your list, OK?'

She stifled a sigh. Always he had to know best. She nodded, lips pursed.

'Who's next, after Bulgaria?'

She thought his smile was meant to be benevolent but she read it as patronising. She wished he'd truly let her be in charge of the corner of the empire that was supposed to be hers. A deep breath. 'East Germany. I want to make a move on East Berlin. I think the dominoes are teetering there.'

Lockhart frowned. 'You're there to make contacts. To take the temperature. Not to start a bloody revolution.'

Genevieve flushed. 'I'm not stupid, Ace. I know this is all about taking soundings.'

'No, you're definitely not stupid.' He broke into an indulgent smile and took a gentle toke on his cigar. 'But you need to learn caution.'

She couldn't help a snort of laughter. 'That's rich, coming from you. Captain Risk himself.'

He looked offended. 'I always calculate the lie of the land before I make my move.'

'That's not how you got your medals at Monte Cassino.' She tempered her sharpness with a smile.

'But it might be how you get your stripes behind the Iron Curtain.'

She recognised a sensible exit point, and no more had been said. And now she was trying to work out what to pack for February in Vilnius. Snow on the ground, meetings with government ministers, knocking a few heads together at Pythagoras Press, maybe a dinner or two, then dressing down to meet the people who had ambitions to be the new masters. Not to mention a few forthcoming publications to hand around like sweets to the children.

It was going to take more than one suitcase, for sure.

★　★　★

When it came to passport control and immigration in Soviet bloc countries, there were definite advantages to being Wallace Lockhart's daughter. Pythagoras Press was a beloved and respected source of hard currency; if they'd had an aristocracy in Lithuania, she'd have been considered part of it. Even flying in on a commercial flight rather than the private jet, Genevieve didn't have to join one of the endless snaking queues at Vilnius airport. She was whisked off the plane ahead of the other passengers and escorted to the terminal by a blank-faced man in uniform. She wasn't sure if he was a soldier, a policeman or state security, but none of those were grounds for concern to a woman in her position.

No matter how often she travelled in Eastern Europe. Genevieve was always struck by two things. Everything was drab. And every public space smelled of cheap tobacco and stale bodies. If those Trots selling *Socialist Worker* outside the Lockharts' buildings had to spend a month in a communist country, they'd run home and vote Tory. Except maybe Cuba, she conceded to herself. At least the sun shone and those ancient American cars that grunted their way round Havana did add a certain faded glamour.

On the far side of the formalities, Genevieve scanned the noisy crowd of eager citizens waiting to meet and greet. On the far left, appropriately enough, she spotted the familiar head of Tavas Nagaitis. He looked exactly as she remembered — same dark brown hair styled like a crash helmet framing the face of a rodent with its bright eyes, sharp nose and little pointed teeth peeking out from a thin smile; same shiny blue suit, white shirt and tightly knotted brown tie. He wasn't holding up a sign with her name or the company emblazoned on it. No need to advertise when they both knew who they were looking for. She waited for him to push through the throng and greet her. No point in lugging a heavy case any further than she had to.

They exchanged meaningless pleasantries in Russian. Genevieve knew she was a little rusty, but experience told her she'd be back up to speed by morning if she spent the evening in her room watching Russian TV or talking to Nagaitis. He led her out of the arrivals hall and she exchanged the intense smell of cigarettes for the equally intense reek of car exhausts, clouds of peculiar sweetness hanging in the freezing air. Nagaitis had parked at the kerb, which meant he'd had to bribe the policeman standing next to his mustard-coloured Kombi. He opened the passenger door for her then stowed her luggage.

'I have a new car,' he said proudly as they set off. 'The last time your father was here, he said he was ashamed to be seen in my old Moskvitch.' He flashed a cheeky grin at her.

'So you can tell him you were picked up in an almost-new Izhevsk. Very smart. You won't see many of these on the road round here.'

'So that's where all the profits are going, Tavas,' she said.

He gave her a slightly alarmed look before he caught sight of her mischievous expression and relaxed. 'I forgot your sense of humour,' he said.

What she'd forgotten were the potholes that made drivers swerve and weave as though they were drunk. Genevieve hung on grimly to the door handle and looked out of the window. They passed ranks of housing blocks that could have been parachuted into any Soviet city without anyone noticing. Then the city park with its statue of Lenin, a copy of the familiar one at the Finland station. Genevieve knew it was heresy, but she always thought Vladimir Ilyich looked like he was hailing a taxi.

Nagaitis, as usual, was determined to remind her of the city sights, choosing his route to accommodate that. The odd couple of Vilnius hove into sight — the white cathedral with its neoclassical pillared portico that could have been mistaken for a museum, and its nearby bell tower, which resembled a lighthouse stranded three hundred miles from the nearest sea. It invariably made her smile; but then in Vilnius, you took your laughs where you could.

112

When they arrived at the Europa Hotel, Genevieve put a hand on his arm to delay him jumping out and getting her cases. 'I'd like to talk to you privately this evening. Is there somewhere we can go for a drink without being overheard?'

He thought for a moment. 'There are bars in the old town that are too busy for hidden microphones to make sense of conversations. With lots of dark corners where we can sit close enough to be private. Is this acceptable?' His eyes were anxious. It wasn't uncommon to see anxiety in people who worked closely with her father. Genevieve was trying to do things differently. Ideally under her father's radar.

'Perfect. How do we do this without attracting attention?'

He gave her a sidelong look. 'You dress too brightly. Imagine you are going to meet the undersecretary for Industrial Production. Do you have a beret? No? Then wear a scarf over your hair. And less make-up, please.' He was enjoying this rather too much, she thought. 'I will knock on your door in an hour. The hotel lobby will be busy then. There is a group of engineers here for a conference, they will be returning from a day touring factories. We can leave without being noticed.'

'How do you know about the engineers?'

He looked pleased with himself. 'We hosted a reception for them yesterday. Pythagoras publish one of their journals.'

It was as absurd as a bad spy movie. But this was his world and she had no choice but to rely on Nagaitis. When he collected her, they made it outside without apparently attracting any attention. He led her through the streets and alleys of the dimly lit old town. Frost stippled the cobbles and their breath clouded the air. Genevieve cast backward looks at every corner but saw no sign of a tail. Ten minutes after leaving the hotel, they squeezed into a tiny corner booth in a crowded bar in the old town with a couple of sweating glasses of beer.

'Is this what you wanted?' he asked.

She nodded. 'It's perfect.'

'You mind if I smoke?'

'Tavas, we're the only table in the room where nobody's smoking, so you'd better.' She waited till he'd lit his cigarette. 'I wanted to talk to you privately because we have some concerns about what's happening in Lithuania. Politically,' she added hastily, seeing the look of panic in his eyes. 'We're happy with how you're running the business here. But we keep our ears close to the ground, and we sense change is coming in the Soviet bloc.' She paused.

A furtive glance to check nobody was paying them any attention. 'Gorbachev,' he said. 'He's a very different kind of leader.'

'We want to pre-empt any potential problems. Any changes that have to be accommodated.' She waited but he said nothing. 'We know there are protest movements gaining momentum. And we want to engage with them, Tavas.'

His eyes widened and he licked his thin lips. 'You say 'we'. Do you mean Pythagoras Press or you alone?'

'My father and I are together in this.' She grinned. 'He knows why I am here. The only reason he's not with me is he's too well known.' She made a small gesture that encompassed the room. 'Can you imagine my father in a bar like this? People would be queuing up to shake his hand. The secret police would have his every move covered and he'd be recognised on every street corner. Whereas I can operate under the radar.'

He finished his beer in one gulp and stood up. 'I need another drink. Would you like one?'

Genevieve shook her head. She watched his progress to the bar, checking he spoke to no one but the barman. When he sat down again, plonking a glass of vodka on the table, she smiled. 'There's nothing to be frightened of, Tavas. We value you. Whatever happens, you'll still be our man in Lithuania.'

'Why do you think I can help you with this? What have I ever done to make you think I am a traitor?' His fingertips were dancing on the tabletop and out of the corner of her eye she could see his leg jumping.

'I don't think you're a traitor. From everything I've seen of you, I think you love your country. That's why I believe you'll already have opened channels to the people who are looking forward to a different future. One where you can be your own masters again.' She let that lie in the open between them.

Nagaitis fussed with another cigarette rather than meet her eyes. He exhaled a stream out of the side of his mouth, drained the vodka and shrugged. 'Miss Lockhart — for a very long time, even thinking what you have just said was impossible.'

'I know. But something is happening now, right across all the Soviet republics. It's not like Hungary in 1956 or Czechoslovakia in 1968, where it was just one country standing up to Moscow. My father has connections right across the Soviet Union and he's convinced that something's stirring, all over the bloc, from the Caucasus to the Baltic.' Genevieve spread her hands in a gesture of openness. 'I'll be honest with you, Tavas. He's not coming at this from an ideological perspective. My father doesn't care what system of government you have, just so long as he can work within it.'

He sighed. 'He is a capitalist.'

'And you've done rather well out of that,' she said drily. 'And if I can make the right connections now, everyone will benefit. Pythagoras continues its profitable relationships with your scientists and researchers. And just as we provided the biographies that painted your communist leaders in bright shining colours for their citizens, we'll do the same for the new regime. They'll need access to friendly media abroad, and we can offer them that too. Everybody will win, Tavas. And your new leaders will know they have you to thank for setting it all up.' In the back of her head, she heard an echo of The Who's 'We Don't Get Fooled Again'. All that stuff about the new boss being the same as the old boss . . .

'You make it sound so easy,' he grumbled. 'You should know that nothing is ever this easy in my country.'

'Set up a meeting, Tavas. Tomorrow, we'll spend the day with your team reviewing Pythagoras business. And in the evening, you'll introduce me to the future.'

His expression was despondent. 'I'll see what I can do.'

Genevieve had a vision of Ace Lockhart's frown and knew what she had to say and how to say it. 'Not good enough, Tavas. Make it happen.' It was her father's voice, alto rather than baritone. But unmistakable in every way that mattered.

17

Just before seven on Tuesday morning, Allie strode down the platform at Piccadilly station to the front carriage of the long intercity train. She always booked the front carriage, ready for a quick getaway when they reached London. The advantage of first class — paid for on expenses — was that she'd get breakfast and coffee on the train. It was a small trade-off for the monthly visit she had to make to attend the news conference of the *Sunday Clarion*.

Over the past couple of days, she'd shaken the trees and uncovered what exactly had happened to her story. She knew who'd made the decision to massacre her copy. She knew the freelance they'd used to wield the hatchet — a man who used to sit at the desk next to hers and whose outrage at being fired while she remained had almost turned to violence. She was armed and ready for the attack. First thing on Tuesday morning, before the schedules, before the conference, she'd be at her news editor's throat.

For a brief moment, she considered the possibility of finding another job. But nobody was hiring in Manchester. She could probably go back to the *Clarion* in Glasgow, but her heart sank at the idea. Apart from Angus Carlyle, who had been bumped up from news editor to editor, she knew the same old faces would be writing the same terrible copy, drinking in the same terrible pubs and demonstrating the same terrible attitudes to anybody who didn't look like them. Bad as things were, they really could be worse. She gritted her teeth and made for the exit.

The overstuffed tube was quicker than a cab in the rush hour. Who knew what it would be like once the Lockhart titles completed their move to the new plant somewhere in the far reaches of the East End? As far as Allie was concerned, that was uncharted territory.

She emerged from the underground at Chancery Lane on to streets that were almost as crowded. But at least the air was fresher than somebody's armpit. Minutes later, she walked into the white marble foyer, flashed her company ID and made for the bank of lifts. Standing next to a silent bunch of people she didn't know, Allie felt gratified yet again at having avoided a move to London. There had been offers over the past few years, both lucrative and professionally tempting. But she recoiled at the prospect of living in London.

It wasn't city life she minded. She'd loved Glasgow, with its grand mercantile buildings, and she'd grown to love Manchester for similar reasons. They'd both been scoured to the bone by the economic policies of the last ten years, but even that couldn't dampen the 'fuck you' spirit they both embraced. Glasgow was defiant, with its approaching City of Culture festival; there were rumours of Frank Sinatra performing at Ibrox football stadium, the very thought of which made Allie grin from ear to ear at its absurdity. And Manchester was clawing its way out of the depths with a combination of music, football and TV production. But the key thing about both of those cities as far as Allie was concerned was how easy it was to escape to the countryside. From the earliest days of their relationship, she and Rona had tried to get out of the city every weekend and into the green lungs of the hills.

118

Sunday afternoon on a windy ridge was the flipside of Saturday-night clubbing.

London with its sprawl, its dirt and its perpetual thrum of traffic offered no easy escape. Allie and Rona had friends in the city who waxed lyrical about the Cotswolds and the South coast; every Friday, they packed up the car with a supermarket shop, sat in traffic queues and arrived in frazzled darkness at their second homes, then did the whole thing in reverse two days later, grumpy teenagers or tired toddlers grizzling in the back seat. And all that talk about access to culture? Allie reckoned she and Rona saw more theatre and visited more galleries in their trips to the capital than their resident friends ever managed. It was fun to visit London, no doubt about that. But living there wasn't an option.

The lift arrived and they crammed in, speaking only to request floor numbers. Allie squeezed out at the sixth floor, squared her shoulders and pushed open the door into the newsroom. At quarter to ten on a Tuesday morning on a Sunday tabloid, most of the desks were empty. It would be half an hour before the reporters and photographers started to drift in. The secretaries were at their desks. The deputy and assistant news and picture editors conferred in tight little shirt-sleeved knots. Nobody looked up as Allie entered.

The man she wanted would be in his office. If the newsroom were a football pitch, Gerry Richardson's glass-walled dugout would have been on the halfway line, perfectly poised to see exactly who was doing what. She knew he would have spotted her seconds after she'd walked in. As she approached, he waved her in with a generous gesture.

119

Everything about Richardson was tight. His skin seemed to have been stretched over his bones; his face looked as if he'd been trapped in a wind tunnel. His thin silver hair was sleek to his head. His body was wiry and spare. Instead of going to the pub at lunchtime, he stripped down to shorts and singlet and went for a run along the Embankment. 'I weigh the same at forty-five as I did at twenty,' he was proud of boasting. He was a genuine Cockney, a working-class lad from Bow. There was a rumour he was part of the notorious Richardson crime family. He never denied it, though Allie suspected it was more wishful thinking than fact. Though he did have the same sadistic impulses the gangsters were notorious for.

She walked in, shrugging out of her coat and throwing it over a spare chair. Before she could get a word out, he held up a hand. 'Before you get stuck in,' he said, 'I know chapter and verse what you're going to sound off about. You're going to bleat about me having your copy rewritten. You're going to whine about sensationalism instead of sensitivity. And you're going to whinge about me handing the rewrite to Owen Prosser because he is something that rhymes with his surname.' He spread his hands and smiled. It made him look like a bad-tempered beaver.

'Why?' she demanded. 'I turned in a great story.'

He curled his lip. 'A great story for a different paper. Allie, you know perfectly well what we do here. We do sensationalism. We do lowest common denominator. We stir the shit.'

'We didn't used to. We used to do journalism.'

He bit his lip. 'Allie. I fought for you.' He gestured upwards with his thumb. 'The boss wanted to keep one of the lads. But I said no. I said, 'Allie Burns is one of the best journalists I've ever worked with.' And I meant it. You get across doorsteps where other hacks get the door slammed in their face. You get people to talk that act like they've taken a vow of silence. But you gotta start dancing to Ace Lockhart's beat.'

'Like a puppet on a string? What if I don't want to?'

He sighed. 'What else are you going to do? Where else are you going to go? If you burn your boats here, you'll struggle, girl.' Hearing him echo her own concerns didn't help. 'I do my best to cover your back, because when it counts, when it comes down to the wire, you're the best. Your Lockerbie stuff? You'd have brought tears to a glass eye. You find stories in Manchester that make London give a fuck, and that's not nothing. But I can't have your back forever. That story you filed last week? You know as well as I do that the *Globe* line isn't a sob story about dying junkies and whores who can't get treatment for their self-inflicted disease.' He shook his head.

She tried to hide her surprise. 'If you're that convinced I'm good, if you're that determined to keep me, why didn't you just kick it back to me and demand a rewrite?'

'Because you'd have done it. And then next week it would have been the same old song. I gave it to Prosser because I knew that would fill you up with rage. I knew you'd be storming the barricades this morning.'

It was moments like this that helped Allie understand how Richardson had climbed the ladder. 'You're telling me this for my own good, are you?' She couldn't keep the sarcasm from her voice.

'Don't be so bloody stupid. I'm telling you this for my own good. I nailed my colours to the mast to give you the northern news editor slot. I'm the one who'll look like a twat if Lockhart makes you walk the fucking plank. Now settle the fuck down, get yourself a desk and give me five lines for conference.' He flapped his fingers at her, indicating the door. Then spoke again. 'No, wait. I only need four from you. Here's number one. Little Weed's wife bolts with champion jockey.' He gave a triumphant wink. 'Owen Prosser's payment for coming back into the fold.'

'Are you serious?' Little Weed, giant hero of the wrestling ring, his fight name a ridiculous nod to the character from *Watch With Mother*. It certainly wasn't a suggestion that he liked a joint. There was nothing chilled about his style in the ring. He made his opponents cry, 'Wee-eed' when he forced them into submission. All Allie knew about him was that he frequented Manchester casinos with his rabbity wife, and didn't like to lose.

'So the story goes. She's fucked off with that little Irish squirt, P.J. Flynn. I tell you, he must have balls of steel. Little Weed could eat him for breakfast and not even notice.' He rummaged through a short stack of papers in front of him and fished out a pale blue square sheet. 'There's the memo. I don't want you to front him up till Friday, though. They've buggered off to Ireland, to some stud farm in the middle of County Bogtrotter. I've got that Irish lass from Belfast tracking them down. I want her to get the wife onside.' He dropped his voice. "My life of hell with the monster of the ring.' Then you can go and see the Weed, don't let on we've got her, and offer him the sob story. Then when you've stitched him up, hit him with whatever she's given us.'

'I do know how to do a showdown, Gerry.' Allie's

mind was already racing through the game plan. That didn't mean she was any happier about what he'd done to her copy. But this wasn't the hill she wanted to die on. 'By the way, I want to take a few days off. Probably the week after next. I need a wee break.'

'Off to the sun with the lovely Rona?' He leered. 'Bikinis and suntan lotion?'

'You're a sick fuck, you know that?' Allie grabbed her coat and tried to slam the door behind her, remembering too late that he'd had it fitted with a hydraulic closer to prevent that very thing. She truly loathed her boss. But she still couldn't deny a lurking sliver of respect for the way he ran his operation. You needed nimble feet to dance with a devil like Wallace Lockhart.

18

Doing what she was told didn't come naturally to Genevieve Lockhart. Though he always made it clear what he expected of her, even her father dialled back his notorious level of bullying when it came to setting her agenda. So she was already chafing against the Lithuanian dissenters before she even met them. It had taken Tavas Nagaitis twenty-four hours longer than she'd demanded to set up a meeting. He had sidled up to her late on Monday afternoon in the Pythagoras Press offices and instructed her to be at the rear of the cathedral the following day at precisely 6 p.m. 'You must go alone and you must not be late,' he said, clearly terrified at having to issue such precise instructions.

'And where will you be?' she demanded.

'I . . . I . . . I will . . .'

'All this time, and you've set it up to be somewhere completely useless,' she snapped. 'You're letting me walk into the lions' den with no cover, no protection.' She could see the sweat on his upper lip and that gave her some satisfaction. 'They're not lions,' he stammered. 'They're harmless.'

'They're plotting against the state. And we both know that's not trivial. How do you know you can trust them not to hold me hostage?'

Nagaitis appeared on the verge of tears. 'No, you're wrong. It's not like that here. The state doesn't have the nerve to arrest them. Truly, they're not a threat to you. They know you can be part of their future. I explained you want to build bridges, to build relationships. To embrace an alternative. They *want* to be your friend, not threaten you.'

Genevieve faked a smile. 'Just testing, Tavas. If you say they're to be trusted, I'll take your word for it.'

But as she slipped out of the hotel in a belted mac and headscarf, trying to look as downtrodden as possible, she couldn't hide the truth from herself. She was heading for a place where her father's influence couldn't protect her. Never mind the secret police, if the dissidents took against her, she had no back-up. To them, the capitalist company that had produced a hagiography of their Soviet-backed leader would likely count as an enemy. She'd have one shot at convincing them she was a good bet.

The streets were quiet now. She walked briskly down the pavement and turned into a narrow alley. If anyone was following her, they'd have to show themselves. She reached the end then doubled back. Confident that she was clear, Genevieve took a circuitous route to the white bulk of the cathedral. She checked her watch and saw she had six minutes to kill. The wide plaza wasn't a place to hang around unobserved, so she set off for the rendezvous.

She found herself walking round what she took to be a cloister. She kept on going, following the path. As she emerged from the lee of the cathedral into a snow-covered area criss-crossed with dark trodden paths, she was suddenly flanked by two men. She slowed and looked over her shoulder. A few feet behind her was a third man. They were all unidentifiable, muffled in hats and scarves over inadequate-looking coats. '*Normalno,*' one said, his voice anxious. '*Nu davay zhe.*'

Trying to calm her, she thought. Telling her it's OK, that she should come with them. Genevieve found them about as threatening as a kindle of kittens. She nodded and let them lead her towards the road, where a battered-looking Lada sat with the engine running. They insisted she sit squashed in the middle of the back seat. It felt like their bulk came from layers of clothes, not muscle. She relaxed a fraction, then they shot off into the sparse traffic. They drove in silence for about fifteen minutes. She could see very little, surrounded by four large men in a small car. She thought they were going round in circles; all she could say for certain was that they crossed the river three times.

At last they pulled up outside a pair of tall doors. The front-seat passenger jumped out, hauled them open and they drove into a courtyard, the snow churned up by tyres. 'Welcome,' the apparent spokesman said. 'We hear you are comfortable speaking Russian?'

'More comfortable than you are with English.' Genevieve reverted to Russian as she got out of the car. 'Thank you for agreeing to meet me.'

They formed a phalanx round her and escorted her to the nearest stairwell. They climbed the dimly lit chipped concrete steps to the second floor and walked into an apartment without knocking. It smelled of cooking and coarse tobacco. In February, she realised, the windows would not have been opened for months. They ended up in a living room furnished with a battered sofa, a pair of unmatching armchairs and a dining table covered in books and papers. Two walls were lined with crammed bookshelves, and stacks of books served as occasional tables for ashtrays. A map of Lithuania was pinned to the wall above a pot-bellied stove that threw out a shimmering circle of visible heat. 'Please, sit down,' the man doing the talking said.

Genevieve remained standing. 'You are clear about who I am?'

Nods all round. 'You are the daughter of the man who owns Pythagoras Press. They publish many lies about our country and its so-called leadership.' The speaker was a middle-aged man with wire-framed glasses, his hair awry now he'd removed his hat. He didn't look like much of a revolutionary. He certainly didn't inspire fear.

She shook her head, impatiently. Time to talk turkey. 'I am the person who runs Pythagoras Press now. And I'm here to make sure we end up on the right side after you have liberated your country.'

★ ★ ★

Later that evening, back in her hotel room, Genevieve typed a report for her father, beginning with the names and the contact addresses of the four men she had spoken to.

Tavas assures me they are the key players among the Vilnius dissidents. They're serious men — one of them is a professor at the university, and they are all passionate about their politics. Their organisation, Sajūdis, was set up last summer and it has connections with similar organisations in Estonia and Latvia. They've been organising mass demonstrations and they're working towards a declaration that the Soviet annexation of their country is illegal. They've won seats in the assembly and the apparently impotent communist government hasn't followed through with its threats to suppress Sajūdis.

The three Baltic states are planning a mass movement demonstration in August — a 600-kilometre human chain two million people strong from Vilnius to Tallinn. If we can play a key role in enabling this, we will be in pole position to benefit from the three independent states that will probably result. Nobody believes that Gorbachev will send in troops to quell these rebellions. I'm not so sure, but I suspect you will have a clearer idea than I have of what he is prepared to risk.

The main problem is that these movements are scattered and fragmented, particularly in their communications. There are somewhere around a hundred and fifty different newspapers and leaflets, all with subtly different agendas — you know how it is with the Soviet left. They make the Labour Party seem cohesive! I explained our proposals to them in some detail — that we will support them with practical help in amalgamating these publications. We'll help put together and distribute news-sheets, flyers and leaflets, and possibly even supply an old printing press (which obviously will not be traceable back to PP). Tavas is confident that we can do this without being discovered or betrayed to the Soviet authorities. He is sure of the discretion of two of his printers who are also active in the dissident movement. And he thinks the authorities don't have the nerve or the resources to attempt to shut the movement down. As we agreed, I handed over $500 as a token of our good faith.

In return, our mutually beneficial relationship in scientific publications will continue on the same terms. And we will also assist in the preparation and publication of the official history of the uprising and whatever biographies of leading figures are required.

On a separate sheet, Genevieve added a handwritten note:

Ace: I'm so impressed that you chose precisely the right moment to strike. They're strong but they still need our support and because we're first to the table, we'll get the richest pickings. Thanks for entrusting this to me. I'm absolutely convinced you won't regret it.
With love,
your Genevieve

She could have waited till she'd returned home to write her report, but she knew from long experience of her father that he would want every detail, and relying on her memory alone was a recipe for harsh questioning. Besides, she wouldn't be able to tell him face to face; by the time she arrived back in the UK, Ace would be cloistered on Ranaig, the tiny

Scottish island he'd bought for a song in the 1960s, when nobody wanted remote islands with no modern conveniences.

In the intervening years, he'd installed a turbine in the Atlantic-facing bay that now supplied electricity for heat, light and cooking. A journalist once asked what he did there and he said, 'I dream big.' But she knew the attraction right now wasn't dreaming — it was the installation of one of the new satellite dishes that would, in theory, beam Sky TV into his cottage. He hated that Rupert Murdoch had stolen a march on him with the inaugural UK satellite channels, but Lockhart couldn't stay away from it. Like a child picking a scab, he needed to see what it was doing, if only to mock. He'd gone to Ranaig to immerse himself in its offering and to plan his return of serve in the tennis match that his relationship with the Murdoch empire had become.

Genevieve would have her report sent up to Ranaig by helicopter, Atlantic gales permitting, and say a little prayer that it would be pleasing enough to push him out of the mood Sky TV would certainly have put him in.

19

Looking at the home of Frannie Sidebottom, aka Little Weed, Allie couldn't help wondering where all the money had gone. He'd been at the top of the wrestling game for years, a regular on Saturday afternoon's *World of Sport*. He was one of a handful of big names who packed out town halls up and down the country, a darling of the old dears who haunted those melodramatic performances. He must have made a fortune. You'd never have known it from his house, Allie thought.

She'd expected one of those Victorian mill owner's bloated mansions that dotted the landscape of West Yorkshire. Either that or their late-twentieth-century equivalent, the sprawling ranch-style bungalow that wouldn't have looked out of place in *Dallas*. She stood at the top of a short flight of stone steps worn uneven by generations of feet and looked down at a meagre cottage and a pocket-handkerchief yard. 'Are you sure you've got the right address?' her photographer asked. Alan Blyth actually lived less than a mile away, on the other side of the steep valley, separated from Sidebottom's village by the railway line and the Leeds–Liverpool canal. Blyth's side was south-facing and prosperous, with a fair few of those mansions. Sidebottom's side was the opposite in every way, blackened terraces huddled round a former mill that now housed a discount furniture warehouse.

'I had no idea he lived round here,' Blyth continued.

131

'Mind, I've no call to be over this side of the valley. You'd have to be desperate to do your drinking in the Scutcher's Arms.'

'I know he likes a night out at the Manchester casinos, but to get through the money he'll have made, it's got to be a major addiction.' Allie squared her shoulders. 'Now he's lost his missus as well. Maybe that's why she walked? Whatever the reason, I don't think he's going to be in the best of moods.'

Allie picked her way down steps made slippery by the thin drizzle coming off the hill in wavering drifts. She didn't check that Blyth was behind her; why would he not be on her heels? She crossed the yard in half a dozen steps. There was no doorbell, just a heavy brass knocker in the shape of a clenched fist. The sound was ridiculously loud for such a small house. There was a long silence and Allie was about to deliver another hammer blow when the door was yanked open. All twenty-two stone and five feet eleven inches of Little Weed stood glowering at her, resplendent in shapeless trackie bottoms and a grubby singlet, a pair of gold-rimmed glasses perched incongruously on the button of fat at the end of his stubby nose.

She got as far as, 'I'm Alison Burns from the *Sunday* —' when he let out a deep growl.

'And you can get the fuck off my property.' His hands clenched into meaty fists and he beat his thighs in a rhythm only he could hear.

'I wanted to ask about your wife. Your side of the sto —'

No words this time. He took a step towards her and shook his head.

'Your fans, they care about you.'

'Fucking vultures,' he roared and covered the

132

remaining feet between them in a split second, fists jabbing at her stomach.

Instinctively, Allie shielded her midriff with her arms and backed away. 'There's no need for this,' she yelped, turning and making for the stairs. She expected Blyth to be at her shoulder but he was already at the top of the steps, heading back out into the street.

Little Weed was at her back, his bulk no impediment to his speed. As she ran, he pummelled her back and sides, every jab a stab of acute pain. Her foot slipped on a step and she fell forward, banging her elbow with a jolt of agony. She scrambled upwards, screaming for help, terrified he was going to throw himself on her as he'd done so often to his opponents in the ring. But he kept enough distance to continue the pounding.

Allie made it to the top of the steps, staggering and swaying into the street. She was aware of Sidebottom retreating as Blyth pulled up next to her, leaning across to open the passenger door. She half fell into the car, shouting out at the pain.

'Jesus, are you all right?' Blyth said, driving away with a screech of tyres.

'Do I sound all right? Do I look all right?' Allie drew in a sharp breath, instantly regretting it. 'Where the fuck were you?'

'When he went for you, I thought I'd better get the car. For a quick getaway.'

'Bollocks you did. You were scared shitless he was going to turn on you, you gutless bastard.' She winced at the effort of shouting at him. 'Did you at least get some pix?'

'I thought it would wind him up even more. I didn't want to make him angrier,' he mumbled.

'You useless shitepoke,' she said, reverting in the

moment to Rona's mother's worst insult. Gingerly she reached into her bag for her mobile. As she pressed the power button, she noticed her fingers were trembling. She stared at the phone, willing herself not to give way, not in front of Blyth. He'd have no hesitation in turning her into a figure of ridicule in the pub. 'No signal,' she groaned.

'I could have told you that,' Blyth said.

'God forbid you'd do anything helpful. Find me a phone box that works.'

'We could go back to mine, it's only a twenty-minute drive. You could have a nice cup of tea.'

Unbelievable. 'Just find me a fucking phone box.'

They drove in silence for half a mile before he spotted a post office with a phone kiosk outside. Allie groaned her way out of the car, feeling like an old woman, and stepped into the box. Because it was in a village, it smelled of air freshener and had no postcards fixed to the windows offering French lessons or massages. It also had a working handset. Allie put in a reverse charge call to Richardson's direct line. Her hand, she noticed, was still shaking. And now she felt sick.

'Allie? Tell me you got something juicy out of Little Weed. The wife's singing like she's auditioning for the Eurovision Song Contest.'

'I got something out of him, all right. I got a beating.'

A moment of silence, then Richardson exclaimed, 'He hit you?'

'He battered me, Gerry. He came after me like a raging bull.'

'What the hell did you say to set him off?'

'Blame the bloody victim, why don't you?' She drew in a breath. Getting angry was too painful. She slowed

134

herself down. 'All I said was, 'I'm Alison Burns from the *Sunday* . . .' I didn't even get '*Globe*' out.'

'And he went for you?'

'To be fair, he only started hitting me when I mentioned his wife. Up to that point, he was just roaring and swearing. Then he started punching me. He chased me up the steps out of his yard, hitting me in the back and the sides. Really hitting me, Gerry.' She heard her voice waver and bit back the next sentence.

'Jesus Christ, Allie. That's bloody awful. Does it hurt when you breathe?'

'It hurts whether I breathe or not, Gerry. He's a fucking mountain and he knows how to cause pain.'

'You need to go to hospital and get checked out, Allie. You might have broken ribs. Or worse. And we'll get the police round to take a statement. He's gonna pay for this, mark my words.'

'No,' she said sharply. Even in the short drive to the phone box, she'd thought it through. 'No police. You know what'll happen there. He'll be all pally with the local lads, they'll charge him with something trivial like breach of the peace and then it'll be sub judice and we'll not be able to write about it. Then it'll quietly get dropped and he'll walk away like he's been freshly laundered. That's not what I want.'

'What are you saying, Allie? I know you know people . . .'

Her laugh turned into an agonising cough. 'That's not the answer, Gerry. What I want is for you to splash on this.'

'What?'

'Little Weed beats up a woman reporter. A pic of me and a pic of him. And trail a turnover to his wife's story inside. The world he moves in, they've got a

135

code. You don't hit a woman unless you're shagging her. Let's humiliate him, Gerry. The people I know, they'll be disgusted with him. He won't dare show his face in a Manchester casino.'

'Are you sure about this, Allie? You're not in shock?' Unusually, he sounded hesitant.

'Never more certain, Gerry.'

'OK, sweetheart. Get Alan to fire over the pix soon as.'

'There are no pix,' she said without expression.

'How come? How can there be no pix?'

'Because Alan Blyth legged it at the first sign of trouble. He left me there, taking a beating at the hands of a man more than twice my weight.'

This time, the silence lasted longer. When Richardson finally spoke, his voice was flint hard. 'I'll deal with him. Bad enough that he didn't take care of you.' A dark little laugh. 'A hundred times worse that he didn't get the pix.'

This was the Gerry Richardson she knew. 'I knew you'd have your priorities right. I'm not going to the hospital unless I start pissing blood. I'm going to get Blyth to drive me home so I can crawl into a bath. And then into bed.'

'That's fine. Do what you need. But don't be a hero. I'll get one of the guys to call you later. You can give him the quotes and he'll pull it together. Don't worry, Allie, we'll give you a good show.' He breathed hard. 'What a bastard. No wonder his wife legged it with the jockey. Now go home. And take tomorrow off.'

Like she'd been planning anything else. Allie clung on to the handset after the line went dead. If Blyth was watching her, let him think she was still on the call. Then she let the tears come.

136

20

The house was cold and empty when Allie closed the door behind her, relieved that she could finally drop the bravado. She would never work with Alan Blyth again, no matter if he was the last available photographer in the north of England. There was no point in a colleague if you couldn't count on them to pitch in when the going got tough. And if you couldn't depend on the pic man to take pix, what was the point of him?

She turned the heating up as she passed the thermostat then stopped in her tracks when she caught sight of herself in the hall mirror. She had no recollection of hitting her head, but the long swelling and the discoloration along her jaw told a different story. She must have cracked it on the step when she fell, the hierarchy of pain meaning she only noticed her elbow. Allie gave the dark purple streak the tenderest of touches and flinched. Just how much of her was going to provoke the same response?

She eased out of her coat, leaving it in a heap on the floor. Just for once, she could be a slob. Step by agonising step she climbed the stairs, glad that Germaine was still with the dog walker and not bouncing around in her usual frantic greeting mode. She started the bath taps, adding the aromatic gel Rona had bought to soothe their muscles after gardening. Then into the medicine cabinet for a couple of ibuprofen, swallowed dry.

Allie had never considered how agonising undressing could be. The day was turning into a whole new encyclopaedia of pain. Getting into the bath was a chapter of discomfort all of its own. Soaking in the warmth helped, but once she'd managed to get out, the slow throb started in her back, her ribs and her elbow. Wrapped in her dressing gown, she slipped into bed, then realised lying on her back was out of the question. She groaned and rolled on to the side without the battered elbow. Her ribs still ached, but the pain was less sharp now.

The women private eyes she read about seemed to recover overnight from a beating. Allie was pretty certain that wasn't how it worked in reality. Apart from the physical damage, she had a feeling there were going to be other consequences. The very thought of rocking up to a stranger's front door to confront them with some awkward question made her shudder. Maybe that would have passed by morning. But maybe not. And what would that mean for her future as a front-line reporter?

Inevitably, as soon as she'd managed to make herself reasonably comfortable, the phone rang. Thankfully, the hands-free was next to the bed and she reached it without too much trouble. It was the chief reporter of the *Sunday Globe*, clearly as uncomfortable with interviewing Allie as she was talking about what had happened. Somehow they stumbled through the necessary questions and answers, and she closed her eyes in relief when the call was over. She'd fulfilled her obligations. All she wanted now was Rona.

★ ★ ★

Rona was not a woman given to quiet entrances. The sharp closing of the front door roused Allie from her fitful doze. For a moment, she couldn't put the pieces together. Then simultaneously pain surged through her and Rona's voice drifted upstairs. 'Allie? Are you home? Why's your coat in the middle of the hall?'

'I'm up here,' Allie said, startled by the weakness in her voice. This wasn't how she saw herself, weak and feeble in the face of adversity.

Rona rushed in then stopped so suddenly she swayed on her heels. 'What the fuck?' she gasped. 'What's happened to your face?' Then she was in motion, hurrying across the room and pulling Allie into an embrace. Allie screamed and Rona released her as if scalded. 'What's happened to you, my love? Have you been in a car crash? Did you fall downstairs or something?'

Allie adjusted her position to ease her discomfort. The thought of reliving the morning almost overwhelmed her. But Rona had to know. 'Little Weed beat me up,' she said, sounding as weary as she felt.

Rona's mouth opened in an O of incredulity. 'He beat you up? How? What happened?'

So Allie took a shallow breath and began again, interrupted every couple of sentences by explosions of anger and sympathy from Rona. When she reached the end, Rona stroked the side of her face that didn't resemble an aubergine.

'I'm going to make him wish he'd never been born,' she snarled.

Allie gave a hollow laugh. 'I think that might be taking on a wee bit too much. Even for you.'

'Not Little Weed — I know my limits. No, I'm talking about that gutless shitepoke Alan Blyth. The people I know in this town — by the time I've finished, he'll not be able to get a gig at a church fete. What a despicable lowlife he is.'

'He is.' Allie's eyes were pricking with tears. She blinked and let them fall. 'I'm so glad you're back,' she said, reaching for Rona's hand. 'I've been feeling so rubbish. Every bit of my body hurts, but I think my pride hurts most of all.'

'Don't be daft. You're amazing.'

'No, I'm not. I'm supposed to handle myself. I keep going over how I could have dealt with him differently, and I keep hitting a brick wall.'

Rona gently wiped Allie's tears away with her free hand. 'It wasn't about you, my love. I think you got somebody else's kicking. Now, at the risk of putting my great big size eights in it, where does it hurt?'

★ ★ ★

By Saturday evening, the answer was still the same: 'Pretty much everywhere.' But Allie was determined that Little Weed wasn't going to spoil her weekend. The only concession she was prepared to make was that everyone should come round to their house rather than go to Alix's as planned. Dosed up with paracetamol and ibuprofen, Allie thought she could probably manage to get through the evening. This would be the first time she'd seen Alix since the disaster of Sunday's paper; she was afraid that to call off the entire evening would send the wrong signal to her friend.

Rona had insisted that Allie was not to move from the table. 'We're getting a takeaway from the Turkish on Barlow Moor Road. I don't want you thinking you have to clear away plates or jump up and get anybody

140

another beer. Just imagine you're a princess.'

'You're taking a big risk, aren't you? What if I get used to it?'

Rona gave a dark chuckle. 'See how far that gets you.'

Jess and Alix arrived together. Rona had warned them about Allie's injuries, but they were clearly both shocked when they saw her. The bruise had spread and darkened into a dramatic shadow across one side of her face. Alix mustered a weak laugh and said, 'You didn't have to go that far to guilt me out of bitching about that travesty of a story last weekend.'

'I told you on Monday, I was shafted,' Allie said.

'And I believed you,' Alix leaned forward and gave Allie a careful kiss on the unaffected cheek. Then she pointed scornfully at the violet velour leisure suit Allie was wearing. 'But looking at that outfit, I'd say you've been shafted in a whole other way.'

'Cheeky cow,' Rona said. 'That's what all the chic set are wearing to do their yoga.'

'That explains why it looks so out of place on Allie.'

'It was a freebie,' Rona admitted. 'I fished it out of the charity-shop bag.'

'It matches my bruises, at least,' Allie said.

'We're going to want the whole sordid story,' Jess added, dumping a bag of beer cans on the countertop.

'Wait till Bill gets here, I don't want to go through it all twice.'

'He's picking up the takeaway,' Rona said. 'He'll be here any minute.'

In spite of Allie's fears, the evening wasn't the endurance test she'd expected. Once she'd got through her account of the attack, punctuated by exclamations of shock and anger all round, they settled into their usual spirited camaraderie.

'You'd be safer coming to work with me,' Bill said. 'I know your fictional private eyes are always getting into fights, but the reality is I haven't had a hand raised to me in anger for years.'

'That's probably because you're a giant blond beardy bear,' Rona said tartly. 'It'd be an idiot that took you on.'

'Speaking of investigations,' Jess butted in, 'I managed to track down Colin Corcoran. I dropped him a note saying you were planning a trip to Berlin and you were interested in meeting up for a chat. And he got back to me.' She rummaged in her bag and produced a postcard. 'There you go. His address and work phone number.'

'Did you tell him why I'm interested?'

Jess shook her head. 'No need. He's a geek. He thinks everybody should be fascinated by the same things as him.'

'Cheers.' Allie took the card. 'I was thinking about going to Berlin next week, but obviously, that's on hold till I can walk down the street without looking like I've escaped from an old people's home.'

'Oh, I don't know,' Alix said. 'Playing the pity card might work in your favour.'

'She doesn't have to be incapacitated to do that,' Rona teased.

Before Allie could respond, the phone rang. 'Stay put,' Rona commanded, getting up and crossing to the wall-mounted cordless handset. 'Hello?' A pause. 'Hi Angus, it's Rona here. I'll pass you over to Allie.' Another pause. 'Me?' Rona cast a glance at Allie. 'Let me take this in the other room.' And she walked out.

'What was all that about?' Bill asked. Allie was never

sure which came first with him; professional curiosity or a natural nosiness that had led him into the right job.

'I've no idea,' Allie said. 'I'm guessing it's Angus Carlyle. He used to be my old news editor back in Glasgow. He's the editor of the *Daily Clarion* now. When I heard his name, it was all about me — that he'd heard what happened and wanted to check I'm OK. But obviously not.'

'I expect he wants to commission something from Rona,' Alix said. 'She seems to be more in demand every time we come round.'

Allie looked at the closed door, puzzled. 'Aye, maybe. But nine o'clock on a Saturday night's a funny time for that. She'll tell us soon enough. Bill, you've been quiet tonight. What's going on in your world?'

He shrugged. 'The usual. Bad people who think they're smarter than they are. But I did meet a genuinely smart financial analyst this week.' He avoided their eyes. 'She's based in Leeds and we're having dinner tomorrow.'

They whooped and teased out of him more details of the latest object of his interest. 'We should take bets on how long she'll manage to be Ms Right,' Jess said, giggling.

'My standards are too high,' he said. Allie wasn't sure quite how genuine his mournful expression was. But the subject was closed down by Rona's return.

'Was that Angus Carlyle?' Allie asked.

'Yeah. He asked after you, said he'd put money on you against Little Weed any day of the week.'

'Eejit,' Allie said. 'So what did he really want?'

Rona sat down and took a swig of her Efes. 'I'm not entirely sure. He wants me in Glasgow on Mon-

143

day for a meeting. I asked what it was about and he said he didn't want to get into it over the phone but it would be worth my while.'

'What is it about you journalists that everything has to sound like a John Le Carré novel?' Jess complained.

'I asked if he wanted to commission something from me, but he just said I'd have to wait and see.' She frowned a question at Allie. 'What do you think?'

Allie shrugged. 'Angus was never a time-waster. If it was me, I'd go and see. What did you have planned for Monday?'

'Just the usual Monday. Write up last week's interviews, see what I can set up for later in the week. Do a bit of gardening if it's not pissing down.'

'You can write on the train,' Allie said.

'And they have phones in Glasgow,' Alix pointed out. 'How can you resist? If you don't go, it'll really bug you, Rona. You know what you're like — you always have to *know*.'

'I think you should go,' Bill said. 'If it makes you feel any better, I'll come round and keep an eye on Allie, make sure she doesn't get into any more fights.'

'I don't need a minder. What about your Sunday-night date?' Allie asked.

He shrugged. 'Priorities, Allie. It's all about priorities. Financial analysts are like buses. There'll be another one along in a minute.'

Rona raised her drink in a toast. 'OK, you talked me into it. Here's to mysterious adventures.'

144

21

When Wallace Lockhart entered any of his company buildings, it was as if he brought a weather front with him. Sunny or cloudy, warm or chilly, calm or tempestuous, the atmosphere in the building seemed to pick up his frame of mind by osmosis. All his senior executives knew to their cost that scattered showers or, as one BBC weatherman stammered, shattered scours, were more likely than sunny spells.

However, that Monday morning, there was a bounce in his step and a lightness in his eyes as he strode into the *Clarion* building on Glasgow's quayside, his camel-hair overcoat billowing around him as if it moved in its own microclimate. He rode his executive lift to the penthouse floor and marched into the biggest office in the building. He subsided into the leather desk chair built to his own specification and frowned at the thin pile of mail front and centre on the desk. Routine matters were handled by others; there were few communications that demanded his personal attention.

Lockhart flicked through the pile. A charity seeking his support, with a scribbled handwritten comment from his PA, suggesting it might earn him favours with the cabinet minister whose wife chaired the board; three sycophantic letters from MPs; a personal note from a retiring division head of Pythagoras Press; and a glossy 8x10 black-and-white photograph of a rough-hewn piece of granite. It resembled a war

145

memorial — a list of names and ages, and below them the legend, *Poladski 1941–44*. Along the bottom margin in thick black marker pen, he read, *All that remains*. Lockhart stared at the image, gooseflesh making the hair on the back of his neck stand up. His PA had attached a Post-It note to the photograph that read, 'No accompanying letter. Not sure what it means?'

Wallace Lockhart needed no accompanying letter to know what the picture showed. The only questions he had were, from whom? And why now?

★ ★ ★

Rona settled into her seat on the train, in front of her a Tandy 100 portable computer and her notebook. She had two features to complete by Tuesday morning. One for each leg of the journey between Manchester and Glasgow, she reckoned. There wasn't enough memory on the 3lb machine for both stories, but she could download the first one to a cassette recorder once she'd finished it. She flipped her notebook open to the starting page of her notes on a pottery company in Stoke-on-Trent whose new designer had transformed their fortunes. It was the one she was least interested in, so best to get it out of the way first. At least it would take her mind off why Angus Carlyle had summoned her to Glasgow.

It was a terrible thing to think, never mind say, but taking care of her bruised and battered lover had forced her not to spend the whole of Sunday brooding about it. Allie had been stiff and sore again after a restless night, but a long bath and a gentle massage with essential oils had given her some ease. She was still reliant on painkillers for any kind of relief, but by the end of the day, Rona could see she was moving more freely.

There had been an endless stream of phone calls from concerned friends once the *Sunday Globe* had hit the doormats and newsagents of the UK. The headline left little to the imagination — in 42-point Tempo Heavy Condensed across four columns — **LITTLE WEED BATTERS OUR ALLIE**. The story was packed with high drama and they'd used a photograph of Allie looking ridiculously young. It was no wonder that her friends and acquaintances were concerned. Recognising how worn out Allie was growing, Rona had started rationing them to ten minutes apiece — including her own mother. Allie had groused about it, muttering darkly about control, but Rona knew it was only a formality.

A couple of neighbours had come round — one with a Tupperware of home-made scones, the other with a bunch of snowdrops from their garden. Thankfully, neither had wanted to come in and draw the full story from Allie.

The one call Rona had wished for hadn't materialised. She'd hoped this was the chance for a rapprochement between Allie and her parents. She'd never understood how they could turn their back on their only child because of who she loved. Rona knew her own family were equally baffled. Her own mother had offered to go to Fife herself and talk to them but Allie had shrugged it off and insisted it was no big deal.

Although Allie had said nothing about it, Rona knew the silence hurt her. It was more than a punishment for something she'd done wrong, it was a rejection of who she was. And that was a heavy weight for anyone to carry. Sometimes Rona wondered if that was the reason Allie threw herself so wholeheartedly into the toughest aspects of her working life. Rona wanted to make it better, but sometimes Allie was a hard woman to help.

And she couldn't help feeling that Allie needed some sort of help. Increasingly, she seemed determined to throw caution to the wind, to take physical and emotional risks without calibrating the likely outcomes. It seemed to Rona that losing her role in investigations had upped the ante for her lover. It was as if she somehow had to prove herself to the world — and herself — in a way she hadn't done when she could point to her successful investigations as evidence that she was making a difference. But believing Allie needed help and getting her to agree were two very different things.

With a sigh, Rona set about deciphering her notes and writing her feature. Whatever Angus Carlyle was going to offer her, the colour supplement who were paying her needed to be fed a slab of copy in the morning.

* * *

Glasgow Central station was buzzing when the Manchester train pulled in. Commuters, day trippers, men and women in suits, even a few hill walkers with rucksacks and boots like Frankenstein. Rona shivered at the thought of the Scottish mountains in February. Not because she was reluctant to get out into the countryside, but because she knew from bitter experience how the weather could turn. Every winter, people died out there, usually because they didn't really believe this was a hostile landscape.

Almost as hostile as walking into her former work-place, she thought with a wry smile. Rona headed for the station toilet where she touched up her make-up and checked her hair in the mirror. She'd gone for high impact; she wanted Carlyle to see she was at the top of the game, not in need of anything he had to offer. She'd bet that the dark blue jacquard Gianfranco Ferre suit with its jewel button and subtle figuring along the bottom of the jacket was a level of couture nobody else in the *Clarion* building would be wearing. Rona allowed herself to acknowledge she wouldn't be wearing it herself if she'd had to pay full price for it, but nobody else had to know she'd swagged it from the back room of *Vogue*. She straightened her padded shoulders and walked out to the taxi rank.

The same bald guy with the toothbrush moustache and the rippling tyres of fat was still in charge of the security gate at the back of the building. He greeted Rona with a generous grin and, 'I knew you couldn't stay away, gorgeous. Did you miss me?'

Some things never changed. 'I've not slept a wink in all these years,' she replied. Being a woman in this building was a joust, always. 'I've a meeting with Angus Carlyle.'

'Oh no, you havenae.' His smile was smug.

Rona rolled her eyes. 'Check your list.'

'I don't need to. You've got an appointment but it's not with the editor.'

Someone was playing games, but Rona wasn't in the mood. 'It's not my birthday, so it's not a surprise party. Can we cut the cabaret and get to the point?'

He looked disappointed. 'Ach, you used to be a laugh, but you're no fun any more.' He nodded towards the entrance. 'Just go straight up to the top floor.'

Rona hid her confusion. She walked into the van-way, as dirty and smelly as it had always been, and into the back lobby. The top floor was the executive dining room, the boardroom and Ace Lockhart. If Lockhart wanted to see her, why not simply ask her? What was the big secret?

The lift doors opened to reveal a capable-looking middle-aged woman with an iron-grey shampoo and set that could have doubled as a crash helmet. 'Miss Dunsyre? I'm Lesley, Mr Lockhart's PA. If you'll just follow me, he'll see you now.'

That was one question answered, at least. Rona followed the tweed skirt and cashmere cardy down the hall, through an anteroom and into a vast office with a view so striking she almost missed the man sitting behind the desk. Not least because he was uncharacteristically silent. Rona crossed the deep-pile carpet towards Lockhart, who seemed transfixed by a photograph he was holding. She cleared her throat when she was halfway there, and he raised his eyes, his expression sombre. Then he registered her presence and at once his face was wreathed in smile lines. The expression didn't make it to his eyes. 'Rona Dunsyre. Thank you for making the time to come and see me. Particularly after the attack on your friend.'

Rona gave him a level stare. 'I didn't know it was you I was coming to see. I was under the impression that it was the editor who wanted to see me.'

'A matter of business confidentiality.' He spoke in a matter-of-fact way that was at odds with his obvious unease. He got to his feet and lumbered across to a tall cupboard that housed a humidor. He took out a

150

cigar then turned back to her. 'Do you enjoy a cigar?'

This was growing even stranger. 'No, I like to taste my food. Why am I here, Mr Lockhart?'

'Ace, please.' He returned to the desk. 'And please, be seated. You are here, Rona, because I am about to make you an offer you can't refuse.' As usual, there was something formal about his English, probably because it was the third language he'd learned.

'That sounds a bit sinister,' she said, sitting down and crossing her legs to their best advantage. *If you've got it, flaunt it.* And when it came to good legs, even at forty Rona still had it.

'I was sorry when you left us. But I understand your desire for wider horizons than the women's page of the *Clarion*. I've been watching you and you've carved out a remarkable niche in the cut-throat world of magazine features. Your work rate is exceptional.' He paused to light his cigar.

'I get bored easily.'

'I'm unhappy about the state of the features departments at the daily and the Sunday paper here. We need someone at the helm with vision.' A puff of smoke. 'Vision and ability. I want to create a new post. Group features editor. With responsibility for both titles. With the remit to develop and edit a colour supplement for the Saturday edition. As well as liaising with the *Globe* titles to ensure they have first option on picking up the best features. And the authority to oversee syndication. If you were to accept this job — and frankly, why would you not? — you would also earn a percentage of the syndication income on your department's product.' More smoke.

Whatever she'd been expecting, it wasn't this. It was, on the face of it, exactly what he'd promised. An offer she'd be crazy to refuse. But she wasn't going to make it easy for him. 'You want me to give up my independence to come back into your fold? Back to Glasgow? I have another life now. I live in Manchester and I like it. I like being my own boss.'

'You enjoy precarity?'

'I don't feel very precarious, thanks all the same. I'm never short of work. I make a good living and I have respect from the people I work for. They know I'll deliver what they need.'

He studied his cigar. 'I know all this too.' He gave her a long appraising look. 'You're forty now. Do you want to still be doing this when you're fifty? Sixty? Only on Friday, you saw for yourself how danger-ous this job can be. Out of the blue, Alison Burns was attacked. Beaten and bruised and not, I imagine, planning to return to work immediately. How would you manage if something similar happened to you? Or if you became ill?

'You are a woman of a certain age. I'm told the menopause can have catastrophic effects on a wom-an's capability. It's temporary, of course. But it only takes a couple of missed deadlines for you to lose the trust of your commissioning editors. And trust is like virginity — you can only lose it once.'

Rona met his eyes. 'And why would I trust you not to sack me at the first hot flush?'

He lifted his shoulders in a heavy shrug. 'Because I give you my word?'

She raised her eyebrows and pushed a tendril of hair behind her ear. 'Forgive me if I'm sceptical. I saw at close quarters what you did to your Manchester operation. You gave them your word their jobs were safe not that long before they weren't.'

This time, his smile reached his eyes. It was almost tender. He tore off a Post-It from a pad and scribbled something on it. He paused, letting the suspense build. Then he passed it across the desk to her.

Rona's eyes widened. 'That's the salary?' She couldn't keep the incredulity from her voice. It was four times what she had earned running the women's page. And that had been a generous amount.

'And if you were to be made redundant, your pay-off would be proportionate.'

She gave him a cool look. 'You really want me.'

'Because you are the fucking best.'

There it was. The sudden vulgarity, the shocking contrast to his customary formal urbanity, calculated to wrong-foot the listener. He stood up. 'I don't expect an instant answer. You must go home and talk this over with Ms Burns.' He glanced at the massive lump of gold on his wrist. 'Twenty-four hours from now should be enough.' He waved her away. 'Off you go. Make the right choice, Rona. You won't regret it.'

22

Genevieve Lockhart had always liked Prague. Eastern bloc shabbiness might have diminished but hadn't managed to destroy the grace and beauty of the old city. And she'd always felt the spirit of dissent and the possibility of something different just beneath the surface, in spite of the crushing of Alexander Dubek's Prague Spring in 1968. The tanks of the Warsaw Pact hadn't entirely destroyed hope, even though the Czech citizens still endured a regime dubbed 'reluctant terror'.

In Prague, Genevieve didn't have to play cat and mouse with the authorities as she'd done elsewhere. At dinner in the British embassy, she'd listened to her hosts talk of the bridges they'd been building with the Charter 77 activists. Václav Havel, the man behind so many dissident initiatives, was a regular guest at the embassy dinner table. 'We invite him often,' one of the diplomats said. 'But we never know whether he'll turn up or be under arrest again.'

She'd been in luck. Havel had arrived in time for coffee at the end of the evening. The ambassador had introduced them and she'd managed to steer him into a quiet corner.

She'd started with an apology. 'I know you probably think Pythagoras Press is hopelessly compromised, but there is another way to look at things.'

Havel looked sceptical. 'It's hard to see what that might be. Your company has shored up this

154

oppressive regime with hard currency in exchange for the intellectual capital of our scientists.' His voice was cold and the warmth she'd seen in his eyes earlier had disappeared.

It was an argument she was prepared for. She'd sparred with her father to strengthen her rebuttal of this very point. 'Your government is interested in profit to an almost capitalist degree. They need that hard currency because they've won over your people with economic growth and consumer goods as a trade-off for repression. So if the scientists are no longer an obvious profit centre, their labs will be closed and their equipment sold off. It's hard to acknowledge, I know that. But Pythagoras is what lets your scientific community flourish.'

'Change is coming,' he said. 'You know that as well as I do. We won't need you.'

'You'll need us even more,' Genevieve insisted. 'You're a writer. You understand the importance of communication. I've seen what is produced here. The worst quality of wood pulp paper that tears and turns yellow. The cheapest inks that fade in the blink of an eye. Even if you could afford better supplies, we can turn around high-quality publications far more quickly than your printing facilities can. Installing new presses and building up new publishing houses will take time and money. You can't let it be a priority or you'll be accused of feathering your own nest.'

'Maybe so. But we will not be beholden to a media tycoon from another country.'

'My father's roots are in Eastern Europe. He grew up here. He's never forgotten that, and neither should you. And he believes in the old saying, 'Hearts starve as well as bodies.' Let me show you what I can do,

155

Václav. As a token of good faith, we'll put *perestroika* to the test. We'll publish one of your books right now and distribute it here in Czechoslovakia. You choose which title. I guarantee, you'll see the sense in working with us to communicate with your audience. We're with you.'

He scratched his head, frowning. 'Why would you risk this?'

'Because you risk so much more, every day. We want to show you that we're part of your future, not just the past. Give me a chance.'

He studied her, his eyes shrewd. 'Not one of my books. I must be like Caesar's wife.'

'So, what?'

'A collection of short stories from some of our younger writers. What do you say to that?'

It wouldn't have the clout of Havel's own work, was what she thought of that. Thinking on her feet, she said, 'Will you write an introduction? To speed it on its way?'

Havel considered. 'That would be worthwhile. Perhaps.' 'I'm only here for two more nights. Can you get the material to me before I leave?'

He shook his head, but his face said yes. 'You strike a difficult bargain, Miss Lockhart. To achieve this, we will be putting ourselves at no small risk.'

She put a manicured hand on his arm. 'You've demonstrated so many times that risk is something you're not afraid of.'

'But are you? What if you are stopped on the way out? Your bag searched?'

'I am Pythagoras Press, sir. As far as the state is concerned, I am their friend.'

He drew in a sharp breath. 'And you think there is

156

nobody in this room who will report to the authorities that you had a private conversation with me this evening in the British embassy? Miss Lockhart, your father's name is powerful. But even that has limits.' And he walked away, leaving her unnerved.

And now here she was at the airport, waiting for a flight to take her back home, a bundle of manuscripts tucked into her hand luggage among a swatch of Pythagoras publications. The stories had somehow found their way into her hotel room the previous evening when she'd been at a formal dinner that included two government ministers.

She told herself she wasn't worried about being searched. Thanks to Pythagoras and its dollars, she was considered a friend of the regime. More, she was someone whose smooth passage should never be impeded. Of course she was. Every time Havel's words crept back into her head, she pushed them away. Tonight she'd be in Glasgow, toasting her latest success with her father.

If Ace had ever had any doubts about his daughter's abilities, they must have been dispelled by now. She was three for three with the Eastern bloc so far. Lithuania, Hungary and now Czechoslovakia. Genevieve Lockhart was pretty sure there was nobody — apart from Ace himself — who could have matched that.

She checked out the VIP lounge, which was barely different from the rest of the spartan airport. There was nobody who caught her attention for more than a passing moment. Not even a possible ship that might pass in the night. That was the trouble with being her. She didn't want to end up like Ace, married to his empire. She wanted the empire, of course. But it would be wonderful to have someone to share it with.

Where exactly was she supposed to find someone to match her achievements, someone who could see past the wealth to the woman?

One thing was certain. It wasn't going to happen on this side of the Iron Curtain.

★ ★ ★

Allie swam reluctantly into consciousness on Tuesday morning. She half turned before her body reminded her that still wasn't a great idea. Still dozy, she opened her eyes then snapped to attention when she realised Rona wasn't lying next to her, blond hair spread across the pillow. Neither was Germaine.

She didn't believe she could possibly have slept through the pair of them getting up and out of the house. So where was Rona? She'd called from Central station the previous evening to say she was on her way home, refusing to tell Allie what the summons had been about. Allie had intended to stay awake, but the combination of painkillers and whisky had put paid to that. A glance at the clock revealed it was only half past seven; nevertheless, Allie swung her legs out of bed and used her abs to propel her upright. She was definitely moving better, but she wouldn't be running round Chorlton Water Park with Germaine any time soon.

She made her groggy way down the hall to the spare room, pushing the door open to reveal Rona sprawled face down like a starfish, Germaine lying between her feet, tail waving in delight at the sight of Allie. The dog jumped off the bed, making Rona stir and mumble, and bounded over to her other mistress, headbutting her painfully in the thigh. 'Oof,' Allie exclaimed. 'Behave, you big lump.'

Rona pushed herself upright and gave a slow smile. 'That's no way to speak to the woman you love.'

Allie crossed to the bed and eased herself into a sitting position next to Rona. They kissed softly; even after the best part of ten years, it was still how they started and ended each day they were together. 'Why are you in here?' Allie asked.

'When I got back, I came through to the bedroom and you didn't even stir. I thought sleep would be a lot better for you than listening to me going on.'

'So what have you got to be going on about? What did Angus want?'

Rona ruffled Allie's tousled dark hair. 'I can't talk without coffee, you know that. Come on, hirple your way to the kitchen and I'll get a brew going.'

'You're such a player of games,' Allie grumbled as she followed Rona at a slower pace. She pestered Rona for answers while the coffee brewed, but Rona refused, her teasing morphing into a more serious response.

'I need you to listen carefully,' she said, when they were finally sitting at the kitchen table equipped with caffeine.

'OK, I'm listening. What did Angus want that's so serious?'

'I didn't see Angus. I was whisked straight up to the ninth floor.'

Light dawned on Allie. 'Wallace Lockhart.'

Rona nodded. 'Wallace Lockhart himself.'

'What did he want?'

'Me,' Rona said flatly. 'He wanted to make me an offer he thinks I can't refuse. Group features editor on a massive salary, control over syndication and a cut of the proceeds.'

Allie took a moment to make sure she'd heard correctly. 'Are we talking the *Clarion* titles or the *Globe*?'

'The *Clarion*.'

So, Glasgow, then. 'I don't understand. Why is he doing this?'

'He thinks features are where the future is and he wants to beef it up now and throw a colour supplement into the mix.'

'You know I think you're brilliant, right? But why you?'

'He said I'm the fucking best. And you can't argue with that.'

Allie grinned. 'He's on the money, of course. I didn't expect this, though. I mean, you love writing, not running the shop, don't you?'

'I'd be strategising, not doing the nitty gritty like you're stuck with these days. And I'd demand some writing too.'

'But it's Glasgow. You'd be based in Glasgow.'

'Yes.'

'But our life's here now. Our home. Our friends.'

Rona stared into her coffee. 'I know that, Allie. Here's the thing, though. I miss Glasgow. I miss my family.' She looked up and Allie saw the naked confusion in her face. 'Manchester is great, but it's not my home. I miss hearing Scottish voices. I miss being able to take the culture and the shared history for granted. I miss the humour. I even miss the creative fucking sweariness.'

Allie couldn't make sense of this. 'You never said.'

'You never heard. It was always there in the spaces.'

What did that even mean? 'I thought you were happy here.' She wrapped her hands round her mug, as if

160

that would anchor her on solid ground.

'I'm happy with *you*. And I like our life. But Scotland's been changing while we've been gone and I think it might be time to go home.'

23

Rona's words had wounded Allie. 'Sounds like you've made your mind up already,' she said.

'That's not fair, Allie. We're a partnership, you and me. I want this to be a decision we take together.' Rona reached out and took hold of Allie's hand in a tight grip. 'This is not me looking for an escape hatch.'

Allie's face twisted in an incredulous expression. 'That never crossed my mind.' 'Good, because it shouldn't have. But moving back home? That was always in the back of my mind.' Allie pulled away and went for the bread bin. 'I'm starving. Toast?' Rona sighed. 'As a diversionary tactic, I've seen better. Tactical toast it is.'

Allie had the grace to laugh. 'I think better when my stomach's not rumbling.' As she dealt with bread and butter and the disgusting orange cheese spread they'd developed a secret taste for, she spoke slowly. 'Let's break it down, pros and cons. This is an amazing job offer on the face of it. It's not like if you turn it down there'll be another one along in a minute.'

'I know. And it's exciting.'

'But is it more exciting than what you do now? What you love?'

Rona filled her cheeks with air and blew out noisily. 'I do love what I do. But — and it's only a wee but at this point — I don't love the chasing like I used to. The pitching ideas, the standing them up, the running around doing the interviews — it's starting to feel like there's nothing new under the sun. Everything feels like I'm doing it for the second time. Or the twenty-second time.'

'Don't I know it,' Allie said ruefully. 'At least when I was running investigations, there was genuine novelty. People are always coming up with new kinds of villainy. But the news beat? It's not 'one damn thing after another', it's the same damn thing again and again. Variations on a theme. I can see the attraction of walking away from that into a fresh challenge. So that's a definite plus.'

'Then there's the geography,' Rona sighed. She bit into a piece of toast to buy time. Allie waited. She was determined to let Rona navigate this one. 'OK, I'll be based in Glasgow. But it's an executive job. I can push for a four-day week. I could come down to Manc for the weekends.'

Allie shook her head. 'That's easy to say now. But there'll be things you need to stay across on the weekends. Glasgow is European City of Culture next year. There'll be experimental Swedish operas and German expressionist dramas and interpretive dance versions of *Goodbye, Yellow Brick Road* you have to sit through. Gobsmacking Scottish art exhibitions and sweaty rock gigs at the Apollo —'

'The Apollo closed four years ago, Allie, get with the programme!'

'OK, OK. And then there'll be those weekends when you get invited to somebody's amazing big hoose in the Trossachs with a five-star chef and vintage burgundy on tap.' There was mockery in her voice but they both knew it disguised a genuine apprehension.

'We could do alternate weekends? You drive up on a Saturday night, back down on Monday night or

Tuesday morning.'

'I still think we'd start off with the best of intentions and we'd be down to a weekend a month in no time at all. And that's not what I want, Ro.'

'It's not what I want either.'

A long pause, the crunch of toast, the scrabble of Germaine scratching her ear. 'And then there's her,' Allie said, pointing at the dog. 'That works because one or other of us is usually here. And we've got a dog walker, and Alix in emergencies. I can't have her if I'm here alone. So she'd have to go with you. It'd take about three days for her to become the Dunsyre family dog. They all love her.'

As if to confirm these fears, Rona dropped her last mouthful of toast in the general direction of Germaine, who captured it before it hit the floor. She stood up and stared out of the window. Allie thought how ridiculous it was that after all these years, Rona managed to wrongfoot her with a stylish elegance, even in a crumpled pair of stripy cotton pyjamas. She couldn't imagine what the loss of that dailyness would do to her existence. She didn't want to try.

Rona turned to her with a quick movement. A smile twitched at her mouth. 'I'll tell him no. The price is higher than I can afford.' She spread her arms out at her sides in a kind of shrug, a gesture straight from the second act of a screwball comedy.

'No!' Allie jumped to her feet then yelped. 'Ow, bloody hell! No, Rona. You can't turn your back on this. You'll never get another chance to stamp your character right across a group of papers. You can do amazing things. For women, for gay people, for all the other people that don't get a voice. You're smart enough to do it with subtlety. You can make a

164

revolution happen.'

Rona gave a sarcastic laugh. 'You think Ace Lockhart will let me start a revolution?'

'I think you know how to dress it up so he won't notice till it's too late.' She stepped forward and wrapped her arms round her lover. The familiar smell of her hair always made Allie feel she'd come home. 'You're amazing, Ro.'

Rona nibbled her earlobe. 'I love you, Allie Burns. That's why I'm going to tell Ace what to do with his dream job.'

If Rona had thought even for a moment that they'd come to a conclusion, she'd been swiftly disabused of the notion. The discussion carried on through first Rona's shower and then Allie's; during the short and perforce slow walk with Germaine; and through their second round of coffees. Just before ten, Allie said, 'I need to check in with the newsdesk.'

'You are *not* working today, Alison Burns,' Rona said, her stern face matching her words. 'No way.'

'I'm not going out on a job,' Allie explained. 'I'll do the calls and brief the freelances, that's all. I've had three days of doing nothing constructive —' As Rona opened her mouth, Allie raised a palm to stop her. 'No, Rona, a jigsaw is not constructive. I need to keep my brain active and besides, I feel like my body's starting to heal.'

Rona rolled her eyes. 'You're impossible. Burns.'

'I'm not done with this conversation, by the way. Do not speak to Lockhart until we've had a chance to finish round two.'

They shared a complicit smile and went their separate ways to their offices at opposite ends of the house. Allie pulled the sheets of freelance story memos from

165

her fax machine, but after the first read-through, she couldn't have outlined a single one. Instead, Rona's news rolled round her head on its own treadmill of headlines.

Allie shook her head, as if flies were buzzing around it, and started reading the memos aloud. That did the trick and she sorted them into her three paper trays labelled, YES, MIBBES, and FUCK NO. She condensed the YES memos into pithy short paragraphs, the MIBBES into single sentences, and typed them all in a list for conference. She hooked up the modem and listened while it sang its electronic signature tune and transmitted her schedule to London. She'd hear nothing back till after conference, which was fine with her. Allie gave a piercing whistle; it took Germaine less than thirty seconds to scamper down the hall, ears alert for the promise of a walk.

They had just long enough to walk up to the row of local shops where Allie bought a loaf of granary bread and a couple of salmon fillets for dinner. She took it as a sign of recovery that she'd regained her interest in food. Her loss of appetite had distressed her almost as much as the various aches and pains.

She'd been back at her desk for less than ten minutes when the phone rang. 'Are you sure you're up to it?' Gerry Richardson demanded. 'I can't have somebody running the desk who's off her tits on painkillers.'

'Thanks for asking, Gerry, I'm feeling much better. I have had two paracetamol but I don't think they're interfering with my judgement.' Sarcasm might be the lowest form of wit but it always made Allie feel better.

'Yeah, well, I'm glad to hear you're none the worse.'

'I didn't say that. I still feel like I've been kicked by a horse. I'm not prepared to go out on any jobs this

166

week, but I'm OK to manage the desk.'

'Fair enough. As far as the schedule goes, I'm up for 1, 3, 4 and 6. The rest you can bin unless you can actually track down some pix to go with that kite-flying number 2. We clear on that?'

Allie marked up her schedule sheet accordingly. 'You not interested in the *Brookside* story?'

'Nah. You know me and Scousers. It's got to be bloody good to get past my in-built Cockney prejudices.' A half-chuckle, cut off in the throat. 'I am, however, sending you a memo for a story I need you to put your best freelance on. It's an absolute cracker and I have it on very good authority. I just need you to get a snapper and a hack staking out the house to see who comes and goes.'

'Who is it?' It wasn't like Richardson to hold back.

'You'll see soon enough, darling.' And that was that. Dead air. And an endearment that made Allie's flesh creep but not for the usual misogynist reason. Gerry Richardson only resorted to blandishments when he was about to shove the blade in to the hilt.

The fax machine beeped and trilled, the tones signalling the arrival of a flimsy memo from the London newsdesk. Allie tore the sheet from the feeder and read it. The colour rose from her neck to engulf her face as the memo's full offence hit her squarely.

It couldn't have come at a better time.

24

Allie's anger blocked her residual muscle pains sufficiently for her to storm the length of the house at speed. Without knocking, she barged into Rona's office. Her partner turned, startled, hands still poised above the keyboard. They tried to respect each other's working space and working day except in emergencies, and it was reasonable to assume they'd already had that day's share. 'Get on the phone to Ace Lockhart and tell him you're taking the job,' Allie announced through narrowed lips.

'What?' Rona was bewildered.

'I'm coming with you.'

'I don't understand. What's changed all of a sudden?'

'I'm about to hand in my resignation, that's what's changed.' Allie collapsed on to the day bed where Rona alleged she had her best ideas.

Rona shook her head. 'You're going to have to back up, doll. And take a deep breath, for starters. You're the colour of a red pudding. And that's not a good look.'

'That double-dealing bawbag Richardson, that's what's changed. He was obviously counting on me not coming back to work for a few days. Read this.' Allie thrust the fax at Rona, who stretched to reach it.

She smoothed out the crumpled edges and read the faint print on the thermal paper.

Memo to Gerry Richardson, Sunday Globe news-desk

Exclusive from Andy Thomas, Anglezarke News Agency

Hi Gerry. I've got a cracking exclusive from a very good Northerners contact. If you recall, this contact produced the 'Cornershop Connie in Cocaine Scandal' and also 'Three in a Bed at the King's Head' last year. She doesn't deliver often but when she does, they're always absolutely copper-bottomed. And the series is currently riding high in the popularity stakes, running Corrie and EastEnders hard thanks to the adoption storyline.

Turns out Timmy Tarleton (who plays Denzel Delamere, as if you need me to tell you) is gay. He's got a boyfriend who's more than a dozen years younger than him (Timmy is 30, so that's illegal for a start). The lad's called Jason Thom, and he's a runner on the show.

As if that's not enough, Tarleton's got AIDS. I've got a photocopy of his HIV test result, and pix of the two of them out clubbing together in Manchester. My source is solid on this one — she's close to Tarleton and she's decided to tell me because she's disgusted at his behaviour. She can't go on the record, for obvious reasons. We can quote her as 'a Northerners insider', though. According to her, if we stake out Tarleton's house, we'll get happy snaps galore — he's got a swimming pool annexe on the back of the property with glass walls. It's hidden from view from the road and the neighbours but there's plenty of shrubbery to get a snapper into.

I can't do the story myself because there are a couple of Northerners cast members who might have an idea who my source is and this would burn her because so few people know about the AIDS diagnosis.

Rona's face tightened in anger. 'This is a bare-faced provocation. After what he did to your copy last week, he knows how much this would anger you.'

'Like I said, he was calculating that I'd still be off sick and not reading my faxes. That he could get it away without me knowing anything about it till it was in the paper.' Allie shook her head. 'It's completely vile. It's homophobic and it's cruel. This story will destroy Timmy Tarleton's career. Nobody in the public eye can survive this kind of outing. Punters don't make a distinction between HIV positive and AIDS.' She stared glumly at the floor.

Rona sat down next to Allie and put an arm round her. 'Why is Richardson trying so hard to pick a fight with you?'

'Because I was never his choice. He always thought investigations was a waste of money. Weeks, sometimes months to stand something up that would only get a show in the paper for a couple of Sundays. So when Lockhart slashed the northern staff, Gerry wanted one of the lads to run the shop. It's an open secret. It didn't much matter which one. He wanted a yes-man who would churn out the sleaze and the crap to order.' Allie sighed. 'I thought the fact that it had been Lockhart who chose me was my insurance policy.'

'So it was.' Rona kissed her cheek. 'Richardson

knows he can't fire you. So he's decided to make your position untenable.'

'Looks like it. But the trouble is, the big picture. This is the kind of story the editor wants to run with. He's competing with Murdoch in the dash for the sewer. I'm not really the target here. I don't flatter myself. Driving me out is the bonus. They'd be running this story regardless of whether I was in post or not.' Allie tipped her head back and blinked a couple of tears out. 'And if I don't jump ship over this, it'll be something else next week. And the week after. I've been kidding myself that I could thole it. But I can't, Ro.' She buried her face in Rona's shoulder and wept quietly.

They held each other for as long as it took Allie to collect herself. Then she straightened up and swiped her eyes dry with the back of her hand. 'I never thought a soap star's sex life was the beach I would die on,' she said with a brave attempt at a laugh. 'I'd better go and write that letter of resignation.' She stood up. 'So, the curtain comes down on my life in tabloid journalism.'

'I think you're maybe being a wee bit melodramatic there. You're born to the breed, Allie. You might not write any more of this kind of shite. But you're still going to find great stories and write them, and some of them might find a home in a red top. Never say never again, doll.'

'Listen to you, Mr Bond. Right now, I can't think of anything beyond telling Gerry Richardson where to stick his job. Only more eloquently.'

'Go and do that,' Rona said. 'And by the time you've composed your nuclear warhead, we'll be ready to figure out what comes next.'

'Oh, I'm not going to do this over the ether. I want to see the look on his face when I stick it to him.'

171

She glanced at her watch. 'I can make the two o'clock from Piccadilly. I'll catch him in the pub. He always takes a break for a sneaky Scotch before he delivers his close-of-play bouncers.'

'Allie, no! You're in no fit state to do this.'

'Watch me.'

★ ★ ★

The Copy Taster was the perfect journalists' pub. Tucked away in an alley off Fetter Lane, it was within a few minutes' walk of Fleet Street itself, easily accessible to the hundreds of journalists who still worked around the fabled Street of Ink. The windows were stained glass, each piece too small to permit a view of the interior. Inside, it was panelled in dark wood with furnishings to match; a thin layer of smoke added to the colour palette. There were three separate bars, each of which had booths and half-hidden nooks where private conversations could be had. You could be feet away from your boss and not know it in the Copy Taster.

But Allie knew where she'd find Gerry Richardson at five o'clock on a weekday evening. He'd be in the Subs Bar, the farthest of the three from the door, tucked away in the second booth on the right, a large Bells in front of him. Not even a single malt, she'd thought with amused contempt when she'd first discovered what he drank.

It was a busy time in the pub, the air thick with smoke and gossip, and Allie had to squeeze and wince her way through, exchanging pleasantries, insults and inquiries about her bruises from several acquaintances. Refusing a couple of offers of drinks on the

172

way, she pushed on to the Subs Bar. Her heart was pounding, the adrenaline coursing through her; she was grateful, knowing its benefits as a short-term painkiller.

Allie paused for a moment on the threshold, muttered, 'Fuck it,' under her breath and took the last few steps that brought her face to face with her boss. Richardson was flanked by the chief reporter and another of his cronies, heads close, voices low. It took a moment for them to register her presence and Richardson looked thunderstruck. 'What the fuck?' he exclaimed. 'What are you doing here, Burns?'

'I wanted to make sure you couldn't claim you'd fired me,' she said, projecting her voice to cut through the hubbub.

'What are you talking about?' Richardson tried to stand up but he was trapped behind the booth's table.

'I resign, Gerry. I'm far too good a journalist to carry on working for an ignorant bigot who's too stupid to realise how stupid he is. If brains were shit, Gerry, you'd be constipated. I've worked for some bloody good news editors over the years, and you're so far from being one of them, you might as well be in fucking Australia.'

'Are you pissed, Burns? Or are you off your face on drugs?' he spluttered. 'You come in here, talking seven shades of shit —'

'I've never been more sober. I'm done, Gerry. You've fucked me over for the last time.'

The chief reporter sniggered. 'That's what you dykes need, a good fucking over.'

Allie rolled her eyes. 'Really? Is that the best you can do? No wonder the subs have to rewrite your copy every week.' She leaned her fists on the table. 'I mean

173

it, Gerry. I've won awards for my journalism, but I'm absolutely fucking positive I won't win so much as a raffle under your leadership.'

Now there were a couple of cheers from staff on rival papers. 'Let him have it, Burns. Both barrels,' a Glasgow accent shouted.

'You ungrateful bitch,' Richardson shouted, two splashes of scarlet on his thin cheeks. 'I fucking saved you from the scrapheap. And this is the gratitude I get?'

'You didn't save me. Lockhart told you to keep me on. It's chapped your arse every day since.'

'I told him you were a waste of fucking space, with your high-horse politics and your cunt-struck attitudes,' he hissed.

Allie laughed. 'Is this the bit where you tell me I'll never work in this town again? Fuck off, Gerry. Away and take a flying fuck at a bag of nails.'

She turned on her heel and marched out, head high, to a chorus of cheers and applause. She knew it wasn't a measure of how much she was liked but of how much Gerry Richardson was loathed. Right then, she couldn't have cared less. This was an exit that would go down in hack legend, and that was enough.

25

It was late when Allie arrived home, tired and aching but still buzzing from her resignation. She collapsed next to Rona on the deep sofa that dominated their living room. Enough space for two to sprawl and a dog to curl up alongside. Rona had brought back a bottle of Lanson Black Label from the evening dog walk because this change was something to celebrate. Allie had phoned her from the train with the broad-brush version and she was desperate to hear the details of Allie's confrontation. But Allie was making her wait. 'Your news first,' she insisted. 'What did Lockhart say when you accepted?'

' 'Clever girl.' I told him I wasn't a girl, I was a woman. He just laughed. On another day, he'd have gone ballistic.'

'I think he puts on different personalities like other people put on clean clothes. The bullying, for example. He turns it up to the max when he thinks it'll get him where he wants to be. But if he thinks bribery or charm will work better, like with you? He just slips his arms into the charming jacket. You think he calls the lovely Genevieve a clever girl?' Allie chuckled.

'Probably. And she probably lets him get away with it when it suits her. She's a chip off the old block. I've seen her turn on a dime.'

'You never said.'

'Never came up. It was at a charity dinner, I was there doing a big puff piece about one of the donor companies. She was backstage, doling out the Lockhart charisma. Then the designer dress she was supposed to be wearing arrived and it was the wrong frock. It was too late to deliver the right one, and she turned like a viper. Someone from the charity ended up having to swap dresses with her and she was all sweetness and light again. It was an instructive moment.' She topped up their glasses. 'I wouldn't want to mess with that lassie.'

'We all might have to mess with her eventually. One day, all of us will be hers.'

Rona pulled a face. 'Hopefully not any day soon. In the meantime — how are we going to work this out?'

'When does he want you to start?'

'The first Monday in March.'

'You're kidding? That's less than a fortnight. Surely you've got jobs booked in after that?'

Rona shrugged. 'He says he's happy for me to fulfil any outstanding obligations. But he wants me in Glasgow, at my desk. He's offering me a very generous relocation package, which is all the more generous since I'm planning on staying at Mum and Dad's till we get things sorted out. Once we sell this place, we'll have no trouble finding somewhere lovely in Glasgow.'

Allie sighed. 'I'm going to miss you. The newsdesk secretary rang me to say Richardson's insisting I work out my notice. All three months of it. But I'm not planning on knocking my pan in. I'm not running around the country day and night for him. I'll do the absolute bare minimum. Less, if I can manage it.'

Rona chuckled. 'What's he going to do, after all? Fire you?'

'Aye, right. I can get on with selling the house. At least I'll have three months' salary as a cushion while

I figure out what I'm going to do next. And I can tee up some stories to nail down once I'm a free agent. Plus I'm still going to Berlin to chase down that drugs trials story.'

Rona chinked her glass against Allie's. 'Good on you. But he'll never sign your expenses chit for that.'

Allie shrugged. 'I can bankroll it myself. I'll more than cover the outlay when I sell it on to a proper newspaper.'

They drank in silence, watching the flames of the gas fire, each lost in thought. Allie knew Rona was keeping her excitement tamped down for her sake. Just as she was doing the same with her fear. Hopefully they'd meet in the middle. Sooner rather than later.

★ ★ ★

The bloody printers had been stirring things up again in the Glasgow building. They'd got wind of the London plans to bypass compositors and have journalists type their stories directly into the computer system. The London print unions were still chastened by what Rupert Murdoch had done to them, but in Glasgow, the natives were always more restless. It had taken an appearance in the press hall by Lockhart himself to calm the bolshy bastards down.

He'd run through a smorgasbord of threats and sweet-talking promises, and finally the presses had rolled on time without too many hostages to fortune. Anyone would think they wanted the bloody paper to shut down, he thought as he stomped down the hall to his office.

He threw himself into his chair and called the

kitchen. 'Bring me macaroni cheese with crispy bacon,' he demanded.

'And garlic bread on the side. And a pint of Coke.' And if he was still hungry, he'd have some of that delicious Scottish vanilla ice cream he had delivered from Fife.

There were a couple of items of mail on his desk. He picked them up and flicked through them. The usual crap. Until he reached the final item. It was a garish postcard featuring four smaller photographs around the central image of a tall clock tower. A red banner across the top read *BIAŁYSTOK* in thick black letters.

He felt a quickening of his pulse and a tightening across his forehead. With a sense of dread, he turned it over. The message was unequivocal and terrifying: *YOU ARE NOT THE ONLY ONE LEFT.*

26

It was strange to wake up without Rona. It wasn't that they were joined at the hip; they were often separated for a night or more by the demands of work. But she'd always known that Rona would return, and more or less when. This time, the house felt differently empty. The hanging space of Rona's wardrobe was half empty, the shelves denuded of lingerie and sweaters. There was a faint lingering presence in the sheets and pillowcases, but only as Allie turned over, readying herself for sleep, when the ghost of Rona's perfume assailed her. She'd never had a problem with her own company when she was single; it disturbed her that she'd finally discovered what loneliness meant.

Dealing with Gerry Richardson had been a relatively pleasant diversion. She delivered her schedules every Tuesday, with stories already assigned to freelances. When he tried to give her stories to run herself, she managed to knock them down. The more ridiculous ones she didn't even bother to pursue. He'd tried to refuse her holiday leave in a typically vindictive move, but a quick call to her union rep had crushed that attempt to dust. Allie had been pleasantly surprised by the support from the Father of the Chapel, as the rep was archaically called. He'd suggested taking the *Globe* to an industrial tribunal for constructive dismissal. She'd vetoed that. 'I want to be able to work again,' she'd said. 'But I appreciate the thought.'

A banging from outside reminded her that the

estate agent's board was due to go up that morning. Allie had been taken aback at how much the agent thought the house was worth, though he'd sounded a note of caution. 'It may take a while, but you'll eventually get your asking price, at the very least,' he'd said. 'Chorltonville is very distinctive — all these lovely Arts and Crafts houses built to individual designs. They're not to everyone's taste, but people who love them *really* love them. And you've made the garden very special. I can see that even in winter.'

Allie thought she would mourn the garden even more than the house. She'd never paid much attention to horticulture before they'd moved here. Her parents had a small back garden that featured a succession of garish flowering plants, and her flat in Glasgow had had no outside space. She'd never imagined turning into a keen plantswoman in her thirties, but she and Rona had embraced their large plot, and had taken to incorporating the gardens of stately homes into their Sunday hikes. They'd made notes and tracked down specialist nurseries. And now they were walking away from it all.

That day, it was Allie's turn to pack her bags. She had an early afternoon flight to Berlin Tegel, the first stage of the investigation she'd been planning for what seemed ages. She'd tried to persuade Paul Robertson to talk to her in more detail about the aborted drug trial but the Edinburgh doctor had hung up on her. She couldn't blame him, after the travesty the newsdesk had made of her AIDS story. In his eyes, she was the enemy who had tricked him into trusting her.

Thank goodness Jess had believed her when she'd explained what had happened. Fortunately she still had her original copy so she could show both Jess and

Alix that it was she who had been betrayed, not them. Allie had spent time with Jess learning all she could about drug trials; even better, Jess had agreed to write to Colin Corcoran to ask whether he'd talk to Allie about Zabre Pharma's ground-breaking use of East Germany for drug trials.

He'd replied saying he didn't want to talk about his employer and risk getting into trouble. 'Typical. No backbone,' Jess had complained to Allie. 'Have you got some cuttings that might persuade him you're one of the good guys? Maybe one or two of those investigations you did? The less controversial ones, obviously.'

'I thought they were all controversial,' Allie muttered. 'OK, I'll sort out something anodyne from my back catalogue.'

'And I'll send him the Little Weed story, play on his sympathy a bit.'

And somehow, it had worked. Something Jess had sent him had changed Colin Corcoran's mind. He called her the night after Rona had left for Glasgow. It had been the one thing that had lifted her spirits that day.

She'd expected him to be gung-ho about Zabre's research programme, but instead, he'd been hesitant and laconic. When she'd asked about the AIDS drug trial, he'd been non-committal. Now Allie feared she might be wasting her time and that she'd have to find another source if she was going to get anywhere. But then he'd said, 'If you're ever over in Berlin, I'll give you the full tour.'

It had been completely unexpected but Allie seized the moment. Trying not to sound over-enthusiastic, she told him she was planning to visit Berlin very soon. He sounded pleased. 'I don't get many visitors,' he said, suddenly shy. 'Could you maybe bring me some HP sauce? I can't get it here for love nor money.'

Allie wrapped the bottle carefully in a plastic bag and stuck it inside a sock. If this was all it took to win over Colin Corcoran, it would be the cheapest door-opener she'd ever managed.

* * *

Dr Frederika Schroeder poured three glasses of beer and raised hers in a toast. 'To Wallace Lockhart's fortune.' Her two companions grinned and clinked their glasses against hers. Hans Weber and Berndt Fischer were her wingmen, the trusted lieutenants in the radical Green movement that had been carefully forging links with their opposite numbers in the East. Change was coming; Fredi could feel it in her bones, and she was determined to be leading the charge when it arrived.

They'd come from a meeting at an artists' cooperative near their office in West Berlin. It had been a gratifying audience, whipped up to enthusiasm by Fredi's charismatic performance. With her shock of blond hair and her long legs that strode back and forth on the platform, she looked as exciting as she sounded. Both men were sufficiently under her spell to have reluctantly accepted that they'd never be her lovers; Fredi invariably spoke of sex with men in tones of dismissive amusement.

They were wrestling with a thorny problem — how to fund the Green revolution. By its nature, they didn't have natural sponsors among the German industrial complex. The likes of BMW and Siemens saw them as the enemy. Even the few companies who claimed to care about the environment were reluctant to fund Fredi and her colleagues. But now, there seemed to be a pinprick of light on the horizon in the shape of Genevieve Lockhart.

A couple of weeks ago, she'd turned up at one of their meetings at the university. Fredi had spotted her in the audience because she didn't fit. She was older than most of the kids in the room. And Genevieve's idea of dressing down was still far too smart and stylish for the student followers of the Greens. To Fredi's practised eye, she stood out. And it didn't hurt that she was really rather lovely. She decided she'd make a point of speaking to her after the meeting.

It hadn't turned out that way. Rather, it had been Genevieve who had sought her out. She'd walked up to Fredi with absolute self-assurance and said in immaculate German, 'My name's Genevieve Lockhart. I run Pythagoras Press, the academic publisher. We're thinking about launching a journal covering environmental science and I was told you would be someone worth speaking to.'

Delighted, Fredi turned on her best smile and said, 'Whoever you spoke to knows what they're talking about. Come and have a drink and we'll talk.'

On the way to the bar, they'd scooped up Hans and Berndt. This, Fredi thought, could finally be the connection they'd been craving. And who knew? Maybe Genevieve Lockhart would be a good fit in more ways than one.

★ ★ ★

Tegel was surprisingly quiet in the early evening. Allie emerged with her carry-on bag into the main concourse, which she'd thought resembled a dough-nut the first time she'd visited the city. She saw no reason to change her opinion. Whichever direction she headed in, it seemed impossible to end up near the taxi rank. Eventually she found it and gave the driver an address on Giesebrechtstrasse in Charlottenburg. They'd stayed in this hotel when Rona had been despatched by GQ to write the words for a photo essay on Berlin's punk scene. It was quiet, comfortable, clean and central; all the things Allie loved in a hotel, especially when she was working.

The other plus point in the small hotel's favour was its proximity to Haus der 100 Biere, a short walk away at Mommsen-Eck. They'd stumbled on it and fallen in love with its traditional interior. Not to mention the challenge of a menu of the promised hundred beers from round the world and more than a dozen on tap. Allie had discovered the joys of Rauchbier, a smoked beer that reminded her of the bouquet of Islay malt whisky; Rona had preferred the local Berliner Weisse. After only a couple of days, they'd begun to feel like locals.

So Allie had arranged to meet Colin Corcoran at the bar at seven. She was there in good time and secured a small corner table where she reckoned they wouldn't be overheard. She ordered a Rauchbier, slightly anxious that it wouldn't taste as good as she remembered. Thankfully, she'd had no reason to worry. She was a third of the way down the glass when a tall man with a slight stoop and a prominent Adam's apple edged his way across the pub towards her. He pushed his oversized glasses up his nose as he approached, his hand continuing to his thin mouse-brown hair. 'Allie Burns?' he said hesitantly.

'Dr Corcoran, I presume.' She stood up, smiled, and held out her hand. He took it in a surprisingly assured grip.

'Colin, please.' His smile seemed pained.

'Have a seat, Colin.' She waved at the waitress. 'Thanks for coming, I really appreciate it. What would you like to drink?'

He glanced up at the waitress and said something in fluent German. All Allie recognised was 'Radler', the German equivalent of a lager shandy. Either he wasn't much of a drinker or he was being cautious.

'I don't usually do this kind of thing,' he muttered.

'What? Drink with strange women?'

He gave her a quick glance, clearly uncertain where flippancy fitted in the conversation. 'Talk about my work with journalists. I've seen enough to know you don't always get things right. Sometimes deliberately.'

'And yet you're here.' Allie smiled. 'Did Jess vouching for me make a difference?'

'A bit. But mostly I realised there's a deal to be made here. I have something you want, and you can help me with something I want.'

'If it's payment —'

'I don't want money,' he blurted out.

'OK,' Allie said, conciliatory. She paused while the waitress delivered his drink in a hefty glass tankard. 'I'm listening.'

He took a long swallow of his drink then burped delicately behind his hand. 'Before I tell you that, I'll give you an outline of what I've got to offer. Zabre are roadtesting an anti-retroviral drug that they hope will slow down the development of HIV into full-blown AIDS. Do you understand what I'm saying here?'

Allie nodded. 'Jess explained it to me.'

'Now AIDS is springing up in Africa and elsewhere, this is potentially a massive global market. We moved the trials here because it gives us much more control over the information that comes out of the trial. Nobody in the GDR leaks to the press.' A cynical twist of the lips. 'But I *can* give you the inside information and if you play ball with me, it will be backed up with documentary support.' His chin jutted upwards.

'OK, that's clear enough.'

'Before we go any further, I need to ask you. What happens to people like me?'

'You mean, whistleblowers? People who act out of principle?'

'Whatever you want to call us that makes you feel comfortable. What happens to people who betray their employers when the circus leaves town?' Another long pull of his drink. His long thin fingers were beating a silent tattoo on his glass.

'There's no template. In a very small number of cases, they face a police investigation of their own, if they've broken the law. Some of them move to another company in the sector — it's a way of advertising how clean you are, if you hire somebody who's already demonstrated their integrity. Some write a book.' She shrugged. 'And some of them just slip out of the picture altogether. Make a new life somewhere else, doing something completely different.'

'They're not a target for vengeance?'

Allie smiled. 'Only in films. Once you've talked, there's no point in that. You've already spilled the beans. There's no benefit in trying to shut you up.'

He turned his head and looked out of the sliver of window visible from their table. Then he turned back to face her. He seemed somehow bigger, as if courage had inflated him like a hot-air balloon. 'OK then, let's deal. Here's what I need from you.'

It was the last thing Allie expected.

27

'Tell me you're not going to do it,' Rona said, her voice crackling over the international phone line.

'It'll be an adventure.' Allie leaned back on the pillows.

'I'm not going to wait twenty years for you to get out of a Soviet jail,' Rona said. 'How quickly it fades. There's you, promising to love me forever, but at the first hurdle, down you go.'

'Don't joke about it.'

'It'll be fine. I can't back out now, the poor sod has got everything lined up. My visa, my letters of accreditation.' 'I wish you'd told me this last night and not waited till the last minute.'

'I tried to call you but you were out. And your mum didn't know when you'd be back. 'I don't know where she's away to and I don't know when she'll be back. Can I take a message?" Allie chuckled. 'It took me back to my teens, parents gatekeeping their wayward lassie.'

'I'm not wayward. I was at the theatre. Watching a dire tragedy with more dead bodies than *Hamlet*. My mum didn't give me the message till this morning, that's why I didn't call you back last night. Maybe just as well. I wouldn't have slept if I'd known what you're planning.

I'm scared for you, Allie. I can't imagine having to be without you.'

'Don't worry. Well, don't worry today. This is just

188

a dry run, checking out the logistics. Nothing bad is going to happen.'

'How can you say that? Everybody knows the East German regime is riddled with informants. The Stasi control everything, and you know as well as I do that their show trials are a travesty of justice.'

'I know all that, but believe me, this is watertight.'

'I don't understand why you're doing this.'

A long pause while Allie tried to find the words. 'I need to show the world I've still got the investigative chops. That I've not been ruined by writing for the gutter. I need a big story to remind everybody who I am.'

'So find another one.' Rona's voice held a note of pleading Allie was unfamiliar with. Still she wouldn't budge.

'They're not that easy to stumble across, Rona. If I'm not in the frame for someone to put me on a story, it could be months before I find something this promising. And I can't afford to spend months not earning.'

'Money's not the issue now, Allie. Not with what I'm bringing in.'

Another pause. 'I'm not living off you, Ro.'

'We're a partnership. It doesn't matter which of us brings it in, it's our money.'

You say that now. Too often Allie had seen the corrosive impact of economic inequality. Not to mention the shame she'd feel. 'It's not going to come to that. I'm going to land this story and re-establish myself as somebody who gets to the bottom of stuff people want to keep buried.'

'But Allie —'

'If I don't go through with this, Colin Corcoran

won't let me in on what's really going on. I'll have shelled out for this trip and I'll be coming home empty-handed. And that's not my style.' She forced a little laugh. 'I'll be careful. I promise. Now away you go and put the fear of God into some poor feature writer.'

Allie could hear the frustration in Rona's smile from a thousand miles away. 'I love you, Allie Burns.'

'And I love you, Rona Dunsyre.' Allie gently replaced the phone and sat up.

In spite of her performance for Rona, Allie could feel the uncertainty in her gut. When Colin had hit her with, 'I want you to help me get my girlfriend out of East Berlin,' she'd almost laughed out loud at the preposterous nature of his demand. He'd seen her struggle and immediately gone on the front foot.

'This isn't a joke. This is the rest of our lives. You can do this. I've worked it all out. It's risk-free for you.'

'What? Breaking the law in a Soviet bloc country? Risk-free?' She scoffed. 'And the moon's made of green cheese.'

He clenched his hands, looked down at his fists and moved them under the tabletop. 'I had no intention of talking to you until I saw this.' A sudden movement and he palmed a tightly folded wad of newsprint on to the table. He nodded at it. 'Go on, look.'

She unfolded the front page of the Little Weed story. 'I don't understand.'

'The picture of you. It was like the last twist of a Rubik's cube.'

'You're not making much sense, Colin.'

He took a deep breath. 'You look kind of like my girlfriend. Enough for her to pass for you at a security checkpoint with your passport.'

190

'Are you serious? You're considering taking your girlfriend through Checkpoint Charlie on my passport?'

'It'd work. There's enough of a resemblance, if Wiebke takes off her glasses. It'd be best if you wore a hat, which is totally normal this time of year in Berlin. I have a rabbit fur one with earflaps.' Seeing the look on Allie's face, he hastily said, 'Or a woolly one? Maybe with a pompom?'

'I haven't worn a woolly hat since I spent a weekend at Greenham Common protesting against American Cruise missiles. Neither was an experience I want to repeat. This is a crazy idea, Colin. How am I supposed to get back to the West if you've waltzed off with my passport?'

'I've given that some thought. And I know just how we can do it.'

And in spite of her attempts to shut him up, he told her.

★ ★ ★

Allie sat in the passenger seat of Colin Corcoran's clapped-out VW Golf, trying very hard not to panic. 'We're not going to do anything risky today,' he said for at least the fifth time. She wanted to slap some sense into him, but it was so long since she'd hit anyone she doubted it would have the desired result.

In normal circumstances, Allie was alert to her surroundings, often mentally describing them to herself partly as an aide-memoire and partly as a first step to framing her story. But she'd have been hard-pressed to create any kind of word picture of the approach down Friedrichstrasse to Checkpoint Charlie. At first,

191

all she could see was the ridiculously vulnerable-looking white wooden huts surmounted by the Allied Checkpoint sign. It was absurd to think of this as the last bastion against Soviet invasion. On the surface, it appeared a troop of Boy Scouts — or Girl Guides, come to that — could have overrun it in a matter of minutes.

But she knew that was deceptive. That at the first sign of trouble, the soldiers on guard duty would take up their stations behind the sandbags and return fire. She'd read *The Spy Who Came in from the Cold*. She trusted John Le Carré to tell her the truth.

As they approached, she read the other sign, the one in English, Russian, French and curiously, bottom of the list and in the smallest type, German, advising travellers, 'You are now leaving the American Sector.' Presumably, the authorities thought the locals didn't need telling. Colin pulled up by the first hut and handed over their passports, their visas and the paperwork that identified them as employees of Zabre Pharma liaising with their East German counterparts.

The inspection was leisurely; while the soldiers went through the motions, Allie stared straight ahead at the forbidding white monolith of the East German pillbox with its shallow slit for shooting anyone foolhardy enough to make a run for it. It couldn't have been more threatening if they'd erected a neon sign saying, *Don't fuck with us*. For a wild moment, she considered jumping out of the car and running back to safety. It wasn't too late to call the whole thing off.

The barrier rose and they drove the few yards to its partner on the East German side of the crossing. 'That went well,' Colin said. 'They're used to me now.

192

I'm back and forward three or four times a week. The Ossies won't be quite so pally.'

They came to a halt and the car was surrounded by guards, all making sure Allie and Colin could see their guns. Their faces showed no emotion. Even the youngest of the quartet, who looked no more than eighteen, had the hard stare of a veteran who had seen more than he'd ever care to talk about. Colin handed over the paperwork. One guard looked through it, then walked around the car to Allie's side. Her stomach turned over as he gestured to her to lower her window. She obeyed immediately. Facing Little Weed was one thing; staring down the barrel of a gun was in a different league. One she wasn't certain she wanted to play in. She felt bile in her throat and wished she'd skipped the coffee earlier. But his glance was cursory and he walked away, back straight, shoulders squared. Colin had warned her that they'd take the papers over to the guardroom. 'I've no idea what they check them against, but they love their bureaucracy. Plus they need to get our Stasi tail in place before they let us through,' he'd said. 'Just sit tight and look straight ahead.'

She did as he'd instructed her. Time crawled past, then the guard returned and handed over their papers. Colin passed them to Allie, who noticed they were now adorned with new stamps.

Now she could look around her and take in more details. There was little sign of the supposed benefits of being a Soviet satellite. The buildings were drab, the paint peeling and dirty. Even the structures that were obviously more modern — residential blocks, a school, a clinic — seemed already in terminal decline. They stopped at a junction and Allie noticed a line of graffiti, scored into the plaster about a foot above the pavement, scuffed but still legible. *Keine Gewalt! Glasnost in Staat und Kirche*. The pedestrians walked with their heads lowered against the weather, dressed in clothes that Allie couldn't imagine anyone actively choosing to own. She recalled photographs in the Burns family albums of her parents and their friends around the time of the Second World War, their clothes threadbare and badly tailored. Even they had managed to scrape together a bit of stylishness. Not the citizens of East Berlin. At least, not the ones out on the streets.

'It's not far,' Colin said, turning into a wide thoroughfare. They turned left almost immediately and he negotiated a maze of narrow streets before arriving at a pair of tall wooden gates in a high wall. Colin got out and pressed a bell next to the gate, then looked up at a boxy grey security camera. Slowly, the gates opened. 'They recognise me now,' Colin said, climbing back into the car and driving across a wide courtyard. Parking places were marked out, but most were empty. 'I told you there was nothing to worry about.' He got out and led the way towards the entrance.

'That was the easy bit,' Allie said, conscious that her palms were sweating in spite of the cold. She followed him inside, where more security guards flanked a reception desk occupied by a middle-aged woman whose expression was a mixture of boredom and scepticism. More bureaucracy, which Colin negotiated on her behalf. 'Just keep smiling,' he'd said.

'Better they think I'm an imbecile than an undercover journalist.'

The cover story was that she had been sent by Zabre's head office to write a glowing report of what an

194

amazing resource the scientific facilities of the GDR were proving for researchers in the pharmaceutical world. Judging by the smiles that reciprocated hers, it was credible. The receptionist filled out a pass, stamped it and handed it over. Colin already had a pass, but it had to be stamped. Allie wondered how anyone could read it, so many stamps overlaid each other.

They walked down the hallway, the walls painted a bilious green. There was nothing to indicate what went on in the building behind the closed doors that lined the corridor. A noisy lift transported them to the third floor, and at once Allie was on familiar territory. She knew what labs looked like, and this was definitely one.

'Wiebke's got her own office,' Colin said as they walked past a glass wall beyond which white-coated figures did the kind of things Allie expected scientists to do — stare down microscopes, lean into computer screens, squirt liquid into test tubes and watch it change colour.

'You mentioned that.'

'It's the key to the whole plan.'

'You mentioned that as well.'

Colin stopped at a closed door. He knocked three times and waited. The door opened to reveal a tall woman in a lab coat. She gave Allie a severe look. 'I am Wiebke,' she said, waving them into her office.

Allie took her in and her heart sank. This was never going to work. They were all going to spend the rest of their lives in a gulag.

28

Less than a mile away from Allie's hotel, Genevieve Lockhart was folded into an uncomfortable chair in a lecture theatre listening once more to Fredi holding forth on the need for a revolution. Not the Marxist revolution she might have expected, even on the West side of the wall, but a green revolution. A revolution that would save the planet if they would only turn their backs on the fossil fuels and the nuclear energy that threatened our very existence.

Fredi couldn't seem to stand still. She commanded the stage and the room, striding around in her Cuban-heeled boots, tight jeans and black polo neck. She'd adopted the look as her uniform, and looking around, Genevieve could see half a dozen other women who had copied Fredi's style, with varying degrees of success. But none of them sparked with the charisma that drew in Fredi's audience.

Her style seemed eminently appropriate to the venue, Genevieve thought, smiling to herself. FU Berlin, the West Berliners' riposte to losing their precious Humboldt University to the East. When she'd first been told by her East German manager where to go to connect with this movement, Genevieve had thought it bold of the locals to express their disgust so unequivocally. When it had dawned on her that the initials stood for Freie Universitat, she felt very stupid, and glad she hadn't tried to make a joke of it. The feisty junior professor on the platform had a reputation for wit, but never at the expense of her politics. There would have been no revolutionary course credits for Genevieve if she'd tried to crack wise about freedom. She'd spent enough time in Fredi's company to realise that.

Fredi was building to a climax now. Genevieve knew what was coming. Her new friend had rehearsed tonight's arguments over dinner the previous evening, inviting Genevieve and their two companions to pick holes in what she planned to say. Hans and Berndt had made a couple of minor points and Genevieve had plucked up courage enough to suggest a small addition about Gorbachev's collusion in the Chernobyl cover-up. Fredi had turned the full beam of her attention on her, her dark blue eyes warm and clear. 'Good point, Genny. I like the way your mind works.'

The last couple of weeks had provoked enough of those moments for Fredi to have pulled Genevieve into the orbit of her select inner circle of radical Green movers and shakers. This wasn't how she'd planned to establish a beachhead in East Germany for the aftermath of change, but she had a sneaking suspicion it might work even better than the strategy she'd already honed in half a dozen Soviet satellites.

She'd realised very quickly that she had no chance of evading the pervasive scrutiny of the state in the GDR. She'd never really paid the Stasi a great deal of attention in the past; she'd expected to be continually spied on in a country where people estimated that one in four of the population was connected to the state's surveillance network. And she had been someone they were courting, someone who brought hard currency into their overstressed and overstretched economy. Wise to keep an eye on her movements and her contacts lest she be seduced from the straight and narrow path that East German communism dictated she should follow.

Even those with special status like the Lockharts and their Pythagoras Press had to travel on fixed tramlines. Genevieve had never needed to cross them before, but as soon as she attempted to move outside her proscribed limits, the GDR head of Pythagoras had warned her of dire consequences. She had asked him to walk her back to her hotel so they could speak without eavesdroppers, and told him what the true purpose of her trip was. He told her she had no chance of carrying out her aim of ingratiating herself with the subversives. 'As soon as you speak to a dissident, they will know. And you will be arrested.'

When she'd protested, he'd cut her off, abrupt as he'd never dared be previously. 'Listen to me, Fraulein Lockhart. They will arrest you. And it will take your father and your diplomats several days to discover where you are being held. And they will be very uncomfortable days.'

'They wouldn't dare.'

He'd given her a pitying look. 'I was born here. I have lived here for forty-two years with the constant anxiety of putting a foot wrong. Working for a Western company, even one led by a man as sympathetic to the Honecker regime as your father — that's automatically grounds for suspicion. I am watched. Day and night.' He scoffed mirthlessly. 'For all you know, I could be a Stasi plant and even now your fate could be sealed.'

'This feels a bit paranoid,' she complained.

'Genevieve, I owe it to your father to advise you, this is a crazy idea.' He looked as if he might burst into tears. He had never used her first name before; he had always been Germanically formal. That told her something about the sincerity of his fear.

'What if I think it's worth the risk?'

The last traces of colour left his face. 'If you won't be careful on your own account, then think of the people you'll be implicating. The ones who have no recourse to your father or your Foreign Office. If they arrest you, they will round up the rest of us. Your dissident contacts. My office staff. Me.' He took a deep breath, 'And because they like pressure points, my family. And we will not be treated kindly. Their methods are not constrained by the European Convention on Human Rights.'

She had been shocked by the harshness of his words. She felt the protection of her privilege slip to one side for a moment as she let her imagination loose. But Genevieve was her father's daughter and she wasn't about to abandon her mission so easily. 'So how do I secure the future for all of us? You *know* change is on the way. The old men in the politburo might be in denial, but even in the time I've been coming to the East, I can see things are falling apart. Broken street lights. Potholes in the roads. Nothing in the shops.' They were passing a children's playground and she nodded towards it. 'Even the swings are broken. Moscow's singing a new song, and everybody in East Germany's hearing it except Honecker. You know I'm right.'

He glanced nervously to either side. 'Go west, Fraulein Lockhart. The dissidents here are supported by radical groups there. It's safer to deal through them. Safer for everyone.'

'You mean West Berlin?'

'When the rumours from Chernobyl started to leak out, a group from the Greens reached out. Not the mainstream Greens, a splinter group. More radical.'

Genevieve frowned. 'How do you know this? It's not like you can read about it in the newspapers.'

He sighed. 'My son. He's seventeen and he wants to change the world. He takes stupid risks and I don't know how to stop him. Every time he goes out of the apartment, his mother and I, we can't eat, we can't sleep till he's home again. My only hope is that he can avoid being arrested until things start changing.'

They walked on in silence. 'I'm sorry,' she said at last. 'I had no idea.'

'We live with the habit of secrecy here.' He managed a wry little laugh. 'I tell you all this only because you have already compromised yourself.'

'The cold comfort of Mutually Assured Destruction,' she said. 'Do you know where I can find these radical Greens?'

He shook his head. 'I don't know any details. All I know is that my son justifies his new convictions by arguing that these are the beliefs of university professors. So maybe the university is where you should start.'

Genevieve made one last attempt to shake off the followers she now saw everywhere. She tried the sort of tricks she'd seen in spy movies — jumping on board a tram at the last minute, entering a cinema and leaving by a fire exit, taking off her scarf and using it to cover her hair. But she kept seeing the same two or three faces time after time. They were far better at finding her than she was at losing them.

She conceded, which had never been a course of action she found easy.

200

She'd found Fredi by simply wandering around the university till she found where the students hung out when they were avoiding anything resembling studying. She stuck around long enough to be unimpressed. Genevieve wondered how any of them planned to make a living when they were pushed out of the nest. She'd partied hard at St Andrews and MIT, but she'd worked hard too. Lazing around talking adolescent politics had never been part of her life, from choice. There were other ways to form ideas about the world, she thought. Like talking to people who had actually achieved something.

But at least the posters on the walls gave her a sense of where she might find what she was looking for. There was a debate scheduled for that evening, featuring four speakers. It was billed as *Green/Red: Who owns the future?* Genevieve turned up a few minutes after the advertised starting time and found a seat at the side of the hall.

First up was a bearded Marxist who insisted that the only problem with the Soviet Union was that it was doing Marxism wrong. They just needed to fix that and everything would be wonderful. Fredi spoke next and she was electrifying. She spoke about putting the needs of the planet first, so that humanity could flourish. She was passionate, coherent and convincing. Genevieve was used to politicians pontificating round the Lockhart dinner table. She'd even heard a few who could hold an audience. Tony Benn always made her pay attention. And even though she despised Margaret Thatcher's politics, nobody could deny that now she'd been groomed in her presentation, she

201

could hold the room. But Frederika Schroeder was in a different league.

Genevieve Lockhart smiled and relaxed her shoulders for the first time in days. Fuck the Stasi. She'd finally found what she'd been looking for. The rest would be easy. And so it had proved.

29

Allie woke the next morning, astonished that she'd slept. She'd considered herself towards the intrepid end of the spectrum, even after her run-in with the brutal wrestler. But her first trip behind the Iron Curtain had unnerved her to a degree that had taken her aback. Colin Corcoran's litany of all the reasons to be careful and the consequences of carelessness had left her feeling as if it wasn't just her own life in her hands but also those of her fellow conspirators.

She'd spent the evening in her hotel room, running over what she'd learned and what she had to remember. Never say anything inside a building that you wouldn't happily say to a Stasi officer. Never attempt a joke that touched on anything to do with security. Never attempt a joke, full stop. Never criticise or compare unfavourably to anything in the West. Smile politely but avoid frivolity. Never go anywhere inside the East German pharmaceutical complex unless you are accompanied by a member of staff. And that includes the toilet. Be earnest about the excellent work being done here. And above all, don't even hint at any kind of deal.

Colin had explained that there would be one opportunity for them to go over their plans — in the lunch break, they could take their food outdoors and sit at picnic tables dotted around a potholed area of tarmac between the research labs and the clinical trials building. If nobody joined them, they could quickly run through the plan for the following day.

It had almost worked as a stratagem. They'd found a table as far from the buildings as possible and Colin had started to outline how things would play out. He'd got as far as explaining where and when they'd swing into action when a tubby man in a lab coat over his shirt and tie had plonked himself down next to them. His thin brown hair was arranged in a comb-over so spectacular that Allie couldn't help admiring the skill and dedication that must have gone into it.

Wiebke immediately jumped to her feet. 'This is Herr Doktor Kasimir, who is supervising the clinical trial I am working on. Herr Doktor, I think you have met Herr Doktor Corcoran, who is leading the trial for Zabre Pharma?'

Kasimir nodded. The sun glinted on his square spectacles, making his eyes invisible. 'Of course, we wrote the protocol together.' Behind his back, Colin raised a sceptical eyebrow. 'But who is your distinguished colleague, Herr Doktor?'

'This is Fraulein Burns, who is with our communications team. She will be writing a series of articles for the scientific and general press about the great advances that have been made possible by Zabre's revolutionary collaborative process with you here in Berlin.' They all knew there was nothing Kasimir could question about this introduction. If Allie hadn't already been approved, she wouldn't be here. And the cash that Zabre was bringing to the GDR table meant that she'd have been hard to refuse accreditation.

Allie smiled sweetly. 'It's a great pleasure to be here,' she said. 'I apologise that my German is not very good.'

Kasimir gave a tight little smile. 'I am sure that my

colleagues are making certain all is clear to you.'

'We're giving Fraulein Burns a very exhaustive tour,' Wiebke said.

'There's so much to see here. So much to absorb. It's very impressive,' Allie enthused.

'So much that we must come back tomorrow,' Colin added. 'It's a real treat for me to be able to show off what we're doing here.'

Kasimir's face was stony. 'Let us hope Fraulein Burns paints a picture that will bring other companies to our door. Have you visited the clinical trials wards yet?'

'We are going there next,' Wiebke said.

'I shall accompany you.' There was no discussion, nor was there any option other than to toss the remains of their meagre lunches in the bin and follow him as he waddled off. He'd stuck to them like glue as they made their way through the wards, where patients lay obediently in bed, eyeing their visitors warily. When Wiebke spoke to them about their treatment, they said little, except to express gratitude for being chosen. It was more like custody than hospital, Allie thought, with the medical staff having the authority of prison officers rather than doctors and nurses. The contrast with the AIDS ward in Manchester was startling; the patients without hope had seemed more cheerful than those ones here who were supposedly its recipients.

Kasimir glanced at charts, but he seemed to have little interest in the patients. In contrast, Allie felt his eyes on her all afternoon, gauging her clothes, her hair, her figure. He said nothing untoward, but he didn't have to. She thought he'd have assessed a carcass in a butcher's shop in much the same calculating way.

As the clock crept round past three o'clock, Allie

was relieved to hear Colin say, 'I think we've covered more than enough ground for Fraulein Burns today. When we come back tomorrow, we can look again at any questions that might have arisen.'

Kasimir walked them back to the front desk and stood next to Wiebke till they drove off. 'What a creep,' Allie said.

'Now you see why Wiebke's so desperate to get out,' Colin said. 'Can you imagine what that's like, day after day?'

It wasn't so different from what it had felt like working in a Glasgow newsroom at the start of her career, Allie thought. 'I don't mean to sound snarky,' she said, changing the course of the conversation. 'If I was anybody except the journalist writing this story, this would be right out of order. But I have to ask. Given the constraints of communication, how exactly did you and Wiebke get it together?'

His ears went pink. 'I know it sounds like some stupid Mills and Boon novel, but it was like a spark between us the first time I clapped eyes on her. I don't know how to explain it. Sometimes you just know?' Even in profile, he looked like a puppy pleading not to be kicked.

'And she felt it too? The spark.' Determinedly keeping the scepticism from her voice.

He let out a long breath. 'She did. We couldn't do anything about it to begin with. You've seen how they spy on everybody all the time here. Then Wiebke got a transfer to the team working directly with Zabre and it was quite natural for us to sit together for lunch. The first time we spoke, it was like we'd known each other for years.'

I bet it was. 'And it just grew?'

206

'Yeah. Allie, I know you think I'm deluding myself. To think that Wiebke actually loves a geek like me. You think she's just using me as a route to the West. But it's not like that. She's risking her life to be with me on the other side of the wall.'

'She's also risking your life. How can you be sure about this? Have even kissed her? Never mind slept with her?'

He gave an exasperated sigh. 'Look, I don't expect you to understand. I know she's the one for me. I don't have to kiss her or go to bed with her to know that. Just the thought of what that'll mean for us both? That keeps us going. I am sure about this, Allie. And you'd better be too, because we're counting on you.' A note of steely defiance at the last.

Or course she recognised that Wiebke's was the greatest risk. But if the first part of the plan worked out, Wiebke would soon be well outside the iron grasp of the Stasi. And Allie would still be firmly in the lion's den. 'I must be out of my mind, taking a risk like this for a story, Colin. But before I come back through Checkpoint Charlie, you're going to have to give me a lot more detail than the pair of you managed at lunchtime.'

And so he had. Carefully, he had explained to her that Zabre would use the trials to get the drug approved. Inevitably, when the side effects became clear, it would be withdrawn. But even though a quarter or more of the patients died much sooner than they would have, HIV carriers desperate for life would still be willing to gamble on the drug.

'But if it's withdrawn, how do they get their hands on it?'

'This is where it gets really dirty,' Colin said, his

face screwed up in unhappiness. 'Zabre's not the only one doing this, by the way. They set up shell companies and manufacture the drugs under the counter in places like India and Mexico. Somewhere with low labour costs and ineffective government regulation. Then they sell them on the black market.'

'That's appalling.' And it changed the way she'd have to write the story.

'What did you think was happening?' Defiant now.

'Stupidly, I assumed they'd look at the trials results and try to figure out what the problem was so they could fix it. Not so they could leverage the wholesale exploitation of sick people.'

'You've not had many dealings with the world of pharma, have you?' His expression was apologetic. 'Nothing interferes with the bottom line.' Then he brightened. 'But it gives you an even better story, right?'

Allie shrugged. 'Yes and no. I'll have to be really careful how I write it or the lawyers will have a hairy fit. The flip side of doing anything to grab the money is that you've got a lot of money to throw at protecting your reputation.'

'But it's the truth.'

'Yes, but they're not actually doing it yet. We've just got your word that they will do that. Do you know the details of how this works? You know the names and places where the drugs will be manufactured?'

'I know some of them. Because we've used this route before. Not with anything this dodgy, I promise. But yes. This is why I want to blow the whistle and get out.'

And that was when she knew she had to stick with the story. Never mind the risk.

'Fuck this,' Allie said aloud, forcing herself out of bed. There was nothing to be gained from lying in bed running through all the things that could go wrong. Shower, coffee, rolls and salami, and out on the street to wait for Colin. The journey passed in an uncomfortable silence. Already the process felt curiously familiar, probably because Allie had been concentrating so hard on every detail the day before. It didn't make it any less nerve-racking.

They spent the day trailing around behind Wiebke, giving another performance of fascinated interest. In truth, there were elements of what she was learning that did interest Allie, but the real meat of her story would come afterwards, when Wiebke could provide her with the true records of the trials and the pressures placed on GDR scientists and medics to produce the required results. Not to mention the mounting death toll in the trial. It was going to be a dynamite story, especially coupled with the dramatic escape from East Berlin.

After lunch, they went back to the lab, Wiebke brightly and publicly suggesting that they pay a visit to the room where the gas chromatography was carried out. 'It's on a side corridor, on its own, because it can be quite noisy and distracting to anybody trying to concentrate,' Wiebke explained. 'But I'd like to show you some of the results we've been finding,' she added for the benefit of nearby ears.

They rounded a corner away from the main labs. A short corridor ended in two doors. She knew from Colin's detailed briefing that one contained the scientific equipment; the other was the cleaners' cupboard. The gas chromatograph machine was a blocky metal rectangle the size of a twin-tub washing machine. It dominated the small space and there was barely room for a couple of workstations beside it. The camera above the door was directed at the machine; by staying near the door, they could avoid being seen.

There was no time for hesitation. The two women stripped to their underwear, Colin blushing furiously at the sight. Wiebke struggled into Allie's clothes. The skirt was on the short side but with the coat over it, they thought nobody would notice. Wiebke put on Allie's hat, and took off her glasses. It wouldn't have fooled anyone who knew them, but they all hoped it was good enough for a border guard. Everyone knew nobody looked like their passport photo.

Allie had rolled some fine but strong cord into the bottom of her bag, and she whipped it out. Quickly Wiebke secured her hands behind her back and tied her ankles together, leaning her against the wall. She took Allie's wallet out of her bag and stuffed it in the waistband of her pants; she'd need some reliable form of ID later, for the Stasi. Finally, Wiebke shrugged apologetically. 'I am sorry,' she said, tying Allie's scarf across her mouth.

Colin opened the door and checked the corridor. 'All clear,' he said. The door opened outwards, shielding them from the camera that looked down the hallway from the far end. Quickly, he pulled open the cleaning cupboard door and between them, they shuffled Allie inside. Colin lowered her gently to the floor, biting his lip in apology. He closed his eyes in a grimace. Allie knew what was coming. They'd agreed it had to be done for verisimilitude.

He picked up a wooden scrubbing brush and hefted it half-heartedly in his hand. 'I can't do this,' he protested. 'I've never hit a woman before.'

Wiebke either had fewer scruples or more to lose. She grabbed the brush and smashed it into the side of Allie's face. Her last thought before the door closed and plunged her into darkness was that her face had barely recovered from Little Weed. Maybe Bill Mortensen was right — being a private eye was a lot less risky these days than being a journalist.

With a groan, Allie leaned against the wall. It would be more than three hours before the cleaners arrived on their rounds. Regular as clockwork, Wiebke had promised. Three long hours cramped in a tiny cupboard before she had to give the performance of her life. There was so much that could go wrong, so many stumbles and mistakes that could completely fuck her up. If she brooded over the possibilities of failure, she'd be a gibbering wreck by the time the cleaners opened the door.

Allie took a deep breath and did what she usually did to take her mind off the waiting and wondering her job so often entailed. She started working her way through the Eurythmics back catalogue in her head, starting with 'Love Is a Stranger'. All those miles of singing along in the car hadn't been wasted after all. If she was lucky, the cleaners would arrive before she ran out of lyrics.

If not, she could just start again from the beginning.

30

A few miles and light years away, Fredi Schroeder watched Genevieve Lockhart heading across the bierkeller towards the toilets. Annoyingly, she could almost taste the desire the attractive publisher provoked in her. The thought of holding her close, feeling the curves and planes of her body against her own — that was enough to make her breath tighter in her chest. But for Fredi, the craving for political stardom had taught her to keep a curb on her other appetites. The cause came first, and she'd schooled herself over the years to stifle these yearnings. She hadn't lived like a nun, but she'd disciplined herself never to make the first move. It would be too easy to discount her if they could paint her as a predatory lesbian. She held back and instead of following her own lust, she'd learned to detect that hunger in others. And the direction of Genevieve Lockhart's desire had become clear to her over the previous few weeks.

Now she leaned forward and spoke to the third person sharing their booth. 'It's time, Hans,' she said. 'She's on the hook of the message, and she's on the hook of you. Now we only need to reel her in and then we can get our hands on her father's money. He's exploited people for long enough. It's time we exploited him to make people's lives better.'

Hans swept his thick brown hair back from his forehead, letting a floppy wing settle over his ear. He grinned. 'The sacrifices we have to make for the cause.'

'She's accustomed to getting her own way. You have to let her think she's leading the charge. She needs to believe she's the one with the smart ideas. You understand?'

Hans shrugged. 'I've seen you do it often enough.'

'She's lived her life in her father's shadow. Sure, he's given her a business to play with, but she wants something of her own, whether she knows that or not. We can be that something. And you can be the way in.'

'You're sure about this? It's you she's obsessed with.' He fiddled with the handle of his beer glass, apparently less sure of himself than he wanted her to think.

'She wants to be me,' Fredi said. 'But it's you she wants to fuck. Just make sure she enjoys it, Hans.' She winked. 'Of course, if you think you need some tips?'

He laughed. 'I'm sure you could improve my technique, Fredi, but I think I'll manage.' He caught sight of Genevieve heading back towards them. 'Here she comes.'

'I'll make my excuses and leave in ten minutes or so. Then you're on your own.' She softly sang the opening riff of Bowie and Queen's 'Under Pressure'. 'We're depending on you.'

★　★　★

Allie was halfway through 'You Have Placed a Chill in My Heart' when she thought she heard voices. She'd got stuck in the middle of *Revenge* and had to repeat a couple of numbers till she got back on track and made it through to *Savage*, but she was pretty impressed with her feat of musical memory. And she'd managed to keep moving enough to avoid all but one bout of cramp in her left calf. She was cold, her mouth was uncomfortably dry and she wanted to pee. But the music in her head had managed to keep her fear at arm's length. Until now.

There were definitely voices. Two or three of them, getting closer. Showtime, she thought. The chances of this going south were still uncomfortably high. She kicked the door feebly and the voices suddenly stopped. She kicked out again and this time there was brief chatter before the door swung open. Allie blinked, aiming for woozy and not having to try too hard. Three female faces gaped in astonishment. Allie let herself fall sideways to the floor, grunting as she went.

More chatter, then one of them ran off down the hall. Tentatively, another reached out and untied the scarf. Allie's mouth felt tight and stiff, but she managed to make a dry guttural sound that turned into a harsh cough. The women were asking her tentative questions, but Allie's limited German seemed to have deserted her. She shook her head and moaned.

Boots clattered down the hallway, and suddenly two security guards were pushing the women to one side. One tall, one shorter, both stocky with cropped hair and the smell of old sweat. More questions, this time less friendly. The woman who had fetched the men said something and disappeared again. More questions. They hauled her to her feet and she promptly fell to her knees when they let her go. The woman came back with a cup of water and pushed the men to one side. She held the cup to Allie's lips and slowly let her drink. It was bliss to feel the cold liquid on her

214

tongue and throat. She looked up with piteous eyes. '*Ich kann kein Deutsch*,' she croaked through cracked lips.

The guards clearly had no idea what to do with that particular paradox. They yanked her upright again and this time they dragged her back down the hallway, past the lab and down the stairs to the ground floor, careless of her feet bumping on the treads. The disregard sent her levels of fear shooting up.

They ended up in a small room looking out across the car park. The dusk was kept at bay by a few spotlights ranged along the factory wall. They dumped her in an office chair, still bound hand and foot, and conferred vigorously. Then the short one picked up the phone and engaged in a short conversation. He ended the call and they both stood glowering at Allie, arms folded across their chests.

'*Bitte*,' she said, thrusting her feet out towards them and squirming round to present her wrists. They stared, impassive. One eyed up her breasts, saying something out of the side of his mouth. The other guffawed but neither made any attempt to molest her. It was as if she was a creature from another planet, dropped into their ambit without explanation.

Time drifted past, then everything happened quickly. The compound's gate opened to admit a boxy beige van that drove straight to the main door. As soon as it appeared, the short one ran from the room. She could hear his footsteps recede, then the sound of more voices. The security guard returned with two men in military uniforms, peaked caps low over their foreheads. They looked crumpled and exhausted, only the violet collar patches on their jackets apparently clean and fresh. Stasi, then. More shouting in

German.

'*Ich kann kein Deutsch*,' she tried again, this time doing her best to sound as if she was on the point of tears. 'English,' she said. 'I've been kidnapped. Please, does anybody speak English?'

The two Stasi officers exchanged a look. 'Kein Engels,' one said. He jerked his head to indicate she should come with them. Allie waggled her bound ankles at them. Again, the exchanged look. The one who had spoken took a penknife from his trouser pocket and cut through the cords, managing to nick the skin on her ankle.

'Jesus,' Allie exclaimed, staring at the thread of blood running on to the floor. The officer shrugged, pocketed knife and cord, and dragged her to her feet.

The air outside was a shock, instantly chilling her. The rough tarmac underfoot was a shock too, reminding her just how vulnerable she was. They threw her in the back of the van, a dark metal box with a wooden bench along one side. The van rattled noisily through the streets, throwing her from side to side as it cornered. Fear was gradually overcoming her determination. Now nobody knew where she was. Now anything could happen.

★ ★ ★

Allie ended up in another room without windows. A woman in the same depressing uniform had cut her hands free from their bonds then handcuffed one wrist to the tubular metal chair that was bolted to the floor. She'd fished Allie's wallet out of the back of her pants and pocketed it. She'd ignored Allie's attempts at communication, thrown her a coarse grey blanket then left her alone. More time passed, but this time, there was no escape in mental music. The tension was too powerful for that.

Eventually, the door opened again. This time, the man who entered was wearing a dark suit that looked worn to the point of shabbiness. But his shirt was clean, his tie neatly knotted and his thick dark hair carefully parted. He wore round black-rimmed glasses that magnified his blue eyes, making them resemble a pair of marbles in a child's game. His face was pale, his lips full. There was something of the cartoon villain about him, she thought. But not the comedic kind.

'Do you speak English?' she asked, not having to fake her frustration.

He said nothing, staring at her for what felt like a very long time.

'Where am I? Why am I here? I'm the victim of a crime, and you people are behaving as if I'm the criminal,' she exploded. 'Talk to me. Or find someone who can talk to me.'

He took Allie's wallet from his pocket and laid it on the table. He flicked it open and withdrew the business card she'd had made up for the trip. 'Alison Burns, Communications Manager, Zabre Pharma,' he read, his English heavily accented. 'This is you?'

She nodded. 'Yes. Listen, I've been kidnapped. I was visiting the lab, we're collaborating on a project with your people. One of your scientists, Wiebke Neumann, she was showing me around and the next thing —'

'*Langsam*,' he said. 'Slow. My English is slow.'

Allie breathed deeply. 'Someone hit me on the head.' She touched her face; it felt hot and swollen. 'I passed out. Unconscious.' She mimed unconsciousness.

'When I woke up, I was tied up and gagged.' More mime. 'It was dark. No light. I didn't know where I was.'

'Someone attacked you?'

'Yes, exactly. They attacked me. They stole my clothes. And I think they stole my passport.'

He sat up straight. 'Your passport?'

'My British passport.' She emphasised each word. 'For crying out loud, I've been beaten up and robbed and you're acting as if nothing has happened. I demand to see someone from the British embassy You can't keep me here like this.'

'We only have your word for this.'

Allie didn't have to act her incredulity. 'I was tied up. Gagged. In a cupboard. Is this how you normally treat important foreign visitors?'

He stood up abruptly. 'You will wait here.'

'I don't have much fucking choice, do I?' she said savagely as he made for the door. It closed firmly behind him and she was left to fume alone.

The next arrival was a younger man. Blond, wearing a sports jacket and dark brown cords. 'Fraulein Burns,' he said, sitting down and smiling at her. 'This is a very strange situation.' His English was precise, his accent negligible.

Time to go on the offensive, she thought. 'Tell me about it. I'm here on a business trip, to write about the excellent collaboration between Zabre Pharma and our East German colleagues, and I get beaten up and robbed. In my world, that definitely counts as strange.'

'Tell me what happened.'

She gave him the same account. 'I didn't see who hit me, I was knocked out. That's all I know,' she concluded.

He nodded. 'This gives me a problem. You see, according to our border records, Alison Burns left the GDR at 3.36 p.m. this afternoon. Yet here you are, some hours later, still in East Berlin.'

'Are you being deliberately obtuse? It's obvious what happened. Someone stole my passport and pretended to be me. To escape to the West.' She expelled a harsh breath. 'I keep telling you, I'm the victim here.'

He gave her a long, steady look. 'But are you? From where I sit, you look very much like a collaborator. What a coincidence that someone who looks sufficiently like you to use your passport had the opportunity to attack and rob you. Don't you think?'

Allie felt the gooseflesh of fear on the back of her neck. 'It's not a coincidence, though, is it? I was there yesterday. Plenty of people saw me. Plenty of people knew I was coming back today. You must be able to verify whether anybody from the lab didn't check out of work today. And whether they look anything like me.'

He raised his eyebrows. 'They put their plan into action very swiftly, don't you think?'

She shrugged. 'Given how you're treating me, a representative of a foreign investor . . . if I was stuck here, I think I'd take half a chance if it offered itself to me.'

He took a packet of cigarettes out and ostentatiously lit one. 'Our records show that Alison Burns was a passenger in a car driven by Colin Corcoran. Your colleague from Zabre Pharma.'

Allie went for full-on shock. Eyes wide, mouth open. 'Colin?' she exclaimed. 'Colin drove her out?'

'So you see, Fraulein Burns, it is hard not to imagine

219

you as a co-conspirator. We are not stupid.' He stood up abruptly. 'We will speak again when you are ready to tell the truth.'

'Wait! I demand to see someone from the British embassy.'

His only response was a soft laugh as he closed the door firmly behind him.

31

No bells broke the silence of Allie's midnight. It was eerily quiet in the cell where she'd been deposited earlier, which surprised her. In her imagination, incarceration was a noisy place, filled with shouts and screams, slamming doors and the rattle of keys. But here — wherever here was — the only sound that had disturbed her was the clatter of the inspection hatch in her door opening with a slice of pale yellow light, followed almost immediately by the bang of it closing.

It wasn't completely dark inside; a pair of fat glass bricks were set high in the wall, too thick to see any detail through but transparent enough to allow a faint glimmer of light to penetrate. Allie could just about make out a narrow wooden shelf with a single blanket and in the far corner, a hole in the floor whose stink and surrounding stains betrayed its function. They'd thrown her a pair of coarse cotton trousers and a thin T-shirt and left her to it. As the adrenaline had receded, she'd drifted into fitful sleep, but now she was awake. Awake, cold, thirsty and scared.

She had no idea how long she'd been there. Her watch had disappeared at some point, along with the three-colour gold Turkish love puzzle ring Rona had put on her finger five years before. Allie tried to banish Rona from her thoughts; it hurt too much to imagine how worried she'd be, never mind to wonder when she would see her again. How could she have been so naive, to think she'd just explain herself to the Stasi and they'd let her go?

The truth was, she hadn't really believed that. She'd just told herself a story for comfort. She'd done some reckless things in pursuit of a headline, but she couldn't remember ever having such little heed for the likely outcome. What was she trying to prove? Who was she trying to impress?

The one thing she could be grateful for was that she hadn't been tortured.

So far.

★   ★   ★

There was nothing dreary about Genevieve Lockhart's midnight. Unless you counted Hans Weber's room, which had too many echoes of student bedsits for her liking. Posters for Green rallies, a line of Kraftwerk album sleeves pinned to a corkboard, a map of Berlin with the line of the wall marked in bright green marker pen. But it was clean and tidy; rather like Hans himself.

It had been a few months since she'd gone to bed with anyone and she'd been more than ready for an adventure, especially with someone as attractive as Hans. Being her father's daughter had always acted as an aphrodisiac to a certain kind of man; either that, or the polar opposite. For some men, fucking Ace Lockhart's daughter was a very particular notch on the bedpost, and Genevieve had learned to sniff them out a long time ago. But it limited her choice. She hated the thought that a man wanted her for her money or her name, and it had made her both wary and picky. But Hans didn't seem interested in her father's money or his influence. When she was with

222

him and Fredi, the conversation was exciting and demanding, an exploration of how the future could be different. There had been people like them around when she was a student, but they'd been tediously earnest and, frankly, unattractive. These German radicals were a different breed, and the future they promised wasn't just appealing in itself — it offered fascinating possibilities for her to build a whole new arm of the Lockhart brand.

So she'd given in to Hans' charms and let him lead her away from the rest of the group. In the street outside the bierkeller, he'd drawn her to him and kissed her. Not forcefully, not wet and greedy, but soft and tender, as if he'd been waiting for this for a long time. It woke something in Genevieve that had been tamped down, something she'd only allowed to break out a few times in her life. Her heart raced and she could feel the tightness of desire in her belly.

It was a foregone conclusion how the evening would go. By the time they made it back to his place, they were both beyond waiting. Clothes strewn around them, bodies hot and ready for each other, a mad heat that carried them both over into abandonment. And again. And afterwards, soft laughter and exploration, learning each other with mouths and fingertips.

It wasn't what she'd been looking for when she came to Germany. But she was very happy to have found it here in the arms of this very beautiful and smart young man.

Just as Fredi had hoped she would.

★ ★ ★

Eleven o'clock in Glasgow, and Rona couldn't settle. Germaine was muttering grumpily at the back door, ready for her final walk of the day. But Rona didn't want to leave the house in case Allie called. She knew what the plan had been and all day, anxiety had nibbled at the edge of her mind.

'Are you going to tell me what's eating you?' her mother asked, bustling into the kitchen to prepare the bedtime snack she and her husband always had before bed. Two digestive biscuits with a scraping of strawberry jam and a slice of mature Canadian cheddar, washed down with a small glass of milk. For years it had been Rona's preparation for bed too; now the thought of it made her smile, a reminiscence she had no desire to repeat. 'You've been like a bairn on Christmas Eve ever since you got in.'

'I was hoping Allie would ring.'

'Is she still in Berlin?' Sandra Dunsyre took the biscuit tin from the cupboard, carefully not looking at her daughter.

'I guess.'

'What is it she's doing, again?'

'Good try, Mum. I didn't tell you for a reason. Sometimes it's better you don't know what Allie gets up to. Or me, for that matter.'

'Aye, right. Whatever it is, I can see you're worried. Can you not phone her? Surely she'll be back in her hotel room by now? It's later there, isn't it?'

'If she was back, she'd have called me.' Rehearsing these responses wasn't helping.

'Maybe she didn't want to ring so late?'

Rona didn't dignify that with a response. 'I'll make a quick call,' she said, reaching for the phone and calling Jess's number. 'Hi Jess. It's Rona . . . I don't suppose you've got a number for your pal Colin? . . . No? It's just that I've not heard from Allie and I know they had something going on today . . . No, I'm sure it's nothing to worry about, you know how she gets when she's in the thick of things . . .' A dry laugh. 'Yeah, I know, Berlin's a party city. Be a pal, don't tell her I phoned.' They exchanged a few meaningless shards of gossip and Rona replaced the receiver. She turned back to her mother. 'See? Nothing. If anything bad had happened, Jess would have heard. So away to your bed and stop fretting.'

'Only if you will.'

Rona leaned over and kissed her mother's cheek. 'I'll just take the dog round the block first. If Allie calls, mind and take a message, yeah?'

'Don't be long.' Sandra hugged her. 'She'll be fine. She's already taken her licking for this year. She's not going to bump into Little Weed in Berlin.'

There were, Rona thought, a lot worse than Little Weed out there. And she was pretty sure some of them were in East Berlin.

32

Allie assumed it was morning from the slightly raised level of light. She knew she'd slept, if only because of the stiffness in her back and her limbs. As the door to her cell swung open, she realised that the turning of the lock must have been what had woken her. She sat up abruptly as a stout man in uniform appeared in the doorway. He placed a tin mug on the floor, a thick slice of black bread sitting on top of it like a lid. The door slammed shut and he was gone.

Allie stretched, groaned and got to her feet. The bread felt moist, though that might have been steam from the weak tea in the mug. She didn't care; now her body was awake, she was aware of hunger gnawing at her. She ate half of the bread at speed then caught herself. Who knew how long it would be till they fed her again? On the other hand, what little she'd eaten hadn't eased her empty stomach. 'Fuck it,' she said, and finished the bread, forcing herself to nibble it slowly. The tea was simultaneously stewed and thin, but it was warm and wet, and that felt almost luxurious.

She sat on the shelf, back to the wall, waiting. She'd done the Eurythmics in the cupboard; today she'd give Blondie a run-out. Allie closed her eyes and let the irony of 'X Offender' fill her mind. Somewhere out there, somebody would be looking for her.

★ ★ ★

Colin Corcoran had woken early, but he'd forced himself not to move. He'd never been privy to a better view. Inches away from him, Wiebke lay sleeping, her breath a gentle purr in the back of her throat. To hell with Allie Burns' scepticism about their feelings for each other; they'd barely closed the door on the room Allie had booked for them in her hotel and they were in each other's arms, relief at their escape fuelling their desire.

He'd never been so scared. He could acknowledge that now he didn't have to keep a brave face on for Wiebke. His legs had felt feverishly weak as they'd walked out of the building. The receptionist had barely given them a second glance, reassured by his cheery wave and Allie's coat and hat.

At Checkpoint Charlie, he'd felt his heart hammering in his chest, his breath ragged as if he'd been running. But Wiebke had seemed cool and in control, her hand on his knee as the guards took away their passports and paperwork for scrutiny. He could feel the sweat in his armpits in spite of the chill of the afternoon; the rank reek of fear was all he could smell.

Then suddenly it was all over. Papers returned, barrier raised, West Berlin ahead without obstacle. They giggled like children all the way to the hotel, Wiebke pointing with delight to every hallmark of Western capitalism she caught sight of. 'The colours are so dazzling,' she exclaimed. 'The shop windows are full! And the people, their clothes look so bright and warm.' Her obvious excitement filled him with joy and pride that he'd made it happen for her.

Later, as they lay tangled in the clean hotel sheets, Colin had felt a pang of guilt at the thought of Allie trapped in the cupboard. By then, she'd have been discovered. Right now, she'd be in the hands of the Stasi, facing interrogation. But she wasn't a GDR citizen and she obviously wasn't a spy, so they wouldn't be heavy-handed. He told himself they'd let her go within twenty-four hours. If he hadn't heard from her by tomorrow morning, he'd contact the British embassy in East Berlin. And maybe Allie's girlfriend.

But for now, before the outside world intruded on them, he planned to get his relationship with Wiebke off to the best possible start. She hadn't been faking the passion they'd shared, he knew it. This was the beginning of a brilliant new chapter; the end of humdrum, the start of excitement.

OK, he'd be out of a job. No question of that. But Allie's story would turn him into a brave whistleblower, she'd hinted as much. Coupled with the quality of his track record in the lab, he'd be a great poster boy for any company that wanted to demonstrate their integrity. And Wiebke too — she'd be a real catch for them.

Right on cue, as he itemised the elements of their gleaming future, Wiebke's eyes opened. She blinked and frowned, then turned towards him and smiled. For the first time in his life, Colin Corcoran felt like a hero.

★ ★ ★

Nobody had ever accused Rona of patience. As soon as she'd walked the dog that morning, she'd headed for her executive office in the Clarion building with a list. Her first call was to the hotel in Giesebrechtstrasse where Allie had been staying. No, she wasn't in her room. Her key was still on the board. If Rona would call back in fifteen minutes, they'd check with housekeeping to see whether her bed had been slept in.

She killed the quarter-hour with a trip down to the canteen to collect a mug of coffee, which affronted her secretary, who saw the supply of hot drinks as her exclusive preserve. When Rona rang the hotel again, she was told politely that Fraulein Burns room had not been disturbed since the previous morning. Did Fraulein Dunsyre want to speak to the occupants of the other room on Fraulein Burns' account?

Fuck, yes. Allie hadn't said anything about another room, but there had to be some answers there, surely? 'Please,' Rona said.

A couple of clicks then a long ringtone. Halfway through the fourth ring, a man's voice spoke hesitantly. 'Corcoran. *Guten Tag.*'

Halle-fucking-lujah. 'Is that Colin Corcoran?'

'Who is this?'

'My name is Rona Dunsyre. I work with Allie Burns. You're the guy she's talking to on the Zabre Pharma investigation, right?'

'I can't confirm or deny that,' he stammered.

'For heaven's sake, this isn't bloody James Bond. I know exactly what Allie is doing, and I know all about your mad stunt to get your girlfriend out of East Berlin. Unless you want the sky to fall on your head, you need to talk to me. Now. Is that clear?' It was a tone of voice and a style of address that had reduced experienced feature writers to small children. Colin Corcoran was no match for Rona on the warpath.

'Yes, sorry, I was just being careful. I'm helping Allie with her story, yes,' he gabbled.

'So where is she? Allie, I mean, not the girlfriend.'

A pause. 'I'm not exactly sure.'

'Go back to when you were sure, son.' She heard

muttered voices at the other end.

He cleared his throat noisily. 'You said you knew about the plan?'

'Yes, you were going to pretend you'd attacked Allie and locked her in a cupboard. Bloody madness, but there you go.'

'We did it. Wiebke put on Allie's clothes and we managed to get through the border. We left Allie in the cleaners' cupboard.'

'You left her.' Rona's voice was cold.

'It was her idea,' he said.

'No, it was your bloody idea. So where is she now?'

'I don't know. I've no way of knowing. The cleaners will have found her.'

'And handed her over to the Stasi.'

A long pause. 'I expect so. She was going to stick to the version we'd agreed, that she's been beaten up and abducted.'

'You abandoned her, son. But she didn't abandon you. She arranged somewhere for you to stay. Somewhere safe. Right?'

He attempted to get on the front foot. 'It's what we agreed. In exchange for the story. She knows it's a really big story.'

Rona hoped he knew better than ever to be in the same room as her. 'In that case, you'd best make sure she gets her really big story. You're holed up in your little love nest with your girlfriend, right?'

'Uh huh.'

'I know she was supposed to supply Allie with documentary evidence of what you're both alleging. You've got that evidence?'

'Yes, we brought it out with us.'

'And you've still got Allie's passport?'

'Yes. Wiebke brought her own passport with her too, she needs that to sort out her German citizenship.'

'So what you and Wiebke are going to spend today doing is writing out in eye-watering detail everything you know about this dodgy drug trial. You're going to translate the documents. Then you're going to package all that up along with Allie's passport and give it to the hotel to put in their safe. Am I making myself clear?'

'Yes, but —'

'No buts. If you piss me about, I swear I will call Zabre Pharma and tell them where you are and what you've done. And I'm sure they have friends in the East who'd be happy to come and have a very intense conversation with you and the lovely Wiebke.'

'You can't —'

'I can and I will. If you think Allie is tough, you ain't seen nothing yet. I make Allie look like Little Bo Fucking Peep.'

'I'm sorry,' he mumbled. 'But she was up for it. Truly, she was.'

More fool Allie. 'So make it worth her while.'

'We'll do it.'

Rona put the phone down. She had no more fear of God to instil. She was too afraid on her own account.

33

Years of journalism had honed Rona's ingenuity. When it came to finding routes around publicists and bodyguards to get the interview she wanted, she had many rivals but few equals. Allie always said she'd learned more tactics from Rona than she'd ever picked up from her fellow news reporters. Rona responded by claiming she'd learned a disturbing amount about back-door sources of information from Allie. Together, their principle of helping hands had made each of them all the more formidable.

But for once, Rona was nonplussed. She'd only ever worked abroad on fashion shoots and curated visits to film sets. She had no little black book of translators, fixers on the ground, local correspondents. When it came to prising someone free from Stasi custody — or even confirming that's where they were — she had no idea where to begin. Her conversation with Colin Corcoran had left her feeling frustrated and faintly nauseous. And bloody useless.

The obvious route would be to contact the British embassy. 'Do we even *have* a British embassy in East Berlin?' she muttered. Either way, Bonn or East Berlin, she had no idea who she should speak to. If she told the whole truth about the plan, she'd be admitting Allie had broken the law in East Berlin — would the embassy use that as an excuse to wash their hands of her? On the other hand, if Rona stuck to the planned set of lies and it turned out Allie had broken under questioning, it would get messy in a different way.

There was one other possibility. Rona had been pushing the idea back below the surface every time it had threatened to thrust its way into the daylight. It felt like the nuclear option. On the other hand, doing nothing would be worse. How could she ever look Allie in the eye again, knowing she'd abandoned her?

Rona picked up her phone and dialled an internal extension. When it was answered, she said, 'Rona Dunsyre here. Is he in the building?'

The reply gave her no way out. Rona grabbed her handbag and headed for the ladies' toilet. She stood as close to the mirror as she could get and touched up her make-up. For once, it really did feel like warpaint. Then she marched up the single flight of stairs to the ninth floor.

★ ★ ★

Much as she'd have preferred to stay in bed with Hans, Genevieve knew there was work to be done. She'd arranged to meet Fredi that morning, then she was due to go back across the wall to chair a meeting at Pythagoras Press in the East. But at least Hans was coming with her to see Fredi, and they swung down the Ku'damm hand in hand like teenagers, making the most of the minutes that remained before they had to find their grown-up faces.

Fredi's apartment overlooked a tiny triangle of trees a couple of streets back from the main drag. It was always calm and quiet outside, a sharp contrast with the lively and loud discussions that took place inside. But that morning, it was just the three of them, drinking ferociously strong coffee and making plans for drawing together the protesters and dissidents struggling to stay under the radar in the East. Genevieve could make some things happen via Pythagoras, but she pointed out that she couldn't magic resources out of nowhere. 'It has to be financed somehow,' she said. She'd told them as much several times before but nothing had come of it.

'We know this,' Fredi said. 'Can you persuade your father to direct some funds to the cause? He must know the future lies in the direction we're pushing.'

Genevieve knew that the outside world had no idea of the present financial precarity of the Lockhart empire. It would resolve itself in Ace's favour over time — things always did, in her experience. For all she knew, he'd already turned things around. But for now, if there was any spare cash swilling around in the Lockhart coffers, it wouldn't be coming the way of Fredi and her crew. Their cause wasn't something that would appeal to Ace. She couldn't admit any of that, and not just for reasons of commercial sensitivity. 'That's not how he wants to play things right now.' She shrugged. 'He wants me to build relationships for the future, but he's wary of being seen undermining existing governments.'

'He likes to hedge his bets.' Fredi's tone was acid. 'If we fail, he won't be tainted.'

'But Genny's not like that,' Hans butted in. 'Are you, Genny? You want to be engaged right now.'

'I do, but I need to work out how best to achieve that. I can offer practical help, but we still have to have some money in the pot.'

Fredi got up abruptly and walked to the window, clutching her coffee mug to her chest. 'We'll find a way,' she said.

234

Genevieve didn't doubt it. 'I'll give it some thought too. But right now, I have to go back to my hotel and pick up some papers for my meeting this afternoon. I'll see you both later.' She missed the quick look the other two exchanged as she pulled on her coat. All she saw was Hans' smiling face as he kissed her goodbye.

★ ★ ★

Ace Lockhart kept Rona waiting for ten minutes. Not because he was in the midst of something that demanded his immediate attention, but because he could. She walked in, as well turned out as she always was, but in spite of her immaculate make-up, he detected strain around her eyes and a tightness in her jaw. He knew he'd given her a demanding and wide-ranging job, but he hadn't expected the gloss to have worn off quite so quickly.

'Come and take a seat, Rona,' he commanded with an expansive wave of his arm.

'Thanks for seeing me, boss.' She sat down and crossed one leg over the other. He couldn't help admiring the line of her calf, pointless as he knew that to be.

'What do you need from me?' Because they always needed something. Even when they brought him a bone, there was always a demand tied to it.

A deep breath. 'Your help. On a personal matter.'

He raised his eyebrows. 'Go on.'

'It's complicated.'

'Personal matters requiring my help generally are.'

'It's to do with Allie. I think she's in trouble.'

One corner of his mouth twitched in a darkly ironic smile. 'Trouble seems to attach itself to Ms Burns.

235

Though since she handed in her notice, she seems not to have done anything at all in the service of Ace Media.'

Rona held a blink for a long moment. 'She's pursuing a story. An investigation.'

'Not for the *Sunday Globe*, though. Not for any of Ace Media's titles. And that's not what she's paid for.'

'She stumbled on a story about a pharmaceutical company moving the clinical trial of an HIV drug from Edinburgh to East Germany so they could control the results. It sounded like they were intending to falsify, or at the very least, to massage the outcomes. So Allie started digging.'

'Just like your Border terrier.' He enjoyed the momentary flash of surprise that he knew so much about Rona's life. There was always some entertainment to be had in toying with those of his employees who managed to be interesting.

Rona gave him a flat stare. 'She found a whistleblower who had access to data from the East German pharma company. Long story short, the price of the story was to get the whistleblower's girlfriend to the West. Allie couldn't resist.' She looked pinched and anxious now.

'Clearly, the wheels came off. How catastrophically? Are they all under arrest?' He reached for the half-smoked cigar in his ashtray and lit it with a careless flourish. This was beginning to sound interesting.

'The whistleblower and the girlfriend got clear. They're in West Berlin. She came out on Allie's passport. They left Allie tied up in a cupboard. The story was to be that she'd been beaten up and put out of the way so the other two could get across the border.' Rona pursed her lips. 'Allie was posing as a publi-

236

cist working for the pharmaceutical company so she reckoned she could convince the East Germans that she was the victim. Then they'd let her off and send her back to West Berlin. I told her she was mad if she thought the Stasi would be such a pushover.'

Lockhart nodded. 'You spoke nothing less than the truth. I take it she hasn't turned up.'

'I've heard nothing.' She bit her lip. 'She's not been in touch with her whistleblower, which she would have been if she'd made it out.'

He sucked on his cigar and blew out a long plume of smoke. 'I don't envy her. So why have you brought this to me?' All innocence and bewilderment. 'It's not as if she's claiming to work for me.'

Something sparked in her eyes and she straightened up, planting her feet firmly on the floor. 'Can we not play games here, Ace? You can find some cover story — tell them she's on attachment to Zabre Pharma because you're thinking of investing in them. Or some other credible nonsense. It's not a secret, how much business you do on the dark side of the Iron Curtain. You're connected, all the way to the driver's seat. You've published hagiographies of the top dogs. You've got access. You've got strings to pull. And I need you to start pulling them. This is not some random freelance who's got into a wee bit of bother. This is Allie Burns, who is still, on paper at least, the northern bureau chief of one of your newspapers. It's not going to look good if you leave her to rot in a Stasi cell, is it?'

The converse of emotional blackmail was to seize the initiative and the moral high ground. 'For my journalists, I will move heaven and earth,' he said grandly. 'People will see that Ace Lockhart does not stand idly by while his people are under threat. Naturally, what influence I have will be placed at the disposal of Ms Burns.'

'You mean that?'

'Do you take me for a liar, Rona? Of course I mean it. If anyone can ensure the safe return of your Ms Burns, it's me.' The sparkle of her unshed tears was almost gratification enough. That she would be in his debt forever was, obviously, a bonus. 'It so happens that my daughter Genevieve is in Berlin right now. I will make a phone call, but she can conduct the practicalities.'

'That's it?' Her astonishment was another source of satisfaction. Lockhart loved to surprise his people with generosity when they expected something else.

'That's it. Remember who you're dealing with here, Rona. Where is Ms Burns' passport now?'

'In a hotel on Giesebrechtstrasse in West Berlin.'

He drew on his cigar again. 'Perfect. You will provide me with the details and arrange for Genevieve to collect it. Then she can escort Ms Burns back to the West.'

'Thank you,' Rona said softly. 'I will never forget this.'

She would not be the only one, Lockhart thought. He'd built much of his success on the amassing of favours owed. The only debts he was comfortable with were financial because those were the ones he could find a way around. 'I'm sure there will come a day when you can provide the payment due. One of the secretaries will let you know when there's something to report,' he said, turning away and picking up a thin file from his desk. In his attempt at dismissive nonchalance, he'd disturbed the papers beneath

238

the file, revealing a corner of the photograph of the Poladski memorial. In that moment, all his pleasure disappeared like a valley in a temperature inversion.

'I appreciate this,' Rona said. He turned back to her, his face blank. 'The phone call, your daughter, all of it.'

Her words dragged him back to the present. 'Good. Now go and see that my staff make me some money,' he growled, reaching for the phone. Time to do something that would remind him that the distance he had travelled had built a wall between him and that miserable little *shtetl*.

34

The hotel Genevieve Lockhart used as a base in West Berlin was several steps up the ladder from Allie's. A uniformed bellboy swung the door open for her and the reception clerk greeted her by name. 'Hallo, Fraulein Lockhart. I have a message for you,' she said, handing over a folded slip of paper.

There were gradations of messages from her father. The lowest level was, *Call me when you have the chance.* They scaled up through, *We need to talk; Urgent matters to discuss;* to full red alert — *Call me as soon as you read this.* Today's trumped even that. *Where are you? Get on the phone to me ASAP.*

Her heart sank as the lift rose. It sounded like a crisis and the only one that sprang to mind was that someone on the pensions board of trustees had started probing where the money was hiding. If it was one of the trustees that her father could persuade –or bully — into submission, all might yet be well. But if it was one of the trade unionists on the board, it would be a different story.

Genevieve rushed down the corridor and let herself into her suite. She didn't even take her coat off before she snatched up the phone, secured an outside line and dialled her father's direct number. 'Ace,' she said the second it was answered. 'I called as soon as I got your message.'

'Where have you been? I've been trying you all morning.'

240

'I was meeting the West German radical Greens. The ones who are in bed with the East Berliners.' She tried hard to sound relaxed. 'Is there a problem?'

'It's urgent but not serious,' he said. He sounded relaxed, which was not what she'd expected from his message. 'It's not actually our problem, in the sense that it's not a business issue. But it might turn into one if we don't deal with it swiftly.'

'I see,' she lied. 'What's happened?'

'The northern news editor of the *Sunday Globe* has gone offside on an unauthorised mission and managed to get herself arrested in East Berlin.'

'So, you want me to . . . What, exactly?' She sat down on the bed, slipping out of her leather jacket and feeling her shoulders relax.

'I've made some calls and straightened things out. Nobody there likes to challenge a cover story coming from me. But I need you to deal with the practical personally. So the Stasi can feel flattered that we're taking them very seriously.'

'Ace, I do take the Stasi very seriously.' She allowed some warmth into her voice. 'Even favoured capitalists like us have to tiptoe a little around them.' As she spoke, the mental image of her father on tiptoe nearly undid her.

'I want you to go to Ruschestrasse. They're holding her there. I had to go all the way up to General Mielke, which was exceptionally tedious. When you get your hands on Ms Burns, make sure you let her know how much in my debt she is.'

'And mine, since I have to go all the way over to Lichtenberg. Is this Alison Burns we're talking about?'

'The same,' he growled. 'I wish I'd fired her with the rest of them now.'

241

'You did get some good headlines out of that wrestler beating her up,' Genevieve chuckled. 'So what has she done to get herself arrested?'

'Some half-arsed scheme involving shenanigans at a pharmaceutical company and a fake abduction. She was pretending to be a PR bimbo. She thought she'd play the innocent victim and walk straight back through Checkpoint Charlie without a murmur. Stupid girl.'

'So why are you extricating her from this? Why not let her suffer?'

He guffawed down the phone, making her hold the receiver away from her head momentarily. 'Dunsyre is doing an even better job than I'd hoped. Besides, Burns is still on the books as one of ours. Leaving our reporters hanging out to dry doesn't play well. Even when they're operating off the books.'

Genevieve sighed theatrically. 'OK. I was heading back for a meeting this afternoon anyway. I'll make a detour to the big bad Stasi HQ.'

'Take Dieter with you, he always manages to make things look serious. You'll have to pick up Burns' passport on the way.' He gave her the details of the hotel on Giesebrechtstrasse. 'A fool called Colin Corcoran is holed up there with his East German paramour. He has the relevant documentation.'

'What do you want me to do with Burns once I've got her back to the West?'

'I couldn't care less, as long as she files her copy directly to me. I want to make sure she's not going to cost me more than she's worth. Let me know when you're all back across the wall.'

Genevieve couldn't help feeling that playing nursemaid to a reporter gone rogue was well below her pay grade, but she understood that Ace needed the safest possible pair of hands on such a delicate mission. She supposed she should be flattered that with so many resources at his disposal, he turned to her. It didn't occur to her that it was simply expediency; she was the body with boots on the ground and more or less carte blanche to move back and forth across the wall.

She pulled off her T-shirt and ripped the laundry plastic off a crisp white shirt. She tucked it into tailored jeans and added an Armani jacket to complete an outfit that would dazzle anyone east of the wall with envy. She garnished it with a pair of large gold earrings in the shape of knots, more ostentatious than she'd ever wear back home. If she was there to emphasise the importance of Pythagoras Press, she'd do it properly. Alison Burns would be in no doubt of the power she was relying on.

★ ★ ★

This time, the man in the shabby suit was accompanied by a woman in a Stasi uniform. She had a broad weather-beaten face and a stiff perm that would have withstood any cold wind from the Urals. Her stare made Allie feel both despised and hated. 'You are a spy,' she said without preamble. 'You are here to find out about the advances of science in the GDR and to report back to your bosses.'

This, Allie realised, was turning very serious. 'I'm not a spy. The work being done in your labs is not original. You're working for a Western company. Zabre Pharma. This is their clinical trial.'

'There is no point in lying to us. We know why you are here.'

243

'So if I'm a spy, how did I end up bound and gagged in a cupboard?'

The woman snorted. The man leaned forward and spoke with an air of calm logic. 'You were betrayed by Wiebke Neumann, just as we were. You thought she was on your side. You thought she was your ally in your spying mission. But you were mistaken. She drew you in with promises of information about the advances our researchers are making in this field. But she tricked you.'

Allie felt the tight grip of fear in her throat. 'This is crazy,' she said. 'I'm not a spy. I'm working for Zabre Pharma. I'm here to write about the excellent work your people are doing in running these clinical trials. Better than we can in the UK. I'm here to boost your reputation, not to steal secrets. Secrets that don't exist.'

The woman frowned, her eyes screwing tight. 'You are a liar. Our scientists have developed treatments you cannot compete with in the West. That is why you are here. To steal these new drugs and pretend they are your discoveries.'

Allie had heard about the looking-glass world of the Soviet empire. But she'd never imagined being trapped inside the twisted logic that drove their claims. The truth was turned on its head, but cleverly manipulated to fit their narrative of noble brilliance undermined by the villainous capitalists. 'You're mistaken,' she said.

'Who are you working for?' the woman demanded.

'I told you. Zabre Pharma.'

The woman shook her head, her expression shifting to one of triumph. 'The more you lie, the longer your sentence will be.'

Allie pressed her sweating palms to her thighs. She badly wanted to pee but she didn't dare ask and give them any more leverage. 'What do you mean, my sentence?'

'You will be brought before the court tomorrow,' the man said casually. 'What is it your Prime Minister Gladstone said? 'Justice delayed is justice denied.' Here in the GDR, justice is swift, not like your defective system in the West.'

'There will be a trial and you will be sentenced to a very long period in prison,' the woman cut in. 'We do not like spies in our country.'

'This is madness,' Allie protested. 'I don't have a lawyer, you've not even told me the charges against me. What evidence have you got that I'm a spy, for fuck's sake?' She was starting to panic now. She was alone behind enemy lines and they had all the power.

'You will hear the evidence in court when we —'

The door opened and a uniformed officer marched in. Judging by the insignia and braid, he outranked the woman by some distance. She jumped to her feet, saluting. The man in the suit scrambled to his feet and began to speak. The newcomer wasn't having any of it. He spoke swiftly, his accent one Allie couldn't decipher. He turned to her and said in fractured English, 'You come. Now.' He rounded the table and grabbed her upper arm in a painful grip.

Allie stumbled to her feet, confused and frightened. Was this it? The moment where she disappeared into some anonymous hellhole?

He yanked her out of the room and down the hall, a pair of armed guards marching behind them. Was this how it was going to end? Ignominy and cruelty in an East German jail? No chance for a last call to Rona?

No possibility of escaping through the looking glass?

At the end of the hall, the door opened and she was pushed through so hard she fell to her knees. She was expecting another cell; it took a moment for it to sink in that she was somewhere completely different. There was a carpet on the floor, the walls were panelled in cheap wood, and the man who had dragged her from the interrogation was throwing himself into a leather chair behind an ill-proportioned desk.

What was even more disconcerting was that the only other person in the room was Genevieve Lockhart.

35

Genevieve wrinkled her nose as Allie followed her into the back of the long black Mercedes that was idling outside the Stasi HQ on Ruschestrasse. Passers-by slid their eyes sideways, fascinated by such luxury but also aware that their fascination would be interpreted as disloyalty to the state if anyone noticed and noted it. And there were always other eyes paying attention.

'Tell me these are not your clothes,' Genevieve muttered.

Relief rendered Allie reckless. 'I chose them just for you. Dress to impress, that's my motto.' She didn't bother trying to keep the sarcasm below the surface. 'I've been shut in a cupboard then a cell for hours. I'm sure I smell as terrible as I look. I'm so sorry if I'm offending your sensibilities. Why are you even here, Ms Lockhart?'

'Your gratitude is heartwarming.' 'Oh, I'm grateful all right. I only wondered how come I qualify for such a high-level intervention.'

'Ace Media doesn't abandon its staff.' Genevieve opened the lid of the seat divider and helped herself to a can of Perrier. 'Thirsty? There's some chocolate in there too. Ruschestrasse isn't known for the quality of its catering.' Her smile felt genuine.

Allie wasn't about to be won over with so paltry an offer of hospitality. If Genevieve really cared, she'd have made more of an effort and picked up some sausages and potato salad on the way. But she lived in a world where that wouldn't occur to her because there was always someone to do that for her. 'How did Ace Media know where I was? Technically, I'm on holiday this week. I'm here on my own dime.'

'You can thank your girlfriend for that. She obviously keeps you on a tight leash. When you didn't call home, she rushed off to beg my father to find out where you were and rescue you. I happened to be in Berlin on Pythagoras business, and, like Ace, I'm taken seriously in this godforsaken socialist hell.'

'I feel better, knowing you didn't have to make a special trip. I'd have been OK, but it's good to have the process short-circuited.' Allie reached for a Diet Coke and a bar of milk chocolate. She tried to take her time with the wrapper, but her hunger overtook her and she ripped it off and stuffed a quarter of the bar into her mouth. The sugar rush was blissful and she closed her eyes in pleasure.

Genevieve sighed. 'You're fantastically naive. They were about to give you a show trial and send you to prison for spying.'

'How could they? There's no evidence, because I'm not a spy.'

Exasperated, Genevieve said, 'Oh, for heaven's sake. You were pretending to be something you're not in an East German secure scientific research facility. It feeds straight into their paranoia. Of course you can be turned into a spy for the purposes of propaganda. It's a drama that takes people's minds off how shit their lives are and how nothing seems to change, no matter what they see about Gorbachev and his *perestroika* on their pirated West German TV broadcasts.'

'And you think the UK government would sit on their hands and let that happen?'

Genevieve stared at Allie, as if she was a curious specimen from a museum. 'Are we talking about the same UK government? Led by Margaret Thatcher who thinks Gorbachev is a man she can do business with? Margaret Thatcher whose government passed a law saying schools can't even acknowledge the existence of people like you in the classroom?' She scoffed. 'You would have been so far down the priority list of the Foreign Office. Even if your media friends had kicked up a storm, you'd have been behind bars in Hohenschönhausen for a very long time. And trust me, you wouldn't have liked that one little bit. My father has the power and influence to make all that go away. So stop being so bloody chippy and thank your lucky stars that he thinks your girlfriend's so good at her job that he's willing to put himself out for her. Now, sit still and behave. We're nearly at Checkpoint Charlie and your papers are very definitely not in order.'

Chastened in spite of herself, Allie subsided and finished her chocolate. They drew up at the East German barrier and Genevieve handed over the passports. She spoke to the border guard in fast and apparently fluent German then took out a business card from her wallet. She scribbled a name and number on the reverse and handed it over, all smiles and deference.

'What was all that about?' Allie asked.

'I was explaining that he should speak to a senior figure in the ministry because we are above his pay grade. Though I was much kinder than that. Now we wait.'

Since they'd got their initial sparring out of the way, Allie didn't want to waste the opportunity to see whether she might squeeze something interesting out of Genevieve. 'So what brings you to Berlin?'

That earned a glance of amused incredulity. 'Business. Pythagoras Press has publishing interests all over Europe.'

'But mostly on the eastern side of the Iron Curtain.'

'What a curiously old-fashioned way to put it. Europe is on the cusp of change. So, for example, I'm talking to Green activists on both sides of the wall in Berlin. I suspect we're going to see a lot of changes in the way the Eastern bloc interacts with the EEC.'

'Won't that be a bit awkward, given all those boot-licking biographies of communist leaders you've published down the years? What happens when one of them is deposed? Do you pulp all the remaining copies and pretend they never happened, like the politburo members who've been airbrushed out of photographs?'

Genevieve shook her head in apparent sorrow. 'So easy to mock. Pythagoras has a long and distinguished history of publishing the groundbreaking work of scientists from many countries. Work that would not readily have reached a wider scientific community without the access we provided. To make that happen, yes, we have on occasion created rather more flattering biographies of communist leaders than you'd read in the *Guardian* or the *New York Times*. But it does give their citizens a glimpse into the lives and achievements of their leaders, and I'm not going to apologise for that.'

'Of course you're not. That's not Ace Media style.'

'I'm not sure quite how you can plant your flag on the moral high ground, Allie. You're still on our books.'

'Not for much longer. I'm working out my notice.'

'I hear 'work' is a very loose term for what you're doing.' Again, she scoffed. 'And even when you shake the dust of the *Sunday Globe* from your shoes, the lovely Rona will still be close to the bridge on the flagship. You're still one of us. Pythagoras is still funnelling money into your household budget.'

It was harsh but true. Before she could find a response, the border guard returned. He gave Genevieve a sharp salute and handed over their passports. Only as they crossed into West Berlin did Allie grasp how tightly she'd been holding herself. Her shoulders literally dropped and her jaw relaxed. She had reluctantly to acknowledge to herself that she'd been living on bravado ever since the security officers had marched her out of the cleaners' cupboard and into their guardroom. She'd been in difficult situations before but she'd never seriously believed she was at risk of losing her freedom. It wasn't an experience she ever wanted to repeat. All that mattered now was assembling the story she'd taken these risks for, then getting back to Rona. Though maybe not in that order.

'Can you take me back to my hotel in Giesebrechtstrasse?'

Genevieve nodded. 'That was the plan. Your co-conspirators are still there. You can finish up your interviews with them then write up your copy. I'd advise you to work quickly. My father doesn't like to be kept waiting.'

There was a presumption there that Allie knew she had to kill in its tracks. 'What has my copy to do with your father?'

Genevieve rolled her eyes. 'You'll be delivering your copy directly to him.'

'I don't think so.'

'What do you mean? You're employed by Ace Media. Your copy belongs to us.'

Allie shook her head. 'Only the copy I produce when I'm at work. I told you earlier, I'm on holiday this week. I paid for my own travel, I'll be picking up my hotel bill and any other incidentals.'

'But I've just pulled you out of the monumental hole you'd dug yourself into.' Behind Genevieve's steady tone was an edge of ice.

'I never asked you to. And while I'm grateful for your help, it doesn't change the baseline. This is my story. I uncovered it in my own time, I pursued it in my own time and at my own expense. It does not belong to the *Sunday Globe* or any other Ace Media title.' Allie wasn't giving an inch; no one who had ever worked with her would have expected that of her.

'My father has just stuck his neck out for you. Do you have any idea how embarrassing it will be if you go ahead and write a story that is in any way hostile to East Germany? Never mind how bloody ungrateful it would be.'

Allie sighed. 'I'm sorry about that. But what you just said? That's exactly why I'm not handing it over to Ace Lockhart. He owes more loyalty to Erich Honecker and his government than he does to me or the truth. He'll bury this story because he thinks it will reflect badly on his cronies, which is bad news for his empire.' She leaned forward and tapped on the glass between the driver and the rear seats. 'Stop the car now,' she said to Genevieve. 'I'll walk from here.' It wasn't exactly a grand gesture; they'd just turned on to the Ku'damm and she knew the way from there.

'Don't be so bloody childish,' Genevieve exclaimed. 'I'll drop you at your hotel. I can't force you to submit your copy to Ace, but you'll be making a serious mistake if you turn your back on him. He'll blacklist you from all the Ace Media titles. You'll be cutting yourself off from a huge segment of the market. And he's going to love your Rona a lot less. I'd say she'd be about fifty per cent less secure in her new fiefdom.'

It was a powerful threat. Allie didn't care on her own account, but the thought of putting Rona at risk gave her pause. But Rona had known this wasn't a story for Ace Media and still she hadn't hesitated. And Rona was a brilliant journalist. Ace Lockhart wasn't the only show in town, and he certainly wasn't the only one who recognised Rona's distinctive abilities.

'Maybe so. But she'd love me a lot less if I abandoned my principles after she'd gone to bat for me. And blacklisting people never goes well. You always end up on the wrong side of history.'

Genevieve flushed. 'You're very cavalier with your partner's prospects. I do hope she feels the same.'

The driver turned off the main drag into the side street and purred to a halt outside the hotel. 'Thanks for your help,' Allie said, opening her door. 'Like I said, I do appreciate that.'

'You have a strange way of showing it. I don't expect our paths will cross again. Next time you're stupid enough to jump into a pile of shit, you'll be on your own, I guarantee it.'

Allie got out of the car then turned back to smile at Genevieve. 'Don't be so sure. Maybe your father still has some surprises tucked up his sleeve.' She shrugged. 'But what do I know? Good luck, Genevieve.'

36

It was awkward, walking into her hotel in cheap ill-fitting cotton trousers and a worn T-shirt, sporting a black bruise down one cheek, carrying nothing but her wallet and passport, pretending to a confidence she didn't feel. Allie couldn't remember the last time she'd felt so self-conscious. But hotel receptionists have seen everything under the sun, even in respectable Charlottenburg, and the woman greeted her with a cheerful smile, handing over her room key without so much as a raised eyebrow.

She held it together till she'd double-locked her door behind her, then she subsided on to the bed and shook with sobs, tears running down her face, nose choking with snot as she let the fears of the last couple of days wash away in a wave of relief. Once the storm had passed, she stumbled into the bathroom and saw her face for the first time. Kudos to the receptionist, she thought wryly. Wiebke hadn't been messing around when she clobbered her with the scrubbing brush; Allie looked like the loser in a bar fight. 'This better not become a habit,' she muttered, stripping off the smelly clothes and stuffing them into the bin.

The shower worked almost all of its usual magic; she was restored and more or less in command of herself. Now she could trust herself to speak to Rona without collapsing in a soggy heap on the end of the phone. She wrapped the towel around her, climbed into bed and put a call in to Rona's direct line. 'Rona

254

Dunsyre speaking,' came her greeting. The sound of her voice, bright and familiar, nearly broke Allie all over again.

She swallowed hard and said, 'Thanks for organising the great escape.'

Rona whooped with excitement. 'You're out! Are you safe? Are you OK? Did they hurt you? Fuck, I love you, Allie.' It poured out breathlessly.

'I love you too. I'm OK, Ro. Really.'

'Thank God for that! I've been so bloody worried, so bloody scared.'

'I'm sorry me not listening to you meant you had to go cap in hand to Lockhart. I can only imagine how shit that felt.'

'Never mind that, all I was thinking about was no sex for twenty years while you were locked up in some gulag.'

An unexpected laugh bubbled in up Allie's throat. 'They don't have gulags in Germany, you numpty.' A deep breath, 'I was really scared, though. They said they were going to put me on trial as a spy. Can you imagine? Me, the least likely spy in the universe. Never kept a secret in my life.'

This time, they laughed together. 'Oh, I don't know,' Rona said. 'You never let on what you've got me for my birthday. But honestly, are you really OK? Did they beat you up?'

'No, but the East German lassie we were getting over the wall gave me a helluva clout.'

'What? Why?'

'We had to make it look like I'd really been knocked out and tied up in a cupboard. She took her role a wee bit more seriously than I'd have liked. Two black eyes already this year, and it's only April.'

'Christ, people will be accusing me of domestic violence next,' Rona teased. 'So, when are you coming home? When do I get the whole gory story?'

Allie sighed. 'Soon as I can. I need to sit down with Colin and Wiebke and get everything I need from them.'

'I may have made that slightly easier for you.'

'How?'

'When I was trying to track you down, I told them to write down everything that was relevant and to put it with the papers the German lassie brought out, and to put the whole thing in the hotel safe. Along with your passport. Did you get your passport?'

'I did. Genevieve Lockhart herself picked it up and brought it to me.'

'Wow. Service with a smile.'

'Not so much of the smile. I think she was pissed off at having to run such a demeaning errand.' Allie stretched out, easing her tired back. 'I don't think she'll be inviting me to any of her starry parties any time soon.' She groaned. 'I'm going to have to grovel to the big man, amn't I?'

'For once, swallow your pride. He could have washed his hands of you.'

'Wouldn't have looked good, though. I'm still on the payroll, as Genevieve kept reminding me. I am grateful for his help and I will express my gratitude. But mostly, you're the one I'm thankful for. And I will demonstrate that in person just as soon as I can suck my sources dry and sort out a flight. So let me go, my love. The sooner I get stuck in, the sooner I'll be home.'

★ ★ ★

There was a relief in wearing her own clothes that Allie had never considered before, a familiarity and comfort that she usually didn't have to think about. She walked down the corridor to the room she'd booked for Colin Corcoran and Wiebke Neumann, aware there was a slight swagger in her walk. This, she thought, was how freedom felt.

There was no response to her knock. So she put her face close to the door and spoke clearly. 'Colin, it's Allie. Open up.' A scramble of movement, then the door inched open, forcing her to step back. Colin's anxious face appeared. 'It's really you,' he gasped, pushing the door wide. 'When did you get out?'

'About an hour ago,' Allie said, her voice clipped. 'My partner knows what strings to pull.'

'It's great to see you,' he said. Wiebke peered over his shoulder and her hand flew to her mouth.

'*Scheisse*,' she exclaimed, horrified. 'Was this me?' She pointed at Allie's face.

'Yes.'

She turned to Colin and said something in German. 'She says she didn't mean to hurt you so badly. She's mortified.'

'I'm sorry,' Wiebke said.

'Never mind that. It is what it is. Are you planning on staying in Berlin?'

'Why?' he asked.

'Because I need to be able to contact you, to answer any queries that come up when I'm placing the story, Colin.'

They exchanged a look. 'As soon as Wiebke's West German passport is issued, we're going to the UK,' he said. 'I've given my tenants notice to quit so we can get back into the house in a month or so.'

'She'll have her passport by then?' Allie was dubious; she couldn't imagine any bureaucracy reacting so swiftly to someone who was, in her mind, an illegal immigrant.

Colin gave an indulgent chuckle. 'The West German government passed a law years ago stating that if you were born in Germany, you're German, regardless of whether that was in the West or the East. We went to the government offices yesterday, filled out some forms and handed over Wiebke's GDR paperwork. She'll have her new passport in a matter of days.'

'Amazing,' Allie said, meaning it. 'That's good, that you're going back to the UK. So what we need to do now is go through the story from the very beginning.'

'We've already written a lot of it down. Your girlfriend told us to make notes of all we knew about, and that's what we did. Wiebke, can you go down to reception and get it from the safe?' She nodded and left the room.

'Thanks,' Allie said. 'Colin, I had a lot of time to think about things, stuck in a cupboard and then a cell —'

'I'm sorry, and we're really grateful —'

'Yes, I get that. But I'm even more determined to get this story away with a following wind. It's an utterly heartless exploitation of people who feel they've got nothing left to lose. So I really need chapter and verse from you on the black market operations that Zabre have used before. Names, places, the drugs involved.'

'I understand. I'll check back through my diaries. I always kept a record. Just in case it all went pear-shaped.'

'Nothing like keeping your nose clean.'

He flushed. 'I was too busy focusing on the science.'

'Sure you were.' As she spoke, Wiebke returned. They sat round the tiny table in the hotel room, going through the pages of data Wiebke had stolen. Allie struggled to get her head round some of the detail, but she made Colin repeat his translations till she was certain she had it straight. Then she got them to fill in the big picture of what was going on with Zabre and the East Germans. By then, they were all running out of steam. But Allie wasn't finished. She held out the promise of drinks and food at the Haus der 100 Biere, which was enough of a bribe to draw out the story of Colin and Wiebke's relationship and the details of their dramatic escape. The last act was for Allie to take a series of photographs of the happy couple on the Canon Sure Shot she always carried in her capacious shoulder bag.

Later, in the bar, supplied with food and drink, they toasted each other. Allie knew she had more than enough material for a powerful investigative story and the human interest sidebar that would make it come alive for readers. It had pushed her to the limits, but now it was beginning to feel worth it. She finished her food, drained her glass, then excused herself.

She was so tired she could barely put one foot in front of the other. She knew she should at least make a start on her copy while the interviews were fresh in her mind, but the sight of her bed was too tempting. Her last thought before sleep ran into her like a runaway train was that Ace Lockhart was not getting his hands on this.

37

Genevieve caught up with Hans at the tail end of a radical Greens meeting at the university. Fredi was speaking, clearly winding up with a rousing peroration that drew whoops and cheers from her audience. Genevieve squeezed her way through the crowd to Hans' side and slipped her arm through his. Startled, he turned and she watched his face light up. 'Genny,' he exclaimed, leaning down to kiss her. 'I wondered where you were.'

'Business in the East,' she said. 'I had to make two trips — one to sort out a problem for my father, the other to chair a meeting at Pythagoras. The Checkpoint Charlie guards barely look at my passport these days.'

Fredi reached her impassioned conclusion, raising her fists to the sky. The room erupted. Genevieve wondered again at her new friend's capacity for stirring a crowd. There were no waverers at the end of one of her speeches. They might wake up the next morning wondering whether the world was really as she'd laid it out for them. But on the night, everyone was a true believer. Genevieve envied her that gift. She couldn't help feeling it was a better way to get people on side than her father's attraction to ruling by fear.

Hans drew her to one side of the hall, out of the way of the audience who were trickling out, chattering excitedly to each other. Gradually they made their way to the front, where Fredi was surrounded by a small group of eager acolytes who wanted more. She caught Genevieve's eye and a flash of relief crossed her face. 'I'm sorry, I must go now,' she said, gently extricating herself and embracing Genevieve. 'Get me out of here,' she muttered, linking arms with her.

They made it out of the hall and to a bar sufficiently distant to escape stray audience members. 'That was exhausting,' Fredi said, subsiding on to a wooden bench. 'So many people are coming now, it's really quite daunting to stand up there and lift the room.'

'You? Daunted?' Genevieve said. 'I find that hard to believe. You radiate self-confidence and self-assurance. Nobody doubts a word you say.'

'It's not so easy,' Hans said. 'If we could only find a way to capture Fredi's performance and scale it out. But there's only one Fredi.'

'You could make videos,' Genevieve said. 'You could even smuggle them into the East.'

He sighed. 'We could. But to be effective, they need to have professional production values, and that's one more thing that eats up money we don't have.' He got up and went to the bar.

'I've been thinking about that,' Genevieve said. 'I heard something today that gave me an interesting idea.'

Fredi raised her eyebrows. 'That sounds intriguing. Tell me more.'

'Let's wait till Hans gets back with the drinks so I don't have to go through it twice.'

Fredi frowned. She didn't like to be kept waiting. She glanced over her shoulder and, seeing Hans was being served, she turned her attention back to Genevieve. 'You've come up with an argument to persuade your father to bankroll us?'

Genevieve smiled. 'In a way.' She held up a finger. 'Patience, Fredi,' she teased.

Hans had barely set down the three steins of beer when Fredi spoke. 'Genny has an idea.'

Genevieve couldn't resist taking a mouthful of beer. 'I understand you — damn it, *we* — need money to move this campaign forward. I already explained that I don't believe my father will simply donate money to the cause. He just won't. But I think I've hit on a way to get him to give us money for a different reason.'

'Explain,' Fredi demanded.

'Earlier today, I had to go to the East to facilitate the release of one of Ace Media's journalists. It's a complicated story but at the heart of it was a plan to get a GDR scientist across the wall. A key part of it was pretending the journalist had been attacked and tied up and left in a cupboard while the scientist used her passport to escape. Obviously, the journalist was discovered and she stuck to the story about being the victim of an abduction to get her passport.'

Fredi laughed. 'And did the Stasi believe her for a moment?'

'No, they took her off to Ruschestrasse. They were threatening to try her on spying charges because all this happened inside a research facility.'

Hans drew his breath in sharply. 'She must have been terrified.'

'So how did you come to the rescue?' Fredi demanded.

'Her partner also works for Ace Media, in a senior role. When the journalist didn't call home, her partner spoke to my father and asked him to intervene. He made a few phone calls to the Interior Ministry and they agreed to release her. I had to collect her

262

passport and fetch her.'

'Quite the dramatic day for you,' Fredi said. 'I hope she treated you like a hero. But how does that help us?'

'This was a *fake* abduction. Involving someone my father doesn't really care about. But he didn't mess about, he sorted it out. How much more eager would he be to sort it out if he believed it was real and the victim was his beloved only daughter?'

Fredi and Hans caught each other's eyes then quickly looked back at Genevieve. 'Are you proposing that we stage a fake abduction?' Fredi said carefully.

'Exactly. We wouldn't even have to do much in the way of staging. You just hide me somewhere you're not directly connected to then you send ransom demands to my father. And he will pay up, because he loves me. And I'm all he's got.' She sat back, well pleased with herself.

'You would do this to your father?' Hans was incredulous.

She shrugged. 'It's kind of my money too. Well, it will be one day. At some point, either when he dies or before that, I'll be in charge. I'm just screwing an advance out of him.' She was choosing to ignore what her father had told her about Ace Media's finances when he'd borrowed the pension fund money. But she was convinced of her father's Houdini skills. He'd always pulled a rabbit out of the hat in the past; she was sure he could do it again. If push came to shove, there was more pension-fund money he could borrow. Then somehow he'd extricate them from their travails and make the company stronger than ever. She had no worries on that score.

'He will take extreme measures to avoid paying this ransom,' Fredi said. 'And he will be afraid for you.

You're OK with all of that?'

'It's foolproof. He'll have a few days of angst, and then it will all be over and you'll have the money you need to keep campaigning for a unified Green Germany.'

'It's a crazy idea,' Hans said. 'But it's also brilliant. It could work, Fredi.'

She frowned. 'There are many places where such a plan could go wrong,' she mused. 'But with careful planning, we could succeed.' She looked around. 'But this is not the place to have this conversation. Let's drink up and go back to my apartment. We will turn the music up loud and start to work out how to separate your father from his money.'

★ ★ ★

Ace Lockhart arrived back at Voil House with a sense of accomplishment. He'd exercised his influence with the government of the GDR to a degree that had reassured him he still had the power to shift the needle and change outcomes. And in the process he'd cemented Rona Dunsyre's loyalties to Ace Media. He walked into his home office, threw off his jacket and kicked off his shoes. He poured a glass of the red wine he bought by the label, took a Cohiba Esplendido from the humidor and lowered himself into the chair.

Only when he had his cigar going to his satisfaction did he look at the small bundle of letters on his desk. Almost no mail arrived at Voil House; anything related to Ace Media was filleted out by his staff, leaving Lockhart with personal letters and cards. That evening, there was a letter from a philanthropist he'd met a few times, seeking a donation to his charity supporting Ethiopian Jews still recovering from the famine. Lockhart screwed it into a ball and tossed it in the bin. He was choosy about the charities he supported; he couldn't see the point unless there was a way of finessing something in it for him.

Another letter from Camilla, who used to be his PA. Her eldest child was looking for a summer job, did Ace have some lowly position he might fill? Camilla had packed in her job after her youngest daughter had been left with catastrophic injuries after a car crash. She'd been the best PA he'd ever had, so Lockhart scribbled Find the lad something on the letter and put it in the 'out' tray.

The final envelope in the bundle was addressed in block capitals that gave him pause. It was hard to be precise about printed letters, but they looked disturbingly similar to a hand he'd seen more than once lately. The postmark was smudged but he thought it read 'Glasgow'. Lockhart rubbed the envelope between his fingers. It felt as if it contained no more than a single sheet of paper. He stared hard at it, as if he might suddenly develop X-ray vision. He sucked on his cigar and shrouded his head in blue smoke before finally ripping it open and drawing out its contents.

A single page fluttered to the desk. It was the pale blue top sheet of one of the copy pads his journalists used. In firm blunt capitals, it said, *WE KNOW WHO YOU ARE. WE KNOW WHAT YOU DID. IT'S JUDGEMENT DAY.*

An involuntary shudder ran through Lockhart, making his surplus flesh wobble. He rammed the cigar into the ashtray and let out a roar that held anger and pain in equal measure.

How dare they? Whoever they were, how bloody dare they?

265

38

Because the only flights allowed in and out of West Berlin had to originate in West Germany, Allie was obliged to travel back to Manchester via Frankfurt, which more than doubled the time she had to spend fretting in airports. She'd considered flying to Glasgow, but since it was Friday, she was technically supposed to be back at work the following day. And Rona could skive off at lunchtime and drive down to spend the weekend with her.

Allie explored the Frankfurt terminal from one end to the other while she waited to board her flight. All she wanted was to close her own front door behind her and fold Rona into her arms. Her copy was written, hammered out on her portable typewriter in the Berlin hotel room the previous day. She'd wanted to write the story up while Colin and Wiebke were down the hall in case she stumbled on elements she needed to check or expand on.

It had taken her a good half-hour to reach an intro that satisfied her:

A British drug company is avoiding testing rules by running its trials behind the Iron Curtain. Its goal — to win approval for a revolutionary drug that may stop HIV turning into AIDS.
Early trials in the UK were halted when

adverse results were reported. But desperate HIV+ patients will do anything to avoid their illness developing into the full-blown killer virus so Zabre Pharma knew they'd find a ready customer base for their product if they could get it to market.

It wasn't perfect, but it was enough to start the wheels turning. She'd worked all day on the copy, writing it as a two-part exposé. First the set-up, then 'behind the scenes in East Berlin' as the second part. That had been straightforward; this was a story that more or less told itself. What took longer was telling the human interest story without descending into sickly sentimentality. Colin and Wiebke falling in love when they couldn't even hold hands for fear of being betrayed to the Stasi; their realisation that what they knew could be their ticket to freedom; and the audacious plot to get Wiebke across the border. There was only one sticking point. The three of them had wrangled over their late-night beers about whether to tell the truth about the escape plot or stick to the story that they'd used on the German authorities. Allie had prevailed; she felt entitled to the credit for taking a chance that could have ended up with her being the victim of a spy trial.

Now, the sheaf of copy was safely stowed in her carry-on, a carbon copy in the post to the house in Manchester. First thing on Monday morning, she'd find a home for it. Probably the Sunday Times or the Observer. Anything that wasn't part of Ace Media would do.

Fed up with pacing, she found a news stand tucked away on the main concourse and bought a copy of

267

the *Globe*. In a quiet corner, she scanned the head-lines, only pausing when she saw a story about protest marches in Glasgow and Edinburgh over the new local government taxation scheme that had been imposed in Scotland on 1 April. The date — April Fool's Day — added insult to the injury that it had been introduced a year ahead of its English counter-part. Dubbed the 'poll tax' because every adult was obliged to pay the same amount, 'whether they are a duke or a dustman', as the story put it, it was causing both outrage and hardship. Allie couldn't help a burst of pride that her fellow countrymen didn't hesitate to take to the streets in protest, their lack of docil-ity another reason for Thatcher's Tories to loathe her homeland.

But the poll tax and the government and all its thrones and dominions disappeared like smoke in a gale at the announcement of Allie's flight. In a cou-ple of hours, she'd be on the tarmac at Manchester airport, a hot story in the bag, and ahead of her, the relief of sleeping in her own bed beside the woman she loved. The last vestiges of the terror and stress of the past few days slipped from her shoulders and Allie bounced to her feet, the churn of fear finally banished by the churn of anticipation.

★ ★ ★

Genevieve followed Fredi up a steep staircase to the fourth floor of an apartment building in a quiet side street in Reineckendorf in the former French sector. Their footsteps echoed in the stairwell, an unsettling clatter as they climbed. There were two doors on the top landing, and Fredi unlocked the farther one with a pair of formidable keys she drew from her bag. She held the door wide for Genevieve, bowing ironically as she waved them in. 'Enter the domain of Tante Lisl,' she said.

The apartment was dark and frowsty, smelling of dust and lavender polish. 'My great-aunt Lisl has lived here since 1928,' Fredi said, following them into the living room, a dim cave with thin shafts of light peeping round the edges of the shutters. She flicked a switch and the room sprang into focus.

'Where is she now?' Genevieve asked, prowling round and taking in the framed family photographs and the dusty leather-bound books crammed into tall shelves.

'With her daughter in Kassel. She had a fall back before Christmas, broke her hip. They spirited her away to live with them till she recovers.' Fredi scoffed. 'As if she will ever manage this place again. But she has a long lease and the rent is low so they don't want to give the place up. This will be your safe house, I think?'

Genevieve frowned. 'But it's connected to you.'

Fredi shook her head. 'I never visited here. I used to have *kaffee und kuchen* with Lisl once a month in the Teehaus in the Tiergarten, she loved to get out and about in the city. We don't share a family name, she is a maternal relative. Trust me, Genny, you will be safe here. Take a look around, go on.'

Genevieve left the room and Fredi settled in a wing-backed chair by the stove. She heard the sound of doors opening and closing, water running, a toilet flushing. At last, Genevieve returned, frowning. 'Everything is dusty,' she complained.

Fredi grinned. 'You'll have time enough to learn

269

how to do housework,' she teased. 'But the plumbing works and if I know Lisl, the bed will be comfortable.'

'I don't think I've ever seen quite so many pillows on one bed,' Genevieve said. 'I suppose I can manage here for a few days. There's a radio and a tiny TV in the kitchen. But what am I supposed to do about food?'

'Hans will come after dark.' Fredi jumped up and went through to the kitchen. She opened a tall door that led into a pantry. The shelves were crammed with jars of sauerkraut, pickled vegetables and assorted sausages — Bratwurst, Currywurst, Frankfurters, Nürnberger Rostbratwurst and Knackwurst. On the floor, under the bottom shelf, were bottles of Weissbier. Fredi laughed. 'Come and see, Genny, you're not going to starve.'

She turned and pointed to the kitchen counter. 'The phone is still connected. Tante Lisl refuses to believe she's not coming home.' Fredi turned to Genevieve and pulled her by the hand, pouting. 'Come on, this was your idea. This place is perfect. Just so long as you don't decide to throw any wild parties with Lisl's beer.' She drew her closer, an arm round her shoulders, hugging her. 'You're not getting cold feet?' Fredi said softly, her voice almost a caress.

'It's all been a bit mad, the last couple of days, making plans, working out arrangements. Almost like a game, you know? But now we're here, now this is it . . .' A catch in her voice. 'Don't get me wrong, I've not got second thoughts. I'm not changing my mind. It's just . . . we've totally got to make this work. If it goes wrong, my father will never forgive me. I'll be out of the business, he'll disinherit me. Hell, he'll probably hand me over to the cops.' She buried her face in Fredi's shoulder.

Fredi looked into the middle distance, her expression set and unreadable. 'Then we'll just have to make sure everything goes like clockwork.' She stepped free of Genevieve and gave her the full beam of her charisma in a gentle smile. 'Let's run through it one more time.' She drew her back to the living room, still holding her hand.

They sat opposite each other. 'You have to stay here from now on.'

'But I haven't got a change of clothes or any toiletries,' Genevieve protested.

'I know. But everything must remain in your hotel room. It must look as if you have been taken, not as if you have gone away for the weekend. Give me a list of what bathroom things you need. And make-up. Also, your clothes sizes. I will shop for these.'

Genevieve raked in her bag and came up with her wallet. She took out a wedge of Deutschmarks. 'OK, but nothing cheap and nasty. This should cover the essentials.'

'Thank you. I will be kind to your body,' Fredi teased.

'I'd expect nothing less.'

'So, Hans will come tonight with some bread and milk and coffee and fruit. He'll bring the Polaroid camera and he will take some pictures of you bound and gagged.' That engaging smile again. 'Not painfully, of course. We will send the pictures special delivery to Glasgow. They should arrive on Monday or Tuesday. What I did not tell you earlier, we have a friend in Scotland, he is working to start a Scottish Green Party, and he will deliver them to your father at Voil House, explaining that we are holding you prisoner

271

in Berlin. The letter will say the Red Army Faction's death has been a lie, that it is still alive, that it is acting in the memory of Andreas Bader and Ulrike Meinhof.'

'That's guaranteed to shake him. It really unsettled him when they were on the rampage. I was in my teens back when they were full tilt and it mortified me that I had to turn up everywhere with a bodyguard. What a blight on my teenage social life! Like Ace is important enough to be a target for international terrorists.'

Fredi raised her eyebrows. 'So it's the perfect trigger. Our man in Glasgow will tell him when to expect a phone call, and I will call him from a secure phone and tell him the ransom demand. We will send more photos, make it look like you're having a really shit time. And if you're right about his reaction, he'll do what he's told.'

'You're still planning to send him to his island?'

'Of course. From everything you have told us, it's so isolated, we can be sure we'll be able to control the handover. It's all going to be perfectly fine, Genny. I promise you. It will be like clockwork. And we will finally have what we need to make the change that matters.'

It was only after Fredi had left that Genevieve realised she'd been locked in.

39

Allie tossed the Saturday style supplement aside and stretched. 'We should get up,' she said, snuggling into Rona, who had returned to bed after a trip to the newsagent's for a bundle of papers. They'd drunk coffee, filleted and shared the news and features, and caught up with each other after Allie's German trip. But now it was after noon and the April sunshine was beckoning. 'We need to tidy up the garden,' Allie groaned.

'You also need to call Lockhart,' Rona said. 'You can't keep ignoring him forever.' Their proprietor had called three times the previous evening and four times that morning, according to the answering machine; Allie had studiously ignored each message.

'I'll do it on Monday,' Allie said. 'I'm technically working today. I can't be tying up the line listening to Ace Lockhart ranting at me. Besides, I called the London newsdesk back when they paged me to check I was available in the event of the end of the world.'

'The longer you leave it, the more incandescent he'll be.'

Allie shrugged and snuggled into Rona's side. 'What's the worst he can do? He can't fire me, I'm already working out my notice.'

'I'm not.'

'I know. But I'll grovel. I'll tell him I was so traumatised after what happened to me that I couldn't face reliving it. I'll lay on my gratitude with a trowel.'

'You know that's not going to be enough. He'll want

the story.'

Allie sighed. 'It's not a *Clarion* story, neither the daily nor the Sunday. It would be wasted there. They'll just sensationalise it and everyone will have forgotten it in a week. This needs to be taken seriously, so Zabre can't exploit the sick and dying.'

Rona put her arm round Allie and found a seductive tone. 'Maybe you could give them the daring escape story? How *Sunday Clarion* northern news editor self-lessly risked her life for the cause of true love. You don't even have to mention the drug trial scandal.'

Allie thought about it. Not for the first time, Rona might have found a way through a thicket of thorns to a solution that could keep everyone if not happy, then at least grumpily satisfied. It made her main package a little light on human interest, but she thought she could use some of the interviews she'd done for the AIDS exodus story to give it a tilt in that direction. 'That might work,' she said slowly. 'And it means I can paint him as the white knight riding to my rescue.'

'And that'll be catnip to him.'

Allie kissed her. 'You're a genius.'

Rona returned the embrace. 'I was so afraid I'd never see you again.'

'I had my moments too. When they said they were going to put me on trial the very next day . . .'

'Don't. And please, Allie, don't ever put me through anything like that again. I don't ever want to feel that sick with fear for you.'

Allie pulled her into a tight embrace. 'I know. I can't promise I'll stay out of trouble, but I'll never stick my neck out that far again.'

'Not if you love me.'

'Oh, I love you. Never doubt that.' Allie let her

274

hand stray down Rona's back, following the curve of her spine.

'Stop that, or we'll never get the bloody pruning done.' Rona pretended to be affronted, but pulled away nevertheless. 'I'll have the first shower.'

'What's the point? We're just going to get dirty and sweaty.'

Rona's chuckle carried a freight of double entendres. 'You wish.'

★　★　★

By three o'clock, they'd dealt with the big herbaceous borders that surrounded the hard standing at the front of the house and they'd moved on to the raised beds at the rear of the house. 'Bloody globe artichokes haven't made it,' Rona complained, hoicking out the blackened stems of what had been her pride and joy the previous summer.

'We got caught out by the late frosts,' Allie said. 'And I forgot to wrap them up. Sorry. Are we going out tonight? I could really use a rampage around the dance floor.'

Before Rona could respond, Allie's pager beeped. Moaning, she unclipped it from her belt and scrolled through the message. 'Call Tim Stannage. DOUBLE URGENT.' She frowned. Tim Stannage was the *Sunday Globe*'s chief football writer, based in London. She didn't even have his number programmed into her mobile phone. 'What now?' she sighed, heading for the house, dropping her secateurs on the way.

Months later, she'd trip over them, immobilised and blunted with rust, and be transported back to that afternoon.

Allie kicked off her wellies at the back door and padded through to her workspace. Her office directory was in the top drawer of her desk, and she flicked through to Tim's entry. Home number and mobile phone. She presumed he wasn't at home at ten past three on a Saturday afternoon. He'd be covering some football match or other. Why he needed her, she had no idea. Some trouble at a northern ground, or fighting outside? She keyed in the number and it was answered as soon as it connected. 'Tim, it's Allie Burns. I just got your message.'

'Thank fuck,' he panted. 'There's a bloody mess happening here. I'm at the FA Cup semi-final at Hillsborough, Liverpool v Notts Forest, and there's some sort of crush going on at the Leppings Lane end. People are trying to climb the fence to get on to the pitch, it's complete chaos.'

'Is it not just the usual over-enthusiastic pitch invasion? I mean, did somebody score?'

'Peter Beardsley hit the bar, but that's not what's going on. They're falling on to the pitch behind the Liverpool goal, we could see the crowd getting squeezed before the kick-off, but this . . . I've never seen anything like this. People are going to be seriously hurt here. There's people collapsing in front of our eyes. This is more than a football story, Allie. You need to get your arse over here and check out what the fuck's happening.'

'I'm about forty minutes away, if the traffic's with me.'

'Just get here. Oh God, the crush barriers are collapsing. The ref's stopped the game. The players are going off. Allie, this is a big one.'

'I'm on my way, Tim. Hold the fort for now.'

Stunned, Allie ran to the bedroom, stripped off her gardening clothes, ran her hands under the tap and pulled on chinos and a jumper. She stuffed her feet into a pair of boots and grabbed a jacket and her work bag. On her way down the hall, she picked up wallet and car keys and ran out the back door. Startled, Rona looked up. 'Where's the fire?' she called, only half joking.

'Something really bad going off at the football in Sheffield.' Allie kept running, making for her car.

'Wait!' Rona shouted.

But Allie couldn't. She didn't really know Tim Stannage but from what she'd seen of him, he wasn't one of the blowhards who flagged up a scoop round every corner. Solid, that's how she'd have described him. But he'd sounded on the edge of hysteria. This was no false alarm.

She'd manoeuvred round Rona's car and reached the gateway when the passenger door was yanked open and Rona dived in. 'I can help,' she panted. 'I can dial the phone for you at least.'

Allie nodded and turned out of the drive, mentally mapping the quickest route to the Hillsborough football ground in Sheffield. Round the motorway, the usual bottleneck at Mottram on to the Snake Pass, twisting its way through beautiful Pennine scenery in a blur of oblivion. Allie saw none of it as she focused on the road, throwing the car round bends faster than she ought and overtaking inadvisedly. Rona had seen enough of Allie driving under pressure not to gasp audibly but her jaw was clamped tight and the hand that wasn't gripping the phone was clenched on the grab handle above the door. She tuned the radio to BBC Radio 2, where the news that something was happening at Hillsborough was filtering into their regular football coverage. Too many fans in too small an area; what had looked like a pitch invasion had actually been people struggling to breathe in a press of bodies.

And there were the phone calls. The London newsdesk now knew something serious was happening, and Rona was acting as conduit between them and Allie. Tim Stannage was talking London through events as they unfolded, and office-based London reporters were hammering the phones, trying to get a sense of what was going on. 'They're sending up a team from London,' Rona relayed.

'Sounds like we'll need it. Can you call the top two freelances on my contacts list? I need them on site soon as.'

The radio was reporting a swiftly unfolding disaster. Fans crushed against barricades, dead and broken bodies littering the pitch, the slow reaction of the emergency services and almost immediately, the blaming of the supporters. Before half an hour had passed, police were already explaining that fans had broken down an exit gate, allowing thousands who didn't have tickets to pour into crowded areas.

Allie slowed at the junction with the main road north, waiting for the lumbering bulk of the police Major Incident Vehicle to pass. Incredibly, she'd crossed the Pennines from Manchester in the same time it had taken South Yorkshire Police to get their MIV to the site of what was clearly a major incident.

She turned on to the road that ran alongside the park. Usually quiet, now it was crowded with clots of people, mostly men, moving slowly or milling around with an air of shocked bewilderment. Some were

278

wrapped in their friends' arms, apparently in tears. Now they were driving alongside the stadium, separated by the River Don. 'We need to park up,' Allie said. There was surprisingly little traffic; a couple of buses and a sudden ambulance, shrieking past them and swinging right into Leppings Lane, which was closed off by police as soon as it had passed.

Allie pulled over at the junction. 'Find somewhere to park the car then talk to anybody who can tell you what happened,' she said, getting out.

Rona scrambled across and handed her the phone. 'I'll call you before the first edition deadline,' she promised, swinging the car round and heading back towards the park. Allie keyed Tim Stannage's number into her phone, praying for a decent signal. He answered right away, his voice crackling but decipherable. 'It's Allie,' she said. 'I'm outside the stadium, near Leppings Lane. Where should I go?'

'You won't get in at that end. It's a fucking disaster, Allie. Bodies on the pitch, half the cops are just standing around, it's the fans that are trying to save people's lives out there. Go round the back of the North Stand, that's where they're taking the dead and the dying. There's a gymnasium there, that's what I'm being told. Allie, there are dozens of fans dead here.' His voice broke. 'Never seen anything like it.'

'Tell the desk I'm on the patch,' she said. 'I've got freelances coming too.' As she took off at a run, the ambulance that she'd seen turn into Leppings Lane reversed out and headed down towards the other end of the stadium. By the time she made it to the back of the North Stand, amazed there was nobody there to stop her, it looked like an ambulance park. Emergency vehicles left at haphazard angles, some doors closed, some doors open. Police and ambulance crew milled around. And in the midst, the injured. Some walking wounded, clearly with broken bones; others on stretchers, unconscious. The eerie thing was the lack of blood. Allie was accustomed to road crashes or violent clashes where the blood flowed freely. Not here.

She headed for the entrance to the gymnasium, following a pair of ambulance crew. Nobody stopped her, and she realised that in her casual clothes, she didn't look like a journalist. But in her head, she was in journalist mode. She walked into a scene of terrible disorganisation. No plan had swung into action. Panicked faces. Bodies on stretchers, on advertising hoardings, on the bare floor. The frantic living, trying to rescue the dying. She walked through the dead, trying to make sense of what she was seeing.

Allie drank it all in, trying to shape it in her head. The collision between her human reaction and her professional response forced her to choose between emotional collapse and a conditioned distance that let her function. She had a job to do; recording the horror with as dispassionate an eye as she could manage — that mattered.

Later, when she had to confront that afternoon, it came only in a series of surreal cameos. The chaos of the gymnasium; the young lad in a Liverpool shirt fitting on the floor; the doctor trying to carry out triage with nowhere to direct those who might yet be saved; the shock on faces as they walked in and saw the carnage. And everywhere, the dead, the dying and the ones who didn't know what was happening to them. Policemen moving among the recently alive, itemising their personal effects, counting their money as if

280

that mattered.

The police station pressed into inadequate service as a holding area for the friends and relatives. The ones who had been at the game and the ones who had driven the eighty miles from Liverpool in a state of meltdown, not knowing if their father, their brother, their sister, their son, their daughter or their lover was alive or dead. The overspill into the boys' club across the road, a place so dank and depressing it felt no good news could ever come out of it. And the flood of social workers, clergymen, bereavement counsellors, whose only use was to escort people to their vicarages to use the phone to call the hospitals in search of information about the ones they loved.

The insistence from those who had been there that the fans hadn't broken down an exit gate; the police had opened it and let thousands flood into an already overcrowded area. An insistence denied vehemently by the police, who spoke of drunken thugs without tickets.

The conversations — Allie refused to call them interviews, because they truly were conversations — with people desperate for news, with weeping middle-aged men whose sons had been separated from them in the crush as more people poured into an already overcrowded terracing pen, with parents who wanted only to keep their child alive by talking about them.

The apparently brutal process of identifying the dead; bodies brought back from the hospitals and added to the ones that remained at Hillsborough; ninety-four, the final headcount, captured on grotesque Polaroid snaps pinned to a board in the entrance area of a football-club gymnasium; devastated relatives confronted with the bodies of their loved ones only if they'd picked them out of the macabre line-up, only to be prevented from a final farewell kiss because the bodies were now the property of the coroner.

The vigils at the city's two hospitals; families huddled on uncomfortable chairs, clinging to hope and to each other. Waiting to hear news. The hysterical relief when a son emerged with his plastered arm in a sling, discharged to go home to smothering love and nightmares.

All of this Allie saw and knew she'd never forget. And still she did her job. She filed copy, she liaised with her freelances and the team of reporters sent up from London. She spoke to Rona, who had submitted a series of interviews with fans who had been in the ground, including a heart-breaking one with two young Scousers who had been in the terracing above the fatal area. They'd managed to pull three fans up to safety, but they were weeping at their failure to rescue more.

By the time the final edition had left the presses, Allie was so exhausted she could barely speak in sentences. They left the hospital, turning their backs on the catastrophe. Allie walked to the car at Rona's side, moving like an old woman, every step slow and cautious. They sat in silence in the car, staring out across the city lights. Finally, Rona spoke. 'I don't know how you do this.'

Allie turned the key in the ignition. 'I'm really not sure I have another one of these in me. Lockerbie, the M1 plane crash, now this. Rona, I'm truly scared of what this job is doing to me.'

40

Hans had arrived at Tante Lisl's apartment laden with shopping bags crammed with vegetables, breads and cheeses. Before he could say anything, Genevieve pointed at the door. 'Fredi locked me in. Like I'm a prisoner.'

He looked flustered. 'There's only one set of keys, we don't want anybody walking in on you.' His smile was conciliatory. 'Anyway, I'm planning to stay with you from now on,' he said. Then a moment of uncertainty flickered in his eyes. 'If you want me to?'

Genevieve waited for a moment before putting him out of his misery. 'Oh, I think that will stop me growing bored.'

He dumped the bags and kissed her. 'By the way, I passed one of the neighbours on the stairs. I said Lisl was my mother's aunt and I was borrowing her apartment while I was in Berlin to do some research for my history dissertation. She seemed to think there was nothing unusual about that.'

'Clever. It explains you coming and going. Though she might wonder about the size of your appetite!'

He pulled her into his arms but in spite of the flare of desire she'd felt, Genevieve had kept her eyes on the prize. She'd pushed him away, wagging her finger. 'First, we get the business out of the way, then we have all the time in the world for pleasure. Did you bring the camera?'

Disappointed, Hans rolled his eyes. 'Yes, madame.'

'I think I should be stripped down to my under-wear,' Genevieve said. 'For dramatic effect. Because that shows very clearly I'm not in a position to escape.' As she spoke, she pulled off her sweater and camisole.

'You are too much temptation,' he complained.

'Find something to tie me up with,' she commanded, slipping out of her boots and jeans. Obediently Hans opened the cupboard under the sink and rooted around. She grabbed a straight-backed kitchen chair and looked around for a bare wall. 'We'll have to use the bathroom,' she muttered, dragging the chair down the hall. 'Bloody awful pictures everywhere.'

By the time he'd found some clothes line, Gene-vieve had placed the chair against the white tiled wall. There was, she thought, nothing that could identify the apartment even if Tante Lisl herself saw the picture. 'OK. Now tie me up and make it look uncomfortable. I hope you're not into bondage?'

Hans chuckled. 'It has never appealed to me.'

'You need to get my scarf, it's hanging in the hall. Use that for a gag. There's an outside chance my father might recognise it. He doesn't pay much atten-tion to fashion details, but I've had it for a while and it's possible he's registered it in his brain.'

Hans busied himself with the rope, loosely tying her hands behind her back then looping the rope around her torso and arms. He made a show of some fancy knots around her waist. Then with a pained expres-sion, he gagged her with her silk scarf. 'I'm sorry,' he said. 'I hate doing this. It won't be for long, I promise.'

Finally, he propped a copy of that morning's *Tagess-piegel* against her stomach, the date clearly visible. He quickly took three snaps with the Polaroid camera, and as soon as they had developed, he undid the gag.

284

'Are you OK? Can I get you some water?' he asked anxiously.

Genevieve shook her head, her hair swinging in a thick arc around her face. 'That's really not a pleasant sensation,' she complained. 'Untie me. I need a proper drink.'

Hans did as he was told then reached for her to draw her into an embrace. But Genevieve had spent her whole life under the edict of 'work comes first' and it didn't even occur to her to abandon the maxim. 'Later,' she said sternly. 'First you have to get these photos to Fredi so she can have them couriered to your man in Glasgow. Until he delivers them to my father, we're prisoners here.'

'I can think of worse things, Genny,' he said, wistful.

Genevieve softened. 'Me too, handsome Hans. But first things first,' she added briskly, getting to her feet and stretching. 'And the sooner you leave, the sooner you will return.'

While he was gone, carefully locking her in again, she prowled around the apartment, opening what cupboards and drawers she'd ignored earlier. There was nothing that interested her apart from a beautiful carved wooden box that contained two packs of cards. She brought the box to the kitchen table and laid out a game of patience. It would pass the time till Hans returned. After that, she didn't imagine they'd run out of other games to play.

Genevieve was beginning to think being 'kidnapped' wasn't such a bad thing.

★ ★ ★

Sleep eluded Allie when she finally crawled into bed. Every time it crept up on her, memory surfaced and confronted her with an image she desperately wanted to erase. And every time, she started awake, eyes wide open and gritty, chest tight with the unprocessed stress of what she'd witnessed and what she'd been told. It had been like this after Lockerbie, she remembered. Less so after the M1 plane crash, because she'd arrived after the worst of the carnage had been dealt with. But it had still been weeks before her sleep had recovered.

She was no stranger to the shocks and stresses of the job. She'd known intellectually this was no job for the faint-hearted; she'd learned it viscerally when she was less than six months into her traineeship. She'd managed to turn up at the scene of a murder before the police had arrived to cordon it off. A man stabbed in the doorway of a betting shop. Blood sprayed up the wall and pooled on the pavement. A tight knot of rubberneckers clustered to one side, one man pulling on his straining terrier's leash. 'It was the dog that smelled it,' he kept saying. 'Little bugger dragged me right across the street.' Though it had rocked Allie's self-assurance, she'd written it up and slept the sleep of the adrenaline-crashed.

But as the years had accumulated, so it seemed the impact of the horrors had deepened. She'd meant what she said to Rona: she was afraid of the effect that the sharp end of news reporting was having on her. She'd retreated from that when she'd been running the investigations team and had been the better for it. But that option no longer existed. When she'd worked out her notice, Allie knew she'd have to find another kind of job. She looked around at her colleagues and knew she didn't want to be them when she was fifty, either emotionally frozen or dependent on drink to silence the demons.

Allie sighed and shifted on to her side. Rona grumbled in her sleep but didn't wake up. She didn't have Allie's history with horror, and she'd only experienced Hillsborough at one remove. Or maybe she was just better adjusted. Either way, she was spark out.

Allie gave up the fruitless battle and slipped carefully out of bed. She wrapped her dressing gown around her and headed for her office. There was a shelf of to-be-read books by the door; there would be something there to absorb her and transport her to a different headspace. *Carpe Jugulum* leapt out at her; Terry Pratchett's comic fantasies were a perennial favourite. She read the jacket copy, saw that this featured her favourite characters — the Discworld witches — settled down on the living-room sofa and lost herself in the absurdities of vampires and magic.

By the time Rona emerged a couple of hours later, Allie felt more in command of herself. Rona squeezed in beside her and reached for her hand. 'You couldn't sleep?'

Allie shook her head. 'My head wouldn't shut up.' She waggled the book at Rona. 'So I filled it with beautiful nonsense.'

'Are you going to have to go back to Sheffield today? Or Liverpool?'

'No point. They're both going to be mobbed with media. There's no chance of me teasing out a line that'll hold till next Sunday. The lads who came up from London will be crawling all over it anyway. Obviously I'll keep across it, but as far as getting out there is concerned, I'll leave it till later in the week.

Wednesday or Thursday.'

'Makes sense. What are you going to do about Lockhart?'

Allie pushed her tousled hair back and sighed. 'I presume you're driving back today?'

Rona pulled a face. 'I kind of have to. I'm supposed to be in the office tomorrow. We're working on a dummy for the colour supp.'

'That's what I thought. I don't want to disrupt your working week any more than I have already. Howsabout I come back to Glasgow with you? Then I can grovel to Lockhart face to face and present him with the human interest story? I'm not giving him the investigation — he'll only spike it so it doesn't offend his East German pals.'

'I'd like that. Company on the drive, and we can have a bonus night together.'

Allie's grin was sardonic. 'At your mum's?'

Rona laughed. 'Or we could pamper ourselves and check into a hotel? A couple of nights at One Devonshire Gardens and you might start to feel human again?'

'It'd be a start.' Allie leaned in to Rona, knowing how lucky she was to be with someone who understood how to take care of her. 'Let's do it.'

41

Peter Thomson wasn't at his desk in Glasgow University library stacks that Monday morning. He'd phoned in sick, claiming a gastric upset that had kept him up all night. There was nothing wrong with his stomach, of course, apart from the clench of nerves as he waited for the courier delivery from Germany. He felt anxious and trapped. Between his cheap furniture and his piles of books and pamphlets about the crisis facing the planet, there was barely enough space in his one-bedroomed flat in Govan to move between the rooms, never mind to pace nervously.

Bloody Fredi Schroeder and her magnetism. They'd met at a conference three years before and he'd been captivated by her oratory. Trying to outline that to anyone else had tied Peter in knots more times than he could count. Still, he was slowly but surely building a cadre of supporters who shared his passion for saving the planet from itself. Meantime, Fredi was forging ahead with her crusade. He hadn't wanted to be involved in what felt like a cruel act of extortion but she'd somehow persuaded him aboard.

The hours crawled by until eventually the doorbell rang. Peter snatched the small package from the courier, scribbled a deliberately illegible signature on his clipboard and closed the door in his face. He went back to his work table and sliced the tightly taped parcel open with a paperknife. Inside was another envelope, addressed to Wallace Lockhart, Voil House,

Glasgow. *Personal and Urgent. By Hand.* The calligraphy was obviously foreign in its swoops and angles. Peter was happy about that; anything that drew attention away from him was a plus.

There was also a single sheet of paper, folded once. He opened it, fingers trembling. 'For delivery, as discussed. Confirm by telephone. Good luck.' There was no signature, but he recognised Fredi's style as well as her handwriting.

Peter slipped the envelope into his pocket and pulled his waterproof jacket over his head. It was drizzling outside, the kind of thick small rain that made him feel like he was being smothered by a low-lying cloud. His face was dripping wet by the time he'd reached the end of the street.

Fifteen minutes later, a drookit Peter chained his bike to the railings of Voil House. He kept to the central drive, a wide sweep of well-kempt gravel, in spite of the sign saying, PRIVATE. STRICTLY NO ENTRY.

The mansion was a louring presence in the grey light of the afternoon. Before he could get within a dozen yards of the imposing portico, the door swung open and a large man in a black suit emerged. 'This is private property, pal,' he said in a dark Glaswegian growl. 'Just turn around and walk away and we'll say no more about it.'

Peter stood his ground, aware that he didn't cut much of a figure. 'I've got an urgent letter for Mr Lockhart,' he said.

'Put it in the post.'

'It's to be delivered by hand.' Peter managed to sound firmer than he felt. He pulled out the letter. 'You might as well take it now I'm here.'

A long hard glare. Then the man beckoned him.

'I'm only taking pity on you because you look like a drowned rat,' he said, reaching for the envelope. 'Now away to fuck with you.' He waved his hand in dismissal.

Peter tramped back down the drive, anticlimax dragging his feet. He'd done his bit. And at least he'd had his hood up. If this all went south, chances were he'd keep his head below the parapet.

Bloody Fredi.

★　★　★

Inside Voil House, Allie and Rona were growing restive. Allie had called Lockhart's office first thing on Monday morning and been told he was in London and would be back in the afternoon. 'If you go to Voil House for two o'clock, he'll see you there.'

The two women had turned up promptly just before two and been shown into his office. Now it was after three and in typical Lockhart fashion, there was no sign of him. They'd been served tepid coffee and that morning's Ace Media newspapers but Allie's patience was fast running out.

'Don't let it wind you up,' Rona advised. 'He only does it to provoke a reaction. It's much more satisfying to smile sweetly and look like you're not bothered. I usually take a book with me when I'm summoned.'

Allie swallowed her irritation and flicked through the *Globe* for the third time. Hillsborough still occupied the front end of the paper, stories of witnesses and survivors filling the pages with heart-rending stories. To her satisfaction, the Lockhart papers had downplayed scurrilous accusations from the police about drunken fans robbing the dead and urinating on bodies. The *Sun* had disgracefully splashed these on their front page. But none of the fans or ambulance crew Allie had spoken to had even hinted at anything other than heroic attempts at rescue from those in the stadium. She couldn't help thinking it was a fiction spread by a panicking police hierarchy trying to escape responsibility for their part in the disaster. But she knew there would be an inquiry; surely the truth would come out then and the blackguarding of the Liverpool supporters would be exposed?

It was almost four when Ace Lockhart swaggered in, overcoat flaring out at his sides like a superhero cape. He shrugged it off, tossed it on a side table and made for his desk chair. 'Ladies.' The greeting was perfunctory. 'Good to see you. Rona, I was astonished to see your name among the bylines in the *Sunday Globe*'s coverage of the Hillsborough disaster.' An interrogative pause.

'I was with Allie in Manchester when the call came through. It got me out of weeding the vegetable patch.'

'Good job. I hope you won't be putting in for a casual shift.' They all smiled politely. 'You pulled it together well, Burns. But I expected no less. Now, where's my copy from Berlin?'

Allie took the folded sheets from her bag and pushed them across his desk. But before he could read them, his PA bustled in. 'Sorry to interrupt, Ace, but this has been hand-delivered for you. The man who brought it was apparently very insistent that it was urgent and personal.' She proffered a slightly crumpled envelope.

Lockhart took it with a sigh. 'Another crank. Convinced he's got the story of the century.' Casually, he slit the envelope open and pulled out a folded sheet of paper. Three Polaroid photographs slipped out and landed face down on the desk. He grabbed them, barely glancing at the images. Then he froze, his face flushing dark red. In silence, he studied them closely one by one. He appeared to have stopped breathing. Then he slammed them face down on the desk and squeezed his eyes tight shut. He took a deep shuddering breath.

'Are you all right?' Allie asked, wondering if he was having some sort of stroke.

His eyes snapped open. 'Do I fucking seem all right?' He snatched the sheet of paper and as he read, the flood of colour receded from his face. He looked like a bad caricature of himself, the lines and creases vivid, the bags under his eyes suddenly the most colour in his ashen face. 'Oh. My. God.' The words were almost inaudible.

'What's wrong?' Rona leaned towards him. 'What's happened, Ace?'

He swallowed hard. 'Genny,' he croaked.

'Your daughter?' What on earth was going on with the dashing arrogant princess Allie had left in Berlin only a few days ago?

He said nothing, but pushed the Polaroids towards them. Rona picked them up, holding them so Allie could see. The first was a close-up of *Tagesspiegel*, clearly showing Friday's date. The second was a full-length shot of a woman stripped to her underwear, tightly bound to a chair. The newspaper was propped on her lap. Even though she was gagged with a scarf, she was identifiable as Genevieve Lockhart. A stab of shock hit Allie in the chest. The final photograph was a head shot, Genevieve's eyes tearful and pleading. Now they could see the gag was a silk scarf with a delicate pattern of leaves and stems. For once, Allie

293

had no words.

'Ace,' Rona said. 'This is terrible. What does the letter say?'

He passed it across. Allie could see he was still in shock; in normal circumstances, she thought he's probably have told them to fuck off. She read the note over Rona's shoulder. She could see exactly why it had provoked that state in Lockhart.

The Red Army Faction is not dead, it was only sleeping. How much is your daughter worth, Mr Lockhart? We think half a million pounds deposited in our Swiss bank account. You have three days to get the money together. Otherwise you will never see your daughter alive again. You can see from the photographs that this is not a hoax. Do not involve the police. If you do, we will know, believe me. Any involvement with the authorities will end this negotiation at once. We will call you on your private number on your private island where you cannot be overheard on Wednesday at precisely noon to discuss arrangements for the handover. You would be very foolish to think you can outplay us, Mr Lockhart. The life of your only child is at stake.

42

Allie and Rona exchanged shocked looks. No wonder Lockhart looked thunderstruck. 'What am I to do?' he groaned.

'You must have people who can help,' Rona said. 'You managed to get Allie out of an East German jail, Ace.'

'But you'll have to be careful. They say no police,' Allie cut in.

He buried his head in his hands. Rona looked at Allie, who shrugged helplessly. They waited in silence. Finally, he raised his head, eyes damp with tears. 'You can help,' he said, stabbing a finger towards Allie.

'How? What can I do?' Allie tried not to show the panic she felt.

'You were in Berlin with Genevieve last week, and that's a West Berlin newspaper in those pics. You must know something about what she was doing, who she was seeing.' It came out like an accusation.

'We didn't have that kind of conversation.'

'You met her driver, you can talk to him. He will understand you are to be trusted.'

'You're clutching at straws, Ace,' Rona said, keeping her voice calm.

'Straws are all I have. Burns, you're always shouting about what a great investigative journalist you are. You complain I took that away from you. Well, now I'm giving it back to you.'

'This is not what I do,' Allie said.

'It is now. Rona, are you going to sit there and let her weasel out of this? If anyone can find Genny, it's Burns. She knows how to work undercover. And it's payback time,' he said savagely. 'If it wasn't for me, you'd be in an East German jail, Burns. You owe me.'

An uncomfortable silence. At last, Allie spoke. 'I really don't think I'm the right fit for this.'

'Nobody would take you for a polis,' Rona said, unhelpfully.

'Exactly.' Lockhart stood up and walked round his desk, clumsy and awkward as they'd never seen him. He leaned over Allie, fists resting on the arms of her chair, his face inches from hers. She could see every hair in his perfectly groomed eyebrows, every imperfection in his skin; she could smell the acrid cigar breath. 'You owe me. If it was your woman in those pictures, you'd already be halfway to the airport.'

He was right. That still didn't make her the right person for the task. But it was clear they weren't going to get out of here till she agreed. 'I'll try.' Even as she spoke, Allie thought she sounded ridiculous. But Lockhart's eyes lit up and some colour came back to his cheeks.

Galvanised at the prospect of action, he pushed himself upright and away from her. 'My car is outside. Burns, take it to the airport. My plane is there. Fly to Frankfurt. We will arrange an onward flight to Berlin. Our driver, Dieter, the man who drove you back from the East? He'll meet you at the airport. He always drives Genny when she's there. He'll know where she was going, who she was meeting. Find her, Burns. Find her.' He flapped his hands at her as if he were shooing geese.

Allie shrugged, as if to say, 'It's your funeral' and

296

stood up. As she turned for the door, Rona got to her feet. 'Not you, Rona. You stay here. I need you here,' he insisted.

Allie wasn't sure what he needed Rona for, but she suspected it was some sort of insurance policy to keep her on track. They exchanged a look, Rona giving her a quick nod to indicate her acceptance of the terms. 'Good luck, my love,' she said, her words covering the worry in her eyes.

Lockhart was shouting orders at his PA as Allie left the room. And at once, Allie was caught up in the most absurd mission of her career. Lockhart's Rolls-Royce pulled up at the front steps as she emerged, his driver hurrying out to open the door for her. The luxurious interior was more like a living room than a car, with a glass-fronted cocktail cabinet facing her. She sank back in the seat and wondered how on earth she was going to manage this. At least she'd obeyed the number one rule of news journalism — never leave home without your passport and your press card.

* * *

Allie disembarked from the last flight of the day into Berlin to find a broad-shouldered man holding a card with her name in block capitals. Dressed in a black suit over a black polo-neck sweater, his hair a salt-and-pepper crew cut, he reminded her of Maximilian Schell in *The Assisi Underground*, which she found slightly unsettling.

'I am Dieter, Frau Burns,' he said. 'We were not introduced before. Welcome back to Berlin.'

Disconcerted by her elevation in German eyes from 'Fraulein' to 'Frau', she said, 'If I'm to call you

Dieter, you must call me Allie. We're both working for Herr Lockhart, after all.'

He frowned momentarily, then nodded with a smile. 'Do you have luggage?'

'No, I didn't have time for that.'

Impassive, he said. 'Allie, I am instructed to answer all your questions and provide what you ask for. But first I must take you to your hotel. Herr Lockhart has spoken to them and said that you will be taking over Fraulein Lockhart's suite. It is as she left it on Friday, so perhaps you will find some useful information there?'

'That's helpful.' She followed him out of the terminal as he walked briskly to the car. She almost had to trot to keep up with him. 'What was Genevieve doing in West Berlin before she disappeared?'

'I don't know all she was doing because she only called on me when she needed a driver. She was spending time with political radicals. Environment campaigners, socialists, people who object to nuclear power. She said it did not look good if she arrived in a Mercedes with a driver.' He stopped by that very car, sleek and gleaming under the airport lights, and opened the back door.

'Can I sit up front with you? I'd feel more comfortable with that.'

Dieter clearly didn't like the idea but she reckoned he'd worked for the Lockharts long enough not to argue. He opened the passenger door for her and shut it with a soft click once she was aboard. Once they'd cleared the airport, Allie said, 'What kind of mood was Genevieve in after she brought me back from the East? Was she happy? Tense? Worried?'

He thought for a moment. 'I would say she seemed

excited. She was looking forward to seeing her friends that evening.'

'Do you know what friends?'

He shook his head. 'She did not tell me who she was seeing. Like you, Allie, I am just an employee, not someone to confide in.'

'Do you know who any of her friends were?'

He flashed a quick look at her as they drew up at a traffic light. 'There is a car phone in the back. Sometimes she used it. I heard her say the name 'Fredi'.'

'Was that a boyfriend, do you think?'

He grinned. 'To anyone in Berlin who is interested in politics, Fredi is not a boy. Fredi is Frederika Schroeder. She is the charismatic leader of the Green movement here in Berlin. Not the official Green Party, but the radicals who think the party is too safe, too slow. Maybe Genevieve was spending time with her.' A chuckle. 'Or maybe you're right, she has a boyfriend called Fredi. Also, she spoke to someone called Berndt. Short calls, arrangements to meet.'

It was a start, Allie thought. There might be more clues in Genevieve's room. She hoped that would produce more leads to ask Dieter about. But it was too late to follow anything up tonight. They drew up in front of an imposing hotel entrance and she said, 'Come and have breakfast with me tomorrow. Eight o'clock, yes?'

'I'll see you then,' he agreed.

'Oh, and Dieter? Do you have access to a different car?'

'A different car?'

'This is too conspicuous for what I have in mind.'

A faint smile. 'My wife has a Volkswagen Polo. Nobody would give it a second glance here in Berlin.

I will bring it tomorrow.'

Satisfied, Allie strode into the hotel lobby, feeling decidedly underdressed. She didn't care. She had a job to do and Ace Lockhart was holding his own hostage to make sure she'd do it.

★ ★ ★

By the time she met Dieter for breakfast, Allie had wrung what little information was to be gleaned from what Genevieve Lockhart had left in her hotel room. Given that there was no passport, diary, wallet or handbag to be seen, she thought it was safe to assume that she hadn't been taken from her room without her consent. Wherever she'd been kidnapped, it hadn't been here.

It was hard to know whether any of her clothes were missing. The wardrobe held a couple of dresses, two pairs of trousers and a pair of jeans, a smart blazer and half a dozen blouses, all with labels Allie recognised (thanks to Rona) as being well outside her own price bracket. The chest of drawers contained an assortment of expensive lingerie; it didn't look as if comfort had been the primary consideration. Allie had been half considering borrowing a clean pair of pants, but after checking out Genevieve's choices, she'd opted for the traditional on-the-road reporter's solution of rinsing out her own underwear with shower gel, and draping it to dry over the radiator. Though in this bathroom, she had the even more efficient option of a heated towel rail.

What paperwork was in the room related to the business of Pythagoras Press and meant next to nothing to Allie. Frustratingly, there was nothing about any other interests she was there to pursue.

She'd ended her day with a call to Rona, who saved her the bother of asking Lockhart exactly what his daughter was supposed to be doing in Berlin. 'She's on a mission,' Rona explained. 'Lockhart thinks Gorbachev is losing his grip on the empire. He thinks some of the republics are going to break away from Russia and the Soviet Union will collapse. Pythagoras is his cash cow and a lot of its profit comes from its dealings with Soviet scientists and their work so he's trying to establish links with the dissident groups he thinks could end up running the show once the dust settles. And that's what Genny's been doing for the past few months.'

'That all makes sense,' Allie said. 'But it doesn't explain what she's doing in West Berlin.'

'Lockhart says the key to East Berlin is the dissident groups that have strong links with the radicals in West Berlin. Because the East is so riddled with Stasi informants, it's easier for Genny to build those bridges in the West.'

'And a lot nicer than being based in the East, from what little I saw,' Allie said drily. 'Thanks for that. It feels very weird staying in her suite, surrounded by all her stuff.'

'I bet. Has she got lovely clothes?'

Allie laughed. 'You're so superficial. I don't know about lovely, but they've got some serious labels. She'd give you a run for your money.'

'Maybe, but I bet she doesn't get discount like I do. I'm sorry we missed our second night at One Devonshire Gardens, by the way.'

'Me too. I'd much rather be there with you. Stay close to Lockhart and keep me posted.'

'That's a bit of a problem. He's going off first thing tomorrow on the chopper to Ranaig. He's cancelled all his meetings and he's going to hole up there to get himself set up for the ransom arrangements.'

Allie sighed. 'I'll just have to do my best at this end, then.'

'Take care, not chances, my love.'

Later, as Allie fought to find sleep in the wide bed with its crisp clean sheets, Rona's words echoed in her head. There was, she thought, as much chance of fulfilling them as there was of finding Genevieve Lockhart before the ticking clock ran out.

43

Dieter was waiting for Allie when she walked into the breakfast room. He'd dressed down to match the car; pressed jeans and a black polo shirt. They found a quiet table and worked their way through coffee, rolls and an assortment of cheese and charcuterie. 'I want to take a look at Frederika Schroeder. Do you know where she lives?'

'No, but I know where the office of her organisation is. We can watch the building and I can point her out to you. Then we can follow her and see where she leads us.'

It wasn't much of a plan but there was no better place to start. Their destination was a few minutes away but there was nowhere on the street to park with a view of the storefront the radical Greens occupied. Dieter circled the block a couple of times but had no luck. There was, however, a corner café with an angled line of sight to the office door so they took up a post there. 'As soon as there is a parking space, I'll move the car,' Dieter said.

Allie was on her second cup of ferociously strong coffee when Dieter stiffened like a pointer who sees a game bird fall. 'That's her,' he said. 'The blonde in the black leather coat.' Her back was to them, but when she turned into the building, her profile was clear and he was in no doubt. 'That's Fredi,' he said firmly. Allie's shoulders relaxed a little; now she knew her target.

A spot opened up for the car half an hour later and they moved from the café to slouch in the Polo. It was a long wait. Fredi emerged shortly after noon and set off on foot down the street. Allie jumped out and followed, thankful that there were other people around. As they'd agreed, Dieter took up a position behind Allie. Fredi walked on, apparently unsuspicious, and turned into a bookshop. Allie slowed to a halt and studied the window of the bakery next door. Dieter leaned against a wall and read his newspaper.

Fredi emerged a few minutes later with a book-sized brown paper bag and their little procession carried on. Across a square, round the corner and into a busy bar. Dieter pulled a cap low over his eyes and together they walked in. Fredi had joined a man at the bar, greeting him with a kiss on both cheeks. He caught the barmaid's eye and they soon had glasses of beer in front of them. Allie and Dieter found a table with a good view and she itemised the man in her mind while he ordered a couple of beers from the waitress. Early thirties, at a guess. Medium height, shaggy brown hair, good-looking in an open-faced way, blue eyes set wide apart. Jeans, work boots and a workman's jacket, none of which looked as if they'd ever done a day's manual labour. There was a canvas shopping bag at his feet, a loaf of bread and a cabbage poking out of the top. Fredi took a hardback book out of the bag and waggled it in front of the man. They were close enough for Allie to recognise, to her surprise, the cover of Len Deighton's *Spy Hook*.

The man took the book and tucked it into his shopping bag. Allie nudged Dieter. 'That's an English book she just gave to that bloke. Maybe he's Berndt? When they leave, you follow Fredi and I'll follow him. It

304

might be a wild coincidence, but maybe it's for Genevieve? To keep her from getting bored and difficult?'

He shrugged. 'If you say so. Do you have a pen?' Allie handed one over. He scribbled a number on a beer mat. 'This is my number. My wife will be home. Call her and tell her where you are, and if I have a message for you, I will leave it with her. Talk slowly. She can understand English but not if you speak fast.'

They swallowed their beer in slow silence, waiting for Fredi and her friend to drink up and leave. They were deep in conversation; she seemed to be giving him instructions that he was responding to. Eventually, she drained her glass and clapped him on the shoulder, giving him a smile of maximum wattage. Dieter gave her a moment, then went after her. The man at the bar took another few minutes over the last of his beer then, with a frown, he picked up his bag and left.

Allie followed him to the end of the street to a wide boulevard with tramlines running up the middle. He crossed to the tram stop and joined a short queue. Allie dithered, not sure whether to wait for someone else to join the queue and risk missing the tram, or to go for it right away. In the end, the decision was made for her by the arrival of a tram and she had to run across the tracks to climb aboard at the last minute. Thankfully the man was further down the carriage with his back to her. If he and Fredi really were involved in the kidnap and ransom, they'd either taken steps to protect themselves or else they were ridiculously over-confident. But in her investigative experience, Allie knew only too well how often criminals considered they were much smarter than those trying to catch them.

Five stops later, the man stood up and made for the door. He didn't even glance at Allie as he passed her. As the tram drew to a halt, she got to her feet and exited behind him. Still he paid no attention to his surroundings. He turned into a narrow street of tall apartment buildings, stopping abruptly about halfway down. Allie carried on walking as he put down his bag and struggled with the front door. She registered the house number as she passed and continued to the corner.

She stopped and took stock. The houses seemed to contain eight apartments, two on each floor. There was no way of telling which apartment the man had entered. There was no obvious vantage point from where she could look up at the building and see in through the windows. Frustrated, Allie decided to call Dieter's wife. Now all she had to do was find a phone.

★ ★ ★

Ace Lockhart had always been good at snatching opportunity from the jaws of defeat. He thought of himself as a winner, even when the dice all seemed to be rolling against him. And by sheer force of will or personality, he'd managed to overcome odds and obstacles to reach his present pre-eminence. Sometimes it was by dint of smoke and mirrors but so far he'd succeeded in replacing them with substance.

The trouble was that this time the smoke was dissipating and the mirrors were tarnishing before his eyes. There would never have been a good moment for his daughter to be held to ransom, but this was the worst possible time. There was something inherently catastrophic in a situation where his only escape route lay in the hands of Allie Burns.

There had to be another way.

He had come to Ranaig to escape the background noise of running Ace Media. He needed to think. He hadn't even summoned his staff. There was food in the freezer and the pantry, there were logs enough to see him through a bitter winter and the window that had been broken by that bloody seagull had long since been repaired. He could survive perfectly well on his own with the satellite phone.

It had been raining when the helicopter had landed, but he'd barely noticed. He was already dressed for Ranaig — wide wale corduroy plus fours tucked into gaiters, stout shoes with nailed soles, fisherman's sweater and an outsize waxed coat, topped with a tweed deerstalker. It was a caricature of a Highland laird, but nobody had ever dared laugh. Not in his presence, at least.

The house closed around Lockhart like a comfort blanket. It was the only place he treated with respect. He hung up his clothes, he loaded the dishwasher, he emptied his own ashtrays. Now, he went through to the den and poured himself an uncharacteristically large whisky. He settled in front of the wide picture window in the living room and stared out at the sea. Great slabs of steely water swelled and broke on the rocks in a scatter of spray. There was no visible separation between sea and sky, the horizon lost in a haze of grey. It matched his mood perfectly.

He took the Polaroids from his back pocket and flicked miserably through them again, as if he could will them to transform themselves. Tears welled up at the thought of his beloved Genny in such a cruel predicament. And all because he was Wallace Lockhart, media baron and multimillionaire.

And that was the terrible irony. In the eyes of the world, he was rich beyond dreams of avarice. The truth was hideous and he didn't have enough time to make it beautiful again. His daughter's life was at stake. But the cupboard was bare.

He'd always been a man who seized life by the throat. He'd done whatever it took to survive. But if saving Genny meant exiting the stage, it might be time for his final bow. The last remaining question was whether he loved his daughter more than life itself.

44

It was over an hour before Dieter arrived. She saw him from the corner café where she had settled in at a window table. She hurried outside to meet him. He'd changed his clothes again; grey cords and a cream crew-neck sweater. He made Allie feel dingy in the same outfit she'd left home in the day before. 'No sign of life,' she said, as they got into the car. 'He's not come out. Maybe he's just an innocent guy who likes English spy fiction.'

'But maybe he is more than that.'

'Where did Fredi lead you?' she asked.

'I followed her to an apartment block near the Ku'damm. Her name is on one of the mailboxes, so it appears that is where she lives. It's very typical Berlin.'

'What if Genevieve's in Fredi's flat?'

He shook his head. 'I know the layout of those flats. The living room is big, but the the bathroom is too small to take those photographs. There is a little park opposite and I was able to get a view of Fredi's living room. And I looked through binoculars —'

'Bloody hell, Dieter, that's resourceful.'

He shrugged. 'I keep them with me. Sometimes Fraulein

Lockhart takes a walk with people she is meeting. Herr Lockhart likes me to keep watch over her.' He pulled a face. 'It's supposed to stop something like this happening.'

'So what did you see?'

'Fredi made lunch.' His tone was wistful. 'Also there is no blank wall where it would be possible to place Genevieve. Unless they are holding her somewhere else, I think she must be in the apartment where this man has come.'

'First, we need to discover which flat he is in. Which I'm guessing is easier said than done . . . . It's impossible to see in the windows. Even the ground-floor flats are too high.'

'I have an idea.' He looked very pleased with himself. 'My wife plays the piano for the children's choir of the church. They always are short of money so they collect at people's doors. She will come here on her bicycle. Someone will let her in and she will knock on all the doors to ask for contrisbutions. Mostly they will say no but we will find out where the man is, I think?'

Allie grinned. She was beginning to understand the confidence Ace Lockhart placed in this man. 'That's brilliant,' she crowed, patting him on the shoulder. 'I can describe the background in the pictures and if we're lucky she might be able to tell whether the photographs might have been taken there.'

Dieter looked doubtful. 'It's much to ask.'

Allie knew better than to push. Always better to let them come to you. 'There's a phone round the corner, just past the café.' He nodded and left. When he returned, they sat in silence, eyes on the apartment building, for another twenty minutes. Then a woman on a sit-up-and-beg bicycle came down the street towards them. She wore a dark macintosh, under which Allie caught glimpses of a floral dress, and blond hair peeped out from a headscarf patterned with anemones. She came to a halt alongside the car and propped her bike against the wall. She waggled her fingers at Dieter and climbed into the back of the car, carrying a wicker basket with a lid.

'This is my wife Margarethe,' Dieter said proudly. 'Margarethe, may I present Frau Burns?'

'Please, call me Allie,' she protested, twisting round to offer her hand.

Margarethe took her fingers in a firm grip, blushing the while. 'Hello. I am happy to be meeting you.'

'I am so pleased you're willing to help us,' Allie said. 'We are very grateful.'

Dieter translated rapidly and she blushed even harder. '*Bitte*,' she said, nodding frantically.

He spoke to her in German, his intonation suggesting a question at the end of his little speech. He turned to Allie. 'I told her what we needed to know, and if she could see into the apartment. She is quite clear. *Alles klar, ja, Margarethe?*'

'*Stimmt*,' came the response. Even Allie knew enough German to understand the reassurance of that exchange.

Margarethe opened her basket and handed them both a roll wrapped in greaseproof paper. Beneath them were a bundle of inexpertly produced flyers promoting the *Chor der Kinderkapelle* and a notebook with *Spenden* written in black marker pen on the cover. She closed the lid and exchanged a few words with Dieter. Then with another wave of the hand, she left them and walked firmly across the street.

'She's good,' Allie observed, watching Margarethe pressing one buzzer then another, trying to gain entry. She was successful on the third try and vanished indoors.

'She also makes a good *Sülze* sandwich,' he said,

looking inside his.

'What's that?' Allie peered suspiciously at what looked like small chunks of meat in jelly. There was a sliced pickle laid along the centre.

'I don't know the English,' Dieter said. 'But if you don't like it, I'll eat yours.'

One bite and Allie was sold. 'No chance,' she said. It was good to have something so tasty to take her mind off the anxious wait.

* * *

What Dieter had failed to mention was that Margarethe was a leading light of the local amateur opera. Playing a part was nothing new for her. Four of the first six doors she knocked on gave her a handful of pfennigs. There was no reply at the sixth, but the seventh apartment gave her a whole Deutschmark. That only left the top-floor far door.

Margarethe knocked and waited. She heard the faint murmur of voices but no footsteps came towards the door. She knocked again, more imperiously this time. Hesitant footsteps, then a man's voice demanding that she identify herself.

She loudly told the door that she was collecting donations for the chapel children's choir and everyone else in the building had been very generous. Reading the name by the door, she took a chance and said that Frau Braun had always been very open-handed in her support. How she loved the children singing!

A mutter of voices. Then the rattle of locks and the door opened a few inches. She could see half a face and a flop of brown fringe. Margarethe gave her most glowing smile and thrust a flyer at him. Taken aback, he retreated and she advanced. The door swung open further and she could see down the hall to the dining table. She took in two glasses and two plates before he thrust a five-mark note into her basket and almost pushed her out of the door.

Satisfied, Margarethe almost skipped down the stairs. She'd found the man her husband had described to her. And you didn't have to be a detective to see that whatever was going on in that top flat, it wasn't normal.

Back at the car, she relayed the encounter in exhaustive detail, Dieter translating painstakingly. The more she heard, the more confused Allie felt. Margarethe was clearly talking about the same man. The jury was out on the apartment, since the only walls she'd seen had been crammed with framed photographs and paintings. The odd behaviour pointed in one direction, the muttered conversations in another. If Genevieve was the other person in the flat, why had she not called out for help, or made a bid for freedom? Dieter pointed out that there could be two jailers and Genevieve could be restrained in another room.

Allie groaned. 'You're right, of course. But someone connected with the only definite contact we have for Genevieve is behaving very oddly. And he's definitely not Frau Braun.'

'But the other person in the apartment might be,' Dieter protested.

'So why didn't she open her own door? And deny that she'd ever given money to the children's choir?'

They were good points, but they didn't take them any further forward. Allie sighed. 'There's one thing we know for sure. The kidnappers are going to phone Ace Lockhart tomorrow at noon. UK time, presumably. Now, from what you've told me about Fredi Schroeder, she's not the kind of woman to trust anybody but herself to make that call. She's too smart to use the phone in her apartment or the Green movement's office — she probably thinks the authorities have those phones bugged. So we need to tail her tomorrow morning. If she's making the call, we can be pretty sure we're on the right track.'

'And if she's sitting in a café drinking a mocha and eating a *krapfen*, we know we're back to the beginning.' Dieter looked glum.

'Yes, but then I can speak to her directly. Ask her who else Genevieve hung out with when she was in West Berlin. If she's not in it up to her neck, she'll want to clear her people of any involvement.'

'Are we going to wait here much longer?' Dieter asked. 'Only, Margarethe has to get home for the children.'

Allie looked across at the apartment. There were still at least a couple of hours of daylight. She didn't want to give up yet. 'Margarethe, can I borrow your bike?' she asked.

Dieter and Margarethe exchanged a few urgent sentences. 'You want to stay here with the bike and we leave?' he asked.

'*Stimmt.*'

He laughed. 'You will soon be fluent. You think that's a good idea?'

'Yes. And on your way home, you can call in at the Greens' office. See if they have any bumf —'

'What is 'bumf', please?'

Allie chuckled. 'Leaflets. Newsletters . . . Anything that might have names and photographs. We need to find out this guy's name, check out whether he's

314

Berndt.'

'*Alles klar.* Yes, I can do this. But will you be safe?'

'I can go back to the café. Get something to eat. If our mystery man emerges, I can follow him. And if Fredi Schroeder shows up . . .' Allie shrugged. 'Maybe he's her boyfriend.'

Dieter guffawed. 'That's impossible. She is . . . I don't know the word. *Homosexualle Frau. Lesbisch.*'

Allie gave a wry smile. 'Lesbian. I get it. In that case, probably not her boyfriend. So, can I borrow the bike?'

★ ★ ★

Across the street, on the fourth floor, Genevieve Lockhart was still teasing Hans. 'I can't believe you freaked out at an old woman collecting for a kids' choir.' She giggled.

'She wasn't that old,' he protested. 'How was I supposed to know who was knocking? It could have been the police.'

Genevieve scoffed. 'I told you, my father will not go to the police.'

'It might have been a neighbour who knows Tante Lisl is away. They might have thought we were squatters. That's not so unusual in this city.'

Genevieve helped herself to another piece of bread and spread it thickly with liver pâté. 'But it wasn't the police. You have to relax, Hans. Everything is going to plan. You told me yourself. Your man in Glasgow delivered the letter. When Fredi speaks to him tomorrow, she'll give my father his instructions and he'll deliver.'

'Are you sure? He's such a ruthless businessman,

315

I can't believe he'll just cave in. And even if he does, he'll want revenge, surely?'

Genevieve nibbled a cornichon in a series of tiny bites with her sharp white incisors. 'That tape we made earlier, the one Fredi's going to play to him? He'll cave in all right. He'll be so grateful to have me back, it'll be easy to convince him that revenge might be too dangerous. That you might come after me again, and not for money. The thing you have to remember is that this isn't business, Hans. This is family. This is love.'

'Still, I find it hard to believe he will just accept defeat if he has to pay a ransom. Everything you have said makes me think he is a ruthless man.'

'In business, yes. But there's so much more to him than that. My father lost his entire family to the Nazis in the war. I'm all he has left. He won't countenance the risk of losing me. He'll be stamping round the house like a wounded bear, eaten up with fear and frustration. But he won't take a chance on my life. You have to impress that on Fredi. She needs to sound truly dangerous. She has to make him believe my life really is on the line.'

Hans's expression gave nothing away. He wondered yet again why that thought hadn't crossed Genny's mind. In her shoes, it would have kept him awake at night. He'd have bet Fredi Schroeder had considered it as an option if the alternative was losing her free-dom.

Genevieve pushed her plate away. 'Now, let's go out for a drink.' He looked so appalled she burst out laughing. 'Why not? Nobody here knows who I am. Or who you are, come to that. It's boring, being stuck in here all the time.' He went to contradict her but she put a finger to his lips to silence him. 'Even with you as a beautiful distraction. Come on, Hans. Let's live a little.'

'No, Genny. You have to be serious about this. You can't be seen. Your father may not go to the police but he will have people out looking for you.'

'What? In this obscure suburban corner of Berlin? And who? Dieter, my driver? He's never seen me with you. Or Fredi, come to that.'

'Everyone knows who Fredi is. If he knows you have been mixing with us, your Dieter will know Fredi. That's why I'm here, not her. We have to stay put.' He pulled away from her and hurried down the hall. He took the keys out of the door and put them into his trouser pocket. Then faced her. 'You can't go out, Genny. You have to imagine you really are a prisoner.'

Her brows lowered in anger. 'I don't have to imagine it, do I? Because I am a fucking prisoner.' The glass she threw left a spray of red wine across the polished floor, shattering into shards as it hit the spot on the door where Hans had been only a moment before. Without waiting for a response, she stalked out of the room. The bedroom door slammed loud as a pistol shot.

Hans stood, hands trembling. It felt like Genny wasn't the only prisoner. Slowly, he began to pick up the larger fragments of glass. Fredi would go ballistic when she heard about this.

45

Allie took her time over an oxtail stew with dumplings. It was almost dusk by the time she'd finished her coffee cake, and still there was no sign of the man from the top-floor apartment. The café was almost full now and the waitress was giving her an evil side-eye that wouldn't have been out of place in the East End of Glasgow. She paid her bill and shivered as she exchanged the warm fug of the café for the twilight chill. The rain had stopped and the clouds looked like an old bruise in the setting sun.

She wheeled the bike slowly down the street, her eyes fixed on the windows of Frau Braun's apartment. The lights were on inside and she propped the bike against a lamppost, unfastening the pump from the frame and pretending to inflate her front tyre. There were pot plants along the windowsill, but as she watched, the man appeared, head bowed. A plate rose into sight and disappeared. The angle was tight and limited, but he was washing the dishes, she thought. A second plate, then what looked like a couple of shallow serving dishes. But no more plates. Two people, then?

It still didn't mean there wasn't a prisoner in there.

Then a second head appeared. All Allie could see was the crown of a head of dark hair falling round a wide forehead. Her heart leapt. It could be Genevieve Lockhart. Then frustration kicked in. Of course it could be Genevieve. It could also be hundreds, if not thousands of Berliners. 'Fuck's sake, Burns,' she muttered under her breath. Then the head swung round and the woman kissed the man's cheek. He turned and they embraced, moving swiftly away from the window.

What had she just seen? If it was Genevieve, it didn't look like she was being held prisoner. Was this some massive scam she was pulling against her father to get money for her pet political cause? The father who doted on her and would presumably have given her the money if she'd asked for it? Or was this some random woman squatting in Frau Braun's apartment with her floppy-haired boyfriend?

None of it made sense. And standing underneath a German streetlight as if she was channelling Marlene Dietrich wasn't going to help. She only had one lead left. If Fredi Schroeder didn't make a phone call the next morning, in spite of what she'd said to Dieter, Allie knew she was beaten.

She knew what defeat tasted like. And she was damned if she was going to swallow it again on Ace Lockhart's account.

★ ★ ★

Genevieve emerged from the bedroom as Hans was finishing the clear-up. He'd found a brush and dust-pan to sweep up the glass, he'd wiped down all the wine stains he could see and now he was making a start on washing the dishes. He was, she thought, a thoroughly domesticated animal. He'd never raise a hand to her in anger; he wasn't a jailer to fear.

He glanced over his shoulder at her, anxiety obvious. She lowered her head and smiled at him in imitation of the style that had always worked so well for the Princess of Wales. 'I'm sorry,' she said, the very picture of penitence. 'I let my frustrations boil over. I'm a mover and shaker by nature and training, Hans. I'm not good at sitting on my hands. This is so alien to me.' She came up behind him and put an arm round his back. 'I promise I'll behave from now on.'

'I'm sorry you're struggling. I thought we were having fun.'

'So we were.' She leaned in and kissed his cheek. 'And since it's your job to make sure I don't get bored, we'd better have some more.'

Hans turned and wiped his wet hands on his trousers then pulled her into an embrace. She could feel the hard outline of the keys against her thigh. All she had to do now was tire him out between the sheets, wait till he was fast asleep and then she could help herself to the keys and get out. It wasn't an escape plan; she'd come back to the apartment later. She simply wanted a couple of hours of freedom where she was in control. Maybe she'd find a jazz club or a bierkeller open till the small hours. It didn't matter, as long as it was up to her.

Fredi didn't know her as well as she believed, Genevieve thought as she led Hans to the bedroom. It was never a good move to deprive a Lockhart of choices.

★ ★ ★

Genevieve made it as far as the front door. She was wrestling with the double locks when Hans came running. He grabbed her by the waist and tried to wrestle her to the floor. But her instincts told her never to give up without a fight. She wriggled and punched

320

and kicked and dragged the bunch of keys down his ribs in an agonising move. She even bit his arm as he struggled to contain her without actually hurting her. In the end, his superior weight overcame her and he managed to pin her to the floor. 'What are you doing?' he yelled.

'I only wanted to go for a fucking walk,' she snarled.

'I told you. You have to stay inside,' he panted. 'You have to stay here. Tomorrow — no, today — we have to make ransom demands to your father. This is a serious business, not a game. Now give me back the keys.'

'Fuck off.' Her voice was low and threatening. She was down but not out. She bucked underneath him and he almost lost his balance. What he did lose was his temper. He let go one arm and slapped her so hard she saw sparks of light behind her eyes. While she was still reeling, he dragged her along the carpet and flung her face down on the sofa. Before she could react, he'd grabbed the bundle of cords they'd used to pose the kidnap Polaroids.

Genevieve realised too late what he planned. She tried to stop him, but he had his knee in the small of her back and was twisting her arms up behind her. The agony was excruciating. She felt her arms were going to pop out of their sockets. She screamed in a mixture of pain and frustration as he tied her wrists tightly together. Then he pushed her face into the cushions. 'Shut up,' he hissed. 'If you don't shut up, I'll gag you again.'

She went limp. For now, she was beaten. But when Fredi showed up, she'd make sure this little shit paid for what he'd done to her. How dare he treat her as if this was their plan and not hers? He'd be one member of the radical Green movement who would be left out in the cold.

★ ★ ★

Dieter was waiting outside the hotel in the Polo when Allie emerged at seven next morning, followed by a porter carrying Margarethe's bike. She waited as the porter stowed it in the hatchback of the car, then tipped him and slid into the passenger seat.

'How was your dinner?' Dieter asked.

'More enjoyable than an afternoon watching a flat in the rain.'

'Did anything happen?'

'There's a woman in there with him. I saw the top of her head in the kitchen window.'

Dieter straightened up. 'Was it Fraulein Lockhart?'

'I couldn't tell. It could have been, but I didn't see her face. Just the hair and the forehead, from across the street and four floors down.'

'How could it be her, though? If you have kidnapped someone, you do not let them wander around.'

'I know. I did have one idea. But it's crazy.'

Dieter started the engine and drove into the traffic. 'Do you want to tell me?'

'No. Because it's too crazy. You might just call your boss and tell him he sent a crazy woman to find his daughter, and we both know how well that would go.'

They drove in silence for a few minutes. 'You are not the only one with crazy ideas,' he said.

She was beginning to like Dieter, she decided. 'You show me yours, I'll show you mine.'

He gave a self-deprecating little wave of the hand. 'I thought maybe she fell in love with Fredi. Setting

322

this up would impress her, no?'

Allie was startled. 'Genny's gay?' It was a vibe that had bypassed her gaydar when they'd been together in East Berlin. But as Rona had pointed out mischievously more than once, Allie was always the last to know.

'I don't know. But she was always 'Fredi this, Fredi that.' Like she had a crush.'

Now what Allie had seen made even less sense. 'I thought she kissed the guy in the apartment last night. I could have sworn that's what I saw.'

'Maybe she's just greedy,' he said with a laugh. He turned into the street where Fredi lived.

'I think the word you're looking for is 'bisexual'.' Allie grinned. 'I hadn't even thought about Fredi and Genny,' she added. 'I just wondered if Genny was scamming her dad to get him to pony up for a political cause he doesn't support. Because she understands the importance of that commitment for Pythagoras Press in the future in a way he doesn't.'

"Pony up?' What is 'pony up'?'

'Pay for something. It has the sense of being reluctant. Unwilling. And Lockhart would certainly be unwilling to hand a wedge of cash over to a bunch of radical German Greens. That's not the kind of post-Soviet era he'd fancy at all.'

Dieter found a parking place and they settled in for a long wait. Allie plugged the headphones into her Walkman and pressed play on her personal mixtape of Everything but the Girl. Tracey Thorn's rich voice filled her head, sounding like another instrument in the mix. 'Don't Let the Teardrops Rust Your Shining Heart', right enough. The music let the time pass without ramping up her anxieties. Dieter mimed drinking

323

and she shook her head. Long hours of stake-out had taught Allie to be cautious about her liquid intake.

It was a busy street, a cut-through from one main thoroughfare to another, but even though people went in and out of Fredi Schroeder's building, there was no chance of Allie missing someone so distinctive. And just before 10.15, her patience was rewarded. She pulled off her headphones in the middle of 'The Night I Heard Caruso Sing' and exclaimed, 'There she is.'

'I see her,' Dieter said, not stirring from his slumped position.

Fredi crossed to the kerbside and looked both ways. She checked her watch; her mouth showed her disapproval. As they watched, a battered 2CV passed them, revealing *Atomkraft nein danke* painted across the back. It slowed to a halt alongside Fredi, who immediately got in. They took off with a puff of exhaust and a muttering sewing-machine engine noise. Dieter waited for another car to pass then followed.

'Did you see who was driving?' Allie asked, excited. 'The mystery man from the apartment.'

'I saw.' Dieter was frowning, focusing on staying close without being spotted. They were heading south, she thought. The traffic was heavy and it was hard to maintain contact with the 2CV. He'd let a couple of cars slip between them at the start of the trip, but by jumping lanes a few times, they were right behind their quarry as they turned into Clayallee. They carried on past the vast green lung of Grunewald then, without signalling, the 2CV shot across the oncoming traffic and turned left.

'*Scheisse!*' Dieter braked hard, earning a salvo of horns behind him, and managed to swing round and make the turn.

'Well done,' Allie gasped. 'But honestly, could we have made ourselves any more conspicuous? Where are they going, do you think?'

'Maybe the Free University. Fredi Schroeder is a junior professor there. She will have an office with a phone that goes through the main switchboard.'

Untraceable probably, in other words. Now Allie could see the disreputable 2CV ahead of them. It turned into a car park in the middle of a low-rise U-shaped building. 'Stop past the entrance,' Allie said. 'I'm walking in. Once they've parked, you can find a spot near them.' She leapt out as soon as he'd stopped and started across the tarmac towards the building, scanning the car park for Fredi and her driver. She spotted them, over on the far side, heading for one of the wings of the building. Adrenaline pumping, Allie changed her direction and picked up her pace so she was a mere half-dozen metres behind them when they walked in. She could feel the sweat of anxiety in her armpits and she forced herself to breathe slowly.

They headed for a flight of stairs. Allie hung back till they'd passed the first landing then pursued them. She made it to the corridor in time to see them halt outside a door. Allie hastily turned and walked the other way down the hall. When she heard a door click shut, she turned on her heel, pushing past a trio of students deep in argument. She couldn't be certain which room they'd entered, but immediately realised the clue would be in the name slotted into a holder on the door. Third door along, as Allie had surmised. *Prof. Dr F. von B. Schroeder.*

Her mouth was dry and her palms were sweating. She leaned against the door, ear to the wood, but heard nothing. Then she heard the faintest mumble of conversation and realised it was coming from another room. Allie crept to the next door and listened intently. She couldn't decipher the words, but she was pretty sure it was a man and woman talking. Obviously they'd worked out Fredi's phone might be tapped so they were using a colleague's office to make the call. Fredi was definitely a smart operator.

Allie checked her watch. Almost noon. She hoped anyone passing would assume she was waiting to be admitted. *Fat chance.* Allie pressed her ear to the door and heard the man say something in German. She heard the sound of a rotary dial.

Then, in Fredi's clear and carrying voice, Allie heard, 'Good day, Herr Lockhart.'

46

Ace Lockhart had passed a night of restlessness and distorted dreams which had as much to do with the quart of vanilla ice cream he'd eaten after dinner as with his daughter's plight. Like so many whose early years had been deprived of both food and emotional nourishment, sweet treats were his invariable port of call when his heart was hurting. He'd given up any attempt at sleep as dawn broke.

Showered and shaved and fully dressed, because there were standards that must be maintained, he'd walked out into a soft morning. For once, the air was still, the sea lapping quietly at the sandy bay enclosed by the twin embrace of rocky promontories. It looked so benign, but Lockhart knew from local boatmen that only a fool would attempt to beach a boat there. It was, he'd always thought, a metaphor for so many things in life.

He walked round his domain, an exercise that took a shade under ninety minutes. He was alone with seabirds unaccustomed to the presence of humans. They treated him like part of the landscape, showing little interest and no fear. The last time he'd walked the bounds, Genny had been at his side, animated and full of confidence that she could bend the future to her will. Pythagoras would not merely survive, it would thrive, she'd assured him.

And now? Now she was held captive because he'd wanted to secure his business against an uncertain future. And she might die because he hadn't even secured it in the present. The millions he'd taken from the pension funds — a loan in his mind still — had already been poured into the sinkhole that the New York *Globe* was proving to be. He'd turn it round, he knew he would, and the finances would be restored. But right now, he was out of options. The banks were snapping at his heels and it wouldn't be long before the pensions trustees were doing the same. Nobody would believe it — certainly not the kidnappers — but there was no possibility of Ace Lockhart laying his hands on half a million any time soon.

Surely these kidnappers, whoever they were, wouldn't kill Genny? They must realise they'd never get away with it. The German police had learned a whole playbook of lessons from their battle with the Bader-Meinhof Red Army Faction; much easier to release Genny than to become the targets of a man-hunt. And West Berlin was not an easy place to get out of, if the authorities chose to make it so. No, he would surely be able to persuade them to set her free? He'd been convincing all sorts of people of all sorts of things for the best part of fifty years.

It would be all right. He'd make it all right.

Back at the cottage, he brewed a pot of coffee and toasted half a loaf of bread, loaded the slices with unsalted Normandy butter and smoked salmon, and munched as he gazed moodily at the stream of tel-exes that had come in overnight. The handful of his bespoke vitamin capsules he swallowed made no dif-ference to his mood. So far was he from his usual self that he couldn't bring himself to care about any of the messages. All he wanted was Genny, safe and well and back home.

At five minutes before noon, he walked heavy-footed to his den and sat down, forcing himself to sit up straight and square his shoulders. It made a difference to the timbre of his voice, lending him an authority he didn't feel that morning. He picked up the receiver on the second ring. A strong female voice with a faint German accent greeted him with, 'Good day, Herr Lockhart.'

'You have the advantage of me, dear lady. I don't have your name.'

'Nor will you,' she sparred back at him. 'We will discuss the arrangements for you to pay for the safe return of your daughter.'

'I require proof of life before we even have this conversation.'

'One moment.' There was the sound of clicking. Then a voice. Lockhart recognised his daughter even through the distortion of a tape recording and a phone line. 'Daddy, it's me. You have to save me. They're going to kill me if you don't pay up. I think they mean it.' Her voice rose in fear. He heard her catch her breath before she continued. 'They say you'll need to know I'm still alive. Yesterday morning's splash in the *Clarion* was the verdict in a Glasgow arson trial. You probably OK'd it yourself. Daddy, these people — they scare me.' Another click and the German woman was back. 'Satisfied?'

'Very well. You have my daughter. But I don't have half a million pounds.'

A short bark of scornful laughter. 'You own one of the largest media empires in the world. You are a multimillionaire. How is this possible?'

'All I own is tied up in the business. I don't even own my own home. I rent it from Glasgow City Coun-

329

cil. I don't have that sort of money readily available.'

'Then borrow it. You have businesses for security.'

Businesses mortgaged to the hilt. Some of them several times over. 'That's not how it works. I love my daughter but I cannot give you what I do not have. Release her now and we will forget this ever happened. But if you harm a hair on her head, I swear you will be hounded to the ends of the earth.'

'Really? You can't afford to save your daughter but you can fund a crusade of revenge? Seems to me, Herr Lockhart, that your priorities are, as we say here in Berlin, fucked up seventeen different ways.'

'It's a matter of timing. In six months, it will be a different picture, but now —'

'Are you saying we should let Genevieve go and kidnap her again in six months?' Her incredulity turned to laughter. 'You really don't care, do you?'

'I love my daughter. If I had the cash, I would pay double what you ask to see her safe. But I do not have the money to hand. I don't know who you are, but you must have parents. Would you put them through this agony for the sake of money?'

'This is not about me. It is about how much you love Genevieve. Your only child. Your only living relative.'

Something in him snapped. 'Yes. My only living relative. Thanks to what you people did in the war. I see you have learned nothing from that. Set my daughter free if you have any human decency.'

A brief silence. Then, cold as winter, 'You have until Friday. I will call again at the same time. This will be your last chance.' And the line went dead.

He slammed the receiver down, dropped his head into his hands and wept.

330

47

'This will be your last chance,' Allie heard. Then the phone was replaced. The man spoke enthusiastically. It sounded like ecstatic congratulation. Time to make herself scarce. Shocked by what she'd heard, Allie hurried down the hall and took the stairs at a run. She found Dieter in the foyer, sitting on a bench ostensibly reading a magazine. Allie jerked her head towards the door and he caught up with her outside. 'Where's the car?'

'Two rows down. I can see their French junk heap.'

'Let's go.'

'What happened?' He lengthened his stride to keep up with her.

Once they were in the car, she told him what she'd heard. 'It sounds like he's pleading poverty,' she said. 'It's not a very credible line. He presents the image of being a successful media mogul. He lives a life of extreme luxury — a private jet, his own helicopter, a Hebridean island and all the accoutrements of wealth. He may well not have cash on hand, but it's not a convincing argument to someone on the outside of his world.'

'I would not believe him,' Dieter said. 'He wants the best of everything — but always at a discount.'

'You don't get a discount on a ransom demand.'

As she spoke, Fredi and her companion emerged from the building and got into their car. 'You want me to follow them?'

'Yes, but don't worry if you lose them. I have a pretty good idea where they're going.'

Twenty minutes later, they watched the 2CV turn into the street where Frau Braun's apartment was situated. Dieter pulled up to the kerb and they waited till their targets were inside before he parked in a side street. 'Is this what you expected?'

'Oh yes,' Allie said, releasing her seat belt.

'What will you do?'

'In the world of investigative journalism, we call it the showdown. I'm going up to the apartment to confront them.'

Dieter swung round, alarm on his face. 'This is too dangerous.'

'I'm not scared of a junior professor and her sidekick. It's not *Die Hard*. I think they're the conning kind, not the killing kind.'

'Conning? What is *conning*?'

'Cheating. Lying.'

'It doesn't mean they won't turn on you. I will come too.'

Allie weighed it up. *Face it, your recent track record doesn't bode well for you in a showdown.* It wouldn't hurt to have someone at her back who looked like muscle. And who could also speak the language. 'OK. But let me take the lead. Her English is very good. And if I'm right, there'll be someone else there who speaks English like a native. Because she is one.'

'Why are you doing this?'

'Because we know Fredi is the person demanding the ransom, and her sidekick is in an apartment that isn't his with a woman that isn't Fredi and who might just be Genny. It's not rocket science, Dieter.' She opened the door and got out, then stuck her head back in. 'Come on, let's go before Fredi nips out for lunch.'

They walked down the street, Allie pushing a little swagger into her stride, wishing she wasn't wearing the same clothes for the third day running. Rona would have something to say about that.

Faced with a column of door buzzers, Allie gestured to Dieter that this was his forte. He got a response from the second one he tried. They let him in without comment. 'What did you say?' she asked.

He shrugged, leading the way into the hall. 'That the buzzer for another apartment seemed not to be working, that I knew my friends were home. This is a nice neighbourhood. People are not expecting bad stuff to happen to them.' He stopped at the iron cage of the elevator and raised his eyebrows in a question.

She grinned. 'We'll take it to the second floor and walk up the last flight. That way, they won't notice anything amiss. And I won't turn up red-faced and sweating.'

They stood outside Frau Braun's door, gathering themselves, breathing deeply. Allie felt the familiar mix of emotions. Fear of failure; the electric fizz of adrenaline; and the knowledge that it might all go to dangerous shit like her encounter with Little Weed had. But at least this time she had Dieter at her back. It would be all right. It would have to be. She raised her hand and rapped on the door.

Nothing.

She knocked again, more aggressively this time. Still nothing. They exchanged looks. 'One last try.' Allie hammered with the side of her fist. She stepped back and gestured to Dieter to do what he could.

He surprised them both. '*Öffne die Tür, Polizei!*' he

shouted, banging on the door. This time there was a response. Heels on wood, then the door opened to reveal Fredi. She looked fierce and imperious. '*Was ist es?*' she demanded.

Allie stepped forward. 'Let's do this in English, eh? I know Genny speaks great German, but *ich kann kein Deutsch.*'

'What are you talking about?' No quarter asked or given.

Allie shook her head, working up a pitying look. 'The game's up, Fredi. It's over.' She raised her voice. 'Genny? It's Allie Burns. It's time to go home. Dieter and I will see you back safely.'

Fredi tried to slam the door shut but was thwarted by Dieter's foot. He winced but didn't move. 'Get out of my apartment,' she snarled.

'Good try, Fredi. I don't know what you've done with Frau Braun, but this isn't your apartment. You live on the other side of town. Lovely spot, nice view of the park. Do you really want to swap that for a jail cell?' Allie said conversationally.

Now she'd earned a glare. 'I don't know what you're talking about.'

Allie put on a puzzled face. 'How the fuck did you get to be a professor? So far, you've displayed all the intelligence of somebody who's very low on the criminal totem pole.' She raised her voice again. 'Genny? Time to stop hanging out with the losers. There's only one winning team here and you're not on it. Let's get you back before your dad moves from upset to raging bull.'

Fredi gave a quick look over her shoulder. Her momentary distraction was enough for Dieter. He surged forward and walloped into the door, driving

Fredi backwards and forcing an opening wide enough for him and Allie to push their way into the flat. Recovering herself, Fredi rained blows on his head and shoulders. But Dieter simply chose his moment and grabbed both of her wrists. '*Genug!*' he roared.

She looked bewildered. Clearly nobody had ever dared to treat her like this. 'This is private property,' she stammered.

'But not yours,' said Allie, pushing past her and kicking the door shut. There was nobody in the kitchen or the living room. She carried on down the hall. Bathroom. Probably a spare room. The last door. They had to be there. Allie turned the handle but the door didn't budge. 'Genny? This is Allie. This could be your last chance to salvage your relationship with your father. I don't know what you think you've been playing at, but I know you love him.'

She heard a muffled sound, then nothing. 'Dieter,' she called. 'I need your shoulder again.'

He said something firm and Germanic to Fredi then appeared at Allie's side. 'I think they're in there.'

He took a couple of steps back then threw himself shoulder first at the door. It splintered at the first blow and banged back against a piece of heavy furniture. The scene that revealed itself was not what Allie had expected. Genevieve Lockhart was dressed for outdoors, but she was bound and gagged on the floor, making small animal noises. The man whose face Allie had grown familiar with hurled himself at her, knocking her off balance enough to make it into the hall where his balls had a sudden encounter with Dieter's knee. He doubled up with a thin scream and fell to the floor moaning.

Bewildered, Allie said, 'What the fuck?' Genevieve

managed to turn her head and meet Allie's gaze. The sound that came through the silk scarf might have been any random three syllables, but Allie thought it was probably, 'Let me go.'

'All in good time,' Allie said. 'Dieter, let's get Fredi in here. Then we'll try to make some sense of this.'

He hurried back down the hall and rounded the corner. '*Scheisse!*' he roared. 'She is gone.'

Of course she was bloody gone, Allie thought. 'Over the hills and far away.'

'I will go,' Dieter shouted.

'Leave it, Dieter. We know where to find her if we need her.'

The man on the ground tried to crawl away and she kicked him hard, right where Dieter had already done damage. His face went white and he curled in on himself. '*Genug,*' he groaned.

She turned her attention back to Genevieve, whose eyes were blazing rage at her. First she untied her feet, then her hands. Genevieve tried to scramble to her feet but only made it as far as the rumpled bed. She batted Allie's helping hand away and hauled at the knots fastening her gag. 'You took your time,' she said. 'What kept you?'

So that was how it was going to be. 'Kidnapped, were you?' Allie went for mild amusement.

'Well, obviously. You found me, bound and gagged.'

'In the clutches of your kidnappers.' Flat delivery, holding Genevieve's eyes.

Genevieve frowned. 'Yes. Exactly.'

Allie pointed to the man on the floor. 'People don't usually snog their kidnappers while they're doing the dishes together. Or are you going to be claiming you're channelling Patty Hearst and suffering

Stockholm Syndrome?'

'I don't know what you think you saw, but you couldn't be more wrong. I'm the bloody victim here.'

'We know all about Fredi, but what's your pal's name?'

'How would I know? She never used his name.'

'Oh, come on. Do you think I came up the Clyde on a bike? He's one of the revolutionary Green lot you've been hanging out with. Either you tell me or I let Dieter find it out the hard way.'

'Hans Weber,' the man on the floor croaked. 'My name is Hans Weber. This was all Genny's idea.'

'Don't fall for his bullshit. But we won't be pressing charges. You can just let him go.' Genevieve insisted, as if she had the right of command.

Allie shook her head in a pantomime of regret. She had no investment in covering Genevieve's back. 'The person who gets to decide what happens to those two is your father. He's the one who's been wronged here. By that pair of prize manipulators. And maybe by you too, Genny? It's Ace who gets to decide what happens — let them go, call the cops, drop them in the Spree bound hand and foot —' she paused, enjoying Genevieve's look of horror. 'That last one was a joke.'

She sighed. 'I'm the victim here. Don't try to put this on me.'

'Yeah.' Allie walked back to the old-fashioned phone mounted on the living-room wall. She opened her contacts book and dialled the number she had for Ace Lockhart's private office. Waiting for the connection seemed to take forever but then she heard the ringtone.

'Mr Lockhart's office,' came the familiar voice of his PA.

'It's Allie Burns,' she said. 'Can you put me through?'

'He's not here,' she said. There was an acerbic note in her voice. 'He's over on Ranaig but he's not answering his phone. He had a call booked to the Home Secretary half an hour ago, but he didn't make it. I've had Mr Hurd's office on, very annoyed. I've sent a fax and a telex, but he hasn't replied.'

'You don't think something might have happened to him?'

'We'd have heard. He does have staff, you know.' Huffy now.

Thus giving the lie to the truism that no man has any secrets from his PA. 'If he contacts you, can you pass on this number and tell him it's urgent?' She read the number off the phone dial. 'That's Berlin, by the way. In Germany.'

'I know where Berlin is.' A definite frost now. 'I'll let him know when he surfaces.'

Allie jiggled the receiver rest then dialled another number, one she knew from memory. When it was answered, she said, 'It's me.'

'I was beginning to think you'd gone off the air as well as Ace.' Rona's voice had never been more welcome.

'I've been busy sorting things out.'

'And have you?'

'In a manner of speaking. Yes. But I need to speak to the man.'

'You're not alone. As far as I can establish, he's spoken to nobody since he took that phone call. If he took that phone call.'

'Oh, he did. I can confirm that much. Am I misremembering or did you tell me he'd told the Ranaig staff to stay away?'

338

'That's right. He didn't want to be disturbed. What's going on, Allie? Have you tracked down Genny?'

Allie chuckled. 'Oh yes. Listen, Ro, I think you need to get the staff out to Ranaig. It's not like Ace to go dark. They can tell him Genny is out of the hands of her abductors and if he calls this number, he can speak to her.' Allie read out the number to Rona. 'I'll speak to you later,' Allie promised. 'But I really need to talk to Ace.' She put the phone down and went back through to Genevieve.

'Let him go, Allie. Nobody will thank you for pursuing Fredi and Hans. I will refuse to give evidence against them.'

Hans was stirring. 'Does that other bedroom have a lock, Dieter?' Allie asked. It did, and she asked him to lock Hans inside for the time being. 'And we'll go and sit in the living room and try to work out what in the name of the wee man has been going on here.'

She watched Genevieve carefully as she made her way through. To nobody's surprise, she settled in the most comfortable chair, rubbing her legs to fully restore circulation. Allie pulled up a kitchen chair close to her and sat down. 'So why would anyone refuse to give evidence against their captors? Unless they were in cahoots?'

Genevieve's smile was condescending. 'Because the person who brings them down will bring down the Green movement on both sides of the wall. People are too stupid to differentiate between the radical Greens and the more conservative ones. The whole movement will be tainted.'

'Really? You don't think they'd be heroic martyrs who took radical action?'

Genevieve scoffed. 'You have no idea, do you?

339

Germans are so conservative. It's not so long since the Bader-Meinhof terrorists had the whole country running scared. A lot of people who are contemplating change would take fright at a case like this. And I'm willing to put my own discomfort and fear behind me for the sake of the cause.' Her smile was triumphant.

'Taking one for the team doesn't strike me as being your style, Genny.'

Anger flared in her eyes. 'Things are changing, Allie. You news reporters, you've always got your heads in the here and now, you can't ever see the bigger picture. The planet's in crisis and we need to stop it. The end of the world isn't going to be a singular nuclear disaster like Chernobyl. We're all going to cook in a slow global warming. Like boiling a frog. Fredi's one of the people trying to stop that. Building bridges across stupid constructs like the Wall, like the Iron Curtain.'

'But it takes time to make change, right? Time and money.'

'Obviously.'

'So you all decided to speed things up and extort money from your dad. Nice one.'

Her lip curled. 'You've no evidence of that. Not a shred. Because it never happened. Who's going to believe the loosest cannon in the Ace Media group over the boss of Pythagoras Press who also happens to be Ace Lockhart's only child and heir? And anyway, you've no right to the moral high ground. If you try to push it, I'll point out that it was you who gave me the idea.'

'Me?' Allie laughed. 'How do you work that one out?'

'You've got a very short memory. Only last week I

had to rescue you from the Stasi. After you'd faked an abduction to achieve what you wanted.'

Allie couldn't credit what she was hearing. 'I was doing that to expose a criminal conspiracy that would cost lives.'

'And how is that different from raising money to stop all of us dying?'

'Well, for a start I wasn't betraying someone who loves me. If Ace finds out you were behind this — and let's not kid ourselves, we both know the truth here — it will break his heart. Always supposing he has one.' She sighed. 'Why didn't you just ask him?'

'Because he'd have said no. He'd see no benefit to him. So he wouldn't care.'

'Surely he'd have listened, at least? I mean, one day his empire will belong to you. Why not give you a down payment?'

Genevieve traced patterns on the table with a finger. 'That's not how he sees the world. He lives in the present. Not the past, not the future. It's the here and now that matters.'

'That doesn't make it OK, Genny.'

'Let Hans go, Allie. And don't chase Fredi. They're not bad people. They just got carried away by their love for the cause. You can be the hero, Allie. We can figure out a cover story between us.' She gave a little chuckle. 'And my father will forever be in your debt. Your lovely Rona will have a top job for life.'

'Rona doesn't need favours for that.'

Genevieve shrugged. 'It never hurts to have friends in high places. Come on, Allie. Who gets hurt if we play it my way? My father keeps his money, I keep my status with Fredi's group, you come up smelling of roses.'

Allie couldn't see an alternative to playing it Genevieve's way. It filled her with rage, but she was well and truly over a barrel. She shook her head. 'You really are a piece of work, Genny. An absolute chip off the old block.'

She stood up and nodded to Dieter. 'Let the bastard go. At least we know where to find him and Fredi Schroeder.'

The two women watched in silence as Dieter unlocked the second bedroom door and dragged Hans Weber through the door. 'You can go now,' Genevieve said sweetly. 'I'm sorry you were hurt. Tell Fredi I'll see you all soon.'

He didn't look as if that were an enticing prospect. But he said nothing and stumbled in Dieter's wake to the front door.

'Shall we go, then? Genevieve asked.

'We need to wait here,' Allie said. 'This is the contact I gave for Ace to call us. And I'm not letting you out of my sight till we've spoken to him.' Genevieve opened her mouth but Allie talked over her. 'That's not a negotiation. Genny. It's a red line. And you're not calling the shots here. For once, you do what you're told.'

'You can't keep me here,' Genevieve snarled, making a break for the front door. Dieter strolled after her. 'Give me the keys, Dieter.'

He shook his head. 'I can't do that, Fraulein Lockhart. Your father is my employer and he instructed me to take my orders from Frau Burns.' He folded his arms across his chest and stood in front of the door. She wasn't going anywhere. Not until Ace Lockhart said so.

48

Fiona and Calum Stuart reckoned they were living their best lives. Taking care of Ace Lockhart and his wee fiefdom on the edge of the Atlantic wasn't exactly the hardest job in the world. He was only there a couple of times a month for a night or two; twice a year, he'd spend longer on Ranaig, usually with his daughter. Who was, let's face it, a bit of a princess. Mr Lockhart, though — he knew what he liked and as long as he was well fed and everything in the house worked as it should, Fiona and Calum got along with him just fine.

Since they only had to be on the island when Lockhart was in residence, they spent most of their time based at their cottage on the nearby island of Coll, where there were attractions such as other human beings and a pub. They'd go across to Ranaig in their efficient RIB at least once a week, to keep an eye on the place and carry out routine maintenance and repairs. It was, as their friends on Coll reminded them at regular intervals, a cushy number.

So when they returned from their pub lunch, they were surprised to see the light flashing on their answering machine. Calum pressed the button and waited. The voice from the machine was unfamiliar. 'This is Rona Dunsyre calling from Ace Media. Mr Lockhart went to Ranaig a couple of days ago. But we can't seem to contact him. Can you go over and check everything is OK?' The message ended with a number Calum recognised as that of a mobile phone.

He rolled his eyes and replayed the message, jotting down the number then tapping it into the phone. 'Gonna cost a fortune, calling a mobile phone,' he grumbled.

'Rona Dunsyre speaking,' came the voice down the crackling line.

'This is Calum Stuart. We just got in and picked up your message.'

'Thanks for getting back to me. I'm sorry to bother you but we're a bit concerned about Ace. He went over on the chopper to Ranaig on Monday. He said he needed some thinking space. But he was in touch until this morning. Then . . . nothing. He's not answering his phone, he's not responding to faxes.'

Hesitantly, Calum said, 'Could be he wants a bit of peace and quiet?'

'Normally, I'd agree with you. But we're in the middle of something really important and it's worrying that he's gone off the air. There are some big decisions to be made that only he can make.'

'You want us to go across and check, right?'

'Got it in one.'

'Aye, no bother. I wouldn't worry, if I was you. The boss likes his own company. Sometimes we hardly see him when he's in residence.'

'I thought you were his bodyguard?'

He laughed. 'That doesn't mean babysitter. On Ranaig, you can see trouble coming a long way off. I'll ask him to call you as soon as we hook up with him.'

The sea rippled gently under the fingers of a light breeze when Calum checked the boat. Fiona walked down from the cottage with a basket containing milk and a bag of langoustines, still lazily snapping at their prison. 'Looks like a fine afternoon for it,' she said.

'Wind's due to get up later, according to the forecast.' Calum spoke absently, more than half his mind on the readiness of the engine. Once Fiona was aboard, he turned the key, the engine roared into life and they left the jetty in a froth of foam. It was a great way to spend an afternoon, Calum thought. Even after years of these waters in all weathers, he still felt a surge of exhilaration at the boat moving beneath his feet. He steered by eye, aiming for the tip of Ranaig, where he swung round and into the bay with the barrage and the jetties.

They tied up and disembarked, noticing nothing out of the ordinary. Calum reminded himself to replace one of the boards that had split after he'd dropped a Calor gas cylinder a fortnight before. They walked up the path towards the house but as soon as they breasted the rise, they knew there was something wrong. 'There's no smoke from the wood burner,' Fiona said. 'No way would he let that go out, it's still too cold.'

'Could be he just forgot to bank it up and he's gone for a walk?' Even as he spoke, he knew the chances of that were remote. The boss loved his comforts too much. Calum picked up the pace, striding out towards the house. The back door was unlocked; nothing unusual there. They walked into a cold kitchen. Fiona touched the kettle and the coffee machine; no trace of warmth.

'Something's not right,' Fiona said. They both eyed the closed door leading to the living room.

Calum made the first move. They both noticed an unpleasant smell but there was nobody in the long living room or the den or on the veranda looking out to sea. He looked at the staircase, pursed his lips and began to climb. As he reached the turn in the stairs, he gasped. 'Oh, fuck,' he said.

'What is it?' Fiona was behind him now, peering round and seeing what had freaked out her husband. One sock-clad foot, ankle and lower calf. She'd have recognised that distinctive Fair Isle pattern in a crowd. She pushed past Calum and reach the top of the stairs to discover Wallace Lockhart sprawled ungainly on the floor. The smell was stronger here; whatever had happened to him had made him lose control of his bowels. His eyes were open, the rich brown irises dulled. His cheeks were stained cherry red, with darker patches. She bent down and touched his skin. It was cold.

Slack-jawed, she turned to Calum. 'He's gone. What do we do now?'

49

'There must be bloody good sound insulation in these flats. I can't believe nobody's come up to complain about the racket we made,' Allie said conversationally as they sat around the table eating cold meats and black bread.

'When are they going to call back?' Genevieve asked. 'It's been hours. I need to speak to Ace, to sort this mess out.'

'Rona will call when there's something to report,' Allie said flatly.

'What's Rona doing in the middle of this anyway? She's just a features editor, not a senior executive. Since when did she get to call the shots?'

Allie wished she still smoked. 'She happened to be in the room with me when your dad got the ransom note. We are the only people who know you were supposedly kidnapped. And Rona is still the only person outside these four walls who knows what's going on. She'll ring us as soon as she has anything to report.' As if conjuring the call out of thin air, the phone rang at that moment. Genevieve made a dive for it, but Allie grabbed it first. 'Speak, it's your money,' she said, dodging Genevieve's grasping hands.

'Allie, it's me.' Blessed relief, Rona.

Allie dodged Genevieve again. 'Just a minute . . . Dieter, take her through to the bedroom, please.'

He wrapped his arms around her and frogmarched

her to the bedroom. 'You're never going to work for my father again after this,' she screeched as the door slammed behind them.

'I'm in a madhouse,' Allie said into the phone. 'So, what's the score? Where is the bastard?'

'Can she hear you?'

'Not unless she has the ears of a bat. Spill, Rona. What's going on? Are we all out of a job?'

'He's dead, Allie.'

It took Allie a long moment to process Rona's words and pick up the thread. 'How?'

'According to the bodyguard, it looks like a heart attack. Or a massive stroke. The police are on their way just as soon as they can get their helicopter in the air.'

'Why the police?'

Rona gave a dry little laugh. 'Because it's Ace Lockhart, a man with a thousand enemies and a lot of political friends.'

'Is it suspicious, then?'

'All I know is what the bodyguard told me. He was sprawled at the top of the stairs, no obvious wounds or bruises but stone dead. I haven't told anybody in the office yet.'

Allie reckoned she'd have done the same. 'I don't know how to handle this,' she said softly.

Always good with compassion, Rona said, 'You're smart, Allie. And you've got plenty of heart. I wish I could help, but you'll figure it out. I know you will.'

Allie dropped her voice. 'Make arrangements to get Genevieve and me out of here. We need flights to Frankfurt then the private jet.'

'Consider it done, my love. I'm on my way into the office, I'll see to it there.'

'I'll call you back when I can. I love you.' Allie put the phone down quietly and leaned her forehead against the wall. She'd never been in a situation like this. It was a death knock to the power of infinity. They'd gone from French farce to Greek tragedy in the space of a few minutes. And it was up to her to tell Genevieve Lockhart that the father she'd tried to scam was dead. Maybe as a result of the con trick she'd pulled.

★ ★ ★

Allie went into the bedroom and found Genevieve sprawled on the bed. Dieter was standing by the window, arms folded across his chest. 'So when can I speak to my father?' she demanded.

'I haven't spoken to him yet but there's been a change of plan,' Allie said, wishing she'd come up with a better line. 'I need you to come back to your hotel with Dieter and me.'

'Why? Is this some kind of trick?'

'No trick. We need to get ready to go back to the UK. And it's best if we leave here before Fredi takes it into her head to come back.'

Genevieve looked uncertainly at Dieter. 'I don't know who to trust.' Plaintive, she turned back to Allie. 'I certainly don't trust you.'

Allie spread her hands. 'We're all you've got right now. I promise I'm not trying to trick you.'

'She is on your side,' Dieter said. 'And so am I.'

Sulky now, Genevieve marched back into the living room. She picked up her bag and stuffed the Len Deighton novel and a packet of chewing gum into it. 'Let's go, then. This might be the last job you do for

349

us, Dieter, so make it good.' She put on her coat and stood expectantly at the door.

'Please, Genny?' Allie followed her. 'Don't try to run away. We have to talk.'

There must have been something in her expression that convinced Genevieve, for she simply shrugged and said, 'Don't try to fuck me over. Remember, I can destroy your career in the blink of an eye. And your lovely girlfriend's too.'

★ ★ ★

As soon as they walked into the suite, Genevieve made straight for the phone. Allie dashed to intercept her. 'No, wait . . . Please.'

'How many times do I have to tell you? I need to speak to my father.'

Allie gripped her by the shoulders and forced her away from the phone. 'There's no good way to tell you this, Genny. Your father's dead.'

A look of blank incomprehension. Then a nervous laugh. 'Jesus! Is this another one of your crazy games? Because it's sick.'

Allie swallowed. 'I'm sorry. It's not a joke. Ace is dead, Genny.'

Her legs buckled and she would have fallen had Dieter not rushed forward and caught her. He half carried her to a sofa and gently laid her down. She looked up at him with piteous eyes. 'She's making it up because she hates me.' Her voice wobbling between registers.

'She doesn't hate you. Your father ordered her to rescue you. He told me that himself. He wanted you back and he told me he sent her to get you because she was the best investigator he had.'

Allie sighed. 'I'm so sorry, Genny.'

Her expression was bleak with shock. No tears yet, she was still too deep in denial. 'What happened? Where did it happen? When?'

'He was on Ranaig. Not answering his phone. Ignoring faxes. Rona was the only person in the office who knew what was going on, so she asked the staff to go across and check he was OK. They found him lying at the top of the stairs.' It was such a prosaic way to go for a man who had been so very much larger than life.

Then the tears came. The loud, gulping sobs children make when they feel their world has ended. But for children, there are always new toys, new friends, new possibilities. For Genevieve Lockhart right then, there was only the desolation of loss.

50

Allie walked back from the newsagent's with her daily bundle of papers. Even at first glance, she could see that Ace Lockhart was still high up the news agenda. First there had been the paeans of praise to a titan of the media world, much of it from people who should have known better. Then there were the rumours around the cause of death, finally laid to rest by the post-mortem and the toxicology report.

But the revelation of cyanide had raised more questions than answers. Suicide or — the headline equivalent of a gasp — murder? Those who claimed to be closest to Ace insisted he'd never kill himself. He wasn't given to despair, they proclaimed. His ego wouldn't let him. But who might have murdered him? And how? And why? There were no traces of anyone else on Ranaig — no fingerprints, nothing on the CCTV.

The conspiracy theorists were only just getting going when the truth started to trickle out about the perilously precarious state of the company finances. Ace Media was reported to be teetering on the brink of collapse, thanks to Lockhart's wildly overpriced New York acquisition. Suicide gained traction; everyone agreed Lockhart would have struggled to overcome the humiliation of his company crashing.

Then the killer blow — Ace Lockhart had helped

352

himself to the company pension funds. There was a huge hole in the accounts and question marks over whether they could even continue to pay their existing pensioners, never mind fund the pensions of those still working and making their monthly contributions. Someone had managed to get a comment from Genevieve, who'd been silent as a stone after the first grief quotes.

Pension fund trustee and Ace Media heir Genevieve Lockhart said, 'I was under the impression that this was a temporary loan from the fund surplus. I had no idea the loan was in excess of the surplus.'

Aye, right, Allie had thought. For the first time in her journalistic career, she was relieved and delighted not to have a front-row seat at the gladiatorial arena of breaking news. She'd brought the grieving Genevieve back from Berlin and then stepped away from the whole sorry mess. Rona had suggested she stay close to Genevieve, but Allie had refused. 'She's not my friend, Ro. I don't even like her. Presumably she's got friends of her own,' she said. 'She's always in the gossip columns at some party or another. It's not my job to be her shoulder to cry on. Or to be her troubleshooter. I've hardly got any of my notice left to work out, then I am free of Ace Media. Genevieve Lockhart is not my responsibility.'

Rona had shrugged. 'Fair enough. I'm going to keep my head down till the dust settles and hope there's still a job for me to do at the end of it. But if I have to come back to Manchester and pick up the threads of our old life, I'd have no complaints. I've really missed the day-to-day with you.'

'Me too. I've got a bit of breathing space to look for my next investigation. And maybe even set something up with Bill Mortensen. There is a kind of synergy there — private eye and investigative journalist.'

So she was happy to watch the bonfire of the vanities consume Ace Media. She recalled a line of Bill Mortensen's about the work of a private investigator. 'You deliver the information to the client and step back, the better to watch the lightning strike someone one else's house.'

Back home, she settled down to do a proper deep dive into the papers. Now she was looking for stories on her own initiative, she needed to delve below the headlines in a bid to find the loose thread that might unravel someone else's cover story. She'd barely finished with *The Times* when the doorbell rang. She headed for the door, wondering. She wasn't expecting a visitor or a delivery.

She definitely wasn't expecting the person standing on her doorstep. Pale and somehow shrunken but still top to toe in designer clothes, Genevieve Lockhart stood on the doorstep, eyes meeting hers in a level stare. 'Genny,' Allie said, her voice flat and cool.

'Are you going to ask me in now I've come all this way?'

'I assumed you were just passing.' Allie stepped back and waved her visitor inside. 'Down the hall to the left, we'll sit in the kitchen.' She followed Genevieve into the bright and well-organised space. Genevieve chose the chair with the best view of the room and the garden beyond.

'Charming,' she said.

Allie leaned against the island, arms folded. 'You didn't come 'all this way' to admire our kitchen.'

Genevieve sighed. 'Please, Allie, can you not treat me like the enemy? I'm here to beg a favour from you, not to pick a fight.'

This was so unexpected that Allie found herself pulling out a chair and sitting opposite Genevieve. 'Let me say again what I said at the time. I'm sorry for your loss. It was a terrible shock, I know that. And it's not exactly been easy since. But I don't know how I can help you.'

'It's been a series of shocks.' Her eyes were heavy with sorrow. 'There's no reason why you should believe me, but I had no idea of the disastrous state of the business. Ace was always clever about keeping things out of sight. When we talked business, he always had answers for my questions. And I wasn't shrewd enough to see past the smokescreen. He lied to my face about the pension money, and I never even questioned the truth of what he was saying. But there's one thing I am absolutely certain of. My father would never have committed suicide.'

Pity swelled in Allie's heart. 'You can't know that. He was looking shame and ruin in the face. I don't think he could have lived with that.'

Genevieve managed a thin smile. 'I don't think you understand. He would never have allowed himself to believe he wouldn't recover. He'd faced down all sorts of obstacles in the past. His whole family died at the hands of their neighbours. He dodged and dived through the war, he built an international business on fresh air. Ace was convinced he'd never fall off the tightrope. 'While there's life, there's hope' is a motto that could have been written for him.'

Allie almost admired her invincible belief. But the facts betrayed it. 'So if it wasn't suicide, how did it happen? There's no evidence anyone was on Ranaig with him.'

'I know that,' she said impatiently. 'But with poison, you can set a trap. You don't have to be in the room. You don't even have to be in the same country. You put things in place and then you just wait.'

'What? You inject a bottle of wine or a box of chocolates with cyanide? You don't think that's a bit Agatha Christie? And from what I've heard of Ace, if he didn't think a present was up to his standards, he'd just give it away to the first passing courtier.'

'All of that is true.' There was something of her old spark in her eyes now. 'But what if it was something specific to him?'

In spite of her natural scepticism, Allie was drawn towards the rabbit hole. 'Like what?'

Genevieve dumped a large Cartier tote bag on the table and rummaged around, finally producing a brown glass medicine bottle. She held it out to Allie. 'Read the label,' she said. 'Please.'

Allie did as she was asked. *Wallace Lockhart. Supervitamin supplement. For the patient only.* Beneath the typed label was a printed logo. *Hygieia Health, Geneva.* She opened the bottle and tipped out a few dark green capsules into her palm. They weren't sealed gel caps but the sort that came in two separate halves, one overlapping the other. It wouldn't be hard to separate them and the colour would disguise whatever replaced the original contents. 'A tasteless delivery system for cyanide,' Allie said. 'Very convenient. So it must have been someone close to him. Who would have known? Who would have had access?'

Genevieve scoffed. 'Any competent researcher would know. *Traveller* magazine has a section called

'Travel Essentials — What I never leave home without'. In the January 1988 edition, my father talked about them and there was a photograph to go with it.'

'That's a long time to be laying a plan.'

'Oh come on, Allie. It's in the public domain. I checked — it's in the *Clarion* cuttings file. It can't be that hard to find for someone who's determined. Anyone in the building who wanted rid of him could have known.'

'But how would they have got to his supply on Ranaig?'

'He kept bottles in his private bathrooms in the offices in Glasgow and London. And in Voil House and the London flat. He'd just pick up a spare bottle from wherever he was when he needed it. It could have been done anywhere.'

'And you think this is somehow evidence that he was murdered?'

'The bottle was in the kitchen.'

Allie shook her head. 'You're grasping at straws because you can't let yourself believe Ace wasn't the man you thought he was,' she said kindly.

'He loved me. He'd never have left me to deal with this mess,' she said, a tremble in her voice. 'Allie, the last thing we know he did was have a phone call with Fredi Schroeder. I know that because your Rona told me. He was trying to negotiate my release. Why would he even bother if he was planning to drop me in a sea of shit?'

She had a point. Allie put the capsules back in the jar and screwed it tightly shut. 'For the sake of argument, let's say you're right. How would they gain access to his vitamins?'

Genevieve sighed. 'Like I said, they're all over the

place. Probably New York now as well. At Ranaig. In the galley of the plane. You know what security's like in the offices, anybody could slip inside in the middle of the night and, because it's a newspaper, nobody notices people wandering around the place.'

'But this bottle was obviously in Ranaig, surely?'

'They're all delivered to the London office. He just pockets —' She caught herself. 'Pocketed a bottle whenever he was running low. I don't think access is going to be how you nail this down.'

Allie shook her head. 'I'm not nailing anything down, Genny. This is nothing to do with me.'

This time, her sigh was a deep shudder. 'Can I get a glass of water?'

'Of course. Would you like some coffee? Tea?'

'Water's fine.'

Allie fetched a glass and put it in front of her. 'Sorry, bad host.'

Genevieve took a long draught then dabbed her lips with the side of her finger. 'I came to you because my father trusted you. And the way you treated me? You clearly don't like me, but I realise now you still did your best for me.' She looked out at the garden. 'After everything that's happened, I don't know who to trust. I feel like a goldfish in a tank of sharks. They're all concerned with their own survival. Injured innocence, that's all I see around me. Given how little anybody admits to knowing about the business, it's a fucking miracle we ever get a paper out.'

The vitriol reassured Allie even more than the manifest grief. Whatever had brought Genevieve to her door, she didn't think it was a scam. 'So if it was murder, who's behind it?'

A twisted smile. 'My first thought was Fredi. With

my father dead, she stood a much bigger chance of getting her hands on even more of the Lockhart fortune than she did by kidnapping me. But it doesn't make sense. I haven't been close to her for long enough for her to have come up with so complex a plan then carried it out.'

'It doesn't strike me as her style. And I don't think she has the resources. So we come back to the classic, who benefits?'

'On paper, that would be me. I'm his sole heir. Not even a bequest to his favourite charities. And by my own admission, I didn't have a fucking clue about the state the business was in. I'd be the prime suspect except for two things.'

'Which are?'

'I loved my father. I'm not going to say anything corny like, 'he was my best friend,' because I actually have a couple of those. But he was always there when I needed him. When I was at boarding school, most of the girls didn't see their parents from the beginning to the end of term. But Ace would show up out of the blue and wheedle us a trip to the cinema or afternoon tea. He'd charm the pants off all those dragon teachers and whisk me off for a weekend in Paris or Vienna. He made space for me in an insanely busy life. And he was fun. You probably never saw that side of him. I know he could be overbearing, but it was always because he wanted things to be perfect and he couldn't bear it when people didn't live up to his expectations.'

That, thought Allie, was one way of looking at his monstrous behaviour. 'What's the other reason?'

'It was all going to come to me anyway. And I had no idea it was all going to shit, so why would I want to get rid of the person who was making my inheritance even better?'

'Maybe you did know how bad things were?'

She shook her head. 'My head's been dedicated to running Pythagoras. Which is still a hugely successful part of the business. I'd just embarked on a charm offensive to make sure we could still hold our own if there are changes of regime in the Eastern bloc. I had no hands-on knowledge of the parent company or the juggling that Ace was doing behind the scenes.' She threw her hands up in a gesture of frustration. 'Look, this is all beside the point.' She raked around in her bag again, this time producing an 8x10 cardboard-backed envelope, the kind the picture desk used to send out complimentary prints. She pushed it across the table to Allie. 'Never mind who benefits. What about 'who issued the death threat'?'

51

Allie tipped out the contents of the envelope. There was a black-and-white print of a chunk of granite with one smooth face, with a list of names and numbers. Under them was carved, Poladski 1941–44. Across the bottom, in black marker pen, *All that remains*. She raised her eyebrows. 'Any idea what this is?'

'Poladski is the shtetl where Ace came from. Back when he was Chaim Barak. I think this a memorial stone.'

'Like a war memorial?' Allie said, looking at the dates.

'More like a grave memorial.' Her face was sombre. 'The Nazis emptied the village of Jews. Its very own pogrom. They burned the place to the ground, and the people with it. It's where Ace lost his whole family.'

'I've read the story. How he climbed into the dung-heap.' 'He was resourceful even then. He was the only survivor of the Jews in Poladski.' 'So, for some reason, someone wanted to remind him of that?'

Genevieve scoffed. 'Take a look inside the envelope.'

Allie pulled out a postcard of Białystok and a single sheet of paper that said: *WE KNOW WHO YOU ARE. WE KNOW WHAT YOU DID. IT'S JUDGEMENT DAY*. She turned over the postcard and read: *YOU ARE NOT THE ONLY ONE LEFT*. She gave a questioning look.

'That feels like a death threat to me,' Genevieve said. 'And the letters look the same. See, the way the

361

A is written? The left side is almost 45 degrees, and the right one goes almost straight down.'

Allie shook her head. 'You can't really tell with block capitals. Especially a marker pen, where you don't see the pressure marks on the paper.'

'I should take them to a handwriting analyst.'

'They'll tell you the same thing. But taken together, they do read like a threat from the past.' She pushed them back towards Genevieve, who shoved them straight back at her.

'Keep them. You might need them.'

'I'm not doing this.'

They glared at each other across the table. 'You're not getting it, are you?' Genevieve asked with a curl of her lip. 'Someone murdered my father for reasons I can't fathom that seem to have something to do with the past. You don't do that if you're sane. And if you're crazy enough to kill my father for a reason like that, what's to say you'll stop there? Because he wasn't the only one left, was he? There's me too. What if you'll only be satisfied when our family line dies out? What if I'm next, Allie? How will you feel then?'

The fact that they were so obviously manipulative didn't mean her words lacked power. Allie took a deep breath. 'The official verdict in your father's death is suicide. I imagine he got a lot of hate mail because of who he was.' She waved her fingers at the messages. 'There's nothing here, Genny. It's in your head.'

Tears sparkled in her eyes. 'I thought you were different. I thought you were smart enough to see the difference between the kind of nutters who just let off steam on the page and the ones who mean it.'

'There's not a clue who these are from,' Allie protested.

'Apart from the content. The connection to where my father came from. I've never seen that photograph before. My father has every book about the Second World War that mentions the area where his village was. And I have never even seen a mention of that grave memorial. Please, Allie. You wouldn't be so blasé if it was your father.'

I wouldn't bank on it. 'What is it you think I can do?'

'Go to Poladski. Talk to the people there. Find out if anyone else has been asking about Chaim Barak. If anyone remembers the Barak family.'

Allie felt herself wavering and tried to tamp down the feeling. But Genevieve had been trained by a master to spot any sign of weakness. 'Technically, I'm still your boss, isn't that right?'

'I guess so. I don't think we have to wait for probate to figure that out.'

'So in theory, I could send you to Poladski to do some deep background for a piece about my father.'

'Gerry Richardson might have something to say about that. He's still pissed off that Ace sent me to Berlin without consulting him. Or even telling him what it was all about. He's even more pissed off with me for refusing to fill in the blanks.'

Genevieve smiled with real pleasure for the first time since she'd walked in. 'I think you can safely leave Gerry to me.' A pause, and the smile widened. 'Who knows? By the time you come back from Poland, we might need a fresh face running the newsdesk in London.'

Allie laughed. 'If that's meant to be a bribe, you're well wide of the mark. I'd rather scoop my eyeballs out with a teaspoon than run a newsdesk in London. Besides, I suspect the hovering vultures might have swooped on the Globe and the *Clarion* by then. You do realise you're going to have to sell? You'll be lucky to still be clinging to Pythagoras at the end of this, I'd have thought.'

'Touché. But for now, I'm still the proprietor of the paper you work for. I'll have the private jet sent to Manchester Airport tomorrow morning. I expect you to be in Poladski before the day is out.'

Allie laughed again. 'To the manner born, aren't you, Genny. And what if I say, 'fuck you,' and stay in bed tomorrow? Not much you can do to me, is there?'

'To you? No, not much, it's true. But the lovely Rona, as my father was wont to call her, is still technically on a probationary period. And she does love her new job. Face it, Allie, she loves her new job so much that it's worth spending four or five nights a week away from you. How thrilled would she be if it was you that cost her that job?'

Don't let her under your skin. Allie shook her head. 'I don't believe you'd do that. If I do this, and it's a big if, it's because in my heart I will always be an investigative journalist.'

'If I were to offer the restoration of the investigations department under your leadership, might that be a bribe worthy of you?'

Allie sighed. It wasn't the bribe that tempted her; as usual, it was the prospect, however distant, of uncovering a hidden truth. 'You're not going to give up, are you?'

★ ★ ★

'So she just looked me in the eye and said, 'I don't think you want me to give up, do you?' I tell you, Ro,

364

she went from grieving to flirting in the same time it takes me to go from nought to sixty.' Allie sprawled on the sofa, the phone to her ear, wishing Rona was next to her instead of two hundred and twenty-one miles away.

'You really have a way with women, don't you? I'm guessing you said yes?'

'I said mibbes. I need to do some research before I commit. Like, do I need a visa? Is there anything left of Poladski other than a chunk of granite? Will lovely Allan Little give me the name of his Polish fixer? I don't have a single word of Polish either.'

'I think 'vodka' would probably work. You're going to go, Allie. I know you. And it might help that there'll be a lot of foreign press about the place.'

'Really? Why?'

'I'm rolling my eyes at you. Hell, Germaine's rolling her eyes. How do you not know this, and you supposedly a proper journalist, not a pedlar of fluff like me? They've just agreed to legalise Solidarity and have free elections in June. All the smart money says Solidarity are going to win a landslide.'

'Missed that. How come you know so much about Poland all of a sudden?'

Rona chuckled. 'Nothing else to do late in the evening except watch *Newsnight.* You'd be amazed what I know these days. If you do go, take care of yourself.'

'I promise. How dodgy can it be, snooping around on the Polish–Lithuanian border?'

Rona groaned. 'Fate well and truly tempted, Allie. Don't lose sight of the fact that you might be on the trail of a killer.'

Allie scoffed. 'It's a fantasy. Genevieve's got a bee

in her bonnet and until I crush it underfoot, she won't leave me alone. In spite of technically owning Ace Media, she doesn't seem to know any other hacks she can monster into doing her bidding. I'll be fine.'

Rona sighed. 'I hope you're right, my love. I really hope you're right.'

52

Genevieve Lockhart might like to believe she'd stepped straight into her father's shoes, but it was evident to Allie within hours of their meeting that she had a long way to go before the world jumped when she said so. In the end, it took three days to arrange her trip. She spent most of that time in the Central Library in Manchester, finding out everything she could about Poladski and the killing of Polish Jews during the Nazi occupation of Poland. By the time Eastern Poland fell into German hands, the locals had learned that the penalty for preserving Jewish lives was death. It legitimised an underlying anti-Semitism with appalling consequences. Three million Polish Jews died either in the death camps or at the hands of their neighbours in towns and villages across the country. That equated to about six times the population of Manchester, Allie reckoned. It was impossible to comprehend.

She finally found a couple of pages about Poladski in a book that catalogued the village massacres that had escaped much of the eye of history. It had been a tiny village twenty-five miles north-east of Białystok, a pocket of relatively fertile farmland surrounded on three sides by dense forest. A small lake occupied the fourth side. A population of three hundred and forty-seven souls eked out a living off the land, growing vegetables and some cereal crops, fishing in the lake, keeping a few cows. Even though most of the inhabitants were Jewish, a handful of pigs wandered the muddy lanes and foraged for scraps. Jews and Catholics had lived cheek by jowl, sometimes uneasily but mostly in a kind of truce. Until the war came.

As the Germans swallowed their country, everyone shivered in fear of what was to come. One afternoon, two Nazi officers in a staff car backed up by a couple of infantrymen in a motorbike and sidecar drove into Poladski. They told the village that the Jews were their enemies, and any village caught harbouring Jews would be burned to the ground. That night, about fifty of the village Jewry left under cover of darkness and took refuge in a barn on the far side of the forest.

When they realised what had happened, the terrified villagers turned on the remaining Jews and slaughtered them. Men, women and children. They dug a pit, dumped the bodies in it and set fire to the corpses. When the Germans arrived two days later, they were initially pleased with the remaining inhabitants. But somehow they discovered the Jews hiding in the barn. The Nazi soldiers set fire to it and shot anyone who tried to flee. Then they burned the village too because, they said, the villagers had lied to them. Poladski was erased from the map.

And that was all Allie could find about that specific village. On the second day of her research, she walked down to the bookshop on St Ann's Square and bought the best map of Poland that she could lay hands on. She also bought a book about Solidarity, clearly hastily thrown together by a print journalist whose name she recognised. With luck, he'd give her a flavour of what to expect.

Back at the library, she spread out the map. Poladski still hadn't made it back on to this map, but from the description in the book and the reproductions of maps from 1939, she was able to work out more or less where it was, thanks mostly to the lake. She circled the area and refolded the map, leaving her target exposed.

When she got home, Allie sent the map reference in a fax to Rona's PA, asking her to pass it on to whoever they were hiring as her fixer. 'This is where we need to get to, I think. We'll need a car. And probably a hotel in Białystok.'

A reply came back immediately. 'All in hand. As for a visa — you pay when you arrive. It costs £20 and they take Mastercard. All very straightforward. Fixer details in the morning, via Allan Little.'

Thank heavens for the fellowship of foreign correspondents. Allie thought. You spent an evening in a bar swapping anecdotes with someone, you swapped business cards and you were virtually blood brothers. Even if the bar had been in Soho and not some wartorn outpost of some bastard or other's empire. She was sorted.

★ ★ ★

They flew into Okecie airport on the outskirts of Warsaw in the early evening. Even the VIP arrival protocol guaranteed by a private plane involved standing in a line of heavy smokers waiting to pay for their visas, but when Allie spotted the length of the other queues, she felt an embarrassed satisfaction at her privilege.

By the time she emerged from the baggage hall, it was properly dark. But there, as promised, was Olga Nowak, her designated fixer and translator, casually leaning against a pillar. One hand held a cigarette; the other, a drooping sheet of paper with BURNS in large black letters. Allie dragged her suitcase behind her and introduced herself. Olga peeled herself off the pillar and gave a crooked smile. She was wearing jeans and a brown belted raincoat that she managed to make look chic. Her dark hair was cut in a precise bob, her lipstick was a scarlet slash and she wore an olive green beret at a rakish angle. 'Good to meet you,' she said. 'I hope we are going to be friends. Follow me, please.' She reached for Allie's case.

'It's OK, I can manage.'

She smiled and persisted. 'I'm sure you can, but it is bad manners for me to stroll ahead while you have a satchel and a suitcase.'

It was easier to give in. They walked into mild evening air heavy with the smell of exhaust fumes, tobacco smoke and fried onions and made their way to the car park. Olga stopped by a shit-brown Lada Niva. 'It's not pretty but it's good for the countryside,' she announced, opening the back and putting Allie's case aboard. 'They call it the bastard love child of a Renault 5 and a Land Rover.'

'Fair enough.' Allie climbed in. It smelled of the ubiquitous stale smoke with an underlying note of garlic sausage.

'We have two choices. Białystok is about two and a half hour's drive. I estimate we will be there by ten. Or we can stay here in Warsaw, have a nice dinner and leave in the morning.'

'Tempting though a nice dinner is, I'd like to get started on the job first thing.'

Olga nodded her approval. 'I thought so. Your people have booked us a pleasant hotel in Białystok, and I have made some sandwiches if you are hungry.' She opened the glovebox and pointed to a paper bag.

370

'Salami and cheese on black bread.'

Allie grinned. 'I think we're going to be friends, Olga.'

★ ★ ★

The hotel felt like a hangover from a bygone age. The furniture was too heavy and ornate for the rooms. Everything was slightly shabby, from the brocade on the chairs to the threadbare rugs. The mattress was soft and the pillows hard. But Allie had stayed in worse, from Dundee to Doncaster. She and Olga met downstairs in what appeared to be the breakfast room. They ate their sandwiches and drank the vodka that the night clerk brought them with great ceremony.

'This will do?' Olga asked.

Allie nodded. 'It's not like we're on our holidays.' She opened up her map and explained where they were going. 'I know this is a very long shot, but I'm looking for someone — anyone — who was in Poladski at the time of the massacre. I'm not trying to find someone to blame or asking them to incriminate themselves. All I need is to make them trust us enough to tell us the truth.'

Olga downed her second vodka and shrugged. 'No big deal, then, huh?'

'No big deal.'

'What exactly are you looking for? It will help if I have an idea.'

Allie took out her copy of the memorial stone picture. 'I want to find this, for starters. I'd like to know who put it up and when. And why. I'd love to find someone who knew Chaim Barak. The one who got away.'

'I'm not confident, but we can try.'

'I'm a bit more confident that you. Because I think someone else came digging up the past here. And not too long ago. I think they found someone who knows a story that hasn't been told yet about what happened in Poladski.'

'And this is what your boss at Ace Media wants you to find out?'

'It might be. On the other hand, it might be something very different. Either way, it's a story, and we both get paid.' Allie clinked her glass against Olga's. 'Here's to digging up the past. Without fear or favour.'

53

According to Olga, Białystok had a beautiful historic centre, complete with a palace. 'But we won't see any of that today,' she said. 'We came round the outside of the city last night so we would be nearest our destination.'

'Don't worry about it, we've got palaces back in Scotland. By the way, your English is remarkable.'

'My mother is English, that's why. She met my father when he was a pilot in the Polish squadron in the RAF. After the war, they got married, moved to Poland and started breeding little Poles. I am the fifth and last of them. We're all at least bilingual. I also speak Russian and French.' Olga's driving was as spirited as she was. It involved a certain amount of swerving and a generous use of the horn, but it never interrupted the flow of her sentences.

'You shame me,' Allie said. 'I've got bits and pieces of French and German, but I couldn't hold a conversation in them.'

'It's too late now. You have to train your brain in shifting between them when you're a little kid. Your brain is too set in its ways now. But you are fortunate. English is spoken everywhere. Even our Polish pope speaks excellent English.'

They left the city and its traffic behind in a matter of minutes and headed along a wooded road with scarcely another car in sight. Every few minutes, there would be a gap in the trees leading to clearings with what Allie assumed were farmhouses on their edges. After a few miles, Olga turned on to a single-track road, still lined with trees. 'You sure this is the right road? I didn't see a signpost.'

Olga nodded. 'According to the map. I checked again this morning before we left.' She pointed at the odometer. 'Three kilometres then we turn left.'

The woods gave way to a series of flat fields, a huddle of farm buildings at their heart, and then their turning was upon them. After a few hundred metres, the tarmac ended and they were on hard-packed earth with gravel that had been ground into it. The Lada's suspension made for an uncomfortable jouncing ride and Allie clung on to the dashboard. They came upon two cottages on the left then rounded a bend and all at once the lake was before them.

'So, here is the boundary of Poladski, I think.' Olga drew to a halt and they both contemplated what filled the windscreen. The sun filtered down through thin high clouds, giving the flat surface of the lake a metallic sheen. It was shaped like a kidney bean, tall conifers reflected in either end. Beyond it lay an area of rough scrub with occasional outcroppings of stone. Even from that distance, they looked too regular to be the natural products of geology. The track continued round the lake, but it was in poor condition; deeply rutted, with tufts of coarse grass growing up the middle.

'You want to drive on?' Olga asked.

'I think I'd like to walk,' Allie said, climbing down, glad she'd packed the lightweight walking boots she'd bought for their Italian holiday the previous autumn. They walked side by side round the tip of the lake, the birds of the forest raucous as they passed. As they

374

grew closer, they could see the ridged outlines of buildings just above ground level, the stone covered in moss and the kind of plants that cling to solid rock against all odds. They looked like lines scribbled in a child's jotter, the lie of innocence only recognisable to those familiar with the history of the place. Still, there was no ominous atmosphere hanging over the site, no sense of anything terrible having happened here. If she'd come across it on a walk, Allie would have dismissed it as an abandoned village, left behind by the vicissitudes of time and change. She'd seen enough examples of that in the Highlands, thanks to the Clearances. It was always a desolate sight, though there was nothing to mark it as sinister.

She walked on, scanning the remains. Then her eye was caught by what she sought. A little higher than the other stones, a lip of granite. She crossed the uneven ground, drawn by it, until she was facing the memorial. A long list of names, covering both faces of the stone. The front of the stone, facing the lake, matched the photograph.

But among the names on the obverse was one that shouldn't have been there. It was a heart-stopping moment for Allie. How could Chaim Barak be among the dead of Poladski when he had escaped to become a decorated war hero and change his name to Wallace Lockhart? It had to be a mistake, surely? Nothing else made sense. But it was an odd mistake, nevertheless.

Puzzled, she counted the names; forty-nine, including eight other Baraks. Were these the Jews who were murdered in the barn? She got out her camera and photographed the stone from every angle, then walked down to the edge of the lake and took several shots of the remains of Poladski.

Olga joined her. 'What now?'

'We canvas the neighbours.' Allie said, the irony clear in her voice. 'Which I guess means those two cottages we passed on the track.'

★ ★ ★

A thin column of fragrant woodsmoke rose from the chimney of the first of the two cottages. There was no response to Olga's knocking at the front door. She shrugged and pointed to the side of the cottage. 'Let's try around the back.' A narrow path led between the house and a thicket of *rosa rugosa* covered in buds that were on the point of opening. They emerged in what seemed to be a well-tended market garden. A man and a woman were working on a patch near to the cottage. He was digging, she was raking manure into the soil. Olga called a greeting and they both turned, surprise and curiosity on their faces. Olga said something more and they nodded and walked over, wary. 'I said we'd like to talk to them,' she explained. 'They probably think we're from the tax office or something.'

The couple stopped a few feet away. They were dressed in matching patched overalls, their faces lined and weather-beaten. Allie reckoned they were in their sixties, which meant they might remember Poladski as it had been. Olga spoke at some length, then held up a hand to give them pause. 'I told them you're a writer and you're interested in exploring what happened in the Białystok area when the Germans took over.'

And so the awkward four-way interview began. Olga asked questions, the couple answered, Olga translated, Allie asked the next question, Olga translated, and so it circled round. No, they hadn't lived here when the village was razed to the ground. They'd built the cottage when they married in 1959. Nobody bothered with them, it was just a bit of land nobody wanted.

Yes, they knew about the memorial. The rabbi who had served the Poladski Jews had been at a meeting in Hrodna when the massacre happened. He'd come back to the smoking ruins and ended up in the Białystok ghetto. He'd survived the Treblinka death camp and after the war, he spent years raising money for the memorial. No, he wasn't still alive, he'd died in a car crash about ten years before. Dead end, thought Allie.

Yes, they'd heard some people had escaped from Poladski. Not the Jews, obviously, the Nazis saw to that. But some of the other villagers, they'd hidden deep in the forest. Later, one family moved into the cottage next door, it was just a ruin then but they rebuilt it with stone from Poladski.

Yes, one of them still lived there. But he'd be no use because he was born after the war was over and he was peculiar. Didn't like his neighbours, never mind strangers. The rest were dead or scattered to the four winds. One was even in America. Or was it Canada?

It wasn't much of a thread to tug on, Allie thought. It would help if she knew what she was looking for. Her scattergun approach wasn't bearing much fruit. She turned to Olga. 'The account I read said the Nazis discovered the Jews. Ask if they know anything about that.'

Olga translated the question. The couple exchanged an uneasy look. The husband started to speak, but the wife interrupted, a suspicious frown on her face. 'Why do you want to know about this?' Olga translated. 'All these years, nobody ever cared about Poladski and

377

now, two of you in the space of six months come asking questions.'

Allie felt the leap of her heart that came when a story began to open like a flower in front of her. 'Who came asking questions?' Her impatience while Olga asked and the woman answered was almost unbearable. There seemed to be a lot of back-and-forth for such a simple question.

At last, Olga said, 'A man came. He had an extraordinary story. His mother died last year from cancer. When she knew she was dying, she told him that he needed to know his true history. She was born in a Jewish family in Poladski the day the Nazis came. Her mother was terrified about what might happen and she persuaded her gentile neighbours to take care of the newborn. Then she went to the barn with the rest of her family. All of them. But the baby girl survived.' She paused to clarify something, then continued. 'The family moved west, and kept moving. They ended up in Germany, in the West. His mother went to England to be an au pair, she got pregnant, married the father and stayed. All his life, her son thought she was German. He had no idea he was a Polish Jew until she told him when she was on her deathbed. He came here to find his family, only to find his family had died in a terrible betrayal.'

Allie was slack-jawed with astonishment. 'A betrayal? What does she mean, a betrayal? What I read, it didn't say anything like that. It sounded like the Nazis went looking and found the barn.' She waited, impatient, for Olga to conduct the back-and-forth.

The woman shook her head vigorously and spoke with some vehemence. Olga listened, then said, 'No, she's adamant about it. Somebody — one of their

378

own — betrayed them. He bartered their lives for his freedom, she says.'

'Jeez. You couldn't make this up, could you? So what happened? With the young man?'

More to-and-fro. 'There wasn't much they could tell him. They'd heard the betrayal story but they didn't know any details. But they do know one survivor of the massacre. Her name is Anna Mikolaska. She comes here every year on the anniversary even though she is in her seventies. Now, her son brings her in his car. They always give her a cup of tea.' Allie took a deep breath. 'Do they have an address for her?'

Olga asked and was answered with a shake of the head. Allie didn't need that translated. Then the woman spoke again, to her husband, a question. He nodded. More words to Olga. 'They say she lives in Krynki. It's a small town on the Belarus border.' They exchanged a look.

'Can't be that hard to find, right?'

Olga nodded. 'We could do that.'

'Ask about the man who came. Did he give a name? Can they describe him?' She waited yet again.

'His name was Thomas, but they can't remember his family name because it was something English that sounded weird to them. He looked to be in his twenties. Dark hair and eyes, slim build. Quite tall.' Olga pursed her lips. 'Could be anyone.'

'Could be a killer, Olga. One last question. Does the name Chaim Barak mean anything to them?'

Olga put the question. They shook their heads without hesitation. 'Thank them for me, Olga.' Allie turned away and looked across the lake. 'If I'm going to make any sense of this, we absolutely need to find Anna Mikolaska.'

54

Back in the Lada, Allie asked, 'So, how hard will it be to track down Anna Mikolaska in Krynki?'

'Old lady in a small town? I don't think this will be too difficult. We'll be there inside an hour, easily. Then I can set to work. This is a crazy story, right?'

'It's certainly crazy. But I don't think it's shaping up to be the story my boss wants to hear.'

'I've been doing this job for the best part of ten years now, and I think editors don't care what the story is as long as it makes the readers sit up and take notice.'

'True. But they don't usually have a dog in the fight.'

Olga darted a quick frown at her. 'What does this mean? I don't know the expression.'

'Sorry.'

'No, it's good for me to expand my knowledge of idiom.'

'It means they have a personal stake in the outcome.'

Olga digested this piece of information. 'So how is it that your boss has a dog in the fight?'

Allie sighed. 'It's complicated. I'm not avoiding answering you, but I think once I hear what Anna has to say, I'll be able to explain it more simply.'

Olga raised her perfectly shaped eyebrows. 'OK. You don't have to tell me anything that is awkward. I'm nosy by nature, I can't help it.'

'Me too. That's why I'm so good at my job.'

Olga laughed. 'I like to hear a woman who is confident.'

Allie stared out of the window at more trees and fields, the occasional farmhouse. 'I think I'm good at my job because I don't feel confident. Every time I get a result, I feel the pressure of expectation on my back. So when I start on the next job, what I feel mostly is the fear of failure. I'm acutely aware of the people who would love to see me fall flat on my face.' A wry smile. 'Most of them men, but a depressing number of them women.'

'I know this feeling,' Olga said. 'When I started working with foreign journalists, back in Gdansk in 1981, I experienced so much hostility from men. They called me a whore and accused me of taking work away from men. I told them to fuck off then proved I was better than them. Now they ignore me to my face. I know they still talk about me behind my back but it doesn't matter because I have a reputation now. And I get the best jobs, like this one.' She took one hand off the wheel and gave Allie a friendly punch on the shoulder. 'Like the Americans say, sisterhood is powerful.'

As she spoke, the landscape began to change. The houses were closer together; still with land around them, but more like smallholdings than full-scale farms. The houses themselves were mostly covered in cement rendering, often with corrugated iron roofs but some were timber-framed and a few stone-built. They passed one or two modern buildings that looked like offices or schools. There were few people around and the town didn't have an air of prosperity. They soon arrived in the centre — a tree-lined park like the hub of a wheel, roads radiating off in all directions. Olga pulled up outside a small convenience store and said, 'I think it's best if you stay here. A foreigner asking questions in a small place like this — they'll be anxious and unwilling to help. I can be the smiling Polish person looking for an old friend of my grandmother.'

Allie shook her head. 'You're right. Bring me back a bar of chocolate, would you?'

Olga disappeared into the shop. When she emerged five minutes later, she was carrying chocolate, a bottle of what looked like orangeade, a large bag of potato crisps and a salami. Allie leaned across to open the door for her and Olga passed her purchases across. 'A chocolate bar wasn't going to do it,' she said. 'So much for the friendly shopkeeper. He's the grumpiest man I've met in a long time, and believe me, I thought no one could beat my Uncle Pavel on that score.'

Allie tore open the crisps. 'Did you get anything useful from him?'

Olga climbed in and took a handful from the bag Allie offered. 'Not really. He doesn't know his customers by name, why would he? They don't spend more money if he calls them by their names. I did get something, though. You remember that massive church we passed on the way in? There's a café next door where a few of the older people play cards in the afternoon.'

'That's worth a try. But is there not a voter's roll? I thought you were coming up to elections soon? Surely there must be some sort of list of who's entitled to vote?'

Olga scoffed. 'Even supposing I was allowed to see it, as someone who doesn't live here, it'll be a work in progress. Nothing is ready for the election yet. Everybody is still a bit stunned that it's going to happen. When I started working with the journalists covering Solidarność, I never thought it would get this far. I thought they'd be crushed under Jaruzelski's boots. It's exciting right now, it feels like we're on the edge of something but mostly I don't dare to believe it. So, no convenient list, I'm afraid.'

The cathedral of St Anne was by far the most spectacular building in Krynki. Its pale stone gleamed in the thin sunlight, the twin neo-Gothic spires the nearest thing the town had to a skyscraper. Olga drove past and found the café with no difficulty. It was, Allie observed, the only business in sight. The frontage was a long plate-glass window and between the notices posted on the inside, they could see most of the brightly lit interior. A couple of tables were occupied by quartets of old men staring at hands of cards, glasses of tea next to them. Three other tables looked like delegations at a headscarf convention. They watched the women for a few minutes. They seemed to be talking among themselves with no formal distinction between tables. Nodding sagely, shaking their heads and tutting, laughing and nudging each other in the ribs, they seemed to be having a fine time. Three of them appeared to be knitting scarves in depressing shades of brown and beige.

'Looks good to me,' Allie said. 'How are you going to play it?'

'Granny's friend won't work here. If Anna is one of them, I won't be able to extricate her from the group. But if I mention Poladski, she'll wonder what's going on — a second person needing to know about that piece of history in the space of a few months. I have

383

one thought that I can maybe make work. I can say I'm from the regional government and there's an irregularity in her voting application. I need to see documentary proof that she was born in Poland. Then hopefully she'll take me to her house. And we can explain the truth?'

Allie scratched her head. 'You think that will work? Will she not freak out when we explain what we really want to talk about? It would freak me out if I'd been lured back to my house by someone posing as a government official.'

Olga clearly didn't like opposition. 'Maybe. Do you have a better idea?'

'Possibly,' Allie said. 'What about this? Wait till one of the women leaves on her own, let her get a bit down the street then do your, 'Excuse me, granny's friend, I was told I'd find her in the café, it's a surprise, can you point her out to me?' Think that might do it?'

Olga considered. 'Yes,' she said, drawing it out to four syllables. 'But what if the woman we stop is Anna Mikolaska?'

Allie shrugged. 'You've got a ten to one chance of that. I'd go with odds like that. And if it is Anna, we come clean. Tell her we know about Thomas's visit and we didn't want to freak her out in front of her pals.'

Strategy agreed, they sat in the Lada eating crisps and chocolate and drinking orange soda. Allie couldn't quite believe she'd found a brand of soft drink that out-sugared anything in Scotland, home of terrible teeth and unhealthy eating. Half an hour passed and nobody emerged. Then an old man tottered into sight, a walking stick in each arthritic fist. He walked into the café and tapped one of the card players on the shoulder. The man looked up and broke into a broad smile when he saw the newcomer. He stood up and made a great show of inviting the new arrival to take his seat. He swiped a short stack of coins into his hand, said something to the players then limped across the room, hauling on a disreputable canvas jacket as he went.

'What do you think?' Allie asked.

'I think he might be even easier than one of the women.'

'And at least we can be sure he's not Anna.'

Olga let the man walk a dozen metres down the street then drew level with him and started talking. They came to a halt and even from that distance, Allie could see Olga was dialling the charm up to eleven. The man was nodding, then turning and taking come steps back towards the café. He pointed and they exchanged a few more words. Olga went into effusive thanks mode and even leaned in to kiss him on both cheeks. He smiled like a happy child and went on his way.

'You see the one with the red headscarf with the yellow pattern? That's Anna Mikolaska,' Olga announced triumphantly. Then she extended a hand for Allie to shake. 'You were right. Best strategy.'

'Now all we have to do is follow her home,' Allie said. 'And hope she doesn't call the police.'

55

Olga moved the Lada farther down on the other side of the street as a precaution. 'We should do the follow on foot,' Allie said. 'There are so few cars on the streets here, we'd be easy to spot.'

'You think we're invisible on foot?' Olga was scornful. 'I look like the big city, you look like a German hiker. We'll have to hope Anna has poor eyesight and an unsuspicious mind.'

Another half hour passed. Then a trio of women emerged, Anna among them. They set off together, filling the width of the pavement. They were headed in the direction of the Lada but on the other side of the street, and luckily they were too engrossed in their conversation to cast more than a fleeting glance at Olga's car.

Allie waited till the women were about twenty metres down the street, then said, 'OK. Now.' They strolled in the same direction as the women, staying on the opposite side of the street. At the first junction, the three women stopped. One kissed the others on both cheeks and peeled off to the left. Allie and Olga froze, but Anna and the other woman kept on walking.

Another junction, another farewell. This time, it was Anna who turned off into a narrow street on the right. Allie speeded up, in case Anna's house was close to the corner. It would be a bastard to lose her now. Olga caught up with her just as Anna was turning into a single-storey house about halfway down the street. Allie fixed it in her mind's eye then backed up, almost trampling Olga. 'Just in case she looks around. I often do before I open the front door,' she explained as Olga danced backwards. 'Let's just give her a few minutes to settle.' She looked around. 'Talk to me, as if we'd just met on the street. I don't want any curtain-twitchers to wonder what's going on. Strange women in the street following our old woman — must be something criminal going on. Talk to me about the election.'

For five minutes, Olga gave Allie the beginner's guide to Polish politics, interrupted by frequent questions of doubtful value. 'OK, enough, already,' Allie said. 'Let's do it. I'm counting on you to get us in. Tell her it's about Poladski and the man who came to talk to her. Tell her I'm writing a book and I think he might be part of the story.'

Olga looked dubious. 'OK. What if she says no, she doesn't want to talk to us?'

'Ask her if I can use her bathroom.'

'What?'

'It often works for women. Men, they tell to go behind the nearest hedge. Women, they take pity on.'

Olga shook her head, grinning. 'You're an interesting teacher, Allie.'

Anna Mikolaska's house was a small brick bungalow that looked like a child's drawing of a house. Front door flanked by two identical windows and a dormer in the roof with a curved lintel that made it look like an eye. The paintwork was in need of refreshment, but the garden was well-tended and neat, with clusters of primroses and violets alternating along the borders. A mature forsythia dressed the side of the house in a

387

yellow waterfall. 'Nice garden,' Allie remarked as they waited for her to respond to the doorbell.

Olga was ready with a warm greeting when the door opened. Anna Mikolaska had bright brown eyes like a blackbird, nestled among laughter lines. Plump cheeks, iron-grey hair in a cottage-loaf bun, and a mouth that revealed several missing teeth when she replied to Olga. Allie tried not to smile like a lunatic. She heard 'Poladski' a few times and saw Anna frown.

'Tell her she's my last chance of uncovering a very important truth,' Allie urged.

'I've got this,' Olga snapped before continuing the pitch. Allie hated not knowing what was happening. This was potentially the most crucial part of the whole enterprise and she had no idea what was being said. It ran counter to what she often said of her own work: 'I don't get paid the big bucks for working a six-day week. I get paid the big bucks for the five minutes when I talk my way across a doorstep that nobody else can get past.' This time, she wasn't the one doing the business and it was maddening.

After what felt like forever, Anna cocked her head on one side and shrugged with hands and shoulders. She stepped back and waved them in. Allie inclined her head in thanks and tried out her new single word of Polish. '*Dzięki.*'

Anna said something and Olga laughed. 'She said you're obviously not Polish.'

'Hey, I tried. I was being polite.'

They followed Anna into her kitchen. It was only just big enough for a table with three chairs set against lurid wallpaper with drawings of vegetables, a heavy oak dresser and a line of cupboards. The sink looked out across the back garden, filled with the familiar array of vegetables in the early stages of growth.

'She wants us to sit down and she's going to make us tea,' Olga translated.

Allie did as she was told and tried not to tear her hair out while Anna pottered round her kitchen finding exactly the right cups and saucers and brewing the tea. Finally, they were all served and Allie said, 'Have you told her I'm writing about Poladski?' Olga nodded. 'OK, so tell her I know about the man called Thomas who came to find out about his family. Ask her what she told him. Emphasise that nobody's done anything wrong, that I need to find out the details for what I'm writing. And tell her I know how hard this must be for her. And does she mind if I record it?' She took out her recorder and waved it at Anna.

Olga's tone was reassuring. Anna listened, nodded and waited till Allie had set up her recorder. Then words tumbled out of her. Olga tried to keep up but Allie could tell it was demanding. 'She says it's good that somebody is finally going to tell what happened in her village. What the Nazis did was an atrocity, a war crime, but nobody cares about a little Polish village in the forest. She says she knew the family that took the Jewish baby in. They were good people. The husband was a miller. People came from surrounding villages to get their grain ground. The wife was the village herbalist, she was a wonder with plant medicine, Anna once had a terrible skin rash and the wife made an ointment with sage and marigold petals and it cured her in no time.' A deep breath.

'They had no children of their own, it was a sad story. She couldn't carry a child for long. So they were happy to save the baby girl's life. They packed up and left that night. Anna didn't know what happened to them afterwards, not until the man came to see her. She was sad that his mother had died, but she was pleased to see the young man, he looked just like his real grandfather, his Jewish grandfather. She told him all about his Jewish family, who were also good quiet-living people, devout and serious but always ready to help their neighbours even if they weren't Jewish, which is why the miller and his wife were willing to take on the daughter.'

Allie butted in. 'Ask if he said anything about Chaim Barak.'

Olga stopped the flow and asked the question. 'He told Anna that he had discovered there was a survivor, Chaim Barak. That he'd tried to make contact with him, but he didn't respond. And when he came to Poladski he was confused because Chaim Barak's name is on the memorial. And Anna said, his name is on the memorial because he's dead. He died along with the rest of his family in the barn. And this lad, he was very insistent. He said Chaim Barak was alive and well and a multimillionaire. And he had some photocopies with him, a whole bundle of them. He showed her where it said Chaim Barak and Poladski, in a big magazine story, it said Chaim had escaped by hiding in a dungheap, and there was a picture of the man called Chaim Barak in a uniform getting a medal from a general.'

Anna had paused for dramatic effect and when Olga stopped speaking, she hooted with laughter. And off she went again, Olga struggling to keep up. 'Anna told him, a dungheap would have been the best place for him, that was not Chaim Barak. That was Szeloma Michnik, she'd know him anywhere. He was in her class at school. That picture with the general?

390

That was Michnik, no mistaking him with his handsome face and his film-star eyebrows. And she wasn't likely to forget him in a hurry. Because he was the betrayer. The one who bargained for his freedom in exchange for telling the Nazis where the Jews were hiding. He led them to the barn. And they burned it to the ground with everyone inside. Including members of his own family — his mother and his two sisters. He was always out for himself. Full of big talk about how important he was going to be one day. He didn't give a damn for anyone else.'

Now tears were spilling from her eyes. 'And that's why the Nazis burned the whole village and slaughtered so many of us. If they hadn't known about the Jews hidden in the barn, they'd just have done what they usually did, they'd have gone through the village killing the Jews, and that would have been bad enough, but they'd have spared the others and not burned every house in the village. So what Michnik did wasn't simply to betray the Jews in hiding. He destroyed so many other lives. Anna was with a few of the villagers who got away, they knew the forest better than the Germans. But Anna lost people that day. Her brother. The boy she was going to marry. Her two best friends.

'And the young man, he told her Michnik is a rich man who owns newspapers and magazines and sits at dinner with politicians and movie stars.' Anna wiped her eyes roughly and blew her nose as Olga spoke. 'And he's a hero, they say.'

'What did the young man say about this?'

Anna sighed. She took a long drink of her cooling tea. 'He was shocked,' Olga said. 'He said he'd only wanted to find out about his parents. That was why he'd tried so hard to see the man who had called himself Chaim Barak. He'd thought the reason Barak didn't want to speak to him was that he's a greedy man who only does things to benefit himself. He never dreamed that he was the man who had betrayed his entire family to the Nazis. Anna asked him what he could do about it. Could he expose the truth about him? He said he didn't know. He didn't have that sort of power. But he swore that he would find a way to make him pay.'

This was gold, Allie thought. 'Can you ask her to repeat that, just to be sure?'

Olga spoke and Anna nodded vigorously. 'She says he promised he would find a way to make Michnik pay the price for his betrayal.'

There was only one more question Allie needed an answer for. 'Does she have a surname for Thomas? Does she have contact details?'

Olga asked the question. And Allie held her breath.

* * *

'I knew it was all going too well,' Allie sighed as they set off back down the road to Bia.ystok. 'How the hell do we find an Englishman called Thomas?'

'It's easy,' Olga said. 'Trust me. We have his first name. We know he is English and we know when he was here. And we know where he was staying in Białystok. He will have had to hand over his passport, they will have a record.'

Allie scoffed. 'We *think* we know where he was staying.' She relived the tense moments when Olga ran through the names of all the hotels she could think of in Białystok. Finally, Anna had lit up at the mention of the Hotel Branicki. She was *almost* certain that's where he said he was staying, when they were making small talk at the start of their conversation. She remembered it because it was in the old town and she'd thought her husband was going to take her there for their twenty-fifth wedding anniversary, but he didn't. Instead, they'd gone to a hunting lodge.'

'It's interesting to me that he was willing to give her some personal details early in that conversation,' Allie mused. 'And then, after she'd told him the truth about Chaim Barak and Szeloma Michnik, he got very canny about what he let slip. I wonder whether he was already making a plan in his head about the price he was going to exact from Michnik.'

'Don't you mean Wallace Lockhart? The man who was your boss until he supposedly committed suicide?'

'I'm glad you said 'supposedly'. When his daughter told me she was convinced he'd been murdered, I told her she was crazy. That he couldn't face the shame of his empire crashing round his ears and everyone knowing what a crook he was. Turns out, maybe she was right.' She rolled her eyes. 'God, I hate being wrong.'

Olga chuckled. 'But being wrong is a better story, no?'

'Just for once, it might be.'

As they reached the outskirts of the city, Olga took pity on her. 'Why don't I drop you at our hotel? There's nothing you can do at the Branicki and going in two-handed might make it harder for me to get the information we need.' She gave a little smile. 'It's never good to have a witness to bribery and corruption.'

56

It felt to Allie as if the piece of paper with Thomas Raventhorpe's address was burning a hole in her heart, never mind her pocket. Throughout her flight back to the UK from Warsaw, she kept taking it out of her pocket and staring at Olga's neat handwriting, as if this time it would give her a clear answer to the question of what to do next.

She'd already decided to sneak back into Manchester by the back door of a commercial flight into Heathrow then a train, rather than discuss her travel arrangements with Genevieve. She wasn't ready to talk to her yet. Rona was driving down that evening; they'd have the weekend to talk through what Allie should do next.

On the tube between airport and station, Allie briefly considered simply rising to the surface of the city and taking a cab to Thomas Raventhorpe's address south of the river. But she wasn't ready for that conversation — or confrontation — either. She needed to find some clarity.

It was a relief to be back in her own home, after a week of hotels and unpredictable coffee. Allie brewed an espresso and walked out into the garden, taking stock of the changes since she'd been gone. The pieris was showing off in its full glory of reds and cream and green, the magnolia stellata was still waving the last of its slender petals in the light breeze, the rhubarb and the sage were both burgeoning, and everywhere needed weeding. She sat on the bench at the bottom of the garden and tried to distract herself with thoughts of whether she should plant for the autumn, given the estate agent had left a message saying they had a potential buyer.

It didn't work. Anna's testimony rumbled round her head, and still she couldn't make her mind up what to do with it. Every time she thought she'd arrived at the most just conclusion, a voice in her head said, 'Yes, but . . .' Whatever route she chose meant casting herself in the role of judge, jury and lord high executioner, one way or another. None of that made her feel comfortable.

The early evening chill drove her back inside and she walked up to the shops on Beech Road to stock up on fresh vegetables, cheeses and smoked chicken from the deli. Even so short a walk shook something loose in her head, and when she returned, she sat at the typewriter and started writing the story as it made most sense to her. She knew even as her fingers moved automatically over the keys that this was provisional. But it was a way of ordering events that let her understand which elements were most important and how to transition between them.

By the time Rona arrived just after eight, Allie was feeling calmer, though no less uncertain about the way forward. When Rona walked in, they clung to each other wordlessly. Inhaling Rona's familiar distinctive smell, Allie finally felt she was home. When they moved apart at last, Rona said, 'Let me get Germaine. She's in the car. I wanted you to myself for a minute.'

Eventually they settled on the big sofa, each with a glass of wine, Germaine between them. 'Tell me all about it,' Rona said.

So Allie did. 'And I don't know what to do about it,' she concluded.

Rona reached across and stroked the back of her neck. 'Let's run through the possibilities,' she said.

'There's the very basic story that I can easily tell — the truth about Ace Lockhart and what he did in Poladski. Leaving Thomas Raventhorpe out of it altogether. It'll leave Genevieve incandescent with rage.'

Rona gave a little laugh. 'So there's an upside. She's driving everybody mad, storming round the place pretending to be Ace, acting like there's not this massive financial fraud at the heart of everything. I'm amazed the Fraud Squad haven't been crawling all over the pension fund offices, never mind the rest of the business.'

'Aye, but I'm not sure I want to be the distraction from all that.'

'True. OK, next option.'

Allie refilled their glasses. 'I think Thomas Raventhorpe possibly murdered Ace Lockhart.'

'That's a big claim. How?'

'Somehow he put a poisoned capsule in among Lockhart's vitamins and just waited it out. He doesn't even have to have gone to Ranaig, he could have sneaked into one of his offices. Though there's probably more security in Ace Media than there is on Ranaig. And if that is what he did, it means he'll have a perfect alibi for when Lockhart actually died. And he wouldn't have cared when it happened as long as it did happen.'

'Would that work?'

'Sure. Stomach acid dissolves the gelatine casing,

the cyanide is absorbed by the stomach lining. It would kill him very quickly. Certainly within an hour. I checked with that nice forensic chemist at Strathclyde Uni.'

'Wow. That's cold, though. But how would he manage it?'

'He's a PE teacher, Rona. If he didn't know before how to use a boat, he'd have no problem getting someone to teach him. The good bit about Ranaig is that somewhere there's going to be a record of him chartering a boat between the date he got back from Poland and the date Lockhart died.'

'How would he get into the house? Lockhart was paranoid, he'll have had security cameras and alarms, surely?'

'Probably. Or maybe he thought Ranaig was secure enough in itself, stuck out there on the edge of the Atlantic. If I was going down that road, I'd need to speak to the husband-and-wife team that look after the island.'

'And where would he get the cyanide?'

Allie shrugged. 'There are ways. Cyanide salts are used in gold mining and other industrial processes. You can distil it from the kernels of peach or apricot stones, or laurel leaves, apparently. It's not easy to get your hands on but it's not impossible. And maybe he wanted to use the poison the Nazis used to murder millions of Jews? A kind of poetic justice.'

'It's going to be bloody hard to prove.'

'That's not the issue, Rona. The issue is whether that's the right thing to do. Ace Lockhart was a terrible man.'

'He did rescue you from the Stasi,' Rona said mildly.

'Only because it suited him. He didn't want to lose

397

you. Rona, what we know now is he betrayed friends and family to save his own skin. He was a ruthless bully, an exploitative employer who destroyed people's lives in less obvious ways than Nazi death camps. The latest crime that we know about is stealing people's pensions, leaving them penniless. I'm not sure I want to set the law on the man who rid the world of Ace Lockhart.'

'Not to mention the wrath of Genevieve. She'll take his life apart in a bid to exonerate her father. And Anna Mikolaska. Genevieve will throw the full weight of Ace Media at her, accusing her of all sorts of lies and deceptions. She's desperate right now. There's no way she's going to have her father painted as a villain who deserved to die.' Rona pushed Germaine to the floor and pulled Allie into a hug. 'The key question is, who does it serve to accuse Thomas Raventhorpe? Who benefits?'

'I'm not sure that's the right question. Surely we're not saying murder is OK? Who are we to decide that some killers shouldn't pay?'

'Allie, step back a minute. We don't even know for sure that he's a murderer. Maybe it really was suicide. Or maybe it was murder but it was nothing to do with Thomas Raventhorpe. Maybe whoever sent those messages to Lockhart was just another nutter trying to upset him.'

It was persuasive, Allie thought. Especially since she'd had time to wonder what she'd have done in Thomas Raventhorpe's shoes. Finding out the hidden truth of his family history, only to discover that the man responsible for his parents' death was a decorated war hero and a man who wielded immense power in the daily life of his country . . . what would that do to anyone? She knew she'd have felt murderous, held back not by morality but by practicality. Every day, seeing Ace Media publications on the news stands, seeing Ace Lockhart strutting through British public life, a walking illustration of Faulkner's comment that 'The past is never dead. It's not even past.'

How could she condemn him for what would have been her own instinctive response? In spite of the gulf between her and her parents, she'd want revenge on anyone who killed them in cold blood. How much worse would she feel if Ace Lockhart had wiped out her entire family line?

The only time she'd previously been involved in a murder, it had been straightforward. Even though unveiling the killer had damaged other lives, there was no possible mitigation of circumstance that gave Allie a moment's hesitation. This was different.

Allie heaved a sigh. 'All I can do is fall back on what I know. I need to talk to him. I won't know what I need to do until I've sat down with him and let him have his say. And pushed him on all the points I don't trust.'

'It is what you do best, my love. And you've got great instincts. Hell, you chose me,' Rona said, trying to lighten the moment.

Allie chuckled. 'I don't remember doing much in the way of choosing. It was more like you happened to me, in the way weather does. No point in fighting it.' She sighed again. 'Let's have the weekend together. Sleep on it, let it lie.' She sat up abruptly, almost spilling both of their wine glasses. 'Let's go dancing. The city'll just be waking up, we can be the oldest swingers in town!'

Rona stood up and hauled Allie to our feet. 'We'll

dance like we don't give a fuck,' she shouted. The dog fled to the kitchen and they fell into each other's arms, laughing. 'Not one single fuck,' Rona whispered in Allie's ear. 'We'll be the queens of the world.'

Allie hugged her tightly. 'For one night, at least.'

57

Thomas Raventhorpe lived in the middle floor of a converted Edwardian semi-detached house in Streatham. The house looked solid and well cared for. The front garden had been abolished in favour of a tarmacked parking area, big enough for two small cars. Late on Monday afternoon, she was perched on a wall by a bus stop on the other side of the road. She had an idea of what Raventhorpe looked like, but no details. She didn't know when he'd get home from school but at least a PE teacher wouldn't have homework to mark in the staffroom at the end of play.

The buses came and went, her refusal to board earning her a couple of odd looks. She'd spent the weekend with Rona doing exactly what they used to do — clubbing, walking in the Derbyshire hills, gardening, eating well, getting slightly drunk and enjoying each other's presence — and it had been the best possible antidote to Allie's fretful state. Being reminded of what she valued was what she'd needed.

A few minutes after six, a man walked up the street from the High Road, a sports holdall slung over his shoulder. He fitted the broad description she had of Raventhorpe, but then, so did approximately one in six of the men who had walked past in the previous hour. The difference was that this one turned off the street and walked up to the front door of the house where Thomas Raventhorpe lived.

Allie jumped off the wall and dodged the traffic to

make it to the other side as the man was closing the door behind him. She ran up the steps, giving her best smile and said, 'Thomas? Thomas Raventhorpe?'

He turned, a quizzical look on his face. He was good-looking — regular features, deep-set eyes, a thick mop of dark hair. 'I'm sorry, I don't —'

'We've not met. My name's Allie Burns. I've spent the last few days talking with Anna Mikolaska, and she suggested I should talk to you.' Get Anna's name in there, build a bridge.

'I don't understand. Talk to me about what?'

'Sorry, I should have said. I'm a journalist. I'm writing a piece about the massacre at Poladski. And Anna said I should talk to you about the loss of your family.' Walk across the bridge, keep the reassuring smile plastered on.

'I don't know . . .'

'If it's a bad time, I can come back. I just think that it's important that we name the guilty. And that we remember how thin the veneer of civilisation is. If we forget the past, it's all too easy to repeat it. And nobody wants another Poladski. Or all the other massacres like it.' A dash of guilt and obligation, always a good seasoning.

'I suppose . . .'

'You can help me make the story touch people. Won't take long, I promise.' A lie, but who was going to call her on it. 'Nobody should ever have to endure what your family did.'

He capitulated. 'OK, you'd better come in.' He led the way upstairs and unlocked a door on the landing. There was no hallway; they walked straight into his living room. A sofa, a dining table and four chairs, a stereo system with speakers the size of small fridges, and sports equipment stacked in the corner: a hockey stick; racquets for tennis, badminton and squash; a long lacrosse stick; and a surfboard. A framed England rugby jersey hung on the wall with an indecipherable signature. A pair of sweatpants had been tossed over one chair, and a line of trainers sat next to the door. But it was clean, and had none of the detritus of most of the young men she'd known. No beer cans or pizza boxes, no overflowing ashtrays or takeaway tinfoils. He flashed her a quick apologetic smile. 'Sorry, it's not very inviting, I know.'

'It's fine. You should see my place if I'm not expecting company. Or rather, you shouldn't.'

'Do you want to sit at the table? It's easier, if you want to take notes, I think?' He fussed around, pulling out a chair for her then stood with his arms dangling. 'Do you want tea, or something?' Now they were in his home, he'd grown noticeably tense.

'No thanks. Let's just have a chat. Do you mind if I record this? In the interests of accuracy. My shorthand never fails to make my colleagues laugh out loud.'

'I suppose that's OK.' He perched opposite her. 'I'm not quite sure what you think I can bring to your story. I mean, Poladski happened twenty-odd years before I was born, I didn't actually *know* anybody who died there.'

'I understand. Anna told me how you found out your connection to Poladski, but could you tell me in your own words?'

He linked his fingers together and put his hands on the table. 'My mother was dying from cancer, last November. She said she had to tell me the truth about my past. I had no idea what she was talking about. I knew the story of how her family had fled from the

Nazis, how they'd made it to safety in Germany. But she told me that she wasn't their daughter. That her family were Jewish and they knew they'd be lucky to escape what was happening to all the Jews in Poland. So they'd given her away.'

'That must have been hard for them.'

'They wanted her to live. That was more important to them than keeping her in the Jewish faith. After the war, years after the war, she decided she would try to find out if my birth family had survived. She made some inquiries and that's when she found out about the massacre. She knew then that her parents were dead, because they were going to the barn.' His voice caught. 'You know about the barn?'

'Yes, it's a horrific story. Did she know anything else?'

He nodded and got up. 'Just a minute.' He left the room and came back with an A4 brown envelope. 'By chance, she read a magazine article about Ace Lockhart, right? She only bothered with it because of the headline.' He took out a small bundle of clippings and handed the top one to Allie.

FROM POLISH MASSACRE TO MEDIA TYCOON she read. It replayed Ace Lockhart's origin myth — Chaim Barak hiding in the dungheap to escape the Nazis, escaping to join the Polish Army, decorated for valour at Monte Cassino. And the rest. There were photographs — Lockhart getting his medal, Lockhart launching Pythagoras, Lockhart with his wife and baby Genevieve. She looked across the table at him. 'No wonder you wanted to meet him.'

'Yes. I thought he was the one person who could tell me about my family. How they lived. Maybe even how they died. So I wrote to Mr Wallace Lockhart.'

404

Contempt dripped from his voice. 'I wrote to him at all his addresses. London, Glasgow, even his stupid little island. I wrote three times. I didn't get a single reply.'

'That must have been frustrating.'

'It was. So I decided to go to Poladski and see whether there was anyone else still alive from that time.' His face screwed up in an expression of pain. 'All I wanted was to find someone who could tell me about my grandparents, right?'

'What happened?'

'Have you been there? Have you seen the memorial stone?'

'Yes. I know what you saw.'

'I couldn't make any sense of it. Chaim Barak's name carved on the memorial stone? Among the dead people? I thought it must be some kind of mistake. And if it was, it should be put right.' He shook his head. 'There's a couple of cottages down the road. I'd hired a local teacher to translate for me and he asked the couple who live there if they'd come from the village, but they were outsiders and they'd never heard of Chaim Barak. They told him about Anna, though. So we went to Krynki and he asked around till we found her.'

'She's a lovely person. I don't know how she could bear to rebuild her life after what happened.'

'I know. We asked her about Chaim Barak and she said he'd died in the barn. So I showed her the article about Lockhart. Obviously she couldn't read it, but she said right away that Lockhart wasn't Barak. I thought at first that something had got lost in translation, but we went through it all again. There was no doubt about it. The man in the picture wasn't Chaim

Barak, he was some guy called Szeloma Michnik. Which was weird, right? But then it got completely, off-the-page messed up. She told me Szeloma Michnik hadn't just escaped the massacre — he'd been the one who led the Nazis to the barn. This . . . this utter bastard had killed my family. And he'd stolen a dead man's name to make sure he never had to pay for it.'

There was nothing synthetic about Allie's sympathetic expression. 'I imagine you were really upset.'

'I was appalled. Not only had Michnik not been held to account for what he did, he'd used what happened in Poladski as a springboard to his success. I was disgusted.' His voice broke.

'And you decided to make him pay.' Not a question, just a very compassionate gaze.

He looked away. 'I'm a gym teacher, not a ninja. How could I do that?'

'I'm not sure. And any evidence would be circumstantial, I suspect.' It was out there now. Raventhorpe seemed thunderstruck. Too thunderstruck to tell her to turn off the tape. Allie dialled her voice down to maximum understanding. 'Thomas, I think you'd already taken the first steps while you were still with Anna. Why else would you not have given her your contact details? She's your one link to your past, and you don't leave her the means to get in touch? Doesn't make sense to me.'

His mouth opened and closed. Then he said, 'I was so gobstruck in the moment, I wasn't thinking straight. I . . . I've been meaning to write to her, but I've been busy.'

Allie made a show of turning off her tape recorder. The one on the table, at least. The back-up in her bag kept on turning. 'This is just you and me, Thomas. I think you decided to make Wallace Lockhart pay the price for what he did to your family. And the other Jews of Poladski. I think you got yourself over to Ranaig and somehow you planted a cyanide capsule in amongst his vitamins. And then you waited.'

He scoffed unconvincingly. His face pinked with sweat, even though the room was cool. His fingers twisted round each other compulsively. 'How dare you? That's crazy.'

'I agree, but it worked. And like I said, any evidence will be purely circumstantial. I'm guessing you hired a boat somewhere up the west coast, but that proves nothing except that you're a bit of a nutter who likes sailing the rough waters of the Atlantic when spring has barely sprung. I've no idea where the cyanide came from, but you're evidently a good planner and it'd be a struggle even for the cops to unravel that trail. How am I doing so far?'

Raventhorpe shook his head. 'That's a fantasy,' he gabbled. 'I don't know why you're accusing me of this, I could sue you for slander.'

'Good luck with that. Without witnesses, it's impossible to prove. But you've no need to threaten me.' Allie realised she had come to a decision. 'Look, I'll level with you. When I came here, I didn't know what I was going to do. I've been a journalist for a dozen years now, and I like to think I'm a pretty good judge of people. I thought I'd make my mind up which story to write once I'd spoken to you. And the bottom line is I've no longer got any intention of writing a story that makes you look like a murder suspect. The Fatal Accident Inquiry has ruled Lockhart's death a suicide. There would need to be compelling evidence to overturn that. And I'm not going to even hint that there might be something there if the police started to look more closely.'

He glared at her. 'Why would you do that? I thought you people were all about headlines and exposing people?'

'There's a big enough headline in telling the truth about Ace Lockhart, believe me. I'm not condoning what you did. But there's that saying, 'Revenge is a kind of wild justice'. And I sometimes think when the law lets you down, that's all that's left.'

They stared at each other, taking the measure of the moment. Raventhorpe broke the silence. 'Do you mean that?'

Allie nodded. 'Provided that I can use you and your family in my story. I'll write it in a way that's safe for you, you have my word on that.'

He looked away. She thought he was weighing up non-existent options. She'd backed him into a corner but as corners went, it was probably comfortable enough to live with. 'How do I know you'll keep your word?' he said to the wall.

'You don't. But I worked for Ace Lockhart for five years and I saw enough of him to know the world's a better place without him. I'm one of the people whose pension fund he stole. At the time he bought the *Sunday Globe*, I had the job I'd always dreamed of. Over the years, that job was destroyed. All my pleasure and pride in what I do has been eroded. So I don't owe his memory a damn thing.'

'Fair enough,' he said slowly. 'I don't know much about journalism, but I think you're going to need more from me about my trip to Poladski and what it all meant to me?'

'Yes,' Allie said. 'Not today, because we've both got

a lot to take in. But soon, yes.'

'Give it a month. If nobody's come hammering at my door shouting about murder, I'll know you've kept your word and I'll cooperate with you. Is that fair?'

She was liking him more and more. 'It's not like people are going to lose interest in Ace Lockhart any time soon. Yes, that's fair.' He extended a hand and they shook on it.

Shaking hands with a killer hadn't been how she expected to end her day. But to her surprise, she was fine with it.

58

Allie managed to catch the last train to Manchester. She hadn't been able to call Rona from the train because there hadn't been a good enough signal on her mobile for long enough to manage it. Besides, she definitely didn't want everyone else on the train listening in to what she was saying.

As soon as she walked into the empty house, she poured herself a large Ardbeg and curled up on the sofa with the phone. Rona answered on the first ring. 'I was trying not to be anxious,' she said. 'You'd think I'd have stopped fretting about radio silence by now.'

'I hate making you anxious, but I love that you still care. Sorry I didn't call before I got on the train but I only just made it.'

'So how did it go?'

'I think he did it and I think nobody would be served if anybody tried to prove it.'

'Wow. You sound very definite about that, my love.'

'I am. I'm going to get a terrific story out of this, unmasking Lockhart as the appalling human being he was. I understand what drove Thomas Raventhorpe and I can't find it in my heart to blame him for being a one-man Nuremberg. I'll get the human interest line from him, but no suggestion that he had anything to do with the death. Genevieve's not going to be happy but even she can't overturn a Fatal Accident Inquiry verdict by sheer willpower.'

Rona chuckled. 'Genevieve's already having a very

bad day. She'll hardly notice one more burning coal.'

'What have I missed?'

'A lot. A big lot,' Rona said, clearly relishing it.

'Stop teasing me and tell me.'

'It's been a hell of a day at the office. First thing, it was announced that the banks had moved to put Ace Media into administration till a buyer can be found. By ten o'clock, the place was swarming with little men in grey suits, counting beans and demanding answers from all and sundry. Then there was an emergency board meeting. I'm told it was a rocky one.'

'I don't see how it could be anything else. What happened?'

'The version I heard is that they told Genevieve in no uncertain terms that until probate goes through, nobody can vote Ace's shares. And then they voted her off the main board *and* the board of Pythagoras.'

'Jeez, that's going to sting. Pythagoras was her baby. When I was with her in Berlin, she was always banging on about how much profit they contributed to the company.'

'Allie, they've taken all her toys off her.'

'So how did that go down?'

'The words 'cup of cold sick' were used by my source. She told them they were a bunch of useless old wankers and a waste of skin. Among other things. But credit to them, they stuck to their guns. Security stood over her while she cleared her desk then they escorted her from the building. And when she asked where her car was, they pointed out the car belongs to the company. She had to stand around in the vanway while Fat Bob in security called her a taxi. Suddenly half the newsroom found an urgent reason to walk through the vanway.'

411

'Probably heading for the pub for a celebratory drink.'

'Nobody's in a celebratory mood, Allie. People are scared they're going to lose their jobs. Finding a buyer's going to be tough. The only one who can afford it is Rupert Murdoch and even Thatcher's corrupt cabal won't be able to get that past the monopolies regulator. There's a lot of folk worrying about their last byline and their expenses sheets. Technically, I'm still on probation. I could be packing my bags and heading back to you any day now.'

'That wouldn't be all bad, would it?' Allie flirted to mask a moment's uncertainty.

'I'd love to be back with you in our lovely house, but I won't deny I'd be disappointed to lose this job. I've barely begun to get the hang of it. But we won't starve, Allie. We're too good to be skint.'

Allie contemplated their mortgage and their outgoings and found she didn't feel quite as optimistic as Rona. 'Yeah, we'll manage.'

'That'll be a lot harder for Genevieve. Because while she was waiting for her taxi, a team from Strathclyde Police Fraud Squad arrived and took her off to Pitt Street for questioning.'

'You're kidding? They arrested her?'

'Not yet. Just 'helping with inquiries'. But there'll be no shortage of backroom boys at the Clarion dying to shovel the shit on to her to cover their own backs.'

'Interesting mixed metaphor there.' Allie snorted with laughter.

'Oh, fuck off, Margaret Atwood. Oh, and I forgot to tell you the cherry on the cake. The *Evening Times*, who have better contacts on the city council than we do, ran a splash tonight about the council beginning

412

eviction proceedings on Voil House. So she's home-less as well as jobless.'

'Ach, she'll land on her feet. Her sort always do. She'll find some sugar daddy to replace her real daddy.'

'Probably. Allie?' Rona sounded hesitant. 'You know what you said after Hillsborough? That you didn't think you could do this any more? Did you mean it? Even after coming up with a brilliant story like this? Because there's no thrill like nailing a big one is there?'

'I meant it, Ro.'

'So what are you going to do?'

Allie smiled. 'I don't know yet. But whatever it is, I'll knock it out the park.'

14 May 1989

PROFIT FROM LOSS

How a drug company is risking lives for cash

By Alison Burns

A drug company have moved a controversial drug trial behind the Iron Curtain to avoid UK watchdogs.

Zabre Pharma were testing Zarovir, a treatment they hope will slow down the transformation of HIV into the lethal full-blown AIDS.

Desperate victims of the disease willingly pay huge sums for any remedy claiming to offer effective treatment. So if a drug like Zarovir were proven to work, it would be a goldmine for the manufacturers.

The drug trial was originally launched in Edinburgh – known as the AIDS capital of Europe – but insiders report that several of the patients died.

One of the doctors involved in the trial, who asked not to be named, said, 'Zabre said it was to be expected because HIV/AIDS takes such a toll on the system. And that the patients concerned hadn't observed the protocol properly. I told them the trial should be stopped and withdrew my patients.'

But the trial wasn't stopped. Instead it was moved to East Germany where the government has tight control over patients in medical clinics.

Wiebke Neumann is one of the East German researchers. She risked her life to smuggle out key documents past the Stasi (the East German secret police) to back up her case. She revealed that when patients suffered adverse effects, they were moved off the trial and replaced by new candidates. (Cont. p4)

ACE LOCKHART'S DARKEST SECRET

By Alison Burns

Disgraced media tycoon Wallace 'Ace' Lockhart hid a secret far more abominable than stealing the pensions of his workers.

He stole the identity of a dead man and lived a lie for almost fifty years to hide this shocking truth.

He claimed he'd escaped a Nazi execution squad by hiding in a dungheap before escaping to join the Polish Army and win a medal at Monte Cassino. But the reality could not have been more different.

When word arrived that the Nazis were on their way to the tiny Polish village of Poladski, forty-nine of the Jews who lived in the village hid in a barn deep in the surrounding forest.

One of their number, a young man called Szeloma Michnik, led the Nazis to the barn in exchange for his freedom. The German invaders set the barn ablaze with everyone inside.

The few who managed to escape were mown down in machine-gun fire.

The Nazis returned to the village, slaughtered the rest of the population as retribution then razed Poladski to the ground.

In a bid to escape the consequences of his treachery, Michnik assumed the name of Chaim Barak, one of the youths who died in the barn. He later changed his name to Wallace Lockhart.

Thomas Raventhorpe (27) lost his grandparents that day. He said, 'Michnik stole my family history from me. My mother escaped the pogrom because she was a newborn. My grandmother handed her over to a Catholic couple who escaped and made it to Germany.

'I owe everything to the kindness of that couple, but I've lost all connection to my real roots. Michnik – or Lockhart, if you want to call him that – should have paid for his actions. I'm angry that he was able to take his own life when his crimes became inescapable. My grandparents had no choice, thanks to him.'

One of the few survivors of the Poladski massacre, 72-year-old Anna Mikolaska, spoke vividly of the day the Germans came. (cont. p2)

415

LOCKHART HEIRESS CHARGED WITH FRAUD

Genevieve Lockhart implicated, say police

The only child of disgraced media mogul Wallace 'Ace' Lockhart has been charged with multiple counts of fraud.

Lockhart killed himself in April rather than face the disastrous collapse of his empire. He stole £400 million from the company pension funds, as well as taking dozens of other unauthorised 'loans' from the business.

Recent revelations about his betrayal of Jews to Nazi killers have further tarnished his reputation.

Genevieve Lockhart, 31, was in charge of Pythagoras Press, the scientific publishing arm of the company. It has emerged since Lockhart's death that this successful business was founded on research Lockhart looted in Germany at the end of the war. It also published flattering biographies of many Soviet leaders which airbrushed their unsavoury pasts.

She will appear for a preliminary hearing in Glasgow Sheriff Court tomorrow.

416

FREEDOM!

BERLIN WALL FALLS

Thousands flee GDR tyranny

East Germans teemed across the Berlin wall in their thousands last night as the citizens on both sides of the divided city breached the wall that had divided them since 1961.

Jubilant celebrations filled the streets as the East Germans fled their drab lives under Soviet domination.

The flood of people was triggered when Gunter Schabowski, an East German official, announced that permanent relocations would be available at all checkpoints, with immediate effect.

The tsunami of people took the authorities by surprise when they flocked to the wall after hearing the news on the West German news channel that can be picked up on both sides of the city.

By 11 p.m., the checkpoints had all been opened and graffiti was appearing along the wall's 97 miles. People danced and sang, strangers embraced and there was a spirit of freedom in the air.

(See: Pictures pp.4, 5, 6)

417

Acknowledgements

Memory is a tricky thing. We all build our own mythic history, and the older we become, the fewer people there are left to contradict us. Writing a novel set in the recent past has been a cautionary reminder of the inaccuracy of my own recollections. More than most of my novels, the Allie Burns series has demanded I rely on a combination of books, newspaper libraries, but most importantly, human sources.

I gathered snippets from many friends, but I particularly owe thanks to Dame Mariot Leslie, former British ambassador to NATO; Bridget Kendall, Master of Peterhouse College, Cambridge and former BBC diplomatic correspondent; Allan Little, journalist, broadcaster and former BBC special correspondent; and Professor Niamh Nic Daeid, professor of forensic science at the University of Dundee. They were all generous with their time and their recollections. The BBC documentary *Choose Life: Edinburgh's Battle Against AIDS* was an invaluable resource, as was the newspaper collection at the National Library of Scotland, whose staff always go the extra mile.

Any mistakes are uniquely mine . . .

I'm lucky to have a great team at my back. Jane Gregory, my agent for thirty-six of my thirty-seven novels, and her colleagues at DHA take the best possible care of my work. My editors — Lucy Malagoni at Little, Brown, supported by Amy Hundley at Grove Atlantic and Stephanie Glencross at DHA — always help to make the books better. Anne O'Brien continues to copyedit with supreme skill and a sense of humour. From design to sales and marketing, Little, Brown give me confidence that *1989* will have the best following wind as it sails forth. My publicist, the incomparable Laura Sherlock, makes sure my diary runs on well-oiled wheels and my family thank her for it!

I'd also like to pay tribute to Thalia Proctor, who would have worked on this book had she not died so prematurely earlier this year. I knew Thal for more than twenty-five years, first as a passionate bookseller and later as an editorial colleague. She was a unique presence who always brought light into the room, and all of us who knew her as a vibrant member of our crime fiction community miss her.

Playing and hanging out with my fellow band members in the Fun Lovin' Crime Writers — Luca Veste, Stuart Neville, Doug Johnstone, Chris Brookmyre and Mark Billingham — has given me some of the best new memories of recent years. Cheers, guys!

My final thanks go to my partner, Jo Sharp. Not only is she my most stalwart support, she makes me think, she makes me laugh and she makes me proud — she's just been appointed the Geographer Royal of Scotland, for heaven's sake. How cool is that? Maybe that's how she always finds me when I'm getting lost.

My *1989* Top 40

In no particular order, this is the forty-track rotation I used to get my head into the world of 1989. But they are specifically Allie's choices, not all mine, and they drift further back into the decade than the year itself.

I hope they transport you into the right frame of mind for Allie's story.

1. 'The Only Way Is Up' — Yazz & the Plastic Population
2. 'A Little Respect' — Erasure
3. 'Love Is a Stranger' — Eurythmics
4. 'Orinoco Flow' — Enya
5. 'Somewhere in My Heart' — Aztec Camera
6. 'Blue Monday' — New Order
7. 'Every Day Is Like Sunday' — Morrissey
8. 'I Want Your Love' — Transvision Vamp
9. 'Fast Car' — Tracey Chapman
10. 'I Don't Want to Talk About It' — Everything But The Girl
11. 'Sisters Are Doing It for Themselves' — Eurythmics & Aretha Franklin
12. 'Real Gone Kid' — Deacon Blue
13. 'Ride on Time' — Black Box
14. 'I Drove All Night' — Cyndi Lauper
15. 'Cubik' — 808 State
16. 'Suspicious Minds' — Fine Young Cannibals

17. 'Wrapped Around Your Finger' — The Police
18. 'Stop!' — Erasure
19. 'Would I Lie to You?' — Eurythmics .
20. 'I Wanna Dance with Somebody' — Whitney Houston
21. 'Brilliant Disguise' — Bruce Springsteen
22. 'Crockett's Theme' — Jan Hammer
23. 'Where the Streets Have No Name' — U2
24. 'Letter from America' — The Proclaimers
25. 'Luka' — Suzanne Vega
26. 'What Have I Done to Deserve This' — Dusty Springfield & Pet Shop Boys
27. 'Don't Leave Me This Way' — The Communards
28. 'Radio Free Europe' — R.E.M.
29. 'Nothing's Gonna Stop Us Now' — Starship
30. 'Walk Like an Egyptian' — Bangles
31. 'Come On Eileen' — Dexy's Midnight Runners
32. 'Dancing in the Dark' — Bruce Springsteen
33. 'The Whole of the Moon' — Waterboys
34. 'I'm Gonna Be (500 Miles)' — The Proclaimers
33. 'Pull Up to the Bumper' — Grace Jones
36. 'The Boys of Summer' — Don Henley
37. 'What's Love Got to Do With It?' — Tina Turner
38. 'Brass in Pocket' — The Pretenders
39. 'Graceland' — Paul Simon
40. 'Let's Dance' — David Bowie